Dante's Wedding Deception
by Day Leclaire

Kiley O'Dell wasn't at all what Nicolò had expected.

But then, neither had he expected the tidal wave of desire that slammed through him, rendering him blind and deaf to everything but the woman standing in the doorway of the elegant hotel suite. He saw her mouth move, but all he heard was the roaring that filled his ears, demanding that he take this woman and make her his. That he put his mark on her in every way possible. That he possess her, binding her to him until neither of them could escape.

No. He flat-out refused to accept even the possibility that this might signify The Inferno.

No. Way. In. Hell.

Mistaken Mistress
by Tessa Radley

What was it about this woman? Joshua asked himself as his mouth closed over hers. Why her...?

This was Alyssa Blake, the woman who had humiliated him in print, compromised his reputation and the future of the Saxon's Folly winery.

The woman who had been his brother's lover...

To desire such a woman was *his* folly.

He forced himself to slow down, told himself he was in control of his senses, his tightly wound body. Told himself he could control this reckless desire as easily as he controlled his vineyard. Told himself he could take his pleasure with her, and then watch her walk away, with no regrets.

He almost believed it...

Available in September 2009 from Mills & Boon® Desire™

DANTE'S WEDDING DECEPTION
BY
DAY LECLAIRE

MISTAKEN MISTRESS
BY
TESSA RADLEY

◉™ MILLS & BOON®

First published in Great Britain 2009
Harlequin Mills & Boon Limited,
Eton House, 18-24 Paradise Road, Richmond, Surrey TW9 1SR

The publisher acknowledges the copyright holders of the
individual works as follows:

Dante's Wedding Deception © Day Totton Smith 2008
Mistaken Mistress © Tessa Radley 2008

ISBN: 978 0 263 87111 1

51-0909

Harlequin Mills & Boon policy is to use papers that are natural, renewable
and recyclable products and made from wood grown in sustainable
forests. The logging and manufacturing processes conform to the legal
environmental regulations of the country of origin.

Printed and bound in Spain
by Litografia Rosés S.A., Barcelona

DANTE'S WEDDING DECEPTION

BY
DAY LECLAIRE

Dear Reader,

I have occasionally heard people say that they'd like to relive a portion of their lives and change the way they behaved, or make different choices. To start over. To take that other fork in the road. But would you be willing to wipe your life's slate clean if it meant forgetting your past? All of it, even the good parts? It's an intriguing fantasy. Imagine. All the foolish, traumatic, silly, sad, funny, tragic incidents in life…gone in the space of a heartbeat. Would you do it?

And even more interesting… How much of yourself would be left once that slate was cleaned? What if you could only go with your gut instincts and behave the way your heart dictates? How much of who we are is determined by genetics and how much by environment? Those questions so intrigued me that I was driven to write this story and explore the possibilities. To find out if love could overcome the uncertainties and trauma of an empty past.

That's the premise behind *Dante's Wedding Deception*. This love story is one of the most unusual I've ever written and one of the most satisfying. As the Dante family troubleshooter, Nicolò Dante is forced to give up control and trust in the Inferno, something he doesn't think possible…until he meets Kiley O'Dell. But love has a way of changing everything and everyone, whether they remember who and what they are…or not.

Enjoy!

Day Leclaire

To Donna Totton, for being the best sister-in-law in the world…and for your constant support and assistance. Thank you!

Prologue

Nicolò Dante anticipated trouble the same way he anticipated marriage—one part dread, and two parts determination to find a way out of the whole unfortunate mess.

Some men found a certain inevitability to the sorry state of "wedded amiss." His two brothers, Sev and Marco, had eventually succumbed to the entire process like the not-quite-proverbial rams to the slaughter. Well, not him. He had enough trouble in his life without looking for more.

And right now that trouble took the form of Kiley O'Dell.

"We need you to look into this," his eldest brother, Sev, instructed. "According to the documents Caitlyn uncovered, there's a distinct possibility that this woman may own a substantial interest in Dantes' fire diamond mine."

Such a simple statement, yet the implications were dire, and could cause endless problems for Dantes' jewelry empire, an empire whose fame was built on the lure of fire diamonds. They could be found nowhere else in the world, except deep within the bowels of a Dante mine, and they were coveted by everyone from royalty to heads of state to the local shopkeeper around the corner.

Nicolò's expression darkened. "Our dear sister-in-law should have kept her nose out of those old papers. They've brought us nothing but grief." He lifted an eyebrow in question. "Does Marco have no control over Caitlyn?"

Sev shook his head in disgust. "You really don't have a clue, do you?"

"I'm probably the only one who does." Nicolò leaned a hip against his older brother's desk. "What's the point of being so damn charming, if he can't use some of it on his own wife? He tricked her into marriage, didn't he? Now that he's got her, the least he can do is keep her out of trouble."

Sev crossed his arms across his chest, his burnished gold eyes brilliant with laughter. "Keep digging that hole, bro. Your Inferno bride will be delighted to bury you in it when you eventually come across her."

"Forget it." Nicolò made a brisk slicing movement with his hand. "As far as I'm concerned the family curse—"

"Blessing," Sev corrected mildly.

"Blessing? Hell, it's more like an infection."

Sev tilted his head to one side and considered the description. "That's an interesting analogy, although I'd say The Inferno is closer to a melding."

Nicolò allowed a hint of curiosity to show. "What was it like when you first felt The Inferno for Francesca?"

"Are you finally admitting it exists?"

"I'm willing to admit you and Marco believe it does," Nicolò conceded grudgingly.

"And Primo."

Nicolò dismissed that with a swift shake of his head. "Our grandfather is the one who has perpetuated the legend all these years. It offers a convenient excuse to explain lust, no more and no less."

"Now you sound like Lazz," Sev said. "But if that were true, Caitlyn never would have been able to distinguish between Marco and Lazz, considering how difficult it is to tell the two apart. And yet, she picked out her husband without any doubt or hesitation. And she did it under the most extreme circumstances. Wasn't that enough to convince you?"

Nicolò couldn't deny fact. Nor could he rationalize what he'd seen that day. But that didn't mean he'd allow Sev to draw him into a discussion about the veracity of The Inferno. "You still haven't explained what it's like."

An odd smile drifted across Sev's mouth and his eyes seemed lit from within, filled with an unsettling combination of pleasure and satisfaction. "When I first saw Francesca, I felt a physical pull, as though we were somehow connected by a thin tenuous wire. The closer we moved in proximity, the stronger the connection between us. It kept growing until it became so powerful I couldn't resist it."

"That's it? You felt physically attracted?"

"Shut up, Nicolò." There wasn't any heat behind the demand, just amused impatience. "Do you want to know, or don't you?"

"I asked, didn't I?" Though why he bothered, he couldn't say. Horrified fascination, perhaps. Or perhaps forewarned was forearmed. The instant he felt anything similar, he'd get the hell out. Get out long before he did something as outrageous as Sev—like blackmail his future wife into first leaving their competitor and working for Dantes, and later still agreeing to a pretend engagement. Clearly The Inferno did strange things to the men and women it mated. "Something happens when you touch, doesn't it?"

"A shock."

At the reminder, Sev kneaded the palm of his right hand with the fingers of his left. It was a habitual gesture, one Nicolò had seen both his grandfather Primo and his brother Marco imitate. They all claimed it occurred as a result of The Inferno, a lingering residual from that first touch. Even Caitlyn rubbed her palm periodically.

"A shock like static electricity?" Nicolò prompted.

"Yes. No." Sev grimaced. "It's a shock, yes. But it doesn't really hurt. It surprises. Then it seems to meld us. Complete the connection. After that, it's done. There's no going back. You've been matched with your soul mate and you're permanently joined for the rest of your lives."

Damn. Nicolò didn't like the sound of that. He preferred having his options open, to have a variety of choices. In his position as Dantes' troubleshooter, he required the freedom to jump from one creative opportunity to another should the need arise. Experiencing such a total loss of control didn't appeal to him at all. The Inferno stole that control, forcing its will on unwilling subjects. And though he didn't mind bending on occasion, so long as it happened to be in the general direction he was headed anyway, he resented like hell the concept of being broken, stripped of power and forced along a path not of his choosing.

"Well, with luck The Inferno will be clever enough to leave me alone," Nicolò said lightly. "Now tell me what you've discovered about Kiley O'Dell."

"Nothing."

Nicolò's brows tugged together. "What do you mean…nothing?"

"I mean that since the question of who actually owns the fire diamond mine broke in *The Snitch*—"

"Damn interfering gossip rag."

Momentary amusement flashed across Sev's face. "Now you sound like Marco. Not that it matters. Apparently, the O'Dell woman reads *The Snitch*." His amusement faded. "She's come forward demanding a meeting to discuss the situation. A meeting you're going to set up. Unfortunately, we haven't been able to get any substantive background info on her. At least, not yet."

Nicolò stared, appalled. "You expect me to go in blind?"

"I don't see what choice we have. Listen, just hear her out. Primo bought that mine fair and square. Find out why she thinks her family might still have a legitimate claim after all these years. Then stall while we put some investigators on this." A fierceness settled over Sev's face. "I don't have to tell you how much we stand to lose if Kiley O'Dell's claims prove genuine."

"Dantes will go under." Nicolò didn't phrase it as a question.

Sev nodded. "Everything we've worked to rebuild over the past decade will have been for nothing. We need to find out what proof the O'Dell woman has that she's a legitimate owner in the mine and then keep her happily oblivious while we find a way to take her down."

Nicolò's expression hardened. "Then that's what I'll do."

"Nic—"

"I understand how important this is." It was probably the most delicate job he'd ever handled, as well as the most difficult. "I'll find a way to keep her off balance."

"Tread lightly." At Nicolò's questioning look, Sev elaborated. "Her claim could be genuine. We don't want to do anything to set her against us. We want an amicable resolution, not a pitched battle."

Nicolò shook his head. "Then she shouldn't have started this war. Because one way or another I intend to finish it."

One

Kiley O'Dell wasn't at all what Nicolò expected.

But then, neither did he expect the tidal wave of desire that slammed through him, rendering him deaf and blind to everything but the woman standing in the doorway of her suite at Le Premier. He saw her mouth move, but the sound refused to penetrate the roaring that filled his ears, a roaring that demanded he take this woman and make her his. To put his mark on her in every way possible. To possess her and bind her to him until neither of them could escape.

No. He dropped his head and fought the sensation, fought for all he was worth. He flat-out refused to accept this feeling, flinching from the very real possibility that it might signify the start of The Inferno.

No. Way. In. Hell.

This woman spelled trouble from the top of her dainty red head to the tips of her tiny red-coated toenails. And he refused to allow trouble into his life, his bed, or his heart. No matter what it took, he'd put an end to this sensation. It couldn't possibly be that difficult. It only required a single, simple solution. All he had to do was figure out what that solution was and The Inferno would pass him by.

Lifting his head, he took a second to study Kiley O'Dell, using every scrap of creative skill at his disposal to search for a way out of his latest predicament. But nothing came to him and he simply stood and stared at her.

Her name suited her. She stood no taller than a minute, with a taut, lithe figure that packed just enough curves in just the right places to tempt a man to explore every inch of that creamy white skin. She wore her hair long and it fell in heavy strawberry-blond curls to the middle of her back. She also possessed the most stunning pair of pale green eyes he'd ever seen, eyes that dominated her triangular-shaped face.

"Mr. Dante?" she asked, clearly repeating herself. Her cultured voice contained a low, musical quality that fell easily on the ears. "Is there something wrong?"

"Nicolò."

He shoved the single word from between clenched teeth. Did she have any idea how hard he struggled to act with a modicum of propriety while instinct clawed at him, urging him to snatch her up in his arms and carry her off to the nearest bedroom?

Possibly, since a hint of wariness crept into her regard and a pulse kicked to life in the hollow of her throat, betraying her instinctive response to him. A response not all that unlike his own, if he didn't miss his guess. A streak of color highlighted her arching cheekbones and he could almost smell the whiff of desire that perfumed the air between them. Oh, yeah, this wasn't good.

She recovered far swifter than he. "I'm Kiley O'Dell. Thank you for taking the time to see me."

Everything about her appeared quick and decisive, from the sharp once-over she gave him to the way her gaze leapt from him, to the hallway, and then over her shoulder to the spacious hotel room. He couldn't help but wonder if that last glance was a final check to make sure she'd properly set the scene for their encounter.

"Come on in," she said, stepping to one side.

She didn't bother offering her hand, which suited him just fine. Considering the overwhelming hunger her appearance aroused it would be downright foolhardy to touch this woman. Not with The Inferno currently on the rampage, cutting a swathe of destruction through the Dante males.

Not that he believed in The Inferno. Hell, no. He hadn't when Primo first told the tale. Nor when Sev and Marco tried to convince him they'd both experienced it the first time they'd touched their future wives. And he damn sure didn't intend to start believing in The Inferno now. Not even with this desperate need filling every empty space inside him with a want so huge he could barely contain it all.

"Would you like something to drink?" Kiley tossed the question over her shoulder while she crossed the plush carpet. She moved with a hip-swinging stride that drew his gaze to her pert, rounded backside lovingly outlined by a pair of trim black slacks. He caught back a groan. Was it deliberate…or another aspect of the stage she'd set for their meeting? "I have sodas," she continued. "Or something stronger if you feel the need."

Whiskey. He'd kill for a double shot of single-malt. "I'm fine, thanks."

"Do you want to talk first or get straight down to business?"

"What's there to talk about?"

That had her turning around. A crooked smile tilted her mouth, giving her an almost gamine appearance. "We could take a stab at making this a friendly get-together. You know, exchange the usual pleasantries people do when they first meet."

Okay, he'd play along. "Like?"

"Like… Tell me what you do at Dantes, Nicolò."

"I solve problems."

Laughter gleamed in those odd green eyes, turning them spring-leaf bright. "And I'm your current problem?"

"I don't know." He lifted an eyebrow. "Are you?"

She shrugged. "Time will tell."

She folded her arms across her chest and leaned her hip against the back of a richly upholstered divan. She took her time, studying him at her leisure. Searching for a weakness? he couldn't help but wonder. If so, she'd have a long, fruitless time of it. The moment stretched, thin and sharp as razor wire. She broke first.

"It's your turn," she prompted gently.

"My turn…what?"

"To ask a question." She released a tiny sigh. "That's how this works, you see. When you're getting to know someone, you exchange pleasant chitchat in order to ease the tension."

"Are you tense?"

"You're kidding, right? You don't feel it?" She punctuated her questions with her hands, their movement through the air as brisk as everything else about her, yet graceful for all that. "Hell, Dante, it's thick enough to scoop out of the air and dish up for dessert."

So she felt it, too. It wasn't just his imagination. "Is that what you suggest? That we move straight to dessert?"

"Is that your way of resolving our problems?" she countered. Heat and awareness broke from her in splashy waves, building on his own. "Do you really think you can seduce my share of the mine out from under me? Is that your creative solution to this particular problem?"

Yes. "No."

"Good. I'm relieved to hear that."

"Because you don't have a share of the mine." He took a step closer to her, just to gauge her reaction. She didn't move, but he could see the slight tautening of the muscles across her shoulders and the momentary widening of her eyes before she forced herself to relax. *Gotcha.* She was good at this little game she played, but he was better. "Since you don't own any part of the mine, getting you into bed won't make any difference to the eventual disposition of your claim."

To his surprise, she laughed, the sound light and unfettered. "I'm so glad we have that out of the way."

"Funny. It still feels like it's right here between us."

It was her turn to take a step closer, to push at the electrical current sizzling between them like a live wire. "Shall we get it out of the way, Dante?" she dared. "It would be easy enough."

She reached for the first button of her blouse and thumbed it through the hole. Then a second. And a third. The deep V of her neckline revealed an intricate heart-shaped locket on a thin silver chain. Then he caught a flash of vibrant red, a sharp note of color trapped between the milky whiteness of her skin and the unrelenting blackness of her blouse. Before he could stop himself his attention dropped from her breasts to her low-riding slacks. Did she wear a matching bra and panties set? Did she conceal hellfire and brimstone beneath the pitch-black of her clothes?

He slowly looked up, his gaze clashing with hers. How long would it take him to find out? Judging by the hungry expression on her face, not long at all. Her fingers hovered above the final two buttons.

"Finish it."

His voice sounded as though it had been put through a shredder. He deliberately took the final step that separated them. Only the merest breath of space held them apart, that space awash with turmoil. Desire roiled there, along with mistrust and suspicion. It was a desire he intended to destroy, while nurturing the mistrust and suspicion.

"Finish it," he repeated. "And show me your true colors."

She jerked back. Where before her movements flowed, now they stuttered. Color stained her face and turned her eyes evergreen dark with horrified disbelief. She fumbled in her effort to rebutton her blouse, jamming the wrong buttons into the wrong holes.

"What the hell was I thinking?" she muttered. The question seemed aimed at herself rather than at him. She shook her head as though to clear it before demanding, "What are you doing to me, Dante?"

"You're the one doing the striptease, lady. Don't blame me if I expect you to put up or shut up. Now do you have proof to back up your claim that you own part of Dantes' mine, or is that what you were in the process of showing me?"

He'd rattled her, something he suspected didn't often happen with the self-possessed Ms. O'Dell. "You feel it, too," she insisted quietly. "Don't try and tell me I'm imagining things."

"And yet, I'm not the one taking off my clothes."

To his surprise, amusement rippled past the heat and turmoil and gentled the flames. "Too true, Dante. I'll have to watch my step with you. It would appear you bring out the wanton in me, though who knew there was any wanton in there to begin with." She shook her head in disgust. "Live and learn."

Taking a deep breath, she circumvented the divan she'd

been leaning against earlier and gestured toward the coffee table in front of it, one littered with papers. She waved him toward a second divan, situated opposite the first.

"So, let's get down to business. You want proof. Here's my proof." She picked up her first batch of papers and shoved them across the table toward him. "My grandfather was Cameron O'Dell. He and his brother, Seamus, were the original owners of the fire diamond mine that your grandfather, Primo Dante, eventually purchased. I've just given you copies of my grandfather's birth certificate, his death certificate and a deed showing that he was a legitimate half-owner of the mine."

Nicolò leafed through the papers. "My understanding is he died before the sale to Primo was finalized."

"True. But that would have merely transferred his share of ownership to any surviving children—my father, to be specific." Kiley tossed another document in his direction. "Here's a copy of Grandfather's will confirming that fact."

"Do you have your father's birth certificate proving he was born before Cameron died?"

Another piece of paper came sailing across the table. "Right here." She rested her elbows on her knees and leaned forward. Her locket swung out from beneath her misbuttoned blouse. It was a curious piece of jewelry, thick and chunky, consisting of fragments of silver that had been laced together to form the heart. "Your grandfather may have paid off Seamus, but my great-uncle didn't have the right to sell my father's share of the fire diamond mine, despite what he may have claimed."

Nicolò took his time studying the documentation even though he suspected he'd find everything in perfect order. A con artist would have made certain of that. What he hoped to uncover while he pretended to read was the slip in logic. It didn't take much thought to key in on it.

"Why has your family waited so long to bring this matter to our attention?" he finally asked. "Why didn't you file a lawsuit decades ago in order to get your fair share?"

"I didn't know that I might be an owner. As for my father…" A hint of some painful memory came and went in her eyes. "I can't ask him that question since he died when I was little more than a baby."

Nicolò allowed a hint of sympathy to show. "You were raised by your mother?"

"What difference does that make?" she asked in sharp retort.

He lifted an eyebrow. For some reason what he intended as a throwaway question had provoked an unguarded response, and clearly a defensive one, which made it all the more interesting. It told him a lot. Without even intending to, he'd hit a hot button with her. It showed him how tight a control she kept over her words and emotional responses. Until now.

"You were the one who suggested we get to know each other better. That's what I'm doing." He pushed a little harder. "Tell me about her. What's her name? How did she make ends meet after your father died?"

Kiley's mouth tightened. "I think you're stalling."

He shrugged. "Believe what you want. I'm just trying

to figure out whether she's in on this little scam or if you came up with it all by yourself."

"It's no scam."

"So you say. But I suspect Seamus will tell a far different story."

Her movements slowed, fluttering to stillness like a bird settling to its nest. It was a "tell," an unconscious look or movement—or lack thereof—that betrayed a lie. He'd always had an innate ability to pick up on them, a prime reason his brothers refused to play poker with him. He could always tell when they were bluffing, just as he could with Kiley.

She moistened her lips with the tip of her tongue, a second, more obvious "tell." "Seamus?" she repeated.

Nicolò took a stab in the dark. "According to Primo, he's still alive." He offered an expansive smile. "Tell you what. Why don't you sit tight for the next few days and enjoy the amenities Le Premier has to offer, while I track him down? I'm sure he can clear up this confusion in no time."

"Give me my papers." The words escaped, raw and harsh.

Without a word he gathered them and passed them across the width of the coffee table to her. Their fingertips touched during the exchange, just the merest glancing brush of skin against skin. A brief flash of electricity burst between them, sizzling for an instant, but not quite catching. Nicolò shot to his feet.

"What the hell are you trying to pull?" he demanded.

She shrank back against the divan, her eyes huge

and vivid in a pale face. "I don't know what you're talking about."

For the first time in his entire life, Nicolò ignored instinct and went with pure suspicion. "Sure you do. You read *The Snitch,* didn't you, Ms. O'Dell? You read about the diamond mine, no question there, since it's what prompted you to contact us. But you also read all about the Dantes and their little Inferno problem. And it gave you the most brilliant idea. Let's gather up these old family papers, you tell yourself, and see if you can't fake a case for partial ownership in the fire diamond mine. And if that doesn't work, let's see if you can fake The Inferno."

She shot to her feet. "You are hands-down certifiable."

"Then how do you explain that little pop of electricity?"

"How the hell should I know? Maybe your brain short-circuited." She hugged the documents to her chest. Giving him a wide berth, she skirted the coffee table and crossed to the door of her suite. "I think you should leave."

Nicolò followed her to the door. "I'm not going anywhere. Not until we have this out. Because, we're not done here. We're not even close to done."

"Yes, we are. First thing in the morning I intend to contact my lawyer. Until then, get the hell out of my room."

He leaned in close, so close he could feel the tiny charges of electricity skipping off her and latching onto him. Pulling and tugging him toward that ultimate commitment, attempting to sear him with that final fateful touch. "This isn't over, you know," he told her.

Her breathing grew jagged and he could see his want reflected in her eyes, a mate to his own, just as he could sense their heartbeats thundering as one. He almost sealed her mouth with his, the temptation nearly overwhelming. It took every ounce of self-control to pull back at the last second. Without another word, he opened the door and stepped into the hallway. The door slammed closed behind him.

Nicolò stood there for a moment. He could still feel her, right through the damn door. She was leaning against it, fighting the same attraction he fought, telling herself, just as he did, that what she felt was insane. Impossible. And to be avoided at all costs. He shook his head in disgust. *Right there with you, Gorgeous.*

Nicolò headed for the bank of elevators and took a car to the main floor. Once there, he hesitated. The lobby offered a spacious sitting area, with groups of chairs arranged in cozy settings. Large, carefully tended ferns, bushes and even a few ornamental trees created oases of privacy.

He eyed a set of chairs that were discreetly screened, while still offering a prime view of the elevators. Instinct kicked in again, growing too loud to ignore. In his thirty years of existence, he'd learned not to question that gut-deep demand. It always signaled something his subconscious had picked up on that his conscious mind hadn't caught up with quite yet.

Giving in, he took a seat and waited. It didn't take long. No more than five minutes later Kiley came barreling out of one of the elevators with that brisk, hip-swinging stride he now realized was her natural way of walking. She wore her hair up and had thrown on a black jacket to match her slacks. Very businesslike. She made a beeline for the concierge, her foot tapping impatiently as she waited for him to answer her question.

Nicolò sensed a purpose behind her actions. She had a destination in mind and he intended to find out where… and with whom. It would be interesting to see if she had a partner in crime. The concierge must have given Kiley the answer she needed, for she rewarded him with a broad smile that seemed to cause the man's brain to short-circuit the same way Nicolò's had earlier. Then she spun around and started toward the lobby doors. And that's when disaster struck.

Even though there was absolutely no reason for her to notice him or glance his way, even though he was practically buried in a jungle of shrubbery, the instant she came level with his position, she stiffened and her step faltered. Whatever connection had been forged in those few minutes they'd spent together crackled to life, sending out tendrils of awareness.

Time slowed and stretched. The chatter of voices and clatter of humanity grew muffled and distant. Even the light seemed to dim, leaving just the two of them within its brilliant embrace. With unerring accuracy, Kiley's head swiveled in his direction and her gaze locked with Nicolò's. The instant she spotted him, her eyes widened in shock. Acute distress followed on the heels of her shock.

Her distress caused an unexpected stab of concern

that threw him off stride. He didn't want to feel anything for this woman. Unfortunately, he couldn't deny fact. During their brief time together, something had sparked to life, and it was more powerful than anything he'd ever experienced before.

Time resumed its normal pace and Kiley shot toward the entryway and whisked through the glass doors embossed with Le Premier's name and logo. Nicolò followed, instinct urging him to run, the hunter giving chase to his prey. He hit the sidewalk outside the hotel just as she reached the corner intersection. People were still crossing, though the crossing light blinked a bright red hand of warning. She threw a quick glance over her shoulder. Spotting him, she darted into the crosswalk just as the light changed.

He saw it coming before it happened. A cab broke around a slow car, accelerating directly toward the intersection. Clearly, the driver didn't realize Kiley was there. Nicolò thought he shouted a warning. He knew he broke into a run. The driver didn't spot her until the very last instant. He hit the brakes at the same instant she tried to leap out of the way, but it was too late. The cab's bumper clipped her with just enough force to send her somersaulting into the air before connecting with the pavement. Even as Nicolò pelted toward her, he reached for his phone. He depressed the keys without even looking and barked the information at the emergency operator the moment the call went through.

He reached her side and knelt down. She didn't move. Didn't even seem to breathe. From what he'd

seen of her fall, she'd been sent flying toward the opposite sidewalk and hit her head on the curb. Vibrant blush-
red hair flowed around her, still shimmering with life,
while her pallor warned of something far different. Her
locket rested against her cheek like a kiss.

"Kiley!" He didn't dare touch her, though he wanted
to. And then he saw it, the slow, steady rise and fall of
her chest, and he almost lost it.

"I didn't see her." The driver of the cab appeared,
staring down at Kiley and wringing his hands. Un-
abashed tears rolled down his bearded face. "She came
out of nowhere."

"I saw what happened. It wasn't your fault."
Nicolò's mouth tightened. The blame was all his, not
the cab driver's.

"Is she—" The cabbie broke off, swallowing hard.
"Is she…?"

"No. I've called for an ambulance."

As though in response, sirens wailed in the distance.
A small crowd gathered around them and Nicolò kept
them back with a single terse command, followed by a
look so black that it sent most of the onlookers scurrying on their way.

The police arrived minutes later, the ambulance
shortly after that. Nicolò watched helplessly as they
secured the area and tended to Kiley. He vaguely remembered giving his identification. Vaguely recalled
claiming Kiley as his own, because on some visceral
level he knew that she was. Her well-being had now
become his responsibility.

All through the hideous ordeal, he watched the EMTs stabilize her, watched them attach endless medical equipment to her, watched them fit her head and neck with protective devices. And the only thing he could think about was that if he hadn't followed her, she'd never have run. She'd never have been hit by the cab. Never would have been injured.

He'd been so caught up in proving her a con artist that he'd put her life in danger. Based on the grim glances he saw the emergency personnel exchange, he may very well have killed her. He closed his eyes, forcing himself to face facts.

There was a connection between them whether he wanted it or not. That spark of electricity they'd experienced earlier hadn't been part of her con. She'd been as surprised by their physical reaction to one another as he had. The truth was… This woman could be his Inferno mate. Since they'd never fully touched, he couldn't be one hundred percent positive. But he doubted they needed complete contact. Deep inside he sensed the truth, sensed it with every fiber of his being.

The Inferno had sent him his soul mate. Granted, she wasn't the one he'd have selected for himself. But by driving her to act so impetuously, he could very well have destroyed their future "might have been" before he ever got to know her. He'd claimed he didn't want an Inferno bride.

It looked like fate had given him exactly what he wanted.

Two

"Have you lost your mind?"

Nicolò glanced over his shoulder toward the hospital waiting room to make certain they couldn't be overheard. Spying a few curious looks, he addressed his brother Lazzaro in Italian. "No, I haven't lost my mind. It's my fault she's in here. If I hadn't been running after her, she would never have—"

Lazz waved that aside with a sweep of his hand. "You told me that already," he replied in the same language. "So now, in addition to having a claim on our fire diamond mines, Kiley O'Dell can sue you for chasing her in front of a cab. Is that what you're telling me?"

"Yes. No." Damn it. Why did Sev have to send the logical Dante? "You don't understand."

"Then explain it so I will. And while you're at it, explain to me why they're calling you Mr. O'Dell."

Nicolò folded his arms across his chest. "I need regular updates about Kiley's condition. And since they only discuss a patient's condition if you're a relative, the hospital staff may be operating under the misunderstanding that I'm her husband."

"They *what?*" Lazz shoved a hand through his hair while he fought a perceptible battle for control. "Don't tell me this is another one of your creative solutions."

"You never complained when my 'creative solutions' worked to Dantes' advantage."

"Damn it, Nicolò!"

"Look, it just happened, okay? They needed information about her and since I had her purse with her identification and medical cards, they leapt to a conclusion I didn't bother correcting, especially since it works to our advantage."

"It works to our advantage right up until someone recognizes you. It isn't like the Dantes are exactly low profile here in San Francisco. Our faces have been plastered all over the gossip magazines in recent months, or have you forgotten that minor detail?"

"Sev, you and Marco, may have been prominently featured in *The Snitch,* but I've been maintaining a low profile. As for Kiley... I plan to play the part of Mr. O'Dell for the time being. Eventually, I'll straighten everything out. Until then—" Nicolò handed his brother Kiley's purse "—get her information and give it to our private investigator. Tell Rufio that I need anything and everything he can discover about her as quickly as possible."

"I'm already ahead of you. I put him on it yesterday."

Nicolò nodded. "Perfect. Also, send someone over to Le Premier. Considering the amount of business we throw their way I don't think the hotel will give you too hard a time about packing up her belongings and checking her out. I want regular updates on this, Lazz. And once Rufio's done gathering any surface info on her, I want him to dig for more. Tell him to dig deep. I want to know everything from what size clothes and shoes she wears right down to what brand of makeup she uses. Everything," he stressed. "Got it?"

"Why? What are you planning?"

Nicolò didn't dare answer that one. "It's still fluid."

"Aw, hell."

"Look, when I have all the details figured out, I'll let you know. Also, stop by my place and feed and walk Brutus, will you? I don't know how long I'm going to be hung up here."

"You've pulled some wild stunts in your time, but this…" Lazz shook his head. "This one makes all the others seem almost normal."

"This stunt won't last long. As soon as she wakes, the jig'll be up and I'll have to finagle some new plan."

"Like a way to get us out from under a massive lawsuit?"

Nicolò's expression fell into grim lines. "That's only a possibility if she ends up blaming me for the accident as much as I blame myself."

"You better hope like hell she doesn't."

The sudden appearance of a nurse saved Nicolò from having to reply. "Excuse me, Mr. O'Dell?"

"How's Kiley?" Nicolò immediately asked, turning his back on his brother.

Compassion darkened the nurse's eyes. "All I can say for certain is that she's stable. The doctor would like to see you and I'm sure he'll fill you in on the particulars." She inclined her head toward a nearby hallway. "If you'll follow me?"

He instantly fell in step with the nurse, only realizing afterward that from the moment she showed up he'd completely forgotten his brother even existed. Turning a corner, the nurse opened the door to a small conference room barely larger than a cubicle. A doctor sat at a table, making notes in a tight, rapid scribble.

Flipping the chart closed, the man rose and offered Nicolò his hand. "I'm Dr. Ruiz."

"Just give it to me straight. She's alive, right?" Nicolò demanded tightly.

"Alive and stable," Ruiz confirmed. "But she took quite a hit. It was miraculous, given the circumstances, that she didn't break anything. She has various lacerations that we've stitched up and a deep hematoma to her left hip. It's going to be quite painful and make it difficult for her to get around comfortably for a while."

"And the bad news?"

"As you're aware, she experienced a head trauma. A concussion. There's been some minor swelling to her brain, but she's responding to the medications we're giving her to reduce it and all the scans are clear."

"Is she awake?"

The doctor shook his head. "She woke briefly and seemed highly agitated and disoriented. Since then she's been unconscious."

One of the skills that made Nicolò so good at his job was an innate ability to read people. "What aren't you telling me?" he asked.

Ruiz's mouth compressed. "I'm sorry, Mr. O'Dell. Head traumas can be tricky. Until she wakes, we won't know the full extent of her injury. She may be perfectly fine, with perhaps a slight loss of memory from around the time of her accident. Or it could be far more extensive. You should prepare yourself for the worst, and hope for the best."

"When can I see her?"

"She's in intensive care. You can peek in for a minute or two right now. Then I suggest you go home and get some rest. We'll call if there's any change."

Ten minutes later, an ICU nurse escorted him into one of the dozen three-sided rooms that comprised the unit. Kiley appeared small and frail in the bed, with various wires and tubes connected to her, while a dirge of machines beeped softly in the background. He wished she would open her eyes so he could see the vivid color brimming with that unsettling combination of hot awareness and keen intelligence, so he'd know that she'd fully recover from her injuries.

He felt the kick that urged him to go to her, to link

their hands and complete the bond he felt between them. But he couldn't. Wouldn't. As though sensing a similar awareness despite the drugs sedating her, she stirred restlessly. Clearly, The Inferno—if that's what it was—called to her, as well, for she muttered in whatever twilight land she occupied. Within moments a nurse appeared in response.

"She senses you," she said, before offering a sympathetic smile. "You'll need to go now. If you'll leave a phone number we'll call you with any updates."

He did as instructed but found he couldn't wait for them to contact him, and returned to the hospital first thing the next morning. The ICU nurses all turned to watch him with broad grins that gave him a second's warning before he stepped into Kiley's room and heard her attending doctor say, "Here's your husband now."

Both Nicolò and Kiley froze, staring for an endless moment at each other. Then she shook her head in wild-eyed disbelief. "That's not possible," she denied in no uncertain terms. "There's no way he's my husband."

Nicolò bit back a curse. "Dr. Ruiz—"

"Don't panic, Mr. O'Dell." The doctor tossed a reassuring glance over his shoulder. "We warned you that she might have memory issues."

"No. I'd remember if I'd married him," Kiley argued.

"It's all right, Mrs. O'Dell," the doctor said in a soothing voice. "Your loss of memory is a result of your accident."

Nicolò shut his eyes. Time to 'fess up. "She's not—"

The doctor spoke at the same time, his voice rumbling over top of Nicolò's confession. "Kiley, you don't even remember your own name," he said gently. "It's perfectly natural that you wouldn't remember you have a husband. I suggest we take this slow and easy. Your memory could come back at any point. Hours. Days. Possibly weeks. In the meantime, we can move you out of ICU and into a regular room while we run a few more tests."

"Why won't you listen to me?" Kiley's gaze landed on Nicolò before flinching away. Tears filled her eyes and her voice rose with each word, growing steadily more shrill and hysterical. "I'm telling you this isn't my husband. He can't be. I'd know if he were."

Ruiz signaled to one of the nurses, who began to prepare an injection. "Mr. O'Dell, I'm afraid I'm going to have to ask you to leave. Once she's had time to calm down and get accustomed to what's happened, you can come back."

Nicolò inclined his head. "Of course. If you'd just give me a second…"

He acted without thought, running on sheer instinct, responding to a call no one heard but him. Crossing to Kiley's side, he reached down to take her hand in his. Behind him, Ruiz voiced an objection, while Kiley hissed in dismay as she drew back in a vain attempt to avoid his touch. He ignored everything but the demand screaming through him, one that insisted he finally act on the urge that had been clawing at him since the moment he'd met this woman.

He forcibly took Kiley's hand in his.

The Inferno struck with more ferocity than Nicolò

believed possible. Even the machines trilled in momentary alarm before subsiding again into a steady rhythm. Never before had he experienced such a powerful connection. It felt as though every emotion he possessed flowed from his hand into hers before slamming him with a backwash that left him drowning in desire.

He responded without thought. Without giving her time to protest, he bent down and took her mouth in a kiss of utter possession, hard against soft, determination overwhelming uncertainty. She tasted even sweeter than he'd imagined, soft and warm and—after a momentary hesitation—receptive. No. More than receptive. Eager.

He couldn't resist. He swept inward, taking advantage of her unstinting welcome. Never had he felt such a reaction when he'd kissed a woman, as though every aspect of the touch and taste of her had branded him. A certainty filled him, a certainty that no other woman would ever be quite right for him, except this one. The softest of moans, hungry and eager, slipped from her mouth to his, welcoming him home.

And in that moment he could no longer escape the simple truth. This woman belonged to him.

Kiley froze at the first touch of her husband's hand, overcome by a sensation so all-consuming, it rendered her speechless. Fiery heat shot from palm to palm, almost painful in its intensity, before settling into a warm, steady connection that soaked deep into that point of melding. Second by second, with each beat of her heart, desire pierced straight through flesh and sinew and bone, until it invaded every part of her. It seemed to lap through her veins, filling her to overflowing with a heavy, irresistible want.

And then he kissed her.

It was a first kiss, worthy of fairy-tale legends. It was also impossible to compare to any that might have come before, since fate had veiled any such occurrences. Even so, she found it the most incredible experience in her very short memory. His mouth ate at hers, his hunger unmistakable, threatening to consume her with that single, unbelievably delectable kiss. Every instinct she possessed screamed to life, telling her this was her man. That he belonged to her and no one else. Her response came without thought or reason. She opened to him, unfurling like a flower beneath the blazing heat of the sun.

He possessed her mouth and she gave back to him with unstinting generosity. In that instant she didn't care who she was, or who this man claimed to be. All that mattered was that this moment never end. Where before all felt alien and unfamiliar, this she recognized. This she knew. Slowly, he pulled back, his breath escaping in a heated rush, his eyes burning with black fire. And she read in his expression all that she felt, a mating of tumultuous emotions.

She sensed on an instinctive level that she and this man had become permanently entangled, heart, body and soul. But…how was that possible? How could something as basic as joining hands, or exchanging a single kiss, cause such an undeniable reaction? How could this simple contact bind her to a complete stranger with such relentless power?

Her reaction to his touch told her she knew this man, regardless of what she'd claimed only moments before. Slowly she lifted her gaze to her husband's. Or at least, the man who claimed her for his wife.

Her opinion of him hadn't changed in the few moments since he'd first stepped into her room. He remained fiercely handsome, a god of war, with hair and eyes of the deepest ink and a stare that silenced with a stony glare. He wore his hair longer than convention dictated and it fell to his neck in heavy waves. Maybe they would have tightened into actual curls if he hadn't subdued them, no doubt with a single forbidding look, the kind he currently had trained on the nurses and doctors surrounding them.

"Who are you?" she demanded. She waved away his response before it could even form. "I know you claim you're my husband. I mean, what's your name?"

"Nicolò. You call me Nicolò." A smile warmed the stark coldness of his features, touching a mouth that had left an indelible stamp on her own. "Except when you're angry with me. Then you choose a few more colorful terms of endearment."

"And how often does that happen?"

His smile grew, stunning in its beauty. "Often enough. We both have rather…tempestuous personalities."

His gaze lifted to the medical personnel gathered around her bedside and he jerked his head toward the curtain that screened the cubicle. Without a word they filed from the room. It didn't come as any surprise that they acquiesced. She had a strong suspicion that few dared to argue with Nicolò, and those few who tried, didn't hold out against him for long.

"I'd also like to set one fact straight," he said the moment they were alone. "My name isn't O'Dell, it's Dante. Nicolò Dante. When you were first brought in, everything happened in such a confusing rush that I didn't bother to correct the error."

He watched her closely as he gave her this latest piece of information, his penetrating look making it almost impossible to think rationally. "I don't understand," she replied. "If we're married, why do we have different last names?"

He shrugged. "We haven't been married long. And you haven't decided whether or not you want to take on all the baggage associated with mine."

She had questions, so many they spun, jumbled, around in the dark fog of her mind. She seized one at random. "You said we haven't been married long. How long is 'not long'?"

"Only a few days. It was a whirlwind affair."

For some reason that upset her, possibly because she'd hoped for more. Proof of a lengthy, established history that he could document in word and picture. A connection stretching back across the empty recesses of her mind. Something that would anchor her in this confusing world in which she'd awoken. Instead, he could only offer a mere snippet to sum up the whole of her life.

"A whirlwind affair," she repeated. Her eyes narrowed in thought. "Somehow, Nicolò Dante, you don't strike me as the impulsive sort. I'd have pegged you as a very deliberate sort of guy. Someone who gets what he wants when he wants it, no matter who or what stands in his way. Am I wrong?"

At the question, a mask dropped over his face, sharpening the harshly beautiful features into diamond-hardness. "That's quite an interesting observation after only a minute or two of contact. Or have you remembered something about me?"

Dear Lord, how could she have been so foolish as to wed a man like this? The strength of his personality threatened to overwhelm her, something she wasn't certain she could prevent even if she weren't injured and in a hospital bed. She must have been out of her mind to marry this man, to believe for even one tiny second that she could cage herself with a hungry panther and emerge unscathed. Maybe—in that other forgotten life—she liked challenges. Or maybe she was simply crazy. Time would tell.

"To answer your question, I don't remember you at all," she confessed. "I wish I did, because then I'd understand how I came to be in this predicament." She plucked at the sheet covering her. "And in response to your other comment, I'm basing my assumptions about you on how you managed to clear the room with a single look."

He studied her in silence before conceding her point. "You're right. I do whatever it takes to accomplish my goals. But my family will tell you I'm the most impulsive of all of them, since sometimes that's what it takes to

succeed. Split-second decisions. Thinking outside the box.
Finding a creative solution to an impossible problem."

"And us?" she couldn't help asking. "How does our
relationship fit into that dynamic?"

A hint of rueful amusement drifted into his eyes.
"Even if I weren't the impulsive sort, you can tell by your
reaction to my touch, there were other considerations."

She could make a fairly accurate guess about one of
those considerations. "You mean we were attracted
physically." She didn't bother to phrase her observation
as a question. There wasn't any question about her
reaction to him…or his to her, for that matter.

He studied her in silence for a long, uncomfortable
moment. "Apparently, it's far more than a simple physical attraction, Kiley. It goes deeper than that. If it didn't,
my touch wouldn't affect you this way. When you lost
your memory, it should have severed all of the connec-
tions between us." He held up their linked hands. "And
yet, it hasn't."

She blinked in surprise to discover their hands were
still joined. Despite the warning signals screaming
through her system, she accepted the contact between
them. More, she clung to it. "You think I recognize you
on a subconscious level?" she asked slowly. "Is that
even possible with amnesia?"

Again that hesitation, as though he used great care
in choosing his words. Apprehension gathered like a
hard, tight ball in the pit of her stomach, and she
couldn't help but wonder what he wasn't telling her.
Endless bits and pieces she had no way of guessing at,

let alone verifying. Everything about her life, about his, about their past and present, even any plans they may have made for the future—the details were his to select, to shade if he so chose, and she'd be forced to accept them at face value. Only one person held the key to all the information that comprised her former life, a man she had no choice but to trust. Heaven help her!

"Dr. Ruiz said your memory might return, given time," Nicolò said.

He hadn't answered her question, she noticed. Hadn't explained how or why she recognized him on an unconscious level. But his comment roused a far greater concern. "What if my memory doesn't return?"

He didn't sugarcoat it. "Then you'll have from this moment forward." That gorgeous smile flashed again, completely altering his appearance. "I suspect you'll start to regain bits and pieces of your past before too long, especially considering your reaction to me."

"Which reaction?" she asked with a hint of dry humor. "The part where I became hysterical, or the part where I melted into a heap of lust?"

Her question caught him off guard and a laugh escaped his control, the low rumbling sound like distant thunder. "A heap of lust?"

Her cheeks warmed, but she continued to meet his gaze. "Well, what would you call it?"

"The Inferno."

He spoke so quietly, she almost didn't catch his response. She tasted his words on her tongue, repeating them softly. "The Inferno. That's the perfect description for what I'm feeling." Then she made the connection. "Dante's Inferno? Clever."

"I can't claim the description as my own."

"A family joke?" she said, hazarding a guess.

Again stillness settled over him and the gaze he fixed on her, so dark and damning, almost made her flinch. "A memory, Kiley?" he asked gently. "Or just a good guess?"

Understanding hit and she inhaled sharply. "My God, you suspect I'm faking amnesia, don't you?"

His expression never eased. Nor did the manner in which he stared at her. "Why would you do that?"

"I don't know. I'm the one with the memory loss, remember? So, you tell me. Let's start with how I was injured," she requested.

Much to her relief, he didn't weigh his words this time. "You were hit by a cab while crossing the street. I came out of the hotel just in time to see it happen."

Now he did pause, but she suspected it had nothing to do with choosing what to say and how to say it. She could tell how badly the accident had affected him, could glimpse the horror and helplessness he'd experienced in those final few seconds before she'd been hit. She wasn't the only one damaged when she'd been struck by that cab. His life had also been irreparably changed.

It took a moment for him to gather his self-control before continuing. "As I said, what possible reason could you have for faking amnesia? It was a stupid, regrettable accident."

"But there's something more. I can see it in your expression. What aren't you telling me?"

"We had a fight right beforehand." The admission came hard. "You left the hotel in a hurry. If I'd stopped you from leaving, or if I hadn't delayed going after you, I might have prevented the accident from happening."

She couldn't mistake his sincerity and something loosened inside of her. Apparently, even hard, powerful men suffered from vulnerabilities. It would seem she was his. "You blame yourself, don't you? For the accident, I mean."

His fingers tightened around hers. "Yes."

"What good would it have done if you'd been with me?" She offered a reassuring smile. "Chances are we'd both have been hit by that cab."

Again that bleak expression. "Doubtful. It's far more likely that I would have prevented the incident from ever occurring."

The absolute certainty in his voice amused her. "I see I've married an arrogant man."

"That isn't arrogance, but fact."

She laughed, the sound a bit rusty, but it felt good, nonetheless. "I believe you just proved my point," she said.

Kiley couldn't say when she accepted Nicolò as her husband. Not at first touch, despite the undeniable connection between them. She'd still been too traumatized by her loss of memory at that point to accept much of anything. Granted, the unmistakable surge of lust had convinced her that she and Nicolò were two parts of a whole, clearly connected to each other physically. But that hadn't been enough to convince her they were husband and wife.

Perhaps she'd begun to accept their marriage because of the way she'd clung to him throughout their conversation. Or the scorching pain she'd glimpsed when her husband had described her accident. Or maybe it had been something as silly as his admitting that she hadn't decided whether or not to take the Dante name as her own. Whatever the cause, the result was that she accepted one undeniable fact. They belonged together.

"What are you thinking?" he asked quietly.

"I'm trying to remember, but…"

"But, what?" he prompted.

"I'm afraid." It amazed her that she confided in him after only knowing him for mere minutes. Maybe it had been like that when they'd first met. In fact, she was certain it must have been. She could practically see their affair unfold as though part of some romantic dream, where they met and connected and established an instant rapport, both emotional as well as physical. It would explain so much about her current feelings for him. "I'm afraid of what I'll find when I do remember."

"Or not find?"

His perception unnerved her. "That, too."

"Now it's my turn to ask," Nicolò pressed. "There's something else. What aren't *you* telling *me?*"

For some odd reason tears gathered in her eyes. "I'm afraid that if I go to sleep again, I'll lose more of myself, if that's even possible." She whispered the confession, almost afraid of speaking it aloud in case it gave form and substance to the nightmare. "That it'll be like that movie. You know the one? Where she wakes up each day having to start over again?"

"You mean *50 First Dates*?"

"Yes, that's it." Kiley stirred restlessly, an intense throbbing in her hip making her catch her breath before she could go on. "Isn't it ridiculous? I can remember that movie but I can't remember when or where I saw it or who I was with." She shot him a hopeful look. "I don't suppose it was with you?"

To her disappointment, he shook his head. "I should warn you that we don't know each other all that well. Our relationship really is a whirlwind affair."

She offered a crooked smile, attempting to put the merest hint of shine on a bleak situation. "Then it shouldn't take us long to catch up, should it?"

That won her another grin, one that caused her heartbeat to kick up, a fact duly noted by the surrounding monitors. "Not long at all."

A wave of exhaustion hit her and her eyes began to drift closed. "I'm getting so sleepy. It must be that shot the nurse gave me." Her fingers tightened on his. "Will you still be here when I wake up again?"

"I'll be right here. I'm not going anywhere."

So adamant. So solid and reassuring. "Will I remember you?" she managed to ask.

"If you forget, I'll remind you. And if that doesn't work…" He lifted her hand to his mouth and pressed a kiss in the center of her palm. "This is one thing you'll never forget."

"You're right. I'll never be able to forget that," she whispered. "Thank you, Nicolò. I'm so glad you're my husband."

And then darkness captured her again.

Three

"Have you lost your mind?"

Nicolò released his breath in a deep sigh. "I believe that's the same question you asked me last time we had this conversation."

"It bears repeating," Lazz proclaimed. He turned to the oldest Dante brother, Sev, for confirmation. "You can't possibly condone what he's doing?"

"Not even a little," Sev assured. He hesitated for a split second before adding, "Although—"

Lazz shut his eyes. "Oh, no. Hell, no. Do not in any way, shape or form encourage him in this madness."

"It'll give us time to figure out what she's up to," Sev offered. "If she does get her memory back, we'll be prepared. Nicolò will have gathered enough information to put a plan in place."

"Is that straight from legal?" Lazz shot back.

Nicolò fought to keep from massaging his palm. Ever since he'd joined hands with Kiley, he'd been driven by the overwhelming urge to rub the spot where her touch had branded him. It had happened to Sev and Marco after they'd been bonded with their Inferno matches. And now it was happening to him, though he didn't dare let on just yet.

"In case it's escaped your collective notice," he announced, "I'm not asking for anyone's advice or opinion. I'm simply informing you of the latest developments."

"Which includes you continuing to pose as her husband," Lazz barked. "Just what the hell do you suppose will happen when she gets her memory back?"

Nicolò lifted a shoulder in a negligent shrug. "I'll deal with it."

Lazz's twin brother, Marco, spoke up for the first time. "I think the more intriguing question is… What do you intend to do with her if she never regains her memory?" He stared at Nicolò, seeing far too much. "How long do you plan to keep up the pretense? And what do you do with her once you're convinced of her guilt?"

"Or innocence," Nicolò inserted without thought.

Marco's gaze sharpened. "You think that's at all possible?"

Nicolò considered the possibility before reluctantly dismissing it. "No. When we met at Le Premier, I'm positive she was running a con of some sort. With luck,

Rufio can uncover the truth. In addition to checking into her background, I had him collect her possessions from Le Premier."

"What did he discover?" Sev asked.

"Nothing helpful." Which only made Nicolò's suspicions all the stronger. "We didn't find anything to indicate where she came from immediately preceding our meeting, or whether she has an accomplice. We haven't found an address book, PDA, or so much as a business card. Her cell phone is a disposable. And her driver's license lists an old residence. She moved from that location—Phoenix, to be exact—eighteen months ago and left no forwarding address."

Sev frowned. "That alone should give us pause," he said. "No one maintains that low a profile unless it's for a reason. I assume you told Rufio to continue digging?"

"I did. He has instructions to call me with regular updates that I can incorporate into what I tell Kiley about our history together. Until then, I intend to keep her close."

Lazz straightened. "I don't like the sound of that. What history? And just how close are you planning to keep her?"

Nicolò spared his brother an impatient look. "Try applying some of that logic you're so fond of. She's supposed to be my wife, remember? When she's released tomorrow, I'm bringing her home with me. I've already transferred her possessions to my house and have created an entire history of how, when, where and why the two of us hooked up." All three of Nicolò's brothers shot to their feet, arguing at once. He waited until they ran out of steam before speaking again. "She's still recovering from a serious accident. She has no memory and no one to help her...except her husband."

"What if she's faking amnesia?" Lazz asked.

"Or is running part two of her con?" Marco added.

Nicolò's expression hardened. Then he'd see that she regretted playing him for a fool for a long time to come. "All the more reason to have her where I can keep an eye on her. She believes I'm her husband. I intend to play the part to the hilt until I have a damn good reason not to. So far, none of you have offered me one. Once Rufio has figured out the truth, we'll decide how to proceed from there."

"Do you have any idea the sort of trouble this could cause?" Lazz demanded.

Nicolò released a laugh, the sound ripe with irony. "It's going to cause more trouble than you can possibly imagine. Unfortunately, I don't have a choice."

The Inferno had seen to that.

"This is where you live?"

"We," Nicolò corrected gently. "This is where we live."

"Oh, right." Kiley stared up at the elegant turn-of-the-century Victorian. From deep inside the recesses of Nicolò's—*their*—home came a thundering bass woof that succeeded in rattling the stained-glass windowpanes bookending the front door. She swallowed. "What was that?"

"Ah." A brief smile came and went. "That would be a who. Brutus, to be specific."

"Brutus," she repeated faintly. "And what sort of creature is a Brutus?"

"Dog."

"Huh. It sounds more like a cross between a moose and a lion."

"That would be about right." He waited until she swiveled to face him in wide-eyed dismay before relenting. "He's a St. Bernard. Very gentle."

Time would tell. She took a deep breath and faced the front door once again. She slanted her husband a final glance. "I don't suppose you know whether I like dogs?"

"You love dogs," he stated categorically. "And you're crazy about Brutus. Everyone's crazy about Brutus."

"If you say so."

Nicolò slid his key into the lock and opened the door. A series of thuds drummed through the soles of her shoes as Brutus approached at a dead run. He reached the parquet flooring in the foyer and the speed of his forward momentum sent him skidding across the glossy wood. He slid to a stop inches from where she and Nicolò stood.

Kiley remained frozen in place, utterly petrified by the mammoth animal who probably topped her by a solid hundred pounds and appeared capable of swallowing her whole in a single gulp. The top of his head hovered at shoulder height and every inch of his massive body rippled with hard, lean muscle, while his rich, multicolored coat gleamed with health. He was a gorgeous animal, though right now she found it difficult to summon much appreciation for that fact in the face of overwhelming terror.

Nicolò dropped to his knees and performed some sort of ritualistic man/dog bonding game that had her backpedaling as fast as her aching hip would allow until her spine hit the front door. If she could have melted into the wood and out the other side, she would have.

"Nicolò," she whispered.

He glanced over his shoulder and frowned. "What's wrong?"

She fought to speak around a bone-dry throat. "I think the amnesia may have screwed up my dog appeal."

Nicolò came to his feet, creating a solid barrier between her and his dog. "Don't be afraid. I swear, Brutus is the gentlest animal in the world."

"It's just…" She swallowed. "He's so big."

"Yeah, he is," Nicolò agreed. He made a hand signal and in response Brutus dropped instantly to the floor in a sphinxlike pose. "So, we'll take this nice and slow. I'm right here beside you, and I won't let anything bad happen."

"Thanks." He held out his hand and Kiley took it without a second thought. She even allowed herself to be drawn toward the dog, who didn't so much as twitch a muscle. "Why isn't he moving?" It was downright unnerving.

"I've trained him not to." Nicolò offered a reassuring smile. "You're not the first person to be intimidated by his size. So I taught him certain behaviors that make him more approachable and less overwhelming."

"You're going to try and get us to be friends now, aren't you?" she asked with a marked lack of enthusiasm.

"Yup." He sent the dog another hand gesture and Brutus dropped his head onto his enormous front paws. Huge melting brown eyes peered up at Kiley. "Kiley, this is Brutus. Close your hand in a fist and just put it in front of his nose so he can smell you. Don't worry, he'll recognize your scent."

It took every ounce of nerve to do as Nicolò instructed and stoop in front of the huge animal. Closing her eyes and praying she wasn't about to lose half her arm, she lowered her fist to within a few feet of Brutus's snout. The dog's nose twitched and he sniffed her hand. His tail thumped in recognition and he squirmed close enough to lick her. It was as though someone had flicked a light switch. The fear didn't completely disappear, but how could she resist the sweetness exuding from Brutus?

She gave in to temptation and scratched behind his ears. After a few short minutes, her sore hip forced her to her feet and she gingerly stood with an assist from Nicolò. "His coat is so soft," she marveled. "Especially around his ears."

"Don't let him fool you. He's a cagey beast."

"Cagey?"

"It's all about food with this one. Be careful when you're eating because he'll find a way to distract you so he can snitch your meal off your plate." Nicolò interlaced his hand with hers. "Come on. Why don't I take you on the grand tour?"

"I'd love to see the place."

With Brutus leading the way, Nicolò escorted her through the lower rooms, featuring a generous-sized kitchen with a small table set in a bow window, a formal dining room off the kitchen, as well as a beautifully decorated living area. Deeper in, he showed her what was clearly his favorite room, a large den with built-in bookcases, a mile-wide plasma TV and a couch with cushions as soft and comfortable as down.

His cell phone rang right before they headed upstairs and, with a word of apology, he took the call. "What have you found out, Rufio?" He listened for a long minute. "Any family other than…? Got it. No, that's quite helpful, thanks. Just what I needed." He flipped the phone closed and offered Kiley one of the smiles that never failed to ignite a flame of intense awareness. "Sorry. Business update I've been waiting for."

"No problem."

Nicolò paused in the doorway of a large bedroom gilded by late afternoon sunlight. Leaning against the doorjamb, he waited while she circled the room. "This one's yours. I thought you'd be more comfortable having a room to yourself. At least for the time being."

Surprise held Kiley frozen for a split second. "That's very thoughtful of you," she murmured.

She didn't dare tell him that it didn't feel comfortable at all. Instead, it made her feel all the more alone. On the other hand, did she really want to spend the night in his bed? Despite her instinctive reaction to him—an all-consuming passion that defied understanding—

they'd only known each other for a few days, at least to the best of her current recollection. Her husband was being incredibly sensitive by not forcing them into an intimate relationship until she'd had time to adjust to their marriage. This situation must be every bit as difficult for him as it was for her.

Nicolò crossed to the closet and opened the double doors. "Your clothes are in here, as well as in the dresser."

Curiosity filled Kiley and she joined him, eager to see what sort of clothing she normally wore, hoping it might help her pick up clues to her personality. The wardrobe was stuffed full, with something for every occasion, though most of the items still had tags dangling from them.

"Why is everything brand new?" she asked.

"You're a Dante now. You needed clothing to match."

She examined the outfits a second time and inhaled sharply. "Nicolò, these are all designer labels. They must have cost the earth."

He shrugged. "That's what you wear. Take back whatever you don't like. You also warned me that some of them would need to be altered before they could be worn." He gave her an odd look. "I thought you'd be delighted by a brand-new wardrobe."

Did she sound ungrateful? She bit down on her lip, struggling for something appropriate to say. "Thank you," she managed. "These are all gorgeous."

"And yet…" He tilted his head to one side, fixing those unnerving dark eyes on her, eyes that seemed to see straight down into her soul. "I can tell you're less than thrilled."

"It's just a little overwhelming." She spared the closet an uncomfortable glance. "I'll adjust in time," she said, before adding beneath her breath, "Maybe."

So, why the knee-jerk reaction to the unexpected riches? Why did she shrink from the beauty and luxury of what he'd shown her. She couldn't explain it. It just felt wrong, as if she'd fallen into someone else's life and didn't have a clue how to get back to her own.

Nicolò caught her left hand in his and she stilled, overcome by the burn of The Inferno. This she understood. This grounded and centered her. His touch. Her reaction to his touch. That remarkable kiss they'd shared. The need that clawed at her, insisting that they complete what they'd started. More than anything she wanted to walk out of this room and into the bedroom that she'd once shared with him. Where she belonged.

Before she could put thought to action, he said, "There's one other thing missing."

You, she wanted to say. His mouth on hers. His skin against her skin. Taking her and making her his. "What's missing?"

He lifted her hand. "Your wedding rings."

Her eyes widened in alarm. "Did I lose them in the accident?"

"As I mentioned, our wedding was a spur-of-the-moment affair. We were supposed to buy our rings the day you were injured."

"Oh, how sad."

"Don't worry. We'll get it taken care of as soon as

you've recovered. We'll make a special day of it. How about that?"

She hesitated. "Are you sure you don't want to wait until I get my memory back?"

"I hadn't considered that." Again came that penetrating look. "Do you think you'll change your mind about the style between now and then?"

She spared an uneasy glancce toward the closet. "It's possible. Maybe our tastes are formed by our past experiences. I wouldn't want to make any decisions I'll regret later."

"If you change your mind later, we'll simply replace the rings."

"Just like that?" she marveled, before confronting him. "As though they had no meaning? As though one ring is as good as another? Tell me something, Nicolò, is that what you believe? More to the point, is that what I believed?"

He shook his head. "We never discussed it."

"No, of course not. Why would we?" Who could have imagined something like this happening? Or made contingency plans in the event it did. "I'll tell you what, let's stick with something simple. Something along the line of a plain pair of bands. If we change our mind later on, we can choose rings that strike us as more meaningful."

"You don't have to make a decision right now. You never know. You might see something you fall in love with when we go to the shop." He opened the top dresser door and removed a small square box. "Here. This is yours. You were wearing it the day of your accident."

She took the box from him, surprised by the weight of it. Removing the top, she found an intricate silver locket on a matching chain. "It's beautiful." She shot him a hopeful glance. "Did you give this to me?"

"I can't take credit for that, I'm afraid. It's your favorite piece of jewelry. A family heirloom, I believe."

"It does appear old." She turned it over, searching for a hinge. "It looks like it should open, but I don't see how. Do you know?"

He shook his head. "If it opens, you never showed me the secret. If you're curious, we can take it to a jeweler and see if they can figure it out."

"That's a good idea." She held the locket out to him. "Would you mind putting it on?"

He took the necklace and she turned, sweeping her hair aside so he could fasten the chain around her neck. She caught a brief glimpse of herself in the huge antique mirror hanging above the dresser and it gave her a start. From the moment she'd first seen her reflection in the hospital, it never failed to surprise her.

"What is it?" Nicolò asked as he fastened the locket in place.

The instant he finished, she turned her back on her image. "Nothing." She offered a bright smile. "Everything's terrific."

She could tell he didn't buy it. He dropped his hands to her shoulders and forced her to face her reflection once again. "Why do you have so much difficulty looking at yourself?"

"I guess because I see the sort of woman I wish I

were." She released a frustrated laugh. "That sounds bizarre, doesn't it?"

"A little." He eased her hair back from her face so it poured down her back. "You don't have to wish to be the woman you see. You are her."

"You don't understand."

His hands tightened on her shoulders, giving them a gentle squeeze. "Then explain it to me."

"This is so frustrating. I don't even remember what I look like. The first time I saw myself in a mirror—"

"It was like looking at a complete stranger?"

"Yes!" She started to swivel around again, but he wouldn't let her. Instead, she met his gaze in the mirror, his midnight black, hers springtime green. "I keep staring at myself, trying to discover some clue to my personality. And the best I can come up with is that I seem…nice."

"I'd call you beautiful." He tilted his head. "Part pixie and part angel."

The color deepened in her cheeks, betraying her reaction to his words. "I meant character, as well as appearance. I'm pretty. Maybe even more than pretty. But I look…" She stared at herself.

For some reason his expression went blank. "Nice."

She couldn't help grinning. "Yes. Don't misunderstand. That's a good thing. I want to be a nice person. I feel nice." She touched a spot just above her heart, close to where her locket nestled. "Inside."

"Then you must be," he informed her lightly. "Otherwise I wouldn't have married you."

She relaxed within his embrace. "I'm relieved to hear

you say it." Then she stiffened as another thought occurred to her. "But what if I've changed because of the amnesia? What if I'm not the same person I was before? What if I turn into a class A bitch or start throwing temper tantrums or pilfering the silver."

In the mirror, she saw his eyes narrow and it caused her heart to give a small jump. "Are you feeling any larcenous urges?" he asked.

"Not even a little, but—"

"Then you don't have anything to worry about."

She turned and this time he didn't try and stop her. "But... Aren't our personalities formed by the events and circumstances of our past? Since I don't have any background notes to draw from—"

"Then you'll have to rely on your instincts and allow yourself to live your life the way that feels right."

Frustration ate at her. "You make it sound so simple."

"It is that simple. Do what feels right inside." He brushed the back of his hand along the curve of her cheek. "Why don't you rest and I'll order up some dinner."

For some reason, that amused her, which helped break the tension. "I gather you don't cook?"

"I can manage toast, if forced. I leave the kitchen to experts like Marco and my grandfather."

"Marco's a brother?" she guessed.

"One of three older brothers." He ticked off on his fingers. "Sev, the eldest. Then there's Marco and Lazz, who are twins. We were raised by my grandparents, Primo and Nonna. Then there's a slew of cousins and the odd sister-in-law or two."

A sudden thought struck her and she couldn't believe it hadn't occurred to her before this. "What about me?" she asked eagerly. "Do I have any relatives?"

He shook his head. "You don't have any brothers or sisters, and your father died when you were a baby. Your mother's still around, but I haven't been able to locate her. Don't panic," he added, when she started to do just that. "According to what you've told me, it's not unusual for her to take off for weeks at a time. You said she travels a lot."

Her excitement dimmed, replaced by dismay. So she really did have no one. Or next to no one. "It doesn't sound as though I have a very close relationship with my mother, if I lose track of her for weeks on end."

Imagine if she'd never met Nicolò. If they'd never fallen in love and married. She'd have been utterly alone dealing with the aftermath of her accident, with no memory and no family to help her. She shivered in distress. He must have read her thoughts, or maybe they were mirrored on her face.

"You have my family," he told her gruffly, "even if I haven't had an opportunity to introduce you to everyone."

"Our relationship developed that fast?" she asked uneasily.

"You're looking worried again. Don't be. There'll be plenty of time to meet them once you've had a chance to recover."

"And if I don't recover?" she asked, tension underscoring the question.

He smiled. "Since you never met any of them before, it'll be a new experience for both old and new Kiley."

"Huh." The concept intrigued her. "Old and new. That's an interesting way to look at it."

Nicolò frowned in concern. "You're exhausted, aren't you? And I can tell just looking at you that your headache has started up again. Probably from all that worrying." He nudged her in the direction of the bed. "Get some sleep. I'll be close by if you need me."

Without thought, Kiley lifted her mouth for his kiss, only a split second later realizing what she'd done. She caught a momentary glimpse of something dart through his gaze, a hint of surprise mingling with an intense desire. And then his head dipped downward.

Before, in the hospital, he'd consumed her, his need a hard, driven thing. This time the kiss came softly, leisurely, but no less powerful for all that. She shuddered within his hold, reveling in the hot spice of his kiss, as swept away this time as she'd been the first.

He tugged her closer, exploring the curves of her body as he deepened their kiss. He cupped her breasts through the knit material of her shirt, thumbing the tips until they tightened into hard, rigid peaks. Before she could do more than gasp in reaction, he slipped beneath her knit shirt to investigate further.

His hands spread across the narrow expanse of her waist and the inch of sensitive skin between the gap of shirt and jeans before finding her breasts again. He teased them through her bra, the slide of the thin silk across the aching peaks almost more than she could stand. He must have realized as much because he dragged his fingertips in a torturous path to her hips, his fingers just curving around her flanks.

She could feel his erection surging against her belly and his mouth grew more determined, driving instead of teasing. His hands began to move again, restlessly exploring the curve of her backside, lightly tracing the flare of her hips before sliding to cup her where her need burned hottest. She wanted him. Heaven help her, but she wanted him to rip away her clothes and spread her on the bed behind them and give her the relief her body wept for.

She sensed he hovered on the very edge of control. They teetered there for an endless moment, locked together, on the verge of taking that final, irrevocable step. At the last instant, he released her and stepped back. But it cost him, his expression drawn into taut lines of pain.

"Sleep," he told her, the single word shredded almost beyond recognition. "You need sleep far more than this."

Kiley would have argued, but exhaustion fell over her like a blanket and she did as he suggested, curling up on top of the bed. If she'd had any doubts about their relationship, Nicolò had put them to rest in the past few minutes. How was it possible that it only took one touch from the man? A single touch and she melted in mindless desire. No way would she do that unless on some level she recognized and trusted him.

She smiled sleepily. He had a knack for easing her fears and helping her to deal with her memory loss. She doubted she'd have been able to get through this if she'd been on her own. But with her husband by her side, she felt she could tackle just about any adversity. She yawned.

How had she gotten so lucky?

The sound of gunshots woke Nicolò and sent him leaping from the bed and racing into the hallway. It was only then that he realized that the noise came from the downstairs TV. After checking Kiley's room and finding it empty, he headed for the steps, surprised to discover every light in the house ablaze. He followed the trail of lights to the kitchen, turning them off as he progressed through the house.

Earlier, he'd planned to wake Kiley when their dinner arrived. But he'd found her sleeping so soundly, he didn't have the heart to disturb her. Leaving a note seemed the best option, and it had worked, since a quick check of the refrigerator told him that she'd polished off the Chinese leftovers. He was less pleased to discover that Brutus had cleaned out everything else. Greedy mutt. It would seem that this new version of Kiley was an easy touch, and Brutus sensed as much.

Next he turned off the trail of lights leading through the dining room, into the living room and finally to the den. And that's where he found her. She and Brutus were curled up together on his couch, both sound asleep and utterly oblivious to the raging gunfight from a 40s gangster movie playing on the television.

She'd donned one of the nightgowns and robes he'd bought during her hospital stay, the robin's egg-blue setting off the vividness of her hair and the creamy paleness of her skin. She'd forked her fingers deep into Brutus's coat, her hand fine-boned and delicate against the huge, muscular dog. Brutus lay curled protectively around her, his breath escaping in deep, rumbling snores.

The desire Nicolò had felt earlier came storming back, just as messy and uncontrollable and incomprehensible as before. He hesitated, no more than an inch away from ripping off her nightgown and covering her body with his own. She wouldn't resist. Hell, based on her reaction a few scant hours ago, she'd open to him as sweetly now as she'd done then. He took a single step in her direction before he caught the violent purple bruising along the back of her shoulder.

He sucked in a shuddering breath and crossed to turn off the television, which instantly woke Kiley. Or maybe it was his lifting her in his arms that disturbed her slumber. He carried her from the room, much to the annoyance of a disgruntled Brutus.

"Where are we going?" she asked, wrapping her arms around Nicolò's neck and yawning broadly.

Her scent drifted to him, light and feminine and unmistakably her own. "Back to bed," he answered her question.

"Oh." She wrinkled her nose. "I'd really rather not."

That gave him pause. "You prefer sleeping with my dog?"

She hesitated, a heart-wrenching vulnerability sweeping across her face and shadowing her eyes. Nicolò found it difficult to believe she could fake the expression, especially straight out of a sound sleep. But perhaps he wasn't the best judge. At least, not right here and now.

"I'd rather not sleep alone," she confessed. "It's not that I'm afraid. Not exactly. It's just that I don't like being by myself. I'm not used to it."

"I can solve that problem for you."

It was inevitable. It had been from the minute he'd first seen her. First touched her. First claimed her as his own. One way or another she was destined to end up in his bed. Better sooner than later.

"Are you taking me to our bedroom?"

"Yes."

"Will you sleep with me?"

"Without question." Even if it meant an eternity of hellfire and damnation.

She snuggled deeper into his hold. "That's okay then."

Nicolò shouldered through the door to his bedroom suite and crossed to the bed. He deposited her there, struck by how small and fragile she appeared curled up on his king-sized mattress. Maybe that's how she succeeded with her cons, by looking so utterly innocent. She blinked sleepily up at him and smiled.

"Aren't you coming back to bed?" she asked.

"I am. Although, now that I have you here…" He tilted his head to one side and studied her. "What will I do with you?"

Four

"I can tell you exactly what you should do with me," Kiley replied.

Desire flashed through Nicolò. "And what's that?"

Unable to resist, he joined her in the bed and scooped her close, cushioning her head against his shoulder. There was something different about her, he realized. A quality that hadn't been there when they'd first met, as well as a quality that had vanished as completely as her memory. And then it hit him. The cunning he'd seen in that other version of Kiley was missing. And in it's place sparkled kindness and generosity and an openness he suspected would have been utterly foreign to her nature only a few short days ago.

Of course, it could all be an act, a brilliant charade

to keep him off balance. But if she were faking amnesia, he was absolutely certain he'd have caught her "tell," just as he had in the hotel room during their first confrontation. He'd have noticed some small indication of subterfuge. So far there had been none.

She curled into his embrace, fitting her curves to his angles as though it were the most natural thing in the world. As though they'd slept like this a thousand times before. For an instant they both stilled, and Nicolò became intensely aware of the intimacy of their position. He could hear her slow, shallow breathing and feel the slide of silk against his side, along with the pressure of her small, rounded breasts. Cautiously, her hand crept across his chest settling just above his heart.

More than anything, he wanted to flip her onto her back and fill her to overflowing, to take her with mouth and body. To join with her in that ultimate dance of pleasure. Nothing mattered except that he have her here and now, in his arms. He'd worry about the ramifications of his actions later. When Rufio turned in his report proving Kiley's guilt. When Kiley regained her memory. When all his outrageous mistakes hit the fan, he'd find a way around it. Because that's what he did. That's what he'd always done. In the meantime, why shouldn't they enjoy what fate had so generously provided? He should take the offering and enjoy it to the fullest, and to hell with the consequences.

But he couldn't. She'd only been released from the hospital mere hours ago, he reminded himself. She had bruises on top of bruises. And most damning of all…

She was a con artist.

It didn't matter that The Inferno shrieked through him, clawing at him to take that final step of possession. It didn't matter that Kiley seemed equally inclined to make the ultimate commitment. He couldn't trust this woman, didn't dare believe that any of this was real. He'd put his family's well-being at risk if he fell for her game. Though right this minute he almost—*almost*—didn't give a damn.

She stroked her fingertips across his chest in tiny, tantalizing circles. "I know exactly what you should do with me," she repeated. "It occurred to me while I was downstairs." The softest laugh escaped her, her breath caressing his chin and neck and wrecking havoc with his self-control. "I'd like to start over."

Okay, not quite what he'd expected. He caught her hand in his before he lost it completely. "Start over," he repeated.

She nodded, eagerness brightening her eyes. "It occurred to me when I was getting reacquainted with Brutus. You see, I don't remember any of my previous interactions with him."

Maybe because there hadn't been any. The only reason Brutus had recognized her scent when he'd first introduced them was because he'd allowed the dog to sniff some of her possessions after he'd had them transferred into his house. "When your memory returns, all that will be resolved," Nicolò offered. Of course, when her memory returned, *he'd* be the one in the doghouse.

"No. I can't wait for that. I have to live my life

now." She regarded him in all seriousness. "I don't re-member any of my interactions with Brutus, any more than I remember our interactions. I can't ask Brutus what happened."

He found himself giving her back a sympathetic stroke. "But you can ask me."

Determination filled her expression, and perhaps a hint of desperation, as well. "I want to do more than ask. And that's where my idea comes in."

He needed to stop touching her and soon. But even as the thought dawned, Nicolò found himself tucking a strand of her hair behind her ear, his fingers lingering on the silky curve of her cheek. "Tell me your idea."

"You said ours was a whirlwind affair, right?" She waited for his nod of confirmation before continuing. "So that means it wouldn't be too difficult to reenact, right?"

Aw, hell. "Reenact, as in create all over again?" he asked.

She smiled and he suddenly realized that her smile was a tiny bit crooked, her lips tugging ever so slightly to the right. For some odd reason, he found the imper-fection all too appealing. "Exactly. We can recreate our first meeting, and each of our subsequent dates. Best of all, maybe it'll help me remember."

Actually, it was a very clever idea, one that would provide her with endless amusement if she were faking amnesia. Considering they didn't have a history, other than that one disastrous meeting at Le Premier, he'd find it impossible to come up with anything real, which left creating some ridiculous fantasy.

Everything within him flinched from the idea. He'd been dishonest enough by claiming her as his wife. Granted, The Inferno had united him with this woman, and perhaps if circumstances had been different he might have pursued a serious relationship in order to see where it might take them. But no way in hell would he permanently connect himself with a con artist.

The reminder of who and what she was stiffened his resolve. He'd put this game in motion for a reason. A very simple, extremely vital reason. If Kiley O'Dell succeeded with her scam, she could conceivably claim half the value of the fire diamond mine and the Dante family jewelry empire would go under. He had to play out this game until he had proof of her true nature. Unfortunately, his physical reaction to her complicated matters.

"Nicolò?" She looked far less excited than moments before. "What's wrong? Don't you like my idea?"

"I love your idea."

"Then will you do it?"

He was digging himself deeper and deeper into an inescapable hole. How would he justify his actions if Rufio proved her innocence? He couldn't. And when she recovered her memory, those actions would cause her unfathomable pain.

But then…he didn't believe for one minute she was an innocent in all this, not based on her actions and attitude that day at Le Premier. That woman and the one currently in his arms bore no relationship to each other. Until the two melded together once again, he'd follow the course he'd set for himself. For both of them. In fact, if he played this the way she requested, he might be able to prove what she was, as well as the truth behind her claim of amnesia.

"Yes, I'll do it," he agreed. "We'll start all over again."

He could feel her relief. "Where did we first meet?"

"In the park," he answered promptly, following the history he'd scripted in anticipation of this conversation. "I was walking Brutus."

"And what was I doing there?"

"Sitting. You'd just moved to the city in order to begin a new job. Unfortunately, the company folded the week after you started."

"You took pity on me, didn't you?"

The fantasy she'd created to fill in the holes in her memory showed an impressive ingenuity and amazed the hell out of him. Unfortunately, the warmth with which she regarded him left him stirring in discomfort.

"Brutus and I both did," he said, forcing out the lie. "We cheered you up with a rousing game of Frisbee."

"Then tomorrow that's what we'll do. We'll go to the park and play Frisbee."

"Actually, we won't."

"But—"

He shook his head. "You're less than a day out of the hospital. We're not doing anything that risks putting you back there again. Frisbee is out." When she would have argued further, he added, "It was just a brief encounter, Kiley. I have an alternate suggestion, if you're willing."

"Which is?"

"I'll recreate our times together, if that's how you want to play the game." And he was painfully aware that this very well could be a game for her. "In return, you don't ask any questions beforehand. Let events unfold naturally."

"I don't understand. Why?"

"Because this way you don't have any preconceived expectations. You can just be yourself and enjoy the occasion. No…did I do this or did I say that? You can just take it as it happens and respond naturally."

"But, I don't know what's natural for me," she argued.

"Then go with what feels right."

She hesitated, considering, before giving a reluctant nod. "I guess I can do that. Are you sure we can't start tomorrow?"

He shook his head. "We wait until the doctor clears you for normal activity."

She grinned, her mouth taking on that lopsided slant again. "In that case, I'll call Ruiz first thing tomorrow."

Nicolò considered for a moment, then shrugged. "If he gives you the okay, I'm fine with it. But, I'll need a little time to set everything up."

And the first thing he'd set up would be a few "dates" that would help him determine whether or not she truly had amnesia, while giving Rufio additional time to complete his background check. Dates that would prove that she was a woman who craved the good life and all the expensive accessories that went with it. Until then…

He stretched out an arm and flicked off the light. "Try

and sleep." Because heaven knew, he wouldn't. Not with her in his bed, wrapped around him, while he couldn't do more than plant a chaste kiss on her brow.

She stirred against him, threatening to shred his ability for any sort of chaste embrace. Or so he thought until she said, "I—I don't like it this dark."

"I'm right here," he said, reassuring her. "I won't let anything happen to you. But if you'd be more comfortable with the light on..." He reached for the lamp again. "Better?"

"Do you mind?" Her eyes turned so dark they were almost as black as his own. "Ever since the accident—"

"What?" He threaded his fingers through her hair, careful to avoid the stitches from her injury. "Do you remember something?"

"No, it's not that." She moistened her lips. "As long as I can remember—which, granted, isn't long— it's never been this dark or so quiet. Hospitals are noisy, busy places. Until I woke up in your guest bedroom, I don't ever remember being alone before. I...I didn't like it."

It took him a moment to reply. "There's an easy fix to that. From now on, you sleep here with me and we leave a light on."

"Are you sure you don't mind?"

"Not even a little."

He continued to hold her until she drifted off, calling himself six kinds of fool. He watched as she slept, memorizing every curve and angle of her face. She was out cold, no faking that, so relaxed and trusting within his embrace. She'd regained some of her color, her cheeks carrying a light flush instead of that frightening waxy pallor she'd worn during her hospital visit. And her hair fell in heavy curls across her shoulders and his bared chest, the soft, springy feel of it sheer torture. Her lips were parted ever so slightly, making him long to sample them again, to delve inward and invade that honeyed warmth. To see if she tasted as sweet and rich as before or if he'd imagined it.

How could someone who looked so innocent be so amoral? Every instinct he possessed insisted she was telling the truth. That her amnesia was real. If he only had himself to consider, he'd take the risk. But his responsibilities encompassed far more than himself, and that meant he needed to use extreme caution. He had to remain on his guard every second, especially during moments like these. Intimate, private, vulnerable moments that someone experienced in running a con could turn to her advantage.

He closed his eyes, wishing he had the ability to trust. Wishing that he could believe in things like The Inferno and second chances and the goodness of human nature. But in his capacity as Dantes' troubleshooter he'd experienced far too much of the opposite to ever take such a leap of faith.

Even as the thought lingered in his mind, he settled her more firmly within his hold, his embrace equal parts possessive and protective. And as he joined her in sleep, one word sounded louder than all the others.

Mine.

* * *

Three endless days passed before Kiley received the official okay from Dr. Ruiz to resume normal activities. He also gave her the name of a doctor who specialized in retrograde amnesia, though she hoped she wouldn't need his services. Instead, she preferred to trust that with her husband's help, her memory would return on its own. It was just a matter of when.

She wished she could explain how disoriented she felt. Nicolò knew everything about her, while she knew nothing. Nothing about herself. Nothing about her likes and dislikes. Nothing about her personality or hopes or dreams. It put her in a position of reacting to all that went on around her instead of driving or controlling events. It also forced her to trust implicitly, which filled her with uncertainty and fear.

Every aspect of her life ended in a giant question mark. And every time she had to ask a question about herself and the appropriateness of her actions, or about mist-shrouded events from her past or unremembered plans for her future, it left her both dependent and vulnerable.

Well, at least she could state two things with absolute certainty. First, she didn't like feeling either dependent or vulnerable. So with each day that passed, she intended to make strides to put some distance between herself and those particular characteristics. To find a way to win back that control over her life.

And second, despite her inability to recall the details of her previous life, it was clear that her feelings toward her husband hadn't changed. It offered untold relief that she felt such a powerful hunger toward the man at her side. That she couldn't wait to be with him, held safe within his arms. To kiss him again. To relive that joy of loving and being loved. And to uncover all the secrets he kept hidden from the rest of the world, secrets he'd probably shared with her, and her alone, if only she could remember.

She wanted him. Needed him. And she had little doubt that they'd act on those desires before very much longer. Soon she'd experience anew those soul-stirring emotions when he made love to her for the first time. Maybe in those intensely intimate moments her memory would return.

She could only hope.

"I'm sure everything will come back to me if we recreate our dates," she told Nicolò. "It's bound to spark something, right?"

"It's quite possible."

Her enthusiasm dimmed. "Do you think the fact that I haven't had any flashes of recall so far means it won't return?"

He instantly wrapped his arms around her. "Not at all. And now that you've been given the all-clear, we'll see what memories we can shake loose."

They decided to skip their first meeting in the park and move on to their first "real" date. To Kiley's dismay, it didn't go quite the way she'd hoped. The day started off well enough. Her excitement at their implementing her plan carried her through the first couple hours as they toured the delights of San Francisco.

Nicolò took her to all the top tourist spots—Fisherman's Wharf and Ghirardelli Square with its view of Alcatraz Island, for a ride on the cable cars that rumbled through Chinatown and past Lombard Street, topped with a drive through Golden Gate Park. It was an exhausting array of sights and sounds, odors and impressions. Unfortunately, not one place incited more than a faint glimmer of recognition in the murky recesses of her mind, an awareness that she'd read about or seen pictures of the city at some point.

And with every stop, she glanced toward Nicolò, hoping against hope to gain some clue as to that first time. Despite her promise to him, she wanted to ask if this occasion matched the one from the past. Had they said the same things? Had they laughed or talked or shared confidences then, all the important tidbits they weren't sharing this time around because she was too empty to have anything worth contributing?

Eventually, he became aware of her growing silence and sideways looks. "What's wrong?" he asked.

She collapsed on a park bench with a weary sigh. "This isn't working quite the way I'd thought it would."

He joined her on the bench. "You don't remember anything? Not necessarily our time together, but I hoped you might remember one of the places we've been. That it might spark some vague memory."

She shook her head, frustrated beyond belief. "I don't remember a blessed thing," she confessed. "Not any of the tourist spots…" She spared him a swift, reluctant glance. "Not being with you. Ever."

He lowered his head. "I'm sorry, Kiley."

She covered his hand with hers. "None of this is your fault." He opened his mouth to argue and she cut him off. "I know you want to take responsibility for my accident. But you have to admit that if I'd been less impulsive, I wouldn't have been in the middle of a busy intersection where I could be hit by a cab."

She watched him struggle with that for a moment. "Why don't we agree to disagree on that particular subject?" he suggested.

She smiled. "I can live with that." His hand tightened on hers, tugging her close. She slid into his hold with the ease of familiarity and tilted her head to one side in consideration. "So…do we continue with our tour? Or can you think of something else that might help me remember?"

He hesitated, before nodding. "There's one more place that might prompt a memory."

"And where's that?"

He gave her the sort of smile that threatened to melt her bones. No doubt it was the same smile he'd used during those earlier dates, if only she could recall. All he had to do was turn it on her and she could feel everything soft and feminine surrendering to him, softening, urging her to agree to anything he might ask of her.

"Come on. I'd rather it be a surprise."

He drove them from the park into the heart of the city toward the financial district and Embarcadero. Beneath one of the towering skyscrapers, he pulled into an underground parking lot and escorted her to a private elevator that shot them straight to a penthouse suite. When the doors parted, they stepped out into a massive room, which at first glance appeared to be someone's private residence.

Kiley entered ahead of Nicolò, sinking into the thick, plush carpet, the soft dove-gray color giving the area an opulent, yet intimate feel. There were several divans decorated in a subtle pinstripe of gray and white, accented with a narrow band of black, and silk chairs in a rich ruby red. The pieces were simple, yet exquisite. Glass tables were arranged in front of the divans and chairs, sitting slightly higher than conventional coffee tables. The lighting also struck her as different, overhead spots creating blazing puddles of brilliance that struck the various tables, while the seats remained in soft shadow. Plants and elaborate fresh flower arrangements gave the area an added warmth.

"What is this place?" she whispered.

"Dantes Exclusive." Was it her imagination or did his gaze grow as intense as the spotlights?

"Dantes? I don't..." She shook her head in confusion. "Is this your family business?"

"You haven't heard of Dantes?"

She blinked. "Are you talking about the jewelry firm?" He simply continued to watch her and her breath escaped in a soft gasp. "You're one of *those* Dantes?"

"You remember us?"

She regarded him uneasily, seeing her husband in an entirely different light. She'd sensed his power, seen his affluence. But it had never occurred to her that he moved in such elite circles...or that she did. How could she possibly live up to what would be expected of a Dante wife?

"I wouldn't say I remember, exactly," she finally responded. "I know about Dantes the same way I know who the current president is. I retain general knowledge, just not specific memories about my past. I've heard of Dantes. I mean...who hasn't?"

He appeared to accept her comment at face value, though it troubled her that he continued to question her amnesia. She kept feeling as though he was concealing something from her. Was it something he hoped she'd remember...or something he preferred remain forgotten?

"Dantes Exclusive is the part of our retail operation for our high-end clients. It's by appointment only. I thought you might enjoy seeing some of our more select designs."

She managed a smile. Had he sprung this on her last time? Is that why he'd brought her here, today? "I'd enjoy that. Thank you."

He led her through the sitting area, past an impressive glass-and-mirror wet bar offering every possible libation, to a barely visible door set into the wall and protected by an elaborate security system. Nicolò removed a card from his wallet and swiped it across the device, before unlocking the mechanism with a combination of voice and thumbprint. The door clicked open and he escorted Kiley into a glittering fantasyland.

She stared around, wide-eyed. "Oh," she managed to murmur.

"Feel free to look around while I see if any of the family's here."

She looked at him in alarm. "Your family?"

"Don't panic. They won't hurt you. I promise." He

started to leave, then hesitated. "Unless you want to be hermetically sealed in here, I'd look but not touch."

Kiley whipped her hands behind her back and interlaced her fingers. "I wouldn't dream of touching."

The minute he disappeared, she made a slow circuit of the room, feeling more overwhelmed with each step she took. Case after case displayed jewelry sets of stunning beauty. Not to mention astronomical expense. Is this the world to which she belonged? She shook her head. No, it didn't feel right. Surely she didn't live a life of such wealth and opulence.

She paused in front of a particularly gorgeous display. Voices drifted to her from the doorway through which her husband had vanished. Nicolò's low murmur sent awareness rippling down her spine. Then came the higher-pitched reply of a woman. At first Kiley couldn't hear the actual words, but the contentious intonation came through loud and clear. Then the woman raised her voice.

"Forget it, Nicolò," she said. "I won't be party to—"

Nicolò interrupted, speaking at length in a soft, hard voice.

Then, "Okay, fine. But this is the one and only time."

Kiley hastened away from the doorway, worry balling in the pit of her stomach. What in the world did Nicolò want, and why wouldn't the woman he spoke to be party to whatever he'd suggested? Of even more concern, did their conversation involve her?

She paused by another display case, focusing all her attention on the glorious necklace, earrings, and bracelet. She was enthralled by their stunning appeal, despite her apprehension. A moment later, Nicolò entered the room, followed by a tall, elegant blonde with dark eyes. She offered a forced smile that left Kiley feeling intensely uncomfortable.

"This is my sister-in-law, Francesca," Nicolò said. "She's Sev's wife and Dantes' top designer. You're looking at one of her designs."

"It's incredible," Kiley said as they shook hands. "Simple, yet elegant. And—and warm."

Her utter sincerity must have come through because Francesca's smile softened and the cool wariness eased from her gaze. "Thank you. It's part of a collection I created called Dante's Heart."

Kiley turned back to study the display case. "I think it's my favorite of all the ones I've seen here today."

"It's the fire diamonds," Francesca stated. "Working with them makes even the most ordinary piece extraordinary."

"Is that what you call those particular diamonds?" Kiley peered closer. "Oh, wow. I see it now. It is almost as though they're on fire."

She didn't know what alerted her. Perhaps it was the fierce stillness emanating from Francesca and Nicolò. Or perhaps she felt the intensity of their joint gaze. Kiley glanced up at them and slowly straightened.

"Could you please tell me what's going on?" she asked. "It's bad enough that I don't remember. But I also don't understand the silent subtext between you two." She focused on Nicolò. "Is there some reason I'm here aside from your wanting to show me the family business and introduce me to Francesca?"

"I was hoping that seeing the fire diamonds might prompt a memory."

"What memory?"

"Any memory." He tilted his head to one side. "But it doesn't, does it?"

"Not even a little." She offered a strained smile. "I wish I had your talent, Francesca. It must give you such pleasure to create these spectacular—" And then a possibility struck her, one that left her trembling with excitement. "Oh, my God. Am—am I a jewelry designer, too? Is that why I'm here? Is that why you're acting so strangely? Am I supposed to recognize something I created?"

Struggling to contain a wild thrill of hope, she looked around with a hint of desperation before darting toward a wall full of display cases. She scanned them swiftly, praying that one of the sets would jump out and connect with her the same way she'd connected with Nicolò.

"I don't recognize anything. I'm trying. Really I am, but—" She glanced over her shoulder, her gaze clashing with Nicolò's. "Please. Please help me."

He reached her side before she'd even finished speaking and wrapped her up in a tight embrace. "Hell. I'm sorry, sweetheart." He held her close, comforting her with his warmth. "It's nothing like that."

"Oh." Kiley struggled to conceal the magnitude of her disappointment, praying she could blink back the tears before he saw them. She might have hid them from Nicolò, but she had less luck with Francesca.

The other woman joined them and caught Kiley's hand in hers. "I am so sorry," Francesca said. "It didn't occur to me that you'd jump to that conclusion. Though now that you have, it seems such an obvious leap to make. I can't apologize enough for being so cruel."

"Don't—" Kiley could feel her emotions escaping her control. She waved a hand in front of her face. "Ignore me. I probably overdid today and it's all caught up with me at once."

"Nicolò," Francesca whispered, a hint of anger coloring her voice.

"This is my fault," he replied. "I'll deal with it."

He glanced down at Kiley. One look at her face had him swearing beneath his breath. She buried her face against the front of his shirt and he jerked his head at Francesca, who left without a word, though her infuriated expression spoke volumes.

"I'm sorry," he said. "I really screwed this up. I meant for you to look at some of the wedding ring sets and see if anything appealed."

"It's too much, Nicolò. Too overwhelming and way too soon."

"I realize that." He grimaced. "At least, I realize that now."

"Should I assume that our first date didn't end like this?" she asked in a muffled voice.

"With you in tears? No, it didn't, thank God."

She released a watery laugh. "I'm relieved to hear

it." She peeked up at him. "Just out of curiosity, how did it end?"

He closed his eyes, fighting an inner battle. A losing inner battle. "Like this…"

Five

He cupped her face and lifted it to his. And he kissed her. She tasted of sweetness and tears, heat and hope, all mixed with white-hot desire. He shouldn't touch her. He sure as hell shouldn't kiss her. He'd thought that by bringing her here, to the heart of Dantes' wealth and power, he'd catch a glimpse of something. Avarice. Delight. A quick hungry look that she couldn't quite conceal.

But she hadn't shown a bit of that, not even after he'd left her alone in the room and watched her on the close-circuit cameras. If anything, she'd appeared nervous and uncomfortable, as though she'd rather have been almost anywhere other than stuck in a room with countless millions of dollars worth of the world's most stunning jewelry.

She melted against him, her mouth parting beneath his. Unable to resist, he dipped inward. The flames from The Inferno roared to life, raging through him like wildfire. If they'd been anywhere else, he'd have said to hell with it and taken her right there and then. And based on the way she clung to him, wrapped herself around him, opened to him without hesitation, she wouldn't have lifted a finger to stop him.

"I'd like to see you in one of these designs," he told her between kisses. "Clothed in fire diamonds and black satin sheets."

She shivered against him. "That would still leave too much between us. Why don't we skip the diamonds and sheets. I'd rather be clothed in Dante. Or at least, one particular Dante."

"Much as I'd like to accommodate you, we can't. Not until you've had time to heal. Until then…" He snatched another deep, penetrating kiss. "Let's go home."

Disappointment filled her, despite knowing he was being sensible. Cautious. Right now she preferred reckless and passionate. "Home it is," she reluctantly agreed. Though she remained tucked close by his side, she didn't speak again until they were in the elevator, returning to the underground garage. "So, what's your plan for tomorrow?"

An excellent question. Based on Francesca's reaction, he realized he needed to take Kiley away from San Francisco for a short time. Just long enough for Rufio to complete his investigation. It would involve a quick phone call to an old family friend, Joc Arnaud. But

Nicolò didn't anticipate any problems from that end of things.

The Dantes and the billionaire financier had enjoyed a long-term friendship. They'd even designed his wife's wedding rings, as well as the jewelry set Joc had presented to Rosalyn on the birth of their son, Joshua. With luck, he'd assist Nicolò now, allowing him to stay on Joc's private island, Isla de los Deseos, while Nicolò decided how to handle the disastrous situation he'd created.

He pulled out of the garage, sparing Kiley a swift glance. She looked pale and exhausted. He'd pushed too hard today and could kick himself for his stupidity. "I have to call a friend in order to set something up. Fair warning, it might take a day or two."

"Is this another of our dates?"

He forced out the lie. "It preceded our marriage. In fact, it was what convinced you to marry me."

"You convinced me to marry you on our second date?"

"No. After today's disaster, I've decided to move our agenda forward a few weeks."

"A few weeks?" she repeated faintly. "You weren't kidding about our having a whirlwind affair, were you?"

"I did warn you that we didn't know each other very long."

She leaned back against the headrest and closed her eyes. "How strange. I must have been an impulsive person. Which explains the dash to beat out a cab."

"That explains you," he muttered. "Now try and explain me."

"I guess we have to blame it on The Inferno. It does

seem to have a rather strong effect." She opened her eyes long enough to shoot him a look brimming with laughter. "On both of us."

"No question about that," he agreed.

She was right. The Inferno did have a strong effect on both of them. It also created a dozen problems. How did he put an end to the physical need clawing at him? Because when Rufio found the evidence of Kiley's guilt, he'd have to put an end to their relationship. He couldn't—*wouldn't*—join himself with a woman he didn't trust. Not that it would be a problem. As soon as she regained her memory and discovered how he'd scammed her in return, she'd pour ice water on any remaining embers.

And if she didn't regain her memory? He refused to consider the possibility. It would come back. He didn't doubt it for a minute. And when it did, he'd watch a woman with a nature full of sweet generosity transform into a sly, devious creature who made a living by her wits and dishonesty. Perhaps that would put a rapid end to The Inferno.

He could only hope.

Kiley could barely contain her excitement when two days later Nicolò escorted her onto Dantes' corporate jet.

"Where are we going?" she demanded.

He regarded her with a lazy smile that made her long for them to be back in bed where maybe—just maybe—he'd surrender to the passion that continued to scorch them both. So far that hadn't happened. He'd shown a disgusting amount of self-control, determined to wait until the right time and place before making love to her. She didn't have a clue when or where that might occur. As far as she was concerned, here and now would do just fine.

"We're going to Isla de los Deseos," he informed her.

"What a romantic name. What did we do there?"

As expected, he shook his head. "Not a chance. We're going to relax and enjoy ourselves. Nothing strenuous. Nothing that will wear you out. This will give you the opportunity to recoup from your accident. Plus, we'll have the time and privacy we need to get to know each other better."

"We'll also get to reenact the dates that led up to our marriage." She nodded sagely. "I have to hand it to you, Nicolò. Recoup, reacquaint and reenact. Not many are so adept at killing three birds with one stone."

"Four, but who's counting."

She tilted her head to one side, intrigued. "What's the fourth?"

His eyes grew uncomfortably direct. "Recover. As in, your memory."

"Oh, right."

For some reason that put a damper on her spirits. She didn't understand it. She wanted to recover her memory, didn't she? So, why did she shy away from the mere suggestion? Part of it resulted from a vague impression she picked up from Nicolò, as though he knew more than he'd told her.

No doubt there was. And no doubt when the time was right and she could handle the information, both physically and emotionally, he'd tell her whatever dark secrets he kept locked away. In the meantime, no matter how difficult she found it, she'd have to remain patient and wait until he felt comfortable sharing the information.

She slept for long periods of the flight to Deseos, wrapped in Nicolò's arms, held safe and secure. The rest of the time, they talked, the conversation quiet and intimate. He discussed his past while kneading his palm in an unconscious gesture, explained how he'd been taken in by his grandparents after the sailing accident that had claimed the lives of his mother and father. He spoke of Sev and how hard his eldest brother had worked to recover the family fortunes. He told her about the twins, Marco, the passionate charmer, who had tricked his bride into marriage by pretending to be his twin brother, and Lazz, the analytical loner. And he described his grandparents, how after The Inferno struck, Nonna had broken her engagement to another man and emigrated to California with Nicolò's grandfather, Primo.

She could picture Nicolò so clearly as a youth. Feel his pain. Sense his determination to solve the unsolvable, perhaps as a result of being unable to ease his family's sorrow after his parents' death. She suspected that he possessed that same determination to fix her situation. The thought brought a misty smile to her mouth, a mouth he instantly captured with his own.

"I like it when you smile," he told her.

"You say that so reluctantly," she teased. "Are you afraid I'll use it against you?"

"Would you?"

"Yes." She tightened her arms around his neck. "If it made you kiss me again, I'd use it against you on an hourly basis."

She leaned forward to demonstrate when the flight attendant made an appearance, warning that they'd be landing in a few minutes. Kiley released her husband with a disappointed sigh and buckled up just as the plane banked over a lush mountainous island dotting the surface of an aquamarine sea. They landed on a private airstrip and were driven to a secluded cabana sitting within the embrace of a stand of palm trees, steps from a private lagoon.

The cabana took Kiley's breath away. Decorated in vivid colors, typical of the Caribbean, it boasted a bamboo floor and every possible modern convenience. "How long are we staying here?" she asked.

"As long as we want."

She turned in alarm. "I only packed an overnight bag. I don't have enough clothes."

He shrugged. "Not to worry. They don't wear clothes here." He waited a beat before laughing at her expression. "I'm kidding."

"Thank goodness," she said faintly.

"We can buy anything you need."

Her brows drew together. "That seems rather excessive. If you'd just told me, I'd have been happy to—"

"You won't need much. A couple bathing suits. A couple dresses for the evening. We'll check out the shops in a little while."

First the wardrobe full of designer clothes, then

Dantes Exclusive, and now this. She regarded him with a troubled expression. "I need to ask you a question and I'm not quite sure how to phrase it."

"Just be direct," he suggested.

"Are we…rich? Or rather, are you?"

"Yes."

So brutally frank. "Was—was I?"

He hesitated before shaking his head. "No."

She nodded in relief. "That makes sense. This feels…"

His scrutiny intensified. "What?"

"Different," she admitted with a shrug. Then she brightened. "But considering how short a time we've known each other, perhaps that explains it. I'm probably not accustomed to such a lavish lifestyle."

He turned to face her, folding his arms across his chest. She'd always been aware of his impressive size, especially in comparison with her own. But for some reason his current stance made her even more aware of it than usual. "You know that much about yourself, even though you have amnesia?" he asked.

The softness of the question captured her full attention. "It's not anything I remember," she hastened to explain. "It's just a feeling I have. Like I'm out of step or something. Like this isn't me."

"Not you?" He shook his head. "You seem to be operating under a misapprehension that I need to straighten out. You didn't have much money, but you thoroughly enjoyed the best life had to offer."

She couldn't conceal her shock. "I did?"

"Designer clothes and accessories. Five-star hotels."

He caught her hands in his and turned them so she could see the lacquered tips. "Professional manicure and pedicure. An expert hairdresser. They were all part of your lifestyle when we first met."

For some reason his words impacted like a body blow. "I didn't know." Nor did she like hearing the truth. It felt wrong. Unappealing. Superficial. Was that the sort of person she'd been before? "If I was so shallow, why were you attracted to me?" she asked, troubled. "Why would you have married me?"

His fingers interlaced with hers until their palms joined. She could feel the heat from The Inferno build there, melding them together. "It's been like this from the beginning."

Oh, God. She stared at him in distress. "It's physical? Our entire relationship is based on this Inferno we feel for each other? That's it?"

"Would you like there to be more?"

"Of course!" She searched his expression. "Wouldn't you?"

"My grandparents have been married for five and a half decades. I'm well aware there has to be more to marriage than physical attraction. But that takes time to build."

"How do we build it when I know nothing about my background?" she protested, her distress increasing by the second. "Nothing about my history or experiences? How do we find common ground?"

"We start with this—"

He swept her into his arms and ravished her mouth with a kiss that stole every single thought from her head.

Heat bloomed, a messy stream of need that lapped through her veins, bringing a flush to cheeks and breasts before settling in the very core of her. He invaded her mouth, teasing her until she couldn't stand it any longer.

She fought back, deepening the kiss until it was his turn to catch fire, his turn to burn. His turn to lose control. She tugged his shirt free of his trousers and swept her hands underneath. The instant she hit skin she slowed, tracking a wayward path across his chest as she gathered all that heat in her palms. And then she dipped lower, over the rock-hard ripple of abs to the belt that prevented her from a more intimate exploration. She settled for outlining the thick bulge she found there, cupping him as he'd once cupped her. At the last instant, he caught her hands in his and pulled them away.

"We start with this, the physical," he said, gritting out the words. "And we build on it. Together."

She collapsed against his chest and nodded. What a wonderful word. "Together," she whispered.

He made a visible effort to catch his breath. "And the first thing we're doing together is purchasing the clothes we'll need for our stay here."

Kiley wrinkled her nose at him. "That wasn't quite the togetherness I had in mind."

"It wasn't quite the togetherness I had in mind, either." Wry amusement gathered in his dark eyes. "But it'll have to do until—"

"Until when?" she couldn't resist asking.

She'd never seen Nicolò look so conflicted. "Until your memory returns. Until you can make an informed choice."

Iciness replaced the heat of only moments before. An informed choice? What did that mean? And of even greater concern... What had happened between them that prompted him to put that sort of condition on their current relationship? What happened the day of her accident that she no longer remembered? When she first awoke in the hospital, Nicolò had told her they'd fought moments before she'd been injured. Whatever the cause of the argument, it had been serious enough to send her darting in front of a cab. Serious enough that her husband wouldn't make love to her until she remembered.

Was it also serious enough to end their marriage?

Kiley entered the restaurant, Ambrosia, feeling more awkward and uncomfortable than she could ever remember. Her mouth curved in a wry smile. Not that she had much basis for comparison.

At least her bruises were no longer visible, since in the gown Nicolò had purchased, they would have stood out like a neon sign. She skated a hand down the pale green silk that molded to her waist, hips and thighs before flaring outward in a short train, and struggled to appear poised and confident. It took every ounce of willpower not to tug at the strapless bodice, one that revealed more than it concealed.

She associated the elegant gown with "Old Kiley," a woman, based on her husband's description, she neither liked nor understood. Maybe that other version of herself enjoyed a life rich in sensual pleasure. The only sensual pleasure this Kiley cared about was the one she found in Nicolò's arms.

But did her preference match his? She searched his stunning profile. He was a Dante. A man who hobnobbed with billionaire financiers and jet-setters. He had a position to maintain. He'd been so patient with her, but maybe his patience would soon run out. Maybe he'd brought her here in an effort to change her back into the woman he'd first married.

She worried at another possibility, one that concerned her more than any other. Perhaps he chose her originally because she fit into his world, something no longer true. Without a memory of all the little turns of events that led her to develop into the person he married, she could only base her actions on what felt right. And though it broke her heart to admit it, this current getup felt completely wrong. No matter how hard she struggled to fit in, she simply didn't.

Since the moment she'd awoken in that hospital bed and been claimed by her husband, she'd been forced to rely on her instincts. And those instincts—straight down to the very core of her—told her that she bore no relationship to this glossy woman he'd patchworked together for a dinner date with some fancy billionaire glamour couple. Perhaps that had been true once upon a time. But not any longer. Not unless she regained her memory and lost her current self. If this version of Kiley wasn't good enough for Nicolò, she had a terrible feeling it doomed their relationship before it ever truly began.

The knowledge hung over her like the sword of

Damocles, threatening with one swift plunge of the blade to render her from a man The Inferno insisted was her soul mate. A man she knew, deep in her heart of hearts, belonged to her every bit as much as she belonged to him.

Or did he belong to that other Kiley?

The maître d' appeared just then and showed them to a private dining alcove and a few minutes later Joc Arnaud and his wife, Rosalyn, appeared. To Kiley's surprise, Rosalyn proved to be a fellow redhead, although her hair gleamed a deep, rich auburn instead of Kiley's brighter shade. Of equal interest, Joc shared Nicolò's coloring.

The similarity ended there, of course. Rosalyn had the height and curves that Kiley lacked and crossed the room with long, ground-eating strides that proclaimed her as comfortable on a Texas cattle ranch as in a ballroom. She stuck out her hand with equal forthrightness.

"I'm Rosalyn Arnaud," she announced. "Pleased to meet you. And this is my husband, Joc."

"Kiley O—Dante. Sorry." She released a quick laugh as they all exchanged handshakes. "I guess I'm still getting used to my name."

"Nicolò told us about your accident." Rosalyn took the seat Joc held for her and dropped her hand over Kiley's, giving it a gentle squeeze. "I'm really sorry that you're going through such a difficult time."

"The doctors say I could get my memory back at any time."

"In the meanwhile it must make it very difficult to take everything in. You must feel so dependent and vulnerable."

"That's exactly how I feel," Kiley confessed. "I don't know what I'd do if it weren't for Nicolò."

"Right." Rosalyn's gaze flashed in his direction and she smiled sweetly. "At least you have a husband who loves you and only has your best interests at heart. Someone you can trust to protect you."

Joc took the menu from their waiter and handed it to his wife. "Here you go, Red. See what trouble you can get into with this."

She shot a grin at Kiley and leaned in. "That means be quiet," she whispered in a voice that could be clearly heard by everyone at the table. "Not that I ever listen."

Kiley laughed. "How did you two meet?" she asked, intrigued by the unmistakable differences in attitude and polish between husband and wife.

"Joc sent some goons to my ranch in a vain attempt to buy it. I stormed his citadel and explained why that wasn't going to happen."

"And then?"

"Then he kidnapped me—"

"I most certainly did not," Joc argued. "I tendered an offer which you accepted with impressive alacrity."

"—and he brought me here and proceeded to seduce me." Rosalyn helped herself to a breadstick. "It was actually quite enjoyable."

"Coming here or being seduced?" Kiley asked.

Everyone laughed and Rosalyn gave Kiley a look of undisguised approval. "Since it resulted in our son, Joshua, I'd have to say that tips the scales ever so slightly toward the whole seduction number. What about you?"

"Oh, I'm hoping for a big seduction number, too." She waited for the laughter to die down again before asking, "How old is your son?"

"Not quite a year and walking already," Joc answered. "That's why we were late. We needed to settle him for the night and he wasn't in any hurry to settle. Then I had to talk Rosalyn into putting on the fancy duds."

"I'd live in jeans if it were up to me," she confessed.

"You don't—" Kiley broke off, searching for a more tactful way to phrase her question. "I assumed—"

"That we always live and dress like this?" Rosalyn shook her head. "Honey, if it were up to me, I'd never attend another fancy shindig for the rest of my natural born days. That's Joc's thing, not mine."

"A consequence of my position, I'm afraid." Joc glanced at Nicolò. "And of being a Dante, too, I presume."

Nicolò nodded and it wasn't until then that Kiley became aware of how quiet he'd remained all this time, content to sit back and observe. Observe her, she suddenly realized, while kneading his palm in a gesture that grew more habitual with each passing day.

"I'm not on the frontline quite as much as Sev or the twins," Nicolò conceded. "But I'm forced to do my fair share when the occasion demands."

"I doubt I'll ever get used to it," Kiley confessed. "I'm a nervous wreck right now."

Joc's brows pulled together. "Well, we can fix that easily enough." He shoved back his chair and stood. "I'll arrange for dinner to be delivered to our cabana. You and

Nicolò can meet us there in say…twenty minutes? Will that give you time to change into something casual? We'll send the nanny on her way and just relax and eat and have some wine. How does that sound?"

Before Kiley could interject, Nicolò nodded. "Sounds perfect, Joc. Thanks for understanding."

"Nothing to understand," he assured.

They met up twenty minutes later and Kiley thoroughly enjoyed every second of the evening from that point on. After dinner, a demanding wail sounded from one of the bedrooms and a few minutes later Rosalyn appeared with a sleepy baby held close in her arms. At first glance his hair seemed as dark as his father's, but as the two drew closer, Kiley saw it reflected a hint of Rosalyn's deep auburn. He'd also inherited his mother's eyes, the color an unusual violet-blue. He blinked at the assembled group for a moment, taking it all in, before offering a huge grin, proudly displaying a pair of bottom teeth.

Kiley couldn't resist. It was a night of new experiences and fate offered her one more she wanted to add to her collection. "May I?" she asked. "I can't remember ever holding a baby before."

Rosalyn instantly melted. "Joshua's still half-asleep, so I'm not sure how he'll take to you. Just don't be offended if he decides he wants to go to Joc. He's more of a guy's guy than a momma's boy."

Kiley took the baby into her arms, cradling him in her arms, barely daring to breathe. Joshua blinked up at her and she could tell he was weighing his options—

scream his little head off or put up with her. To her delight, he gave her the benefit of the doubt.

"He's almost a year, and yet he still smells so new," she whispered to Nicolò.

He chuckled, joining her on the couch and wrapping an arm around her and the baby. "Try smelling him when he loads that diaper of his."

"Amen," Joc and Rosalyn said in unison.

The rest of the evening passed, possessing an almost dreamlike quality. Contentment settled over Kiley, along with a renewed self-confidence. Maybe she could handle this, especially if all Nicolò's friends were as nice as the Arnauds. She continued to hold Joshua, who promptly fell asleep against her breast.

"Lucky brat," Nicolò whispered in her ear.

"No," she whispered back. "Lucky me."

When the evening came to an end, Kiley reluctantly handed over Joshua and she and Nicolò made their farewells. They followed the lighted walkway from the Arnauds' cabana to their own, enjoying the exotic scents that filled the sultry night air. It gave Kiley a moment to think, to address the whispered concerns that had gradually grown to a shout during the course of the evening. She'd learned two very important facts this evening.

First, that she could act the part Nicolò required of her in order to fit into his world. And second, that she didn't want to pretend to be anyone other than herself, the "real" woman she instinctively recognized as her true persona. Now, she had to convince her husband of that. Nicolò unlocked the door and waited for her to precede him into the darkened interior. She paused in the foyer, turning to face him.

"I can't continue this pretense any longer," she announced.

Six

Nicolò froze, Kiley's words causing bitter disappointment to clash with cynical triumph. *Gotcha*. He didn't know what about tonight had set her off, but she was finally going to admit the truth of who and what she was.

"What can't you do?"

She swiveled to face him, taking a step in his direction that shifted her from deep shadow into a pool of moonlight. "I can't continue living this sort of lifestyle. It feels…wrong. *I* feel wrong."

Okay, not quite what he expected. "You didn't enjoy this evening?"

"This evening—or at least, the second half of the evening—was incredible. But not all the rest. Not the trappings and the facade I'd have to adopt." Worry filled her expression. "Is it necessary, Nicolò? Do I have to become the woman I was before in order for our relationship to work?"

"No." The word escaped before he could stop it. "You can be any sort of woman you wish."

"And you'll still love me?"

The question burned like acid. "My feelings for you won't change."

"Even though I've changed?"

"Give it time, sweetheart."

She took another step in his direction, closing the gap between them. Her hands slipped across his chest and gathered up handfuls of his shirt. "I don't want to be the Kiley you described to me earlier. How can I like or respect her if she's as shallow inside as she is on the outside? I just want to be who I am now. Can you live with that? Can you accept that?"

He wasn't the one who wouldn't accept it. She, herself, wouldn't. Couldn't. Not once she regained her memory. But how did he explain that to her, without telling her the rest? "It's not my decision," he said, regret roughening his voice. "If your memory returns you'll be who you were before. The events that will have occurred since then may alter your perspective, somewhat. But you'll be the Kiley O'Dell I first met."

Tears filled her eyes and she shook her head. "I can almost hear the clock ticking down. Only in this version I don't know who or what Cinderella turns into when the clock strikes midnight. I'm afraid of that other woman, afraid I'll turn into something or someone I won't like."

"I don't understand. Don't you want to remember?"

"Yes. No. The way you act—" She shook her head, her tears catching on the end of her lashes. "The way everyone acts makes me wonder what you're not telling me. Even Rosalyn—"

Aw, hell. "What about her?"

"She was annoyed with you about something. Please don't deny it," Kiley added, before he had a chance to speak. "All that business about being vulnerable and having to trust you. I can read between the lines. I also overheard you and Francesca arguing at Dantes Exclusive. I'm not an idiot, Nicolò. You're keeping something from me. What is it?"

"It's nothing."

The tears fell then, each one impacting like a knife to the gut. "You're lying," she whispered, not even attempting to disguise her pain. "You said we fought right before my accident. Were we about to break up? Is that it? Is that what you can't bring yourself to tell me? Are you just waiting until my memory returns before you put an end to our marriage?"

"We did argue," he admitted. "And it's possible that when your memory returns you'll want to end our relationship."

"Why?"

He shook his head. "Call it irreconcilable differences."

"What happens if I never regain my memory?" she

persisted. "If I never remember, do we continue to pretend there isn't a problem? For how long?"

"You'll get it back." He said it with such flat certainty that she flinched.

"What if I don't?" The question sounded more like a wish and a prayer. "What happens then?"

"I don't have an answer for you."

"That's why you initially put me in a separate bedroom. Why we haven't made love. Why you're insisting that I regain my memory before we do. Because we were on the verge of divorce."

"It was an argument, Kiley. That's all."

She took a step back, releasing him. Her eyes glittered like crystal in the moonlight, leached of all color. She reached for the first button of her blouse and thumbed it through the hole. Then a second. And a third. The deep V of her neckline revealed the intricate heart-shaped locket on its thin silver chain.

It was almost identical to their first meeting at Le Premier when she'd tempted him with that tantalizing striptease. Only this time around, he didn't catch a flash of vibrant red. This time he couldn't tell what color provided such a sharp contrast between the milky whiteness of her skin and the unrelenting darkness of her blouse.

His gaze shot to her face and he searched for some hint to her thoughts, some clue that she was playing him by reenacting that initial meeting. But he saw nothing other than a fierce determination.

She finished unbuttoning her blouse and shrugged it off. It crumpled to the floor behind her. She kicked aside her sandals before tugging at the snap of her jeans. Next came the rending of her zipper, the sound shattering in the dense silence of the foyer. She slipped the denim off her narrow hips, her no-nonsense movements in complete opposition to her provocative actions during their hotel room meeting.

She stood before him in bra and panties. When he made no attempt to touch her, she reached behind her back and unfastened her bra and tossed it to one side. And then her panties disappeared as simply and economically as her jeans.

Moonlight poured over her, silvering the creamy white of her skin and creating interesting shadows beneath the slight curve of her breasts, as well as in the nest of curls at the junction of her thighs. It also spotlighted a small birthmark that rode the curve of her hip, one that reminded him of a flower in full bloom.

Some might have called her figure boyish. Nicolò found it anything but. Her arms and legs were sculpted with lean muscle with just enough curves to make them distinctly feminine in appearance. Her breasts were on the small side, certainly, but they were also round and pert, with the nipples forming perfect pearls that he longed to taste. She was so delicate, her ankles and wrists coltish-slender. And yet, she was all woman, an indomitable woman at that, determined to tempt him beyond endurance.

The Inferno woke with a roar, consuming him in huge greedy gulps, filling him with an insatiable hunger. In that moment he didn't care who she'd been before.

All that mattered was here and now. They belonged together and he refused to deny that fact any longer. He'd deal with the fallout from his actions when Kiley regained her memory. In the meantime he'd take what she so generously offered. Take it and be damned grateful because when she came to her senses, she'd make him pay.

Big-time.

In one swift stride he reached her and swept her into his arms. "I hope you know what you're doing," he told her.

Her arms whipped around his neck and clung. "Not even a little. Not that I care."

"I'll remind you of that at some point down the road."

"I won't forget." Her expression grew fierce. "Not this time."

He shouldered his way into their bedroom and dropped her onto the mattress. She came up on her knees, lost amid the flow of cream silk covering the mile-wide bed. He didn't waste any time. He stripped out of his clothes and joined her. And then he paused. Slowed. Allowed himself to savor the moment.

The moonlight had followed them in here and caught in the long curls of her hair. He could just make out a whisper of blush in the pale color, as well as the merest hint of green in the eyes she trained so steadily on him. "The light?" he asked, remembering how she hated the dark.

"It's not necessary." She cupped his face and lifted upward, fitting her mouth to his. "Not any longer."

He sank into her, home at last. "Are you sure," he murmured between a series of long, drugging kisses.

"Positive."

"No regrets come morning?"

"No regrets ever."

His smile held little humor. "Don't be so sure of that."

"And I'm guessing you aren't going to explain that particular remark, either."

"No." He lost his hands in the weight of her hair. "But there's one thing I want you to know and believe."

Her head tipped back giving him better access to the length of her neck. "And what's that?"

He slid his index finger along the pulse throbbing in her throat before following the same path with his tongue. "It was like this between us from the first moment we met. From the instant I set eyes on you, I wanted you."

"Was the feeling mutual?"

"You know the answer to that."

She smiled, the curve of her lips full of mystery and allure. "I responded the same way as I did at the hospital." It wasn't a question.

"Yes."

"I may have no memory," she whispered. "But I know you. I know your touch and your scent. I know the sound of your heartbeat and how it echoes my own. I know you were meant to be mine, just as I was meant to be yours."

He shook his head. "Kiley—"

She stopped his words with her hand. "I'm serious,

Nicolò. On some level I must remember you. It's as if you imprinted yourself on my heart and soul. Can't we just start over, as though that fight never happened?"

He closed his eyes. "It won't change anything. Not in the long run. Not when you regain your memory."

She shifted, opening herself to him. "I'm willing to take the chance."

The last of his resistance vanished. He lowered himself to her, sliding over her. Skin burned against skin. Curves and angles collided before shaping themselves, one to the other. She was soft, so soft. It took every ounce of control to keep from burying himself in that softness. And then a stray thought took hold.

If her memory loss was real... If she couldn't remember anything of her life before, then she also didn't remember making love. For her this would be another new experience. And even if she regained her memory at some point, this night would, quite possibly, hold special meaning for her. How could he do anything other than make it as unique for her as possible?

He slowed the pace, taking her mouth in slow, deep kisses. And all the while he gave to her, gifted her with quiet caresses and teasing strokes. With whispered words that brought a flush of warmth to cheek and breast. He let her know with every touch, with every appreciative murmur, with every sweep of his hand that he thought her the most beautiful woman he'd ever held in his arms. And she believed him, because it was the truth.

"Is this how it was the first time we were together?" she marveled at one point.

He couldn't lie. Not here. Not now. Not in such an intensely intimate moment when they were both stripped to their bare essence. "This isn't like any other time. This is new for both of us."

"I'm glad. I want it to be different. I want it to be special."

And it would be. He'd see to that. He cupped her breasts, as tantalizing and perfect as the rest of her, and lathed the sensitive tips. She arched beneath him, pressing herself deeper into his mouth. He scraped the tight nipples with his teeth and heard the soft cry of pleasure it elicited. And then he tormented her other breast, feeling the pounding of her heart against his cheek.

The need to taste more of her drew him and he slid downward, sampling the soft indentation of her belly and the small birthmark at her hip, before finding the thick blush of curls that concealed the heart of her. He parted the delicate folds and gave her the relief her body wept for. Her hips rose to meet his kiss, her thighs taut and trembling as she teetered on the knife's edge. He pushed, ever so slightly, and she went over with a cry, all fluid heat and gasping pleasure.

"We're not done, yet," he warned. "Not even close to done."

"I don't want this to ever end." Her hands curled in his hair and she tugged, drawing him up and over her. "I want this night to last forever."

She was so beautiful, still captured within the moon-silvered glow of her climax. "It's not within my power to make the night last forever." He traced her features, one by one. The winged arch of her brows, the wide, vivid eyes, her sculpted cheekbones and pert nose, right down to her sweetly lopsided smile. "But the memory of tonight will last forever."

Her smile faded. "What if I forget again?"

His gaze grew tender. "Then I'll remember for you."

Tears gathered in her eyes. "I'd like that."

He began again, building on what had gone before. Her reaction to him came quicker this time, her responses more natural and fluid. And she gave back in ways that threatened to send him straight out of his mind.

Her quick, clever hands stroked and gripped before flitting away to provoke a new sensation. And she moved—heaven help him, how she moved—with a sensual grace that drove him wild with desire. She flowed over his body like silk, cupping him, tracing a provocative finger of exploration across velvet and steel. By the time she finished she knew every inch of his body. But then, he knew every inch of hers.

Finally, the exploration ended in the ultimate discovery. Making short work of slipping on protection, he parted her thighs and forged deep inside. She wrapped herself around him, clinging to him as though she never intended to let go. And then she rocked upward, surging with him into a rhythm as old as mankind.

Nicolò could feel the white-hot forging of The Inferno, could feel the ultimate completion of the bond between them and the way it expanded until it filled him to overflowing. It didn't matter any longer whether Kiley was con artist or innocent. They belonged together, two parts of a whole. How their affair would ultimately end was a question for another time and place. All that mattered was here and now.

This moment.

This woman.

The creation of this memory, everlasting.

She shuddered beneath him. "No, not yet."

"Now, Kiley. Go over with me."

Their gazes locked, his demanding, hers so trusting it would haunt him forever. He cupped her head as he surged inward, watching her give in and take flight. Feeling her surrender radiate outward until it encompassed her entire body. And he soared with her, losing himself in her heat and warmth. Losing himself in that moment of ultimate completion. Losing himself, body and soul.

"How could I have forgotten that?" she whispered in the darkness. "How is it possible that something so—"

"Perfect?" The word escaped without thought.

"Yes. Perfect." She didn't speak for a long moment, and then added, "I thought when we made love I'd remember. That the strength of it would bring the past back to me."

He couldn't help himself. He froze. "It didn't?"

"No. I only have this one memory of us together. All the other times are—" Her hand fluttered through the air. "Gone."

Her voice broke on that last word and she curled into him, her tears biting into his skin. All he could do was hold her while she wept and allow the guilt to eat him alive. He couldn't doubt her any longer, at least not about her amnesia. Whatever she'd been before was currently trapped in the dark recesses of her mind, perhaps forever.

So where did the two of them go from here? He'd taken her on as his responsibility, claimed her as his own. Worse, he'd taken advantage of her vulnerability. If she'd been a scam artist, what did that make him?

He closed his eyes, flinching from the question. Up until now he could justify his actions. Could claim he was acting for the better good of his family. But what he'd done this night wasn't for anyone's benefit but his own. Hell, he could blame it on The Inferno, could claim that their ending up in bed together was inevitable. But at least he knew all the facts, had taken this step with total awareness and understanding.

Kiley hadn't. Worse, she believed they were married, that when she'd given herself to him, that it had been a wife to her husband. He pulled her close and kissed the top of her head. She murmured drowsily and snuggled closer. No question about what was going to happen as a result of his actions tonight, especially if his "wife" regained her memory anytime soon.

He was going straight to hell.

"What are you up to, Nicolò Dante?" Kiley faced her husband, her hands planted on her hips. Not that she appeared terribly intimidating, an impossible feat when dressed in a minuscule bikini, her modesty barely preserved by the paper thin floral pareo she'd wrapped around her hips. "You have *secret* written all over you."

"A small deviation in plans."

"We're not reenacting another date?" she asked, unable to prevent a small twinge of disappointment.

He shook his head. "Since the one time we attempted it you ended up in tears, I'd rather not. So, I decided to try something else. You gave me the idea last night when you were holding Joshua."

She stared blankly. "I did?"

"You did." He adjusted her hat so her pale skin remained shaded from the powerful rays of the sun. "You commented that holding a baby was a new experience for you. So, I've decided to give you a few more new experiences. They're waiting for you on the beach."

He led her toward the lagoon outside their cabana and she paused halfway across the sand, staring in amazement. A huge table had been assembled beneath a canvas tent, the linen-covered surface overflowing with food, drinks, and even flowers.

"What's all this?" she asked in astonishment.

"These are new memories." He gestured toward the table. "We're starting with appetizers and ending with dessert. There's a little of everything."

It took her a moment to reply. "And the flowers?"

"I had them gather up every variety they had in stock. You decide which ones you like best."

"Oh, Nicolò, this is so thoughtful of you."

She threw her arms around him and lifed her mouth to his. He took his time with the kiss, sparking a return of the passion they'd shared the previous night. Before she could act on it, he caught her hand in his and drew her across the sand to the tent. Once inside, he considered the flowers and finally plucked one from the various arrangements, one she wouldn't have expected.

"Honeysuckle?" she asked. "Do I make you think of honeysuckle?"

He hesitated. "One of my earliest memories is wandering through my grandfather's garden. He has this beautiful pink honeysuckle growing along one of the fence lines. I couldn't have been much more than three, but that scent drew me. It was indescribable. I think I got drunk on the perfume."

She leaned in and inhaled the delicate sweetness. "It's wonderful."

"It was my first flower, my first memory of one. My first floral scent."

"It's your favorite, isn't it? That's why you're sharing it with me."

"Yes. Though I learned to be cautious around a hedge of blooming honeysuckle."

"Uh-oh. Bees?" she asked, hazarding a guess.

"'Fraid so. That day was also my first bee sting."

She frowned. "So one of your favorite memories is also one of your most painful."

"I've discovered that's often the way life works."

"Why, Mr. Dante, you're a cynic."

"Comes with the territory, I'm afraid. As Dantes' troubleshooter I see all the problems. It's my job to fix them."

"Regardless of the cost?"

"Yes." He gave her a direct look, one that seemed to chill the humid warmth of the midday air. "And sometimes that cost is very high."

"You don't have to worry about that now," she told him, her tone taking on a fierce edge. "You don't have to troubleshoot a problem while we're on Deseos. Not here. Not with me. You can relax and enjoy yourself while we have fun playing."

He swept a curl tightened by the unrelenting humidity back from her temple and tucked it behind her ear. Then he anchored it in place with the sprig of honeysuckle. "You, my dear, cause me nothing but trouble."

He said it with such a look of good humor that she couldn't take offense. "Well, as long as I'm already trouble for you, why don't we see how much more I can cause you?" She shot him a flirtatious glance from beneath the brim of her hat. In response, heat flared to life in his dark eyes. "What do you say we dive into that table of new memories?"

The rest of the day was one of sheer delight and endless sensual pleasure. It wasn't just the food or flowers or drink, but who she shared them with. Nicolò. Nicolò, who left her in fits of laughter one minute and in the next moved her to tears with his poignant stories of family. Nicolò, who turned her life golden with a single smile. As the sun slipped away, and the shadows grew long, she went into his arms.

"Thank you for such an incredible day," she told him. She lifted her mouth to his in order to sample the sweetest of all the desserts. This put the final touch on their time together. This made it perfect. His reaction to her was instantaneous. He tugged her close, wrapping his arms around her with a power and strength that reminded her of their night together. He'd put those skillful hands on her the previous evening, used that strength and power—and gentleness—to drive her insane with desire.

She caught his lower lip between her teeth and tugged. With a groan, he opened to her and she slid into rich, lush warmth. Drowned in it. Drowned in him. "Please, Nicolò," she whispered against his mouth. "After all the new, I need something old. Not too old," she hastened to add. "Just a little old. A slight bit repetitive."

"One night old?" he suggested with a soft chuckle.

"Yeah. That should do it."

Without a word, he turned her toward the cabana and they walked hand-in-hand into the dusky interior. One by one, clothes were discarded, creating a pathway of color from doorway to bedroom. There was a different quality to their lovemaking this time. Less desperation. No, she decided with a muffled groan. She still felt desperate, in the best possible way. But there was less uncertainty. She had a better idea what to do and how to do it. And she put that knowledge to work.

Where before he'd taken charge, had guided the pace and rhythm, this time she took the lead. With each stroking caress, her confidence grew, as did her creativity. And then intent dissolved in the face of helpless passion. There was no follower or leader, just the two of them, lost in one another, drowning in glorious sensation. Reveling in touch and possession.

She took him in, hard and deep, moved with him, seeking that moment, that sweet, sweet moment when the melding would come, when two were mated into one. At last it hit, an uncontrollable rolling that crashed over her and sent her up and over. And as she tumbled, helpless beneath the hugeness of it, she realized she'd just experienced something else new, new and infinitely precious.

She'd just discovered how to love.

Seven

Nicolò and Kiley ended up spending five more delicious days and nights on Deseos; bright, shiny moments she treasured and held close to her heart. Although their original plan had been to duplicate the dates they'd enjoyed leading up to their island marriage—dates she still couldn't recall—she much preferred Nicolò's change of plan. Instead of repeating the old, he'd filled their time together with an endless tumble of new sensations, memories she'd always treasure.

Finally the time came for their return to San Francisco and she packed away the memories with as much care as their various purchases. On the return trip, she and Nicolò curled up together, laughing softly over various highlights of their trip while exchanging deep, leisurely kisses.

Once they landed, they grabbed a cab that let them off in front of Nicolò's house. He carried the luggage they'd acquired on Deseos onto the broad, wraparound porch and stacked them to one side of the door before turning to address Kiley.

"My grandparents dropped Brutus off first thing this morning, which means he's going to need a walk. He has a fenced run out back, but it doesn't give him the amount of exercise he requires." He shot her a warning look. "You might want to stand back. Chances are, he'll be a bit exuberant."

Kiley decided to opt for the smarter course and wait on the sidewalk while Nicolò dealt with the massive animal. The instant he inserted the key in the lock she could feel the initial rumblings of the earthquake that signaled the dog's approach. To her amusement instead of greeting Nicolò with their usual bonding ritual, Brutus shot past him and headed straight for her. Between his massive jaws he carried a much abused tennis ball.

Kiley greeted the dog with a thorough scratch behind his ears and picked up the ball he dropped at her feet. "You want to play catch?" she asked.

Brutus spun around, barking in excitement. Then to Kiley's horror, he bounded into the street. Behind her, she heard Nicolò's shout of warning, a mirror to her own panicked cry. She saw the dog hesitate in confusion, then crouch down in his sphinxlike pose, holding perfectly still.

After that, events seemed to unravel in slow motion.

Kiley swung her head to the left and saw a massive SUV heading for the motionless dog. Without a moment's hesitation, she charged toward the road, running on sheer instinct. Pelting toward Brutus, she grabbed for his collar. But even as she did so, she knew she'd reached him too late. She was nowhere near strong enough to drag the dog clear of danger before the SUV hit them.

She didn't see the vehicle's final approach, only heard the harsh blare of horn and the sickening squeal of brakes. She acted without thought, throwing herself across Brutus in a ridiculous attempt to protect him, not that she covered more than half the animal. Then she braced herself for the inevitable impact she knew would follow.

The horn and brakes continued their endless scream of warning and for a brief instant, something flashed through her mind. A memory. A memory that caused such pain and panic that every part of her cringed from it. In that split second of time she wasn't outside Nicolò's house, but found herself in the middle of a different street, where something bright yellow with blue fenders came barreling toward her. Before she could fully grasp the memory, it slipped away, along with all the foggy wisps of that other time and place, of that other Kiley.

The squeal of brakes seemed to last forever before the SUV slid to a stop mere inches from where Kiley had her head buried in Brutus's thick coat. The vehicle came so close she could feel the heat pouring off the engine hovering inches above her ear, and smell the distinctive oil and radiator stench that clogged her lungs and made it impossible to breath.

She vaguely heard the driver shout in a bizarre combination of anger and concern. Vaguely heard Nicolò's response before the driver took off with another punch of the car horn that left her trembling in reaction. Vaguely heard Brutus's whimper, as well as Nicolò's voice coming from somewhere above her.

She couldn't move. Couldn't process thought or any of the reassurances Nicolò offered in that soft, gentle tone. She didn't even think she could feel, until Brutus washed the tears from her face and Nicolò lifted her from her prone position. Then she felt far, far too much. With a wordless cry, she dissolved against her husband, sobbing uncontrollably.

"Easy, sweetheart. You're okay. You're fine now."

"Bru-Brutus?" Her teeth were chattering so hard she could barely get the word out.

"He's fine." A snap of his fingers had the dog scurrying onto the porch, his tail between his legs. Nicolò followed, carrying her as though she were made of the most fragile porcelain. "What the hell were you thinking, running into the street after him like that?" He sounded angry, but even in her current state she understood the anger came from fear.

She sagged against him. "Wasn't thinking. Not even a little. I just—just reacted."

"That's obvious. Did you really believe you could protect Brutus by throwing yourself between him and a two-and-a-half ton SUV?"

She forced out a watery grin. "Haven't you figured it out, yet? I'm indestructible."

"Don't joke," he said, his voice tight and ragged. "You could have been killed. Again."

"But I wasn't. Again."

She pressed her mouth to his neck, inhaling the crisp, masculine scent of him. It stirred the oddest sensation, making her dizzy with need. How was that possible after what she'd just been through?

Nicolò put Kiley down long enough to toss their bags through the door before slamming it closed behind them. Then he picked her up again, intent on taking her to the bedroom. He managed a single step before sagging onto the floor in a jumble of arms, legs, luggage and dog.

"Aw, hell." He wrapped her up tight. Too tight. But he couldn't seem to control his response. "Damn it, Kiley. I thought I'd lost you."

"I'm sorry." Her words tumbled out, nearly incoherent. "I just reacted. All I could think about was saving Brutus. I'm fine. We're both fine now."

"That's twice." He lowered his head and inhaled her, her scent, her touch, her taste. He snatched a half-dozen urgent kisses. "Twice I've watched you come within an inch of dying. And both times I wasn't able to get to you before—"

"I'm okay. I'm safe." She caught hold of Brutus's collar and tugged the dog into their circle. "And so is Brutus."

It was time to face facts, he realized. He didn't know the woman he'd met that day at Le Premier. But whoever she was, she bore no relationship to the Kiley he held in his arms. That woman, the one prior to the accident, wouldn't have risked her perfectly manicured pinky to save his dog. That woman wouldn't have relished the scent of a simple sprig of honeysuckle, or reveled in the experience of holding a sleeping baby in her arms. That version of Kiley was gone, with luck permanently, and he could only thank God for it.

"Brutus, backyard," he ordered. As much as he adored his dog, right now he needed his wife.

No. Not his wife.

At least…not yet.

He cupped her face and covered her mouth in another kiss, only this one held a far different quality. Where before he'd been reassuring himself that he'd reached her in time and she hadn't been harmed, this kiss was life-affirming. Fate had been kind to them both, had protected her not once, but twice. He'd see to it there wasn't a third incident. No matter what it took, he'd protect her from her own impulsiveness.

At the touch of his mouth, she opened to him, welcomed him home. Gave to him. He could feel his self-control slip as he lost himself in his desperate need for her.

"Now. I want you right here and right now."

She eased back and he snatched her into his arms again, unwilling to release her. "Wait," she said. Her laugh bubbled with happiness and desire and the sheer exhilaration of life. "I'm not going anywhere. You can have me wherever. Whenever. However."

"Here. Now. Naked."

Her laughter faded while her eyes heated. "In that case…"

Again she eased back and this time he let her go.

Gripping the bottom of her shirt, she yanked it over her head and off. He didn't wait for her to remove her bra. His patience only stretched so far—no more than a few short seconds. With a flick of his fingers, he had the scrap of silk and lace open and swept aside.

She settled back onto his lap, back where she belonged, her legs cinching his waist. She started on the buttons of his shirt, but he didn't have the patience for that, either. In one button-spewing move, he shredded his shirt from stem to stern. Anything, if it meant having those clever hands of hers on his skin.

Heaven help him, but she was beautiful. Soft and tender and utterly edible. He cupped her, gathered the slight weight of her in his palms. She tilted her head back with a groan, giving him total access to the elegant length of her throat and curve of her shoulders, long silken sweeps of skin that begged to be tasted and caressed. He gave her his full attention, finding every sensitive hollow and curve. And still it wasn't enough.

He tore at the snap and zip to her jeans, dragging them down her hips to reveal the flower-shaped birthmark stamped there, and off the pert curve of her backside. She wriggled clear of his lap just long enough for him to strip her. When he finished, she lay panting on the parquet floor, her skin sun-kissed gold against the dark wood, her hair full of red-hot flames. He ripped open his own jeans and took her hard and fast, sinking deep inside her in one powerful thrust while her cry of ecstasy echoed through the foyer.

He'd almost lost her. He might never have been able

to hold her again. Kiss her. Make love to her. The mere thought left him crazed, gripped by a frenzy unlike anything he'd ever experienced before. He'd never been this desperate to have a woman. Never been so insane with desire that he hadn't cared about the where and when.

Until Kiley.

"Don't stop," she ordered. She clung to him, arms and legs wrapped tight around him, pulling him in until they were one flesh moving in unison. "Don't ever let go of me."

"Never. I swear I'm going to lock you away where no one can ever hurt you again."

She opened her mouth to reply, but instead arched upward, a keening cry ripped from her throat. She surrendered utterly to his possession, giving everything she had and holding nothing back. No hesitation, no subterfuge. Every stray thought and feeling there for him to see, his to accept or reject, more open and honest and giving than he believed it possible for a woman to be.

Her eyes turned a blinding shade of green, burning with an emotion so powerful and all-consuming it hurt to look at her. And as he took her, as he sent her slamming into an endless climax, he realized it was love he saw in her eyes. A soul-deep commitment. And with that knowledge he went over the edge with her, lost to a moment that never should have happened.

It was a long time before he could move again. When he did, he realized that nothing had changed. He had committed a crime beyond redemption and Kiley— He closed his eyes, utterly destroyed. Kiley had fallen in love with him. Gently, he lifted her in his arms and carried her to their bedroom. And all the while, two questions tormented him.

What the hell had he done…and how could he fix it?

Kiley awoke the next morning, deliciously sore, yet thoroughly refreshed. On the pillow beside her, she found a businesslike note from Nicolò warning that he'd be at the office all day. Beneath the first note was a second, and there was nothing businesslike at all about this one. The few short sentences left her in no doubt of Nicolò's feelings about the night before and caused a blush of delight to warm her cheeks.

She grinned like a loon over the second note, while fighting a wave of disappointment over the first. Well, what did she expect? Because of her accident, he'd been forced to take countless days off. He must have mountains of work piled up as a result.

Bouncing out of bed, she spent the morning on domestic chores, unpacking their bags and washing clothes. As the clock edged toward noon she decided to surprise her husband for lunch. During their time together she'd gotten a fair idea of his tastes and made up her mind to create a silly meal loaded with his favorites, everything from chicken Marsala to panzanella, pistachios to bitter chocolate, all easily available with just a few quick phone calls.

The instant the various treats arrived, she loaded them into a basket she found in a cupboard above the refrigerator and decorated it with a sprig of honeysuckle she found growing along the backyard fence. She liked to think Nicolò had started the hedge from a cutting he'd taken from his grandfather's garden, a tribute to that long-ago encounter with his first flower…and first bee sting.

Next, she called for a cab, relieved to discover the driver knew just where to find Dantes' corporate head-quarters. The cabbie dropped her off in front of an impressively large office building and she entered through the revolving doors. Once inside she stumbled to a halt, staring in awe at the spectacular three-story glass foyer. She took her time, admiring everything from the elegant decor to the dance of sunlight off the sheets of tinted windows, to the impressive glass sculpture of dancing flames that hung above the receptionist's desk.

She'd just started toward the desk when an elderly man with a thick thatch of snowy hair approached. "Please, excuse me," he said, his deep voice carrying the lilting cadence of a Mediterranean heritage. "Are you Kiley O'Dell?"

She smiled warmly. "Actually, it's Kiley Dante."

"Yes, of course." He gazed at her with assessing gold eyes, eyes that cut straight through all pretense and yet held an unmistakable glint of kindness. "I believe, my dear, it is past time we met. I am Primo Dante."

Her smile grew and she regarded him in genuine delight. "You're Nicolò's grandfather. He told me all about you and how you helped raise him and his brothers."

"Nicolò, Severo and the twins. Yes, Nonna and I took them in after the death of our son, Dominic, and his wife, Laura." He took her hand in his and leaned in to kiss first one of her cheeks, then the other. "You are on your way to visit Nicolò?"

She indicated the basket she carried. "I thought he'd enjoy some lunch."

Primo's gnarled fingers brushed the honeysuckle blossom decorating the handle. "And what have you brought him?" He listened intently while she listed the eclectic jumble of flavors. "It would seem you know my grandson's tastes quite well. And for yourself? Have you put nothing of your own in here? Or is all this for Nicolò's benefit alone?"

She looked momentarily abashed. "Tapioca pudding," she admitted. She couldn't help laughing at herself. "Who'd have figured I'd develop such a taste for it?"

He chuckled. "You may find it interesting to discover what things appeal when you permit yourself to give them a try without a history to influence your choices."

"Or what things no longer appeal?" she asked.

His gaze grew even more shrewd. "Excellent observation." He gestured toward the bank of elevators toward the rear of the foyer. "Shall I escort you?"

"Thank you. I'd appreciate that."

Primo used a key to access a private car. "You are recovered from your accident?" he asked politely.

"Physically, yes." A slight frown tugged at her brow as they entered the elevator. "I still haven't regained my memory. Although…"

"Although?"

She hesitated, for some reason tempted to confess something to Primo that she hadn't even told her husband.

"I might have remembered something yesterday." She detailed her near-miss from the day before. "Right before I thought the SUV would hit us I had a flash of memory."

"And what was this flash?"

"I suspect it was from that first accident."

Primo gave a slow nod. "That would make sense. The similarity between the two incidents might prompt a return of your memory."

She turned to face him, staring up at a compassionate face lined with a wealth of experience, both good and ill. "And yet, my memory didn't come back, even though for a split second I recalled…something. Pain. Fear. And…"

"And?" he prompted. "What are you afraid to see, Kiley O'Dell?"

"Dante," she corrected. "I know I wasn't certain I wanted to take the name when Nicolò and I first married. But I think it's like tapioca pudding. Things that might not have been to my taste before, are now."

"You are avoiding my question."

She grinned. "You're right, I am." Her smile faded. "I was afraid of whatever I saw. I guess of the accident, of the pain it caused me."

"Or maybe you were afraid of that other life. Maybe when you had the choice to remember or forget, you chose to forget."

His words caused her heart to kick up a beat, possibly because they held the weight of truth. "You think I don't want to remember?"

Primo shrugged. "The mind is a strange thing.

Perhaps it is protecting you. Perhaps when you no longer need its protection, you will remember." Before she could reply, the door slid open and he gestured for her to precede him. "You will find Nicolò's office at the end of the corridor to the left. Tell him it is time for you to meet the family. Tell him it is past time, yes?"

"Yes, it is," she agreed.

He leaned down and kissed her cheeks again, then headed in the opposite direction. Taking a deep breath, she followed Primo's directions, pausing outside a door with Nicolò's name on it. Some jokester had added a shiny gold label beneath his name that read Chief Troublemaker. Her lips twitched and she lifted her fist to knock, hesitating at the last instant.

Was it possible? she couldn't help but wonder. Was she resisting remembering because she wanted to escape those memories? Could it all be tied in with the fight she'd had with Nicolò? Maybe if he told her what had happened it would cause her memory to return. Because despite how their marriage had functioned before her accident, they'd fully bonded since. And that meant they could find a way to work through whatever had divided them. She was convinced of it.

No matter what secret Nicolò kept from her, one thing was certain. The time had come for the two of them to be totally honest with one another, regardless of how painful the process. That decided, she rapped on the door, then turned the knob and walked in.

To her dismay, she found the room crowded with people. Three men stood in a pile, arguing at full throttle. None were Nicolò, though based on the fact that the three shared a physical similarity to her husband, and two of them were twins, they had to be his brothers. Off to one side sat a man with salt-and-pepper hair and a flushed complexion who silently seethed while he listened to the argument. He was flanked by yet another man, this one notable for the very fact that he looked so nondescript.

Finally, she located her husband, leaning against his desk, a grim expression darkening his face. At her entrance, his head jerked in her direction, and if anything, his expression turned blacker still.

He slowly straightened. "What are you doing here, Kiley?" he demanded in an undertone.

The salt-and-pepper-haired man glanced her way and leapt to his feet, pointing an accusing finger straight at her. "That's her! My God, you found the little bitch." He lunged toward her, his forward momentum stopped by the quick action of the three men Kiley had pegged as Nicolò's brothers. "Get out of my way," he roared. "I've waited a long time for this. Just give me five minutes of uninterrupted time alone with her and you can keep the money she owes me."

Kiley stumbled backward, relieved to find Nicolò planted in front of her, his stance clearly protective. "You shouldn't be here." He threw the comment over his shoulder. "Why did you come?"

"I—I brought you lunch. I wanted to surprise you." She swallowed, struggling to control the fear and tension tearing at her. "Surprise."

"Your timing couldn't have been worse."

"Who is that man? How does he know me? Why is he so angry?"

"The man—Jack Ferrell—has leveled some accusations against you. My brothers—" he confirmed her guess by indicating the trio of men who'd been arguing when she'd first entered "—and the private investigator I hired, Rufio, were trying to get to the bottom of the allegations when you arrived."

She stepped out from behind her husband, determined to face the accusations aimed at her head-on. The Dantes and Rufio continued to restrain Ferrell while he ranted in undisguised fury. "What does he say I've done?"

Nicolò hesitated, then reluctantly explained, "He's accused you of scamming him out of a rather substantial sum of money."

"No." She shook her head. "That's not possible. I may not remember the past, but I do know myself. I wouldn't do anything so dishonest."

He turned to face her. "Kiley—"

"Oh, God." The lunch basket slipped from her fingers and hit the carpet, spilling its contents. The can of pistachios landed square on the honeysuckle, crushing the fragile blossoms. The sweet scent drifted up between them, sharp as a bee sting. "You believe him, don't you?"

Eight

To Kiley's horror, Nicolò didn't deny the accusation.

"Ferrell has proof, sweetheart," he said gently. "Granted, it's a bit on the sketchy side, but he insists you ran a con on him involving a fire diamond necklace, one you supposedly inherited from your grandfather."

"Fire diamonds?" For a split second she saw Francesca and Nicolò staring intently at her as she studied the fire diamonds at Dantes Exclusive, waiting... Waiting for what? For her to remember something about this necklace Ferrell referred to? Had they known about the accusations even then? "I don't understand any of this. What necklace does he mean?"

"I don't know. It's something we'll have to figure out together." She closed her eyes at his use of the word *together.* He must have understood how much it meant to her, because he traced his thumb along the curve of her cheek. "Until then, you need to go home."

"She's not going anywhere," Jack Ferrell protested. "I want my money. And I want her to pay for what she did to me. I insist you call the police and have her arrested."

Nicolò spun to face the man. "You signed a binding agreement, Ferrell. One that allows us to settle this matter quietly. It also requires you prove your claims. So far, all we have are accusations."

"She offered to sell me her grandfather's necklace. I put half the money down. But when I went to complete the transaction, she'd disappeared, along with my money and the necklace." He glared at Kiley. "You were slick, I'll give you that. But you won't get away this time."

Kiley shook her head, attempting to reason with the man. "I wouldn't do something like that. You must have me mixed up with someone else."

His lips pulled back in a snarl. "Not a chance in hell. You have a birthmark on your hip. It's shaped like a flower."

She felt every scrap of color drain from her face. Wordlessly, she shook her head.

"No? Come on, gorgeous. Strip down and show us the birthmark. Prove me wrong."

"Get out of here, Kiley," Nicolò interrupted. "I'll be home as soon as I resolve this."

"No. I'm not going anywhere. Not until the two of us discuss this." She spared a brief glance toward the other men. "Privately."

"Think you can sweet-talk your way around him?" Ferrell interrupted. "You're wasting your time. He's not the fool I was. With all the information his P.I. has assembled, I'll bet he sees right through you. No way are you slipping out from under this one. Not this time."

Nicolò spun to face his brothers. "Shut him up, will you? I'll be right back." Without another word, he cupped Kiley's elbow and drew her from the room. "I can spare five minutes. We'll hash out the rest of it when I get home."

One look at his expression and everything went numb inside. This man wasn't her husband, wasn't the man who'd taken her with such crazed desperation on his foyer floor. This was the suspicious stranger from those first hours and days after her accident.

She remained silent while he ushered her into a small conference room. Like everything else she'd seen of Dantes so far, it was a lovely room, but one clearly designed for business. Is that what she'd become? Business? Based on his current attitude, she might as well be.

She fought to gather her self-control, to focus her confusion into some semblance of order, so that at least she'd know what questions to ask. She opened with the first one to come to mind. "Why did you hire a P.I.?"

"I hired Rufio after your accident."

"That doesn't quite answer my question," she pointed out. "But let's start there. Did you hire Rufio because of my accident…or because of our fight?"

"Does it matter?"

"Is what that man was saying—" She gestured in the

general direction of Nicolò's office. "The necklace and the money I supposedly took from him. Is that what our fight was about? The one before my accident?"

"Indirectly."

Anger ripped through her. "Stop it, Nicolò. Just stop all the cagey responses and give it to me straight. I'll believe whatever you tell me." She laughed, a hard, painful sound. "After all, I don't have any other choice. Since I don't remember, I have to accept your version of events."

"The truth?"

"If you don't mind."

"Your grandfather and your great-uncle jointly owned a fire diamond mine, a mine they sold to my grandfather, Primo. When we first met it was to discuss the legality of that sale. You claimed there was a problem with the transfer of title, that you still owned a portion of the mine."

"So we didn't meet over a game of Frisbee?"

"No."

She shook her head in bewilderment. "Why would you invent that other story? What difference does it make how or when we met?"

"It mattered."

Frustration ripped through her. *"Why?"*

He rubbed a spot between his brows where tension had formed a deep crease. "I didn't want to bring it up after your accident because I needed time to find out whether your claim on the mine was genuine. I needed time for Rufio to unearth the truth while you recovered from your injuries. Time for us to get to know one another, to deal with The Inferno, without the mine coming between us."

She frowned in confusion. "I still don't understand. What has the sale of the mine got to do with this necklace Ferrell is going on about?"

"I have no idea. If there's a connection, I haven't found it, yet. Rufio met Ferrell while investigating you and your claims regarding the mine."

"This man, Ferrell, he's convinced I've scammed him, isn't he?"

"Yes."

"And you? What do you believe?"

"We're still looking into it, Kiley."

"But it's possible he's right?" She could see the answer in Nicolò's expression and something infinitely precious died inside. It took a moment before she could form her next question, one almost too painful to ask. "Do you believe I was trying to scam you about the diamond mine?"

"Don't do this, Kiley. Not now."

"Answer me, Nicolò. When we first met, did you think I was some sort of con artist?"

He hesitated, before reluctantly nodding. "I suspected you might be."

"Why?" It was a cry from the heart.

He lifted his shoulder in a shrug, his expression one of extreme weariness. "Nothing definitive. Just a feeling I had."

She wanted to go to him, to wrap her arms around

him and reassure him that it would all work out. But she couldn't. Too much divided them right now, a chasm of doubt and suspicion that she had no clue how to bridge. "If you suspected me of being that sort of person, why did you decide to date me? How did we end up falling in love? How did we end up married?"

He lifted his hand, palm out. "It would seem The Inferno doesn't worry about such minor details as—"

"As moral character?" she cut in.

"Kiley—"

She glanced toward the door, realizing that she was poised to run, to escape an untenable situation. The urge nearly overwhelmed her. Was it gut instinct, or a pattern so much a part of her that it didn't require memory? She fought it with every ounce of strength she possessed. "Is it true? What Ferrell accused me of... Did I do those things? Is that who I really am?"

"I don't know." She could hear the frustration ripping apart his words. "I don't want to believe it, Kiley."

"Then don't." She dared to approach, dared to splay her hands across his chest and gather that steady, life-affirming heartbeat in her palm. "I need you to believe in me, Nicolò. I need you to fight for me. Maybe everything Ferrell says is true. Maybe I am a horrible person."

"No." The word escaped without thought or hesitation and it gave her the first glimmer of hope.

"Okay, was. Maybe I *was* a horrible person. But what if it's all a mistake? Since I can't remember, I can't defend myself. I have to believe there's some other explanation, if we can only find it." She stared up at him, no longer interested in running, but determined to fight. "Please, Nicolò. I need to discover the truth."

"And if the truth isn't what you want to hear?"

"At least it'll be the truth."

She shouldn't kiss him, shouldn't put any more pressure on him. But she couldn't help herself. Just for a moment or two she needed her husband, needed to coax him out from under his troubleshooter persona.

She slid her arms around his neck and covered his mouth with hers, practically consuming him. She felt his momentary resistance, understood it even as it caused her unfathomable pain. And then she felt the give, the gentle slide from reluctance into acceptance, before it transformed into something desperate and greedy and urgent. The flutter of hope gained in strength. He hadn't given up on her. Not yet.

She snatched another kiss, a final one. "I need you to promise me something else," she said.

She could see the shutters slam back into place. "If I can."

"Promise me you'll tell me the truth from now on. When you're done here, we'll put all the cards on the table."

He gave a brief nod. "That's one promise I can make. Until then, go home and I'll join you there as soon as I'm able."

His eyes were dark with pain and haunted by secrets. He lowered his head and kissed her again. There was an unmistakable finality in the way he embraced her, as though acknowledging on some level that their relationship would never be the same again. This time when he released her, he took a step backward, distancing himself physically, as well as emotionally.

"Fair warning, Kiley. You won't like some of those cards I'm going to show you. They may very well end things between us."

There was nothing she could say to that, no way to reassure him or calm her own fears. He opened the conference room door for her and she sleepwalked through it. She headed for the elevators, but found herself continuing past them, unable to convince herself to leave. She never knew how long she wandered the corridors before Primo found her and gathered her up.

Murmuring in soothing Italian, he escorted her to a generous-sized office. He installed her in a large, deep-cushioned chair before crossing to a wet bar. Pouring her a drink, he handed it to her. She cupped her hands around the balloon of the snifter and inhaled the potent brandy before taking a generous swallow.

Primo didn't say anything to her, but resumed his seat at his desk and occupied himself with paperwork. She sat and sipped the brandy, losing track of time. It could have been minutes…or hours. Time flowed in a confusing haze. But at long last she looked up.

"Lunch didn't go well," she announced in a low voice.

Primo set aside his papers and capped his pen. "I assumed as much."

"It's funny. For the past few weeks I've been enjoying so many new experiences. Until today." She pushed out an unsteady smile. "Today…not so much."

"Sometimes we learn more from the bad experiences than the good."

She curled deeper in the chair. "I'm not sure I like that idea."

He cocked a head to one side in a gesture endearingly reminiscent of Nicolò. "Perhaps you have learned what you now must fix. Would that not allow some good to come from the bad?"

"I can fix being a con artist?"

His gaze sharpened. "So. You believe this man, Ferrell."

It shouldn't surprise her that he'd heard about what had happened in Nicolò's office. The Dantes were a tight-knit family. "Ferrell knows things about me. Things he shouldn't—" Her voice broke and she struggled to control it. "What if he's right? What if I really am a scam artist?"

"Are you?" He paused a beat. "Or were you?"

Tears filled her eyes. "Is there a difference?"

"Very much so. One exists in a past you cannot recall. The other may be created in a future yet to come."

His words struck hard, restored the hope that had been so badly shaken. "Thank you, Primo." She uncurled from her chair and crossed the room to plant a kiss on his cheek. "I'm glad we finally met."

He stood and enfolded her in a tight embrace. "As am I."

Nicolò had told her to go home, but she couldn't bear the idea of returning there without him. Instead, she retraced her path to his office, hoping he'd now be available to leave with her. To her disappointment, the door stood open and the room deserted. She entered, intent on scribbling him a brief note. Crossing to his desk, she saw a folder bearing her name on the wooden surface. Curiosity got the better of her and she flipped it open.

And her world collapsed around her.

Nicolò had to be home, waiting for her, Kiley decided as she left Dantes. And when she arrived, she'd have him explain all that she'd found in that damning file, a file currently tucked beneath her arm. There had to be an explanation, other than the obvious one. She couldn't be the person detailed between those pages. It wasn't possible.

To Kiley's disappointment, she arrived to find an empty house, empty except for Brutus, who seemed to sense her despair. He trailed behind her, whining softly, as she wandered from room to room, struggling to come to terms with all she'd learned. From deep within the house, she heard the doorbell ring and for a split second her heart leaped. *Nicolò*. He was home. Then common sense prevailed. Her husband would have used his key.

Leaving Brutus in the den, she crossed to the front door and opened it, surprised to discover a woman standing there, impatiently tapping her foot.

"About time," the woman announced, before sweeping inside. "Do you have any idea how long it's taken me to track you down? I finally tricked your address out of the hospital, though what the hell you were doing there, they wouldn't say."

"Who—" Kiley hesitated, taking a second, longer look.

The woman, a striking blonde, appeared to be in her late thirties, though something about the hardness around her carefully made up eyes and mouth hinted at a handful of years more than that. She matched Kiley's stature, or lack thereof, the only difference between them the extra few inches the older woman carried in the bust line and around the hips. She wore her hair in a short cap of curls that emphasized both her striking bone structure, as well as a pair of vivid blue eyes.

A possibility occurred to Kiley, one she could only pray was true. "I know this is going to sound like an odd question, but... Are you my mother?" she asked, fighting to control a wild surge of emotion.

A single eyebrow winged skyward. "Have you lost your mind? Of course I'm your mother."

"Oh, my God." Kiley threw her arms around the woman, hugging her with tearful exuberance. She needed this, needed something to go right today. "Oh, Mom, you have no idea how happy I am to meet you."

"Now I know you've lost your mind." The woman pried herself free of Kiley's embrace. "What the hell do you mean you're happy to meet me? And—horror of horrors—since when have you called me 'Mom'? Try Lacey, you ungrateful brat. Now where's the damn necklace?"

Kiley fell back a step. "I—I call you Lacey?"

"If you don't pull yourself together, I swear I'm going to slap you, if only to knock an ounce of sense into that brain of yours. I mean, really, Kiley. What were you thinking? What made you believe for one tiny second that you could get away with it?"

"Get away with—" She shook her head. "You don't understand. I was in an accident. I lost my memory. I have no idea what you're talking about."

To Kiley's shock, Lacey burst out laughing. "Oh, that's a good one. You're always scheming, aren't you? Well? Come on." She folded her arms across her chest and set her foot to tapping again. "Explain how this latest one works. I'm all ears."

Kiley stared at her mother in horror. Didn't she believe her own daughter? But then, if the information in the file was correct, why would she? "You don't understand. I'm serious. I have no memory of you, or of my past, or—or anything."

"Oh, you poor dear." Lacey feigned a sympathetic look before spoiling it with a laugh. "I have to hand it to you, sweetie, you're really quite good at this. I'm actually starting to enjoy myself, which is rather miraculous considering my mood when I arrived." She crossed to Kiley's side and linked arms with her. "Now don't keep your dear momma standing in the hallway. Why don't you show me around the place."

Every instinct Kiley possessed screamed a warning. "Why don't we go into the living room," she suggested instead. "Maybe I can give you a tour when Nicolò gets home. He's due any moment."

"Nicolò?"

"My husband."

Lacey's jaw dropped. "You're *married?*"

"Close to a month now." She gestured toward the sofa. "Can I fix you a drink."

"The usual. Make it a double."

"And the usual is…?"

Lacey shrugged. "I should have known you'd be too good to fall for that one. Double scotch. Neat." She waited until she'd been served before leaning forward with a wheedling expression. "Come on, Kiley. Let me in on this one. I can play it anyway you want. Just give me the lowdown so I don't make any mistakes."

Kiley stared at her mother in disbelief. Oh, God. If this was the lifestyle she'd chosen before being hit by that cab, no wonder she didn't want to remember. How had she lived with herself? How had she justified such an unscrupulous existence? "This isn't a scam. I was hit by a cab and I'm suffering from something called retrograde amnesia."

Lacey waved that aside. "Whatever. At least tell me who your mark is."

Mark. With every word her mother uttered, she confirmed the information in the file—hideous, damning information that listed name after name, amount after amount, of people scammed and money taken. "There is no mark," Kiley stated numbly. "There's just my husband."

Lacey snapped her fingers. "Right. The husband. That's one I haven't pulled in a while. Too messy." She gestured for Kiley to continue. "Well? What's his name?"

"Nicolò Dante."

"Dante?" Lacey sat bolt upright. "Nicolò *Dante?*

Have you lost your mind? You think you can take down a Dante?"

"I keep telling you," Kiley said wearily. "This isn't—"

"A scam. Right." She slammed her drink onto the coffee table with such force it made the crystal sing and gathered up her purse. "Well, I don't want any part of whatever it isn't."

"Just answer a question first." Kiley crossed to where she'd left the file. Flipping it open, she removed one of the pages and offered it to Lacey. "Do you recognize these names? Is this information correct? Did I rip off all these people?"

With notable reluctance, Lacey set aside her purse and took the paper. Scanning it, she turned deathly pale as she read. "What the hell are you thinking, writing all this down?" she gritted out. "Do you have any idea what sort of trouble this could cause us?"

"All I want to know is whether or not it's accurate. Did I do those things?"

Lacey shot to her feet, shoving the list back into Kiley's hands. "That's it. I don't know what you're trying to pull, but I won't be party to it. I suggest you burn that paper before someone connects you with it. In the meantime, I'm out of here." She held out her hand. "Just give me the necklace and I'll be on my way."

Kiley stiffened. There it was again. The necklace. No doubt the same necklace Ferrell referred to. She carefully folded the list into fours and slipped it into her pocket. "What necklace?"

"Stop playing games." Lacey's voice could have cut glass. "Your grandfather Cameron's fire diamond necklace."

Kiley stilled. "Then…there really is a necklace?"

"Of course there really is a necklace. Now where is it?"

"I haven't got a clue." Kiley began to laugh. "Maybe when I get my memory back I'll remember that, as well."

"The locket." Lacey's anger ebbed, replaced by a look of cunning. "If you don't have the necklace on you, you've got a safe deposit key hidden in the locket."

Kiley slipped her hand beneath her blouse and fisted her fingers protectively around the silver heart. "So, I'm not just a scam artist. I get top marks for deviousness, too. Lovely." She remembered with painful amusement how crushed she'd been when Nicolò had informed her that she didn't have a close relationship with her mother. How she'd longed for the sort of family ties the Dantes possessed. Right now, she'd have given almost anything to be an orphan. "FYI, I don't know how to open the locket."

"Oh, would you please give this amnesia business a rest? You had me in stitches with it earlier, but enough's enough." She took another step in Kiley's direction, her face lined with grim intent. "Give me the locket. I'll open it if you won't."

"I'm not giving you anything."

"You are such a fool," she ranted. "Do you think I didn't consider setting up the Dantes years ago? Color me with a bit more common sense than you're currently showing. At least I knew better than to make a play in that direction, though I will admit the amnesia thing gives it an interesting twist."

"It's not—"

"I'm your mother, Kiley," Lacey bit out. "You can't fool me. Now, I want that key. Give it to me or I swear I'll take it from you. I'm not playing around here. I don't want to be anywhere in the vicinity when Dante discovers you're faking amnesia in order to scam him."

"To late, I'm afraid." Nicolò stepped into the room, Brutus at his heels. "It would seem that Dante found out a little sooner than you anticipated."

Nine

It took every ounce of self-control for Nicolò to hold his fury in check. At his appearance, Kiley and her mother both spun to face him, identical expressions of consternation on faces that bore a startling similarity. Or they would if Kiley ever acquired the bitter cunning that marked the older woman's features.

Here was the avarice he'd sought in Kiley's face during their visit to Dantes Exclusive. The slyness. The self-indulgence. Finally, he could see what she had worked so hard to keep from him. He only had to meet the mother to uncover it. Beside him, Brutus checked out the newcomer and released a soft growl, one that had her taking a hasty step backward.

"You asked for the truth, Kiley." He stripped off his suit

jacket and tossed it over a nearby chair. "I didn't realize you were the one who would be providing it for me."

"No, Nicolò." Her cheeks turned every bit as waxen as they'd been during her hospital stay, a realization that gave him an unwanted pang of concern. "You misunderstood what we were saying."

He cut her off with a slice of his hand. "Drop the act, Kiley. I'm neither deaf nor a fool. I understood every word your…mother?" He lifted an eyebrow in the older woman's direction, prompting her to confirm his assumption.

"Lacey O'Dell," she offered coolly. She took a step in his direction, hand outstretched, but stopped dead in her tracks when Brutus bristled. She cautiously lowered her arm to her side, and Nicolò couldn't help noting with some satisfaction that it took her a few seconds to recover her aplomb. "Call me Lacey."

He continued to address Kiley, tearing at the tie knotted at his throat. "I understood every word Lacey said. You've been faking amnesia in order to pull off a scam meant to garner you a share of the Dante fire diamond mine."

"I did warn you," Lacey said to Kiley, before fixing him with an assessing gaze.

The pale blue color struck him as ice-cold and lacked the humor and kindness—not to mention the fiery passion—so often reflected in her daughter's. Maybe the difference between the two came from Lacey's additional years of running scams. Maybe this was how Kiley would appear a few years down such a rough and unforgiving road.

"I assume you're Nicolò Dante, Kiley's husband?" she asked.

"Is that what she told you?"

Lacey hesitated, disappointment flashing across her face. "Another lie?"

He stripped away his loosened tie and released the first few buttons of his shirt before it strangled him. "My lie, this time. Conning a con, I guess you'd call it."

Kiley caught her breath in a soft, disbelieving gasp. "No. No, that can't be. Tell me you didn't lie about that, Nicolò." She stared at him, her pleading look one of utter devastation. "Anything but that."

He met her gaze without saying a word. He simply waited. She knew the truth. She'd known from day one, minute one that they weren't married. And she'd chosen to play along every step of the way. No doubt her current performance was for her mother's benefit. Eventually she'd explain why she'd set this particular game in motion and what she hoped to gain from it. In the meantime, he was done playing.

At his continued silence, Kiley closed her eyes in abject surrender. The expression on her face absolutely gutted him, even though it had to be an act. It took her several seconds to regain her equilibrium and confront him again. When she did, her eyes were black with pain.

"We're not married? All those romantic dates you told me about, the seaside wedding, none of it ever happened?" When he didn't respond, she lifted a trembling hand to her mouth. "It's all a lie? All of it? Touring the city. Dantes Exclusive. Oh, God. Deseos. Those incredible, beautiful, romantic nights on Deseos. It was just a game to you?"

He didn't spare either of them. "It would seem we both lied, didn't we, Kiley?" But even that wasn't the complete truth. Because there had been times when he could have sworn there'd been nothing but honesty between them. "No doubt we each have our own special place reserved in hell."

"No! I don't believe you. Some of it had to be real."

Painfully aware of Lacey's keen interest, he cut Kiley off. He didn't want to remember any of it, remember what a fool he'd been. He especially refused to think about Deseos. "Enough. Just can the dramatics, will you? You've won your Oscar. I actually believed you had amnesia, if only for a few weeks."

Lacey blew out a sigh. "That's my daughter for you," she said with exaggerated sympathy. "Just one deception after another."

He turned on her next. "Like mother, like daughter?"

She stiffened, lifting her chin in defiance. "Not at all. Since you listened in on our conversation, you must have heard me say that I wanted no part in whatever scam Kiley's running."

"Very self-righteous of you," he said dryly. "I'd be a bit more impressed if I also hadn't heard you say that you know better than to take on the Dantes. Still, I applaud your intelligence, as well as your keen sense of self-preservation."

She had the unmitigated gall to wink at him. "Thank you."

He removed his cufflinks and pocketed them before rolling up the sleeves of his shirt. Throughout the process, he continued to scrutinize her. "Just out of curiosity, what about the others?"

"What others?" Her movements slowed, stuttering to stillness, and she moistened her lips with the tip of her tongue. The "tell," the unconscious movement that warned him whenever she lied was painfully similar to the one he'd noticed Kiley use in the suite at Le Premier all those weeks ago. "I have no idea what you're talking about."

"I'm talking about the other men you've scammed over the years."

Lacey's eyes went flat and, if possible, even colder than before. "Hmm. I don't think I care for the direction this conversation has taken. So, if you don't mind, I think I'll opt out of it." She crossed to the sofa with a hip-swinging walk and gathered up her purse before confronting Kiley. "I believe you have something to give me."

The odd quality in her tone caused Brutus to leap to Kiley's defense. He muscled his way between the two women, appearing more ferocious and intimidating than Nicolò had ever seen him. With a muffled cry, Lacey stumbled back a few paces.

Kiley reached out and soothed the dog. "I have nothing for you. Do I, Brutus?"

He gave a sharp bark of agreement, one that had Lacey making a beeline for the doorway. Once she was satisfied that she stood a safe distance from the dog, she opened her mouth to argue. Sparing a swift glance toward Nicolò, she thought better of it. Apparently, he looked every bit as intimidating as his dog. It was a comforting thought.

"This isn't over," she warned. "Not by a long shot."

With that, she swept from the room escorted by Brutus, which no doubt explained why her heels tapped a frantic dance across the foyer. A few seconds later, the front door opened and slammed shut again. The silence hung in the air, thick and heavy. Nicolò could see Kiley struggling to find the right words to use on him. The best tack to explain away what he'd heard. He didn't give her the opportunity to settle on a strategy.

He approached, watching the wariness flare in her eyes. "When did you get your memory back? Or did you ever lose it in the first place?"

Her chin shot upward. "I lost it. I still don't remember anything before the accident, despite what you and my mother may think."

He couldn't help himself. He laughed, the sound harsh and ripe with disbelief. "Yeah, right."

She searched his face, no doubt looking for the chink in his armor, a chink he'd make very certain she never found. "There's nothing I can say to convince you I'm not faking amnesia, is there?"

"Not a thing."

Exhaustion settled over her, a visible blanket of weariness. "All right, fine, Nicolò. Have it your way. I'm lying about everything. I faked amnesia. Tell me what I've won. What's my consolation prize?"

He hesitated. "What are you talking about?"

"I must have faked amnesia for some reason." She

spread her hands. "Tell me what I could possibly gain by such a pretense."

"Will half of Dantes' fire diamond mine do? I mean, when we first met at Le Premier that was your original scam, wasn't it?"

"For the sake of argument, let's say it was. Did it work?"

"You know it didn't."

"Why?"

His eyes narrowed in speculation. "What game are you playing now, Kiley?"

"Just answer the question. Why didn't it work?"

"Because your argument that day wasn't logical. You had all the documentation lined up, but it didn't make sense that your family would have waited so many years before coming forward with the claim."

"Huh. Good point." It almost felt as though she were tiptoeing through her analysis, though he couldn't figure out why she bothered. "Okay, so I tried the con on you when we first met at Le Premier and it didn't work. Logically, what would I have done next?"

"Slipped away before I took legal action or involved the police."

"Then why didn't I? How would an amnesia scam work to my advantage? What do I gain by it?"

"You'd inveigle yourself into my life."

"Again…For what end? Money? I haven't asked and you haven't given me any. For the sex? Pretty damn good, I'll admit, but not worth the consequences when you found out about the scam. So, why would I assume such a risk? I had to know you'd take the precise steps you have and hire a P.I. to look into my background. *If* I were faking amnesia."

He folded his arms across his chest. "You tell me. What could you possibly get out of pretending to lose your memory?"

"And there's the rub." For just an instant, humor lit her eyes before fading into something heartbreakingly bittersweet. "I haven't a clue. Maybe I fell in love with you when we first touched. Blame it on The Inferno, if that helps. Maybe I wanted a few days, a few precious weeks, to experience normalcy. No cons. No angle. Just a woman in love with a man with no strings attached."

He steeled himself not to reveal how her words had affected him. "And now?"

She lowered her head as though considering her options. Her hand slipped into her pocket, wrapping around something that crinkled. She froze, so still and silent, while conflict battled across her expression. And that's when it happened. She slowly looked up and he watched a hint of avarice grow in her eyes, watched them take on that hard, knowing look that had been so apparent in Lacey's gaze. She even managed to imitate her mother's flirtatious smile, the tip of her tongue tracing a tantalizing path along her lush mouth.

"I guess my little vacation from reality is over," she purred. "It's been fun. I got some designer clothes out of it, not to mention a trip to an island paradise. Of course, it didn't end as well as I'd hoped. But we'll just chalk that up to misfortune and move on."

"Kiley, what—"

"Don't," she said sharply, her breezy expression shattering for a telling moment. "It would never have worked, Nicolò. You must have known that as soon as you read my file. If we'd tried for anything more than a fling, my reputation would have ruined the Dante name. Just let me go. It's long past time I got back to my old life."

She was right and he knew it. "Fine. No point in dragging this out."

Without another word she headed for the foyer, picking up her purse from off the small hallway table where she'd left it. She hesitated with her hand on the front doorknob. "I appreciate you taking care of me after my accident."

Nicolò leaned against the archway between the living room and foyer. "Before you go, answer one question."

She shrugged without turning around. "Sure."

"Was any of it real?"

She swiveled to face him, but all he could see was Lacey staring at him through Kiley's eyes. "You mean... did I love you?"

"Did you?"

Her movements slowed, fluttering to stillness like a bird settling to its nest and she moistened her lips. "Sorry, Dante. I guess there was some sort of glitch in The Inferno that day at Le Premier. Our bond never took, at least not on my end of things. It may have been fun. But it wasn't true love." And with that, she walked out the door.

The instant it closed behind her, Brutus howled in anguish. "I'm right there with you, buddy," Nicolò whispered. "Right there with you."

Kiley never remembered the hours immediately following her flight from Nicolò's, where she went or what she did. She didn't awake to her surroundings until dusk had settled over the city and she found herself standing in front of a seedy little hotel somewhere in the Mission District.

A quick check of her wallet elicited five hundred dollars and a couple of credit cards. One was maxed out, so she used her precious cash, holding the second credit card in reserve. At least she now had a roof over her head. She huddled in the depressing little room she'd rented, her locket clutched in her hands, determined to come up with a game plan. The silver heart seemed to burn within her grasp, the lacey strips of silver pressing ridges into her palm, as though trying to imprint a message there.

But all she could think about was Nicolò. The expression on his face when he'd walked into the living room after overhearing her moth— No, *not* her mother—*Lacey*. That flash of emotion she'd seen in his eyes when he'd asked if any part of what they'd experienced over the past few weeks had been real. His shock when she'd shoved out the one lie she could ever remember telling him.

She opened her hand and studied the locket, pushing absently at the intertwining strips of silver. But she'd had to do it, had to lie to him. Once she'd had time to absorb that damning information from the file, she realized she couldn't stay. Couldn't allow her relationship with Nicolò to continue, assuming he'd have wanted such a thing. There'd been no other choice but to sever all remaining ties between them.

Even if Nicolò had been willing to overlook her past, she couldn't take the risk that one day her memory would come back and she'd turn into a younger version of Lacey. Couldn't risk the possibility that she'd turn on him and use his wealth and position for her own personal gain. It didn't matter that walking away had broken her heart. After all she'd done to hurt others, it was a small price to pay.

And, regardless of what cost the sacrifice, she'd continue to pay until she put right all she'd set wrong in the past.

The instant she reached her decision one of the small strips of silver slid to one side and the locket clicked open. She stared in wonder at the small key she found nestled inside. If Lacey were right, it was the key to a safety deposit box, as well as the solution to her problem.

Because in that safety deposit box was the means for her to make amends to all those she'd injured over the years.

"Have you lost your mind?"

Nicolò glared at his brother, Lazz. "Why do you keep asking me that same question?"

"Because it bears repeating." He shoved a hand through his hair. "I mean, get serious. Did you not read her file?"

"Yes, I read her file."

"Did you not see the part that said scam artist in big red letters? Hell, it was hard to miss since Rufio also put it in bolded caps."

"I saw it," Nicolò stated between gritted teeth.

"So…what? She scammed every man she ever met, but she's not going to do the same to you because she's your Inferno soul mate?"

"That's part of it."

"And the other?"

"She's changed. She's not that person anymore."

Lazz's mouth dropped open and he floundered a moment before he could speak again. "You have got to be kidding me. You did not just say that."

Nicolò swore beneath his breath. He didn't know why it had taken him a full three hours after Kiley had left before he caught the mistake within the lie. Maybe he'd been so focused on her claiming she didn't love him—and the "tell" that had given lie to that statement—that he hadn't fully processed her comment. But the instant it sank in, he realized that she hadn't regained her memory at all, or she'd have known that they never bonded at Le Premier.

As soon as he'd realized the truth, he'd gone charging out of the house. With Brutus at his side, he'd spent the entire night combing the city for her, but she'd disappeared as though she'd never existed. It was the first time in his entire life he hadn't been able to find a way out of a predicament. He was good at solving problems. The best. But this time he hit a brick wall and it was a wall he couldn't find a way over, under, or around, let alone through.

"She doesn't remember, Lazz," Nicolò insisted. "She still has amnesia."

"How can you possibly know that?" Lazz argued.

"Because she slipped up right before she left. She said we first bonded at Le Premier. But we never did. We just spat sparks at each other. We weren't 'Infernoed' until I took her hand at the hospital."

"Hello. She's. A. Con. Artist. She hasn't changed. And it wasn't a slipup. It was an 'on purpose.' She was hoping you'd catch the mistake. Hoping you'd buy right back into the con. And damn it, Nicolò, you have, haven't you?"

"If that woman's still a con artist, then yeah, I'm buying it. And I'm going to keep buying it until I'm old and gray and we've been married for as many decades as Primo and Nonna." He leaned in, jaw set. "I'm going to find her, Lazz. And then I'm going to marry her. She's going to have my sons—and I say sons because, with the exception of our cousin, Gianna, the men in our family seem incapable of producing daughters. We're going to have four of them, in case you're interested. And anyone who has a problem with that can discuss it first with my right fist and then with my left hook."

He looked around with a hint of defiance, stunned when he caught Sev and Marco's nod of approval. Even better was the expression Primo wore, one that offered unconditional support. "Everyone should receive a second chance," he stated.

Nicolò turned on Lazz again, his determination rock-solid. "So, are you going to help me find her, or are you going to fight me over this?"

"You know I don't believe in the family curse," Lazz muttered.

"Blessing," the others chorused in unison.

Nicolò barked out a laugh, the first one since Kiley left him. "You better start believing in The Inferno, Lazz. So far it's three down. You're the only one of us left."

"And that's the way it's going to stay." Lazz held up his hands before anyone could argue the point. "Fine. You want her, you got her."

Nicolò nodded. "Let's just hope it's that easy."

Ten

Of course, it wasn't easy at all. It took a team effort involving Rufio and the entire Dante family to finally locate Kiley. Nicolò couldn't recall a rougher few weeks. Not that he had anyone to blame other than himself. He'd allowed her to walk out instead of stopping her, and that knowledge had haunted him every single minute since. When the call finally came in from the P.I., he found it a struggle just to form a coherent sentence.

"Where is she, Rufio?" he managed to ask.

"A small dive down in the Mission District bearing the delightful name of the Riff Raff Inn. Not one I'd recommend, especially not for a woman on her own."

Nicolò swore. "What the hell is she doing there?"

"I can't say. Might be all she could afford. Thank God she finally used plastic or we'd have had the devil's own time finding her."

Nicolò closed his eyes. Of course. She'd left with nothing in hand but the funds in her purse. Five hundred couldn't have kept her fed and housed for much longer than a couple weeks, if that. Not in San Francisco. What would she have done if she hadn't had another source of money? Would she have come back to him? Somehow he doubted it.

"Watch the motel in case she leaves," Nicolò instructed. "I'll be there in fifteen."

"You'd better make it ten."

Hell. "Why? What's wrong?"

"Our old buddy Ferrell just got out of a cab. He's making tracks toward the motel and looks like a man on a mission. Do you want me to intercept him?"

"Not unless there's trouble. It can't be a coincidence he's shown up, or much doubt who he's there to see. Follow him and call me back with a room number. I'm leaving now."

He was five minutes out when Rufio called again. "More good news," came the P.I.'s gloomy voice. "By the look of things, Kiley's about to have another visitor."

"Who?"

"Based on the description you gave me, I'm guessing it's Lacey O'Dell. Blonde, blue eyes, five foot nothing. Looks a good bit like Kiley, except…"

"Harder," Nicolò supplied.

"I'd call her cold if she didn't look spitting mad. If

I were a betting man, I'd say your wife… Er, sorry— Ms. O'Dell has done something to seriously tick off Momma dearest."

"Which room is Kiley in?"

"Two-oh-nine. Up the stairs, hang a right. Middle of the hallway on the left. You'll find me near the stairwell. I can see the door, but I'm not close enough to hear anything. Don't want to attract too much attention from those inside."

"Will I have any trouble getting past the front desk?"

"I wasn't sure what sort of reception you might receive when you joined the party, so I dropped a Franklin on the manager. He's suddenly developed a severe case of deaf, dumb, and blind."

"Hang tight. I'm almost there."

A few minutes later, Nicolò swung into a parking space and hustled into the motel. Rufio's bribe worked. The manager didn't so much as lift his head, just gestured toward a worn stairway carpeted in the remains of faded paisley. Nicolò came across Rufio in the hallway, a few doors up from Kiley's room.

"In there," he whispered, pointing. "Decided I better move closer so I could step in if things turned nasty. Got a right little row going."

More than a row. Nicolò could hear Ferrell's voice raised in fury, as well as Lacey's. And then he heard Kiley's cry of alarm and didn't bother with a civilized knock on the door. He crashed against the hollow core panel and sent the door bursting inward.

It took only an instant to assess the situation. Ferrell

and Lacey were in a furious struggle over something
that glittered with unmistakable fire. A diamond necklace. Or rather, what remained of a diamond necklace.
And then he saw Kiley. She was on the floor, a hand
raised to her cheek, one that showed evidence of a
rapidly growing bruise. He was at her side in an instant,
lifting her in his arms and clear of the fray. He didn't
know who had hit her or why, but someone would pay
for hurting her.

"Are you okay?"

"I'm fine." She ran her hands across his chest while
she ate him up with her eyes. "Don't think me ungrateful, but… What are you doing here?"

He pulled a slow smile. "I'm here to rescue you, of
course. Isn't that how it's supposed to work?"

She shook her head, despite the hope dawning in her
expression. "Only in fairy tales. Not in real life."

"In real life, too, sweetheart. Now who hit you?"

"It was an accident."

"Uh-huh." He shot Lacey and Ferrell a grim look.
"Don't go anywhere. I'll be right back."

"Forget it, Nicolò. This is my fight, too."

Together they waded into the fray, separating the two
combatants. Lacey gave a squeak of surprise and broke
away from Ferrell with only minor prompting from
Kiley. The older man backed up several paces, the
remains of a diamond necklace clutched in his hand.

"If you don't want to find yourself eating carpet
with a bruise to match Kiley's, I suggest you hand over
that necklace."

"I'm not handing over anything," Ferrell snarled. "The diamonds are mine."

"I paid you what you were owed," Nicolò bit out. "And a good deal more beside. Or have you forgotten that minor detail?"

Kiley balled her hands into fists. "Why, you lying piece of scum. You told me you didn't receive so much as a dime from the Dantes."

"Look who's calling who scum," he shot back. "I deserve the diamonds for the hell you put me through. You deserve to know what it feels like to get conned."

"I'm not going to warn you again," Nicolò interrupted. "Drop the necklace."

Ferrell glared in frustration. "You don't understand."

"No, *you* don't understand." Nicolò stalked closer, leaned in so the other man couldn't mistake his words. "I'm going to pretend that bruise on Kiley's cheek is a regrettable accident. That it didn't have anything to do with you. While I'm operating under that misapprehension, I suggest you get as far away from this room as possible. You got me?"

Ferrell's hand clenched around the necklace, common sense in a pitched battle with greed. After an endless minute, sensibility won out, though it took on a vindictive edge. "Fine. I'll leave. But you're a fool, Dante. She's just going to use you the same way she's used every other man she's ever met." He shook his head in disgust. "You're going to wish you'd never met her before she's finished with you."

And with that, he threw down the remains of the

necklace and stalked from the room. He attempted to slam the door behind him, but it listed drunkenly on its hinges and wouldn't close.

"Thank you for getting rid of him," Lacey said, offering Nicolò a beaming smile. "You can come to my rescue any time."

"My pleasure, though I'm here to rescue Kiley, not you."

He couldn't help but notice that Lacey's smile was absolutely symmetrical, no adorable tilt to disturb its perfection. She bent down and scooped up the necklace, allowing a brief frown to carve a network of lines between her brows and at the corners of her mouth.

"Damn," she muttered. "What the hell were you thinking, Kiley?"

Kiley shrugged. "You know what I was thinking. And FYI, my plans haven't changed just because of a bruised cheek."

"What happened to the necklace?" he asked. "Where are the rest of the diamonds?"

Lacey jumped in before Kiley could respond. "She grew a conscience, that's what." She shot a sour look at Nicolò. "Your bad influence, no doubt."

"I gather the necklace originally belonged to Cameron O'Dell?" At Lacey's nod, he held out his hand. "Do you mind?"

"Not much left of it." A wistful expression slipped through her gaze. "You should have seen it before Kiley broke it up. It was spectacular."

He scrutinized the remaining diamonds. There were

three of them, two single carat diamonds as well as a gorgeous five-carat stone that had to be one of the most exquisite fire diamonds he'd ever seen. "Magnificent."

"It was."

Unable to last another second without touching some part of Kiley, he drew her to the bed, and urged her down on the edge. Then he lifted her chin and tilted her face into the light. "That's quite a shiner you have there. I was right, wasn't I? Ferrell did this?"

"He didn't hit me on purpose," she conceded. "He and Lacey were fighting to get their hands on the necklace and my cheekbone got in the way of his elbow."

"Ouch." He glanced at Lacey and jerked his head toward the door. "Why don't you get your daughter some ice."

"Oh, of course. Right away." Not a trace of sarcasm rippled through her words, yet she managed to make her displeasure heard loud and clear. Quite a feat. "Happy to help."

As soon as she left the room, he asked, "What's going on, Kiley? How did you end up with the necklace?"

She shrugged. "I figured out how to open the locket."

He lifted an eyebrow. "And the necklace was inside?"

That won him a brief, endearingly lopsided smile. "No, but the key to a safety deposit box was. It took me a while to track down the right bank. But once I had, I found the necklace."

His eyes narrowed at that telling piece of information. Did she even realize what she'd said? By admitting she didn't know how to open the locket or where she'd stashed the necklace, she'd just confirmed she still had amnesia. He let it pass for now. "And after you found the necklace? What did you do then?"

"I used the list, the list from the file I found on your desk."

"What did you use it for?" he asked gently.

She focused on a spot over his shoulder, her face set in determined lines. "I gave the diamonds to the people I—" Her voice broke for an instant before she regained control over it. "To the people I scammed. Ferrell was the last one. I didn't realize you'd already paid him off or I'd never have contacted him."

"I gather he wasn't satisfied with a single diamond?"

"Even the little one was worth twice what I took from him. But he felt he deserved more for his pain and suffering. He wanted all three. Then Lacey arrived and..." She shrugged.

"Then I jumped into the fray. Got it."

Her gaze drifted to his face again. Clung. "How did you find me?"

The Inferno called to him, urging him to lean in and take her mouth, to drink her in like a man lost and parched and desperate for relief. He fought the sensation. Not yet. Not until they'd resolved all the remaining issues. "I've been trying to track you down almost from the moment you left."

"Almost," she repeated.

"Well... I had to come to my senses first," he admitted. "When I couldn't find you, I elicited some help from my family."

"Your family?" She shook her head in disbelief. "They were willing to help you find me?"

"Every last one of them," he confirmed.

She stared in wonder. "But why would they do that? Didn't they know what was in the file?"

"They knew."

"I don't understand any of this."

Before she could ask any more questions, Lacey returned with a bucket of ice. Playing the role of the concerned parent, she filled a washcloth with the cubes and offered it to Kiley. "There you go, sweetheart. This should help."

"Now it's your turn," Nicolò warned.

Lacey released a gusty sigh. "I had a feeling I wasn't going to get out of this unscathed."

"I'm surprised you came back. I half expected you to take off."

"Thought about it," she admitted.

"Why didn't you?"

She gave him a cheeky grin. "You have the diamonds."

Of course. Foolish to think she wouldn't make a final play for them. "Explain the necklace. And Kiley's scam with the fire diamond mine."

She lifted an eyebrow, a calculating expression sliding into her gaze. "What do I get in return?"

"Lacey!" Kiley protested.

"The two little ones," Nicolò offered.

"No way. I want the big one."

"That belongs to Kiley," he said in a voice that didn't

brook any argument. "If you want the little ones, you're going to need to explain since Kiley can't."

Lacey made a face. "She really doesn't remember, does she? If she did, she'd never have given away the diamonds."

"I am still here, you know," Kiley objected.

Lacey patted her shoulder. "Of course you are, dear. I assume you showed Nicolò all of Cameron O'Dell's documentation? Birth certificate, death certificate, will?"

Nicolò waited while Kiley silently fumed, fully aware that she had no idea how to answer her mother's question. Satisfied that the point had been made, he answered, "Yes, I saw all that. What happened to Cameron's share of the mine?"

"He sold it to his brother before your grandfather, Primo, made his offer. He sold it in exchange—"

"For the necklace."

"Exactly. He thought the mine was played out. As did his brother, Seamus, for that matter."

"Got it. And you and Kiley have been using that necklace to run a series of scams. Selling and reselling it, I assume, then either substituting a fake or cutting out before the transaction was completed?"

She hesitated. "Well… Not exactly." She shot a disgruntled look toward her daughter. "I guess since there's no more necklace, I can tell you the truth."

Kiley braced herself. "I'm not sure I can handle much more truth right now."

"All those things in the file?" Lacey shrugged. "It was me. I'm the one responsible."

"No." Kiley shook her head, adamant. "That's not possible. Those people identified me."

"Yes, well." Lacey lowered her gaze and released a light laugh. "They might have done that because I was using your name."

"You—" Kiley took a deep breath and tried again. "You would do that to your own daughter? Why?"

Lacey waved the question aside with a sweep of her well-manicured hand. "A girl's got to survive. And speaking of surviving…" She spun to face Nicolò. "Cough it up, handsome. I explained everything, now I want my diamonds."

He removed the largest of the stones from the band and pocketed it before handing her the remaining two. "I'll be watching to make sure that you don't use Kiley's name anytime in the future," he warned.

"Not a problem. And now, if you'll excuse me, I do believe I've outstayed my welcome. If there's one thing I've learned, it's how to make a graceful exit." She flashed a megawatt smile at both of them. "Don't worry, I won't be in touch."

"I'll see you out," Nicolò insisted.

They didn't speak until they'd reached the foyer. He pulled a business card from his pocket and handed it to her. "I hope you won't need this, but just in case."

She regarded it in surprise. "I don't understand. Why are you giving this to me?"

"Two reasons. When all is said and done, you're still Kiley's mother. Family means a lot to the Dantes."

She shrugged that off as though it didn't count for

much. Which, he supposed, it didn't. Not for her. "And the other?" she asked.

"The other is for the lie you just told in there. Although I wouldn't advise lying to me anytime in the future. I'll always know."

"That's so sweet." She twinkled up at him. "You're actually thanking me."

Before he could debate the point, his soon-to-be mother-in-law swept out the door and disappeared down the street with a jaunty hip-swinging stride. And wasn't the idea of a familial connection with Lacey a depressing thought? He didn't waste any further time on her. After giving Rufio the money to pay for the damaged door, he sent the P.I. on his way. Then Nicolò returned to the room where he'd left his heart and soul.

Kiley stood by the motel window, staring in the direction her mother had taken. He joined her there, taking her hand in his. "I'm sorry, sweetheart. I'm sorry for doubting you. I'm sorry for allowing you to leave. And I'm even more sorry I didn't find you sooner."

"What do you want, Nicolò? I mean, really." She lifted her gaze to his and he flinched at the wealth of sorrow he found there. "As much as I appreciate your helping me out of a tight spot, what is there left to be said?"

"Just one more thing." He cupped her face. "I love you, Kiley O'Dell. I love you more than I believed it possible to love someone. I want to spend the rest of my life with you and I'm hoping that's what you want, too."

"I love you, Nicolò. I do." Her voice broke. "I always have."

"Marry me. For real this time. No more lies. No more deception. From this day on, cards on the table."

She shook her head, pain etched deep in her face. "Even now you're not leveling with me. After all we've been through, you still haven't put all your cards on the table."

"What are you—"

"Stop it, Nicolò. I know she lied. I'm not the victim she made me out to be."

He sucked in a deep breath. "How did you know?"

"I'm not a fool. I read the files. Every last word. Those men weren't describing my mother. They were describing *me*. When I met with them, when I made reparations, they recognized me. They—" She fought to gather her self-control. "They despised me. Me, not her."

"She's no innocent in all this."

"No, she's not. I suppose she tried to make amends by taking the blame for all those scams." Her mouth trembled, ripping him to shreds. "But I can't marry you. Not ever. It wouldn't be right."

He fought the panic turning his insides to ice water. "Don't do this, Kiley. The past doesn't matter."

"You're wrong. If it didn't matter, I wouldn't have given away those diamonds. Trust me. It matters. It matters even more when you have nothing left but your honor and self-respect."

"You're not the person you once were."

"I am that person," she insisted. "I'll always have to live with that knowledge. So will you, and so will your family. So will your friends and associates and customers. And they may not be as forgiving as you when they find out who—*what*—I am."

"Was, Kiley. *Was.* Don't you get it? I don't care. I love you. We belong together."

"Do you think I don't want to spend the rest of my life in your arms? Oh, Nicolò. I love you so much. But I can't be with you. I can't marry you."

"Why?"

The words burst out. "Because one day I'll wake up and I'll remember. And when that happens, I'll turn back into her. I won't have a choice. She's who I really am. Who I'm meant to be. I can't do that to you. I won't."

"Bullsh—" He broke off, drawing in a deep, calming breath. "Do you really believe you have no choice? Do you really believe that you can't change? Do you want to be the woman you were before?"

"No. *No.*"

"Then don't. It's that simple. When you remember— if you remember—you can choose. You can choose a life filled with love and family. Or you can choose to go back to your old lifestyle. I'm betting you'll like your new life far better than your old one."

"It's not that easy," she protested. "It can't be."

"It can and it is." He pulled her close, closing his eyes in relief when he felt the helpless give of her body. It told him he hadn't lost her, that he only had to find the right words to win her. Honest words. Words from the heart. "If someday you remember, if it becomes a struggle, I'll be there for you. I swear it. And so will my family. There's only one thing that matters, Kiley. Do you love me?"

"You know I do." Her breath shuddered from her lungs. "I don't want to be her, Nicolò. I don't ever want to be her."

He understood that she didn't just mean her past self, but the sort of woman her mother had become, as well. "You're not. The person you are now, without the baggage from the past, that's the true woman. Your innate sweetness and strength, your intelligence and humor, your wit. All of those things are what exist at the core of you. That's the real you. That's the woman I fell in love with, the Kiley you would have been if your life had taken a different turn." His arms tightened around her and he put every ounce of grit and determination into his voice. "Well, it did make that turn, sweetheart. Call it fate. Call it divine intervention. Hell, call it The Inferno. But because of your accident, you've been given a chance to take your life in a new direction. With me."

He cupped her face and kissed his way past the tears, losing himself in her passionate warmth. This was the Kiley he knew. The Kiley he'd fallen in love with. The Inferno caught fire, blazing hotter than he'd ever felt it before. It was almost as though by their breaking through the final barriers separating them, by sharing those final pieces of themselves, The Inferno rewarded them with a connection so strong, so utterly complete, that nothing could ever divide them again.

He lifted his head and gazed down at her with unfettered honesty and trust. "Marry me, Kiley. Take a chance. Create a brand-new life with me."

"Cards on the table from now on?"

"All fifty-two of them."

She smiled then, that beautiful, radiant, lopsided smile. "Take me home, Nicolò."

He didn't need any further prompting. Together they left behind the old and forgotten, the sordid and painful, and walked into a future shiny with possibility.

Epilogue

Kiley's memory did return, but not for another twenty years.

It came back on a hot summer day while she played baseball with her husband, her four strapping sons and their various first and second cousins. Nicolò had suggested she play centerfield, "out of harm's way," but she'd insisted on covering third. What she hadn't anticipated was chasing an easy pop fly that took an unexpected curve into a nearby street.

It happened again as it had twice before in her life. She darted out into the street, her glove lifted skyward, only afterward realizing the sheer idiocy of her reckless actions. The driver of the oncoming car hit his brakes and horn at the exact same moment, skidding toward her at a frightening speed. She knew she wouldn't be able to avoid the impact this time, just as she hadn't on that very first occasion when she'd been struck by a cab outside of Le Premier. Ironically, this car was the same bright yellow as the cab had been all those years ago. This time it wouldn't miss her, just as it hadn't then. And this time she'd fully suffer the consequences of her impulsiveness.

At the last possible instant, an arm swooped around her waist like a band of iron and yanked her clear of the oncoming car. With a final blare of the horn, it swept past, leaving her trembling within Nicolò's embrace. Her husband growled out a string of Italian curses before kissing her senseless.

When she surfaced from the kiss, it was to find her sons grouped around her in a tight worried circle, and her husband gazing down at her with a combination of undisguised love and bone-deep terror. It felt as though time caught its breath for a brief instant, pausing just long enough for the rush of memories to finish cycling through her head, cascading over her in a dizzying flood.

In that odd timeless moment she remembered it all. Those crazed early years with her mother. The childhood better off forgotten. The lessons she'd learned at the knee of an amoral parent more concerned with material possessions than character or soul…more concerned with money than the needs of a lonely child desperate for a proper mother. Kiley could see, as though through a thick glass, the string of scams she and her mother had pulled. Could feel the cold emptiness of that life, could feel the spirit draining out of her with each successive con.

"Mom?" Dominic, her eldest, touched her shoulder, fear evident in the deep black gaze he kept trained on her face. "You okay?

"I—"

The past tugged at her. Called to her. Tried to pull her back toward that other person. That person she'd been all those years ago. So many options opened themselves to her, options that for that long-ago Kiley would have been like hitting a million dollar jackpot.

And then she began to laugh. She'd hit the jackpot long ago. She gazed up at her husband, a man she adored with all her heart and soul, a man who'd saved her from that other life. And she looked at each one of the children she'd given birth to, children she'd showered with love and attention, discipline and a strong moral character. And she laughed again, laughed for sheer joy. The diamond on her wedding ring flamed brighter than ever. It was the last diamond from Cameron O'Dell's fire diamond necklace, a diamond that symbolized an end to the old and the opportunity for a new beginning.

Go back? Never.

She picked up the softball laying at her feet and tagged her son with it. "You're out," she told him. "Now, let's play ball."

* * * * *

MISTAKEN MISTRESS

BY
TESSA RADLEY

Tessa Radley loves travelling, reading and watching the world around her. As a teenager Tessa wanted to be an intrepid foreign correspondent. But after completing a bachelor of arts degree and marrying her sweetheart she became fascinated with law and ended up studying further and practising as an attorney in a city practice.

A six-month break travelling through Australia with her family reawoke the yen to write. And life as a writer suits her perfectly: travelling and reading count as research, and as for analysing the world...well, she can think "what if" all day long. When she's not reading, travelling or thinking about writing, she's spending time with her husband, her two sons, or her zany and wonderful friends. You can contact Tessa through her website, www.tessaradley.com.

Dear Reader,

When I first started creating the Saxon's Folly vineyard, I spent a fair amount of time considering what makes vineyards such an appealing setting for romances. I thought about the vineyards I'd visited. About the history behind them. About the people I'd met. The wines I'd tasted. The stories I'd heard. Above all, I thought about the delicate nature of the grape-growing process.

Sunshine. Rain. Sweet plump grapes. The inexorable cycle of the seasons, of vines budding, growing heavy with sun-ripened fruit as summer marches on. Those are fabulous visuals for a writer – especially a romance writer. And then, of course, there are the men who grow the grapes. Gorgeous, rugged men, masters of science and nature…men who, like Joshua Saxon in *Mistaken Mistress*, are part of an ancient tradition. Once I'd found Joshua there was the challenge to match him with a very special woman…a woman who would become a Saxon Bride… Trust me, I had a lot of fun!

I hope you enjoy Joshua and Alyssa's story – you can find out more about new books in THE SAXON BRIDES series at www.tessaradley.com.

Take care,

Tessa

For Lesley Marshall, who is always an inspiration.

One

The annual Saxon's Folly masked ball was already in full swing when Alyssa Blake crept up the cobbled drive.

"Walk tall," she whispered to herself as she skirted the shadows between the rows of parked Mercedes and Daimler cars. "Look like you belong."

The winery's historic homestead came into sight, brightly lit against the dark sky. A triple-storey white Victorian building that had withstood more than a century of fires, floods and even an infamous Hawkes Bay earthquake. With every step the music grew louder, even though Alyssa couldn't yet see the partygoers.

At the top of the stone stairs a large uniformed man blocked the double, wooden front doors. Alyssa came to a halt.

Butler?

Or guard?

She wavered for a moment, her heartbeat quickening as her eyes scanned the building.

Don't panic.

"I've lost my invitation." She practised the timeworn excuse to herself under her breath. It sounded lame. Particularly as she'd never received one of the sought-after silver-embossed, midnight-blue invitations. If the guard took the time to check, he wouldn't find her on the guest list. But would he check?

Perhaps she could sashay past with a smile? What was the worst that could happen? The doorman, guard—or whatever he was—would fail to locate her on the list of invitees and demand her identity? No one would suspect Alyssa Blake, leading wine writer for *Wine Watch* magazine, of gate-crashing the annual Saxon's Folly masked ball. Or at least only the few who knew how much Joshua Saxon, CEO of Saxon's Folly Wines, detested Alyssa after the article she'd done a couple of years ago—and most people's memories didn't extend that far back.

There was a chance the burly doorman would let her in without a second glance. Wearing a long, ruby-red dress and her flamboyant black mask decorated with feathers and diamante studs, it was unlikely he'd suspect her being a gate-crasher. Alyssa hauled in a shaky breath.

She'd made up her mind to brazen her way past the doorman—guard, whatever—when a side door opened and light streaked out into the night. A couple slid out into the embrace of the darkness, laughing. The door swung closed but the latch failed to click shut.

Quickly, like a thief in the night, Alyssa slipped into the enormous homestead. She stood to one side of the entrance hall. Ahead of her, an imposing staircase swept upward.

At the top of the stairs Alyssa stepped into a different world—a world of wealth and privilege where women fluttered like designer-clad butterflies in the arms of men in dress suits and bow ties.

After one glance, she dismissed the dancers. Instead she scanned the vast reception room, searching…searching for the man she'd gone to the lengths of gate-crashing a masked ball to find.

"Have you just arrived?"

She looked up into a pair of glittering dark eyes shielded by a black mask.

"I'm a little late," she managed, her nerves rolling as the realisation sank in that she'd made it to the ball.

"Better late than never."

"Never say never," she quipped, wagging a finger at him.

He laughed. "A woman of strong opinions, right?"

"And proud of it."

His voice was husky, oddly familiar…and terribly sexy. A sweeping glance from behind her mask showed her that he was tall, the broad, hard planes of his body showing to best advantage in the superbly tailored dinner jacket. Dark hair topped his head while a black mask concealed his face. A handsome face, she speculated.

"Dance with me." He stretched an imperious arm out. Mr. Tall, Dark and Probably Handsome wasn't taking no for an answer.

Not that those attributes had any effect on her. She preferred her dates kind, caring and capable…qualities that were becoming harder to find. She stared at the demanding arm.

"I take it that silence means yes?"

Before she could object that it most definitely meant no the arm locked around her shoulder and he propelled her toward the dance floor. She started to object. She wasn't here to celebrate the budding of the new season's vines, she'd come with a purpose…and it wasn't to dance with this sexy, cocky stranger. But nor did she intend to cause a scene and be noticed.

If Joshua Saxon discovered her presence, he'd toss her out before she could even try to explain why she was here. Better not to cause a stir by refusing. At least she would blend in better with the crowd. And she could continue her search from the dance floor.

She let him sweep her into his arms and into the throng of dancers. The covetous glances her partner drew made her reevaluate whether this had been a good idea. Perhaps dancing with him would attract the attention she was so keen to avoid. She assessed him through her eyelashes, measuring what the other women saw: broad shoulders beautifully displayed in a dinner jacket, an uncompromising jawline. She glanced upward into eyes that gleamed behind the black mask.

"Do I know you?" he asked, his voice deep.

She considered that. If he was a member of the wine fraternity, they might have met at a wine show. It was possible he might have seen her during the occasional appearance she made on television, a guest spot on a food show...or perhaps he'd read her *Wine Watch* articles or the column she wrote for *The Aucklander* newspaper. But none of those meant he knew her.

So she shook her head.

"Well, I'm going to enjoy seeing your face when we unmask at midnight—it's a tradition." As a pair of dancers jostled them, he leaned toward her. "Do you have a name, Oh Silent One?"

Alyssa hesitated, transfixed by the way the hard line of his mouth tilted up into a smile. The contrast was intriguing. "Alice," she said finally, using the name on her birth certificate rather than the name she'd reinvented herself under as a teenager.

"Alice?" Those lips curved further, deepening the sensual smile. "Do you feel as if you've stepped through the looking glass, Alice?"

If he only knew.

"A little," she confessed in a low voice.

He bent his head closer. "Does that mean this is the first spring masquerade you've attended?"

"Yes."

"That explains why you're not wearing a costume."

She let her gaze linger pointedly on his dinner jacket. "You're not in costume, either."

He shook his head. "Didn't have time to plan it this year."

A busy man, then. But he didn't need the trappings of a

Robin Hood or a regency rake, she decided. He was commanding enough in his own right.

"Most women live to dress up."

His comment set her teeth on edge. "I am not most women."

He laughed softly. "I'll be even more intrigued to meet you face-to-face at midnight. So Alice, you don't like to dress up, but are you like all the Cinderellas—" he waved a dismissive hand at the beautiful women around them "—here to find a wealthy Prince Charming?" A tinge of cynicism coloured his deep voice.

"Definitely not here to find Prince Charming, wealthy or otherwise." But she shivered at his percipience. She was certainly here to find someone.

"You're not given to much conversation." He sounded far too curious for her liking.

"All these people," she simpered. "I'm not used to it."

His gaze raked her. "I'd peg you as a sophisticated city girl—not someone who'd be nervous around people."

Alyssa glanced down at the plunging V-neckline of her ruby-red dress. She'd better take care…he was altogether too astute. Her pulse pounded in her head. She couldn't afford to be thrown out—this was her best chance. "Perhaps it's the excitement. The music…the beautiful people, the handsome masked man." Her voice was sweeter than syrup. She glanced up through the satin strip of her mask to see how the flattery was going down and caught a white flash of teeth.

"As long as you're not nervous, Alice," he whispered. "That's not allowed."

Alyssa shuddered as his warm breath skimmed her sensitive ear and arousal shot unexpectedly through her.

"You *are* nervous. You're trembling."

She couldn't remember the last time a stranger had had such an immediate effect on her. Safer to say nothing.

"You're the most silent woman I've ever met," he growled, and pulled her closer to avoid a couple dancing with far too much enthusiasm in the mass of bodies.

"Not always." Not when she wasn't watching every word—her normal stock-in-trade—in case she slipped up. This disturbing stranger was far too confident...and she was not in the frame of mind to handle him.

Not tonight.

A flash of red hair caused her head to whip around, and reality came crashing in.

Roland! She couldn't mistake him, not even with a rakish pirate's eye patch. The red hair was a giveaway. He held a slim, dark-haired sprite in his arms. Across the crowded room Alyssa followed the couple's progress over her partner's broad shoulder, saw Roland say something to the brunette and watched her reply.

Alyssa had read that her name was Amy...and she was Roland's fiancée. The two of them slowed and left the dance floor.

Panic surged through Alyssa. She couldn't lose them— him. Not when she'd come so close.

"I'm parched, I need a drink," she said, not caring how abrupt she sounded, and freed herself unceremoniously from her partner's hold.

"What would you like?" Her stranger showed every sign of coming with her.

"I'll find myself something." Alyssa glanced anxiously after her quarry and back to the partner she'd failed to shake.

She mustn't give herself away.

He was much too distracting, too perceptive. She didn't want any third parties overhearing what she had to say to Roland. This was private. Too important. "You don't need to worry about me. I'm sure there are other people you should be mingling with...dancing with."

He wouldn't lack for partners. He danced like a dream... confident...moving with rhythmic grace, a man aware of his attraction and power. She jerked away from him.

His sensuous mouth twisted. "None as interesting as you,

Alice. What would you like to drink? A glass of Saxon's Folly Sauvignon Blanc? I can recommend last season's vintage."

Perhaps letting him get her a drink would get rid of him. "Just water, please."

He beckoned to a waiter who arrived at breakneck speed.

So much for getting rid of him. Alyssa resisted the urge to swear.

"Just water?" His eyes gleamed through the mask. At her nod, he turned to the waiter. "Two bottles of Perrier."

Alyssa forced herself not to look for Roland, but she was anxiously aware that if she didn't find him now, she might lose him again.

"I need the cloakroom," she improvised. "I'll be back in a minute," she flung over her shoulder, and dived into the crowd.

A glance back showed that her Mr. Tall, Dark and Probably Handsome had been detained by two women who each kissed him enthusiastically on both cheeks, the mask clearly an ineffective disguise to the ambitious Cinderellas. Impatience was carved into every line of his tall, muscular body, but he murmured a polite response.

Good, he wasn't following.

Then Alyssa put him out of her mind as she wove her way between men in tuxedos, women in silk and satin dresses, intent on finding the man she'd come to confront.

But Roland—and his fiancée—had vanished.

Alyssa hurried out onto the balcony outside, brushing past Rhett Butler and Scarlett O'Hara flirting in the shadows, and a couple of men smoking alone.

She peered over the white wrought iron railing, through the criss-cross shadows cast by a clump of tall Nikau palms, into the well-lit garden below. Two couples stood under the trees. Her breath caught. But neither man sported that distinctive red hair. Her pulse quickening with urgency, Alyssa hurried along the wide balcony and down a set of steep narrow stairs and slipped through the side door back into the homestead.

Sweeping up the long skirts of her dress, she hurried, peering into rooms she passed. A quick scan of the large dining room with tables laden with finger food failed to reveal Roland.

Roland must've taken his fiancée—Amy—upstairs. Alyssa hesitated, eyeing a staircase that appeared to lead to another wing. The bedrooms must be up there. What if she disturbed them in an…intimate moment?

Her teeth played with her bottom lip. She'd come so far, she couldn't chicken out now. Drawing a deep breath, she moved toward the stairs.

But before she got there, the door on her right swung open and a brunette burst out. Amy. Her colour was high, her hair mussed. Alyssa stopped, and then Roland came rushing into the corridor, his eye patch in his hand, his expression determined.

"Amy, listen to—"

"Roland?" Like a sleepwalker Alyssa reached out and touched his arm. "Roland Saxon?"

She knew exactly who he was but she couldn't help enunciating the name that had been imprinted on her mind for years.

He gave her an impatient glance. "Yes?"

"I'm—" She hesitated, her mind suddenly blank. Everything she'd planned to say withered under the attack of doubt devils. Dare she reveal herself as Alice McKay? He hadn't responded to any of her letters or e-mails, so why should he be any more welcoming now?

He glanced past her to where the brunette had taken the main stairs and disappeared in the direction of the ballroom.

Concerned that he would brush by her and vanish again, Alyssa thrust out her hand and said, "I'm Alyssa Blake. I'm—"

Recognition flared in the eyes that met hers in astonishment. "The journalist who did that hatchet job on Saxon's Folly. Yes, I know who you are."

No, you don't.

Finally, to her immense relief, he took her hand and shook it, before letting it drop. "What are you doing here?"

Alyssa found she was shaking. Roland had touched her. His skin had been warm and solid. Real. She'd met him. At last.

Struggling for composure, she said, "I'd like to arrange to interview you for a feature in *Wine Watch*."

Now she had his full attention, but his expression had shifted to wariness. "What would the focus of the story be?"

"I'm doing a story on how some of the strongest brands in the industry have been built. As the marketing director of Saxon's Folly Wines, I'd like your comments."

"You haven't been too complimentary about Saxon's Folly in the past, Ms. Blake."

"Maybe I've had a change of mind." Please, God, let him believe it. She needed a chance to meet with him one-on-one. They had so much to talk about.

"I don't know—"

"Please." She was practically begging now. "It will be a positive article. I promise."

"Why should I trust you? Joshua believed you were going to do a feature on the estate. Instead you lambasted his management methods."

"Joshua Saxon had it coming," she said heatedly. "He's the most aggravatingly uncommunicative man I've ever interviewed." The man had refused to see her in person, had given her precisely ten minutes of his time on the phone. And during each miserable second of those minutes his terse voice had made it clear that he was doing her a favour. A very junior cellar hand who'd been in the job for less than a week had shown her around the winery. Alyssa had asked him about his job and discovered that the previous cellar hand had been fired under very hush-hush circumstances. A few calls to the disgruntled former employee and she had a different story from the one she'd planned to do. Now she told Roland, "The facts bore me out."

"Joshua didn't think so."

"I did my job."

He looked her up and down. "Some job."

"I tell the public what they ought to know." She knew that sounded pious. So she drew a steadying breath. "Look, this is getting us nowhere. The piece I'm working on now is different. You can even see the copy before it goes to print." Something she'd never offered but she had to see him privately.

He looked dubious. "Why the change of heart? And why ask me now, here at the ball? Why not contact me by more conventional ways, telephone—or even e-mail—to set up an appointment?"

I tried.

You never responded.

She'd tried as Alice McKay. She'd reveal Alice tomorrow. All she could do now was tempt him with the promise of a great profile. He was a marketing man. Unlike his arrogant brother, he knew he needed the goodwill of the press. "It will be great publicity for you, for Saxon's Folly."

But already he was moving past her. Time to give him an ultimatum. She spoke to his back. "Yes or no?"

"Yes, I suppose."

Alyssa knew she'd lost his attention. "When?" Alyssa switched into the familiar role, closing the escape route. "I'm in the area tomorrow. Shall we meet at The Grapevine—" she named a popular café "—in town?"

He turned his head and gave a slow nod, and her heart leapt. At last! Quickly she confirmed a time. Alyssa wanted to punch a fist in the air and yell, "Yes." After all the years…

But instead she smiled sedately and banished her impatience. Time enough tomorrow to celebrate.

Joshua Saxon was frowning. The fascination that his mystery lady in red held for him was fast becoming a compulsion. He'd been holding the two bottles of Perrier, and positioned himself so that he wouldn't miss the lady when she reappeared. But she hadn't.

Either he'd missed her. Or she hadn't been as desperate to go to the cloakroom as she'd led him to believe.

He made for the balcony on the off chance that she'd passed him and gone outside.

As soon as he stepped outside he wished he hadn't. Roland, no mask concealing his features, had Amy pinned against the balcony rail, trying to say something. But Amy was shaking her head wildly, her mask askew, telling Roland she was going home.

Under the hanging party lights Joshua caught a glimpse of tears streaking her cheeks. Roland growled that she wasn't going anywhere.

None of his business. Neither of them would thank him for the interference.

Then he spotted a flash of dark red in the gardens below and all thoughts about his brother's romantic problems fled. Alice. He leapt down the stairs that led to the garden.

"You aren't leaving already, are you?"

She turned, her rich red dress swirling around her legs, every line of her body revealing her surprise.

"Umm…"

"You were." Outraged, he stared at her. Suddenly it had become critically important to know who the provocative woman was, where to find her. But he couldn't tell her that. Instead he said, "You can't leave before the unmasking." He checked his Rolex. "It's only three-quarters of an hour away. And then the real party begins."

"I need to make this an early night."

Joshua almost laughed. Women rarely used that line on him. "The Saxon ball happens only once a year. No early night tonight."

"I have a big day tomorrow."

"Big day?" His curiosity was well and truly captured.

"Work."

She definitely wasn't the most talkative woman he'd ever

met. And that intrigued the hell out of him. Not that he'd
ever admit it.

"Work? On a Sunday?"

She nodded. "Some of us are slaves to demanding bosses."

Her lips curved into an irresistible smile, and Joshua
found himself smiling back. He couldn't imagine any boss
forcing this woman to work against her will. He twisted the
cap off one of the bottles of Perrier he held and handed it
out to her. "At least take the time to finish the drink you
needed so badly."

She looked startled, and a little embarrassed colour stained
the elegant jaw that the mask didn't cover. "Oh, thank you."

"Do you want a glass?" Joshua twisted the cap off his
own bottle.

"No, this is fine."

He gave her a reckless grin. "I probably wouldn't get you
one—you might disappear again." Tilting his head to one
side, he waited for her response. For an explanation of where
she'd been.

But she only drew a sip and said, "Mmm, this is good."

The soft hum of appreciation riveted his attention on her
mouth; the lips pursed against the top of the bottle were full
and lush as she drank thirstily from the bottle. A sudden stab
of sexual awareness pierced him.

"Dance with me," he said brusquely. He wanted to hold her
in his arms again, feel her body against his.

"Here?"

"Why not?" Joshua moved closer. Out here there were no
hordes of dancers to navigate in an overheated room. It was
private in the cool intimacy of the gardens.

She didn't resist as he took the bottle from her fingers and
propped it with his against the base of a Nikau palm. Nor did
she utter a word of objection as one arm slid round her waist
and drew her toward him.

His left hand closed around her right. Their bodies caught

the rhythm first, then their feet started to shuffle against the night-damp grass.

She smelled of jasmine and heady notes of ylang-ylang. On a conscious level Joshua found his vintner's nose analysing the feminine mix of scents, scents only a woman confident of herself, of her sexuality and her place in the world would wear. The man in him responded to the rich, sensual aromas on another—much baser—level.

Her hip slid against the top of his thigh.

Desire exploded through him. A rush of heat chased through his bloodstream, wild and unwanted. He resisted for an instant in time, then he shifted, giving in to the heat, his leg brushing between hers as they moved.

She gave a little gasp, and her body softened into his.

Instantly Joshua relinquished her hand and wound his arm around her shoulders pulling her closer. She was slim and soft in the curve of his arms. He bent his head, nuzzled the smooth skin under her jaw, and heard the sharp, telling little exhalation.

"You smell wonderful," he murmured.

"Thank you." She sounded breathless. "You smell pretty good yourself." She gave an awkward laugh. "Goodness, we should start a mutual olfactory admiration society."

He doubted that her sense of smell ruled her life as it did his. While he didn't have his younger brother Heath's highly developed ability, he'd grown up at Saxon's Folly immersed in wine, and smelling was as natural to him as breathing.

He nuzzled again. "You smell of dewy nights and dark, exotic spices." He heard her breathing quicken. This time he pressed a soft kiss under her jaw. She quivered. "So soft," he murmured throatily.

"Oh." A sigh escaped her.

Joshua took that as license to nibble gently, and she arched in his arms, her response unequivocal.

His hands explored the bare skin of her back. Under his fingertips he could feel the electric tension tightening within her.

But she didn't push him away. By the time he slid his lips across hers she was ready, her lush lips parted.

She tasted fresh and cool. Of mint and the hint of lemon in the Perrier. A powerful surge of hunger swarmed through him. Instead of tasting carefully, proceeding slowly, he yanked her close and devoured her mouth.

A wild sound escaped the back of her throat. Then her hands were raking up the corded muscles of his back, across his shoulders, her touch sparking a rush of energy that pooled in his groin.

His feet gave up all pretence of dancing. Behind his head her fingers rubbed against the exposed skin of his neck, before burying themselves in his hair. He groaned into her mouth. His tongue swept across the soft, slick inside of her bottom lip, tangled with the sleek wetness of her tongue, then plundered the back of her mouth.

Her response was instant and arousing. Her body tensed against his, and desire ratcheted up inside him until he felt that his skin was too tight. Restlessly, he ground his hips against her, acutely conscious of the blatant hardness of his erection straining for freedom. She moved, too, equally unsettled, and Joshua felt arousal kick up to the next level, his hormones telling his head there was only one place where this could end.

His bed.

For a moment he fought the savage urge. Too soon. He'd never bedded a woman he didn't know enough about to be relatively certain he'd still like her in the morning.

"God." He lifted his head, his breathing heavy.

"I should go." But she didn't sound very sure.

"Why?" he demanded, and his voice sounded hoarse to his own ears.

"Because it would be the sensible thing to do. And I'm always sensible." But her breathlessness belied her claim.

"Haven't you ever wanted to do something wild? Something totally out of character? Something that might change the rest of your life?" He murmured the inflammatory words against her lips, knowing that was what he was doing now. Allowing his body to rule his brain and letting go with this stranger was the kind of risk he, who liked his odds very carefully calculated, never took.

"Yes, I did that tonight."

He raised his head a little, trying to read the glitter in her eyes behind the mask, in the pale silver light of the crescent moon overhead.

"By coming here at all," she said cryptically.

"Come with me." Joshua reached for her hand and pulled her toward the house, leading her down a dark passage, through the empty hallway to a set of stairs that descended to his suite.

She baulked. "We can't go down there."

"Hush. Trust me."

She trailed behind him as he hurried down the stairs and past the living room that he shared with Roland.

"I suppose there are etchings you want to show me?" But beneath the bite there was breathlessness.

"No etchings." Joshua veered left toward his destination. "Come here, babe." He didn't bother to switch on the lights before he took her in his arms.

"But—"

He kissed her objections away. And when her hands ran over his back, Joshua groaned out aloud. He couldn't wait for this. Couldn't remember ever wanting a woman this much. He tore off his mask. The expensive Italian-styled dinner jacket landed on the floor, and Joshua yanked the snaps of the dress shirt open.

The touch of her fingertips on the bare skin of his chest was electric. Joshua bit back a curse of pure ecstasy. She drew her palms across his pectorals.

Joshua shuddered.

He drove his tongue deep into her mouth and shifted his hips, knowing she must be aware of how incredibly turned on he was.

But she didn't flinch. Instead her fingers teased, exploring the ridges of his abdominal muscles, brushing his lower belly.

"Woman, you're killing me," he said hoarsely.

She gave a little throaty laugh.

That was enough. His senses on fire, Joshua drew her to the bed and came down on the cover beside her. In the darkness he cupped her head in his hands, her hair soft and silky between his fingers. The ties of the mask tangled in his fingers and he tugged them loose. He kissed her cheeks where the mask had rested…her neck…and moved his lips to where he guessed the V-neckline of her outrageous dress would be.

She wasn't laughing now. Her body arched beneath him, and the swell of her breasts brushed his arm.

"Alice."

She stilled.

Then his hand closed over the fabric-draped softness of her breast. He heard her gasp out loud.

"Ah, Alice, this is going to be good. I promise." Impatiently, he peeled the dress down over her shoulders—and discovered she wore no bra. He bent his head to taste the skin he'd exposed.

"Joshua."

The call jarred Joshua back to reality an instant before the bedroom door burst open. He rolled in front of her, shielding her from the intruder.

Dim light backdropped the figure who stood in the doorway. Joshua snarled, "Dammit, Heath. Can't you knock?"

Two

The bedside light clicked on. Brightness spilled into every corner of the room, hurting Alyssa's eyes.

But she didn't blink. She couldn't take her eyes off the half-naked man on the bed beside her. The high, slanting cheekbones and black eyes were all too familiar. She'd studied photos of him, wondering how someone so utterly beautifully and flagrantly male could be such an arrogant swine.

Joshua Saxon.

No wonder his voice had sounded so damn familiar. She pulled her knees to her chest and yanked the bedcover over her nakedness, then buried her head in her hands, humiliation crawling through her.

"What do you want, Heath?" There was an edge to Joshua's voice as he sat up and addressed his brother.

Through the cracks between her fingers, Alyssa peered toward the door. Heath Saxon. The younger, rakehell brother. He'd been featured in *Wine Watch* as a winemaker to watch. In the photo accompanying the profile, he'd been smiling, tanned. Now he hovered indecisively in the doorway. Until, a flush burning into his pasty skin, he said awkwardly, "Sorry, Joshua, but there's been an accident."

Joshua's shoulders bunched under the open shirt. "An accident?"

Alyssa's hand dropped to cover his.

"Roland's been hurt," Heath said. "We need to go to the hospital."

Roland hurt? Alyssa was off the bed in an instant, pulling up the neckline of her dress.

"Roland's my brother," Joshua said to Alyssa. Then his focus returned to his brother. "What kind of accident?"

"A car accident."

"What the hell happened?" Joshua asked the question before Alyssa could.

Heath shook his head. "I don't know, but an ambulance has taken him and Amy to hospital."

That catapulted Joshua into action. He leapt off the bed, started buttoning his shirt and trod into his shoes. "Do the parents know?"

Heath's eyes darkened. "I told them there'd been an accident, that you and I would go see how bad it was. They're telling everyone the party's over."

"Good move." Joshua headed for the door. "If it's necessary, they can come to the hospital later."

Before he could disappear, Alyssa said, "I'm coming with you."

To her relief both men were more concerned with getting to the hospital than arguing with her. Heath gave her a searching look—then glanced at Joshua and raised his eyebrows. Alyssa knew he was making assumptions—assumptions that were totally wrong. He thought she was Joshua's lover. She didn't bother to disillusion him.

Nor was it the time to get into lengthy discussions about her relationship to Roland...a revelation that she suspected might come as a huge shock to both men. Joshua was not to find out who she was. She didn't need a crystal ball to know that she would be unceremoniously tossed out the house.

She couldn't afford that. She had to find out how badly Roland was hurt.

Once in Joshua's Range Rover, the tension became palpable. Joshua drove like a man with a lethal mission, in total silence, his hands clenched around the steering wheel. Beside him Heath made call after call from his cell phone, growing increasingly frustrated when he couldn't get answers out of the emergency staff.

Alyssa huddled down in the back, doing her best to remain invisible lest either man question her right to be here. She prayed that Roland's injuries were minor. Hopefully he'd be discharged tonight. It would be unbearable if, after all the waiting, she couldn't meet with him tomorrow.

The moment the Range Rover braked outside the hospital, the three of them leapt out, hurrying for the glass doors that led to the emergency room.

Inside the smell of urgency and antiseptic injected dread into Alyssa. As Joshua's voice rose, she heard the nurse murmuring "in surgery" and "someone will be with you soon." Alyssa stopped a distance away. Heath asked a series of short, sharp questions and Alyssa strained her ears to hear the reply. She heard "shocked" and "will need supervision" before Joshua replied, his voice cutting. Alyssa felt for the nurse. He'd used that same voice on her in the past after her story had been printed. It had riled her enough to tell him to get lost before she'd slammed the phone down. But now she hoped it would get the answers they all wanted.

When Joshua came back to where she'd settled to wait, his mouth was tighter than before and lines of strain were etched across his forehead.

"How is my—" Alyssa broke off.

Joshua did a double take. "Your…what?" he prompted softly.

Furious with herself for the near giveaway and fighting to keep her face impassive, she asked in an even tone, "How is Roland?"

Instinct warned her that it was vital not to let Joshua Saxon know how important his answer was to her. He detested Alyssa Blake. As soon as he realised who he'd been kissing…touching…stripping…in the dark, he was going to explode.

"He's in surgery. No news yet about the extent of his injuries." The chair scraped against the polished floor as Joshua threw himself down beside her. "Thankfully Amy got off with only some bruising from the seat belt when the car hit a tree."

Hit a tree? A vision of mangled steel and broken glass flashed across Alyssa's mind. The sound of screams and groaning metal rent her imagination. She bit her lip and focused instead on Joshua's drawn features, the beauty dimmed by the savage line of his mouth. For a moment she felt a sense of kinship with him.

"Joshua?"

He lifted his head at the intrusion and the spell was broken. Alyssa felt the loneliness return, stronger and more pervasive than before. There was no bond between her and Joshua Saxon—at least none that wasn't based on sex. She shook away the disappointment.

Heath was heading toward them. "The nurse says they've finished checking Amy out and it shouldn't be long until she's back here."

"It's a relief that she wasn't hurt. She could've been killed if they're right about the speed the SUV was doing," Joshua said darkly.

"Since when did Roland ever drive slowly?" Heath bit out.

Roland had been driving? Alyssa started to shiver with reaction. If only he'd been in the passenger seat…

She thought back to when she'd spoken to him. Had he and

Amy had a lover's tiff? Would he have had the accident if he hadn't been upset?

"I heard them having a fight earlier in the evening. I considered breaking it up, then decided to mind my own business. My mind was on other things." Joshua glanced at Alyssa, his face blank. "A mistake."

So she was nothing more than a mistake. Tightness filled Alyssa's chest.

"Not your fault," said Heath. "No guy would welcome interference in that situation. You probably had it wrong. Amy and Roland never fight."

Alyssa opened her mouth. "When I spoke to Roland—"

"You spoke to Roland?" Joshua interrupted Alyssa. "When?"

"Just before I decided to leave."

"So before I spotted them on the balcony." There was a peculiar note in Joshua's voice. "What did you talk to him about?"

She stared at him, her hackles rising at his peremptory tone. She was a mistake, was she? Well, her business with Roland had nothing to do with him. "It wasn't important."

Joshua gave her a narrow-eyed glare filled with suspicion that told her he thought it was important. But before he could challenge her, a doctor in a white coat entered the reception, ushering a slender, white-faced young woman ahead of him.

Heath was on his feet. "Amy!"

Heath and Joshua both started forward.

"Are you her family?" asked the doctor.

"Yes," said Joshua.

"No," said Heath at that same moment.

There was a confused silence. The doctor looked from one to the other. "I need to see her family. She'll require observation tonight."

"We'll take care of that," said Joshua.

"I'll take her home now," added Heath, frowning as his gaze scanned Amy.

Alyssa flinched as she saw the scraped skin on the other woman's pale face. Her fine-boned build made her look frail.

"She's very lucky. Only one bruise from the seat belt. There's not even a cracked rib or a broken clavicle where the seat belt restrained her. I have a list of symptoms to watch for. We're particularly worried about concussion…or any form of head trauma. If she displays any of them bring her straight back."

Amy stood, unmoving.

"Come on," Joshua said, putting an arm around her, "Heath is taking you home."

Amy blinked. "Where's Roland?"

Joshua answered, "In surgery."

There was a moment's silence. "Will he be okay?" There was fear in Amy's voice. "There was so much blood…and he was so quiet."

"I'm sure he'll be fine," Heath said soothingly. "You know Roland, he always bounces back."

Amy didn't look reassured. "When will I be able to see him?"

"We don't know yet." Joshua's frustration added a hard edge to his voice. "But I'll soon change that."

"I'm not going anywhere," Amy said with a stubbornness that belied her delicate appearance. "Not until I've heard what's happening with Roland. And Heath won't want to leave, either."

"Don't be a child, Amy," Heath sounded exasperated. "You heard what the doctor said, you need rest and observation. There's already one—" He broke off.

"Patient?" Amy's chin lifted. "Don't worry about me, I won't collapse. You can observe me here. I'm not going anywhere until I've seen Roland."

Alyssa suppressed the urge to cheer the other woman on for standing up to the overbearing Saxons. She knew exactly how Amy felt. She, too, wanted to see Roland with a deep, driving ache. She shifted restlessly.

Joshua's gaze flickered to her before returning to Amy. "Can I get you anything while we wait?" His tone was gentle, not hinting at the frustration he must be feeling at Amy's intransigence.

Amy shook her head violently. "I'm fine."

But even Alyssa could see that the other woman was far from fine. How must Roland's fiancée be feeling, waiting to hear the extent of her beloved's injuries?

The waiting was bad enough for her. She'd only met Roland once. Very briefly. The man she'd been seeking for years...

A strand of hair fell forward. She stared at it. It was dark red—thankfully not the bright red that topped Roland's head, more of an auburn shade. But it was something tangible that she shared with him.

There would be more links to discover once they got to know each other. There must be. After all, Roland was her brother and they shared the same DNA.

A stir at the doorway caused Alyssa to lift her head. Kay and Phillip Saxon—Roland's adoptive parents—had arrived.

"How is he? Can we see him?" Kay's eyes were frantic, and the powerfully built, gray-haired man beside her looked shattered. Everyone swarmed around them. Alyssa saw her chance.

She stopped a passing nurse. "Roland Saxon...where is he?"

"What's your relationship to the patient?" The nurse glanced at the clipboard she held. "Are you the fiancée?"

She hesitated, glancing quickly back to where Kay Saxon was bending over Amy, patting her shoulder. It would be better if she didn't lie outright and simply let the nurse assume she was Roland's fiancée.

"My name is Alyssa Blake, I'm—"

"Alyssa Blake?" Joshua had come up behind her, unheard. Now his angry gaze impaled her.

Uh-oh.

"Are you the fiancée?" The nurse looked confused.

"No! She's *not* my brother's fiancée," Joshua hissed from between clenched teeth.

Alyssa's heart crashed to the floor as she read the disdain

and rage in his eyes. Game over. She could kiss her hopes of seeing Roland tonight goodbye.

"So you're Alyssa Blake, the journalist?"

Suddenly everyone was gathered around. Heath, his eyes almost as glacial as his brother's. Kay and Phillip Saxon. Only Amy remained seated, her face cupped in her hands.

Alyssa's gaze flickered from face to face. "Yes, I'm Alyssa—"

"You told me your name was Alice," Joshua interrupted.

"It is—"

"Alice?" Kay Saxon had gone so white that her lips appeared bloodless.

"Don't worry—her name isn't Alice. She's Alyssa Blake, that bloody journalist who—"

Alyssa cut across Joshua's rant. "What does it matter right now what my name is? Roland is hurt."

"You're right! I've wasted enough time on a journalist in the business of telling lies." Joshua's gaze scorched her. "It's my brother who's important right now. Come, Heath." Joshua stormed past her, his brother in his wake.

Feeling sick, Alyssa started to follow.

"Wait." Kay Saxon grabbed her arm.

Alyssa stopped. Maybe Kay would let her see Roland if she told the older woman the truth. That Roland was her brother. That she'd dreamed for so long of this day…of finding her brother…of meeting him. Warily, she searched Kay Saxon's face for a hint of softness.

"Did Joshua call you Alice?" Kay's eyes held desperation.

"Yes."

"But you introduced yourself as Alyssa Blake to the nurse."

"Yes." Where was this going? Alyssa could feel impatience rising in her. She needed to find a way to get to Roland's side. To hold his hand, absorb his pain.

"Does that mean you're Alice McKay?"

Alyssa froze. "What do you know about Alice McKay?"

"You contacted Roland."

"Yes. He told you?" She'd wondered how Kay and Phillip would feel about her contacting Roland. It looked as if she was about to find out.

Phillip stood behind his wife, a solid wall of powerful flesh she'd have to scale to get to Roland. "Darling, the doctor will be here in a minute to talk to us."

"Phillip…" Kay's hand rested on his arm and Alyssa could see that the fingers were shaking. "Didn't you hear? This is Alice McKay."

After one startled moment when everything seemed to freeze, Phillip recovered and in a low voice demanded, "What are you doing here?"

Roland's parents definitely knew who she was. But neither appeared welcoming. A sinking pit opened in Alyssa's stomach. She lifted her chin. "I wanted to meet my brother."

From across the room, she saw Joshua reappear and an ugly frown disfigured his handsome face when he saw her talking to his parents. Clearly he didn't want them talking to the notorious Alyssa Blake.

"Now is not the time for this. We want you to leave," Phillip ordered.

Alyssa stiffened and fisted her hands at her sides. "Now is exactly the time for me to be here—my brother is in surgery. I have every right to be here."

Kay Saxon took her clenched hands. "I understand how you feel, but Roland wouldn't want you here."

Alyssa's throat closed and she felt perilously close to the tears that she'd been fighting. "What do you mean?"

"He never responded to your letters or e-mails, did he?"

With heavy reluctance, Alyssa choked out, "No, he didn't."

"Doesn't that tell you something?"

"That he didn't get them?"

"He did receive them." Kay's eyes held shadows. "He chose not to reestablish contact."

"But I'm his sister." It was as though she'd ventured into a nightmare world, full of blood and death and unhappiness. All she'd wanted was a brother, a taste of family that most people took for granted. "He can't not want to meet me!"

Phillip Saxon looked around, frowning.

Kay's icy grip tightened around her fingers. "Dear, he's a Saxon—the eldest. Not even his brothers and sister know that he's adopted. Roland didn't want it getting out."

"No!" Her stomach churning, Alyssa rejected what she was hearing. She stared at Kay Saxon, hating the older woman for what she was saying. But then she took in Kay's sincerity and the deeply etched lines of pain around her mouth and the hatred evaporated.

"This is hard enough for all of us right now, Alice. Don't force us to reveal the truth…that Roland isn't a Saxon."

The impact of what Kay was saying pounded into her. Roland had rejected his birth sister in case their relationship took away his Saxon status. How could she stay under those circumstances?

Tears stung her eyes. "I just wanted to see him, hold his hand."

"It would be selfish—and not what Roland wants," Kay Saxon said softly, persuasively. "Right now we have to think about Roland."

Blinking back her tears, Alyssa nodded. "All right."

Relief flared in Kay's eyes. "Thank you." The older woman hesitated. "Do you have a cell phone, Alice?"

Alyssa nodded.

"Give me your number, dear. I'll call you as soon as we get an update."

Alyssa dug a business card out of her bag. Kay took it and pocketed it, glancing past Alyssa as she did so. "Now let's all talk about something else—Joshua is coming."

Three

Joshua made his way over to where his parents stood with Alyssa, Alice—whatever her damned name was.

He was aware of the incongruously glamourous, burgundy dress she wore and how it mirrored the colour of her long hair. Against the rich hue her bare shoulders gleamed like pale pearls.

Angrily he suppressed the flare of reckless want. He'd just taken a call from the surgery team advising that his brother was in critical condition—worse than the medical team had originally believed—and here he was lusting after Alyssa Blake, accomplished liar. It was insane.

But even as he drew closer, she gathered up her bag and rose to her feet. He stopped beside his parents and thrust his hands into his trouser pockets, at a loss to convey what he had learned. As Alyssa started for the doors one hand shot out and snagged her arm. "Where are you going?"

She kept her head down and continued to walk. "I'm leaving."

"Wait…I need some answers."

But she pulled free of his hold and marched toward the external glass doors in a flurry of dark red. Joshua started after her, then stopped as Heath came over and murmured, "Have you told Mum and Dad?"

He shook his head.

His parents must come first.

The next two minutes were a nightmare as he relayed what the surgeon had told him. "It's the internal bleeding they're worried about, and the head injury. Roland wasn't wearing a seat belt. He was catapulted from the SUV. The surgeon said they don't expect to be out for hours."

His mother's eyes stretched wide, shocked. His father straightened stiffly. Heath, his brave, bad-boy brother, was still pale under his tan. Joshua knew they all feared the same unspoken thing—that Roland might die.

Through the glass doors he could see Alyssa Blake's back, bare above that killer dress. She must be freezing. Then he put how cold she must be out of his mind.

All this had started with her arrival.

Anger turned his vision bright red. Leaving his parents with Heath, he stalked forward. The doors slid open and cool, dank night air rushed against his face.

The doors hissed closed behind him. Ahead lay the almost-empty car park. Alyssa didn't spare him a glance.

He drew a deep, steadying breath. "You came with me. How do you propose to leave?"

She brandished a cell phone. "I've called a cab—I need to collect my car from your home."

"You can't be intending to drive back to Auckland tonight?"

"Don't worry, there's not a drop of alcohol in my system." She gave him a sideways glance. "But, no, I won't be leaving tonight. I want to stay near Roland."

He drew another, deeper breath and forced himself not to react. Instead he said as calmly as he could manage, "You must be freezing. Here, take my jacket." He started to shrug off the black dinner jacket he'd grabbed before they'd left the homestead.

But she said, "No, thanks. I'm fine."

"You've got gooseflesh." He touched the skin on her upper arms, and she leapt away as if he'd singed her.

"I don't need it. The taxi will be here in a moment."

"You can give it back to me tomorrow."

She stilled. "Okay, thank you."

He slid the jacket off. It sounded as if it had taken a lot for her to accept his offer of help. Contrary damn woman. Watching her wind the jacket around herself, he relaxed a little as the pale tempting flesh disappeared out of sight.

"Where will you stay?"

Her mouth curled. "Don't worry, you won't need to track me down. I'll return it to you tomorrow."

"I wasn't worried about that."

She named a popular hotel in town.

"And you're leaving tomorrow, right?" Part of him wanted her to leave, never come back. He couldn't help the ridiculous superstitious stab of dread that her arrival had heralded Roland's accident. But there was another part of him, the sybaritic pagan part, who wanted to see her again. Touch her again. Kiss her again.

For one reckless instant he considered doing just that. It would be so easy. One tug, and she'd be up against his chest. He'd feel her body warm against his, he'd taste her lips under his mouth. The cold that froze him inside might seep away under her touch…her kisses.

And then he'd despise himself for it. He shook his head to clear it.

Maybe Alyssa Blake was a witch.

"I might leave tomorrow. It depends." Alyssa gave him a sideways glance.

But Joshua barely heard. He frowned as he took in her red-rimmed eyes, the silvery stains on her cheeks where the wind had already dried the tears. "You've been crying."

Quickly she averted her face.

"Why?"

The look she gave him revealed too little. Secrets, he thought suddenly. He glanced through the glass doors and his gaze landed on Amy, curled up in the chair, her face wearing an expression of intense misery.

His gaze came back to Alyssa and narrowed. Instead of drowning her, his dinner jacket simply increased her up-market city sexiness. She was gorgeous, stylish, smart. The kind of woman Roland had always dated before he'd become engaged to Amy....

And Amy had been upset earlier this evening—she and Roland had fought, even though it was common knowledge they never fought. The uncertain suspicion coalesced into certainty.

Alyssa had been having an affair with Roland.

She must have confronted Roland during the evening, and Amy had found out.

It wasn't important, Alyssa had said when Joshua asked her about her conversation with his brother. He'd known from the flicker in her eyes that she'd been lying. The conversation had been very important.

And now Roland was unconscious....

No wonder Alyssa was upset. Did she feel responsible for causing her lover's accident?

Did she *love* his brother?

He raked his hands through his hair as unruly thoughts churned round and round in his overwrought brain. "Who invited you to the ball tonight? You weren't on the list of official guests—it had to be a personal invitation." From Roland?

"I didn't have an invitation. I gate-crashed." There was defiance in her gaze.

Then she turned away. He heard what she had, the sound of the taxi pulling up at the curb.

But all he could think about was that Roland hadn't invited her. Or she could be lying. Again. "Why? What did you hope to achieve?"

She didn't answer and started to move away.

"Tell me, dammit." Without thought, he reached for her. His hands closed over her shoulders covered with the fine fabric of his jacket. He glared down into her blank features, her lashes lying long and dark against her cheeks. "Tell me!"

She shook her head. "It doesn't matter."

Had she tried to break up Roland's engagement? He struggled to read the beautiful, frozen face. "I think it does."

She didn't answer. He slid his hands down and circled her wrists, gave them a shake to get her to meet his gaze.

Wrapped in his jacket, she stood unmoving. And strangely that made him even angrier. He wanted her to object to his hold, he wanted her to struggle, to see her eyes spit fire at him; he didn't like the limp arms in his grasp, the listlessness in her eyes.

So he softened his grasp and said with quiet menace, "What did you want at Saxon's Folly tonight?"

She hesitated. "I'm sorry, I can't tell you."

He heard the taxi door open.

"Ma'am, did you book the taxi?"

He looked over her shoulder. "The lady's not ready to leave yet."

"But I am," she murmured.

His brows drew together. "I want an answer before you go. What did you want?"

What had happened between her and Roland? Had Roland sent her away—was that why she'd kissed *him* out in the garden? To get back at Roland? Was that why she'd landed in *his* bed?

As revenge against his brother?

He didn't like that idea at all. Yet he couldn't seem to bring himself to release her arm. The pain in her eyes damn near killed him.

He'd never envied his older brother, but now he did.

Whatever happened, if Roland survived the hours of surgery that lay ahead, Joshua wasn't going to allow Alyssa to rekindle whatever affair she and Roland had going. He told himself that his resolve had nothing to do with the wild feeling that Alyssa had aroused in him; he had Amy to think about. Sweet Amy who was expecting to marry Roland in two months' time.

Behind him he heard the doors whisper open.

"Joshua?"

He turned and glared at Heath. "What?"

"Mother wants you."

Alyssa pulled free. "I'll get your jacket back to you tomorrow."

"I don't care about the damn jacket." Inside he seethed. "This conversation is not finished. I'll talk to you in the morning."

She wouldn't flee town overnight, not while the outcome of Roland's surgery was unknown. Secure in that knowledge he turned on his heel and followed his brother back into the hospital.

It was going to be a long night.

The sound of her cell phone ringing shattered Alyssa's restless sleep. The compressing darkness of the hotel room lay like a heavy blanket around her.

It would be Joshua calling to finish the conversation he'd started outside the emergency room. Alyssa dragged herself upright. She wasn't ready for this confrontation. Then she spotted the green digital numerals of the clock radio and her heart jolted with fear. Four-thirty in the morning. Too early to be Joshua.

Her hand trembling, she picked up the phone.

"Where are you staying?" Little composure remained in Kay Saxon's voice.

Alyssa's heart slammed against her ribs in fear as she automatically gave Kay the information she sought. "Is Roland okay?" she asked shakily.

There was an ominous silence. Then Kay said, "I'll send a cab. You need to come now." The phone went dead.

It had to be bad.

With few alternatives—the red dress or a pin-striped business suit—Alyssa threw on the pair of baggy sweats and sweater she'd worn for the drive down to Hawkes Bay and was downstairs in minutes. By the time the lights of the cab cut through the dark gray pre-dawn light she was already out on the sidewalk.

Too soon she'd reached the white hospital building. Inside, everything was quiet. She made for the front desk. "Where will I find Roland Saxon?"

"Are you Alice?" A nurse came around the desk at her silent nod. "Come, I'll take you to him."

Sick with anxiety, Alyssa was led through double-seal doors into a unit filled with beeps and a sense of life-and-death gravity. At the sound of hissing as the ventilator rose and fell, fear shafted through Alyssa.

She took in the couple hovering by the bed.

Kay and Phillip Saxon.

On a high bed lay a prone figure wrapped in dressings, attached to the life-support machines, an oxygen mask over his face, so swollen that he was rendered unrecognizable. Only the shock of red hair sticking out from the head dressing revealed that this was Roland.

"You have five minutes," the nurse whispered. "Only family are supposed to be here—and only two at a time. I've already stretched the rules." Then she was gone in a rustle of starch.

Kay Saxon turned, her eyes puffy. She'd aged in the past few hours. "I'm glad you made it."

"How is he?"

"He's unconscious. I'm not sure how much is induced—"

Alyssa said desperately, "But he's going to be all right."

He had to be.

Kay took her hands. "The doctors don't think so. That's why I called you. I couldn't live with myself if—" Her voice broke.

Cold dread suffocated Alyssa. "They think he's going to *die?*"

Kay hesitated. "They told us to call anyone who might want to see him. They warned us to prepare for the worst."

Her world crashed in. Alyssa fell to her knees, stretching her hands to touch the heavily bandaged hands of the man in the bed.

Her brother.

Her brother who was dying.

Kay sniffed behind her, but Alyssa was crying so hard she couldn't think.

This wasn't how it was supposed to have ended.

She was to see him tomorrow. *Today.* She'd been looking forward to reuniting with the brother she'd been searching for since she was eighteen.

"Nooo!" It was a wail of anguish.

Then Kay was holding her and murmuring to her not to cry because it might upset Roland. As Alyssa's tears subsided, Kay pulled away. "Alyssa, the boys are coming, and I don't want them to find you here. Phillip and I don't want to have to answer their questions. Please, for our sakes—for Roland's sake—will you go now?"

Before Alyssa could answer, the nurse was there, waiting to escort her out.

She wanted to beg for more time. Her throat closed. The words didn't come. Finally, she swallowed and managed to speak. "Give me one minute. To say—" her voice cracked "—goodbye."

Kay nodded and waved off the nurse.

Alyssa bent forward, her lips colder than ice as they brushed the forehead of the man in the bed. She noticed a drip of liquid on his forehead. Water? Another splash. No—tears, she realised. Her tears.

Closing her eyes she prayed. For Roland. For herself. For

TESSA RADLEY 41

a miracle. For all the years they'd missed. Then she kissed him and murmured, "Au revoir."

Blinded by tears, she turned for the door, the room a blur.

Joshua hurried toward the hospital elevator, Heath and his younger sister, Megan, flanking him on either side. The panel above the elevator doors showed that a car was already descending and Joshua found himself drumming his fingers as they waited for the doors to open. Hurry. Hurry.

The doors opened. A nurse exited. Then Joshua saw Alyssa coming out. "How did you get here?"

"In a cab."

"That's not what I meant." He turned to his brother and sister. "You go ahead, I'll see you upstairs."

While he waited for the elevator to depart, he inspected Alyssa's features, taking in the hollows under her eyes, the lack of makeup and the way her glorious hair had been pulled back from her face, as though she'd gotten ready in a hurry. In the tatty sweats she looked nothing like the sophisticated woman he'd met…was it only last night?

"What are you doing here?"

Her eyes flicked away from his. "I came to find out if there was any news about Roland's condition."

Joshua's mouth tightened; he suspected she was dissembling. The suspicion of earlier was back in full force. "Why are you so upset? What's Roland to you?"

She shook her head and didn't answer.

Joshua couldn't help thinking about Amy, brokenhearted and sedated for shock. "Heath had to give Amy a sleeping tablet. He's left her at his home, with his housekeeper watching over her. How could you, Alyssa?"

Alyssa let her hands drop and stared at him blankly.

"She and Roland are getting married in two months. Now it's all gone to hell because you couldn't stay away from Roland."

"What?" Her eyes were stretched wide.

Joshua frowned at the shock in her eyes. He'd surprised himself with the outburst. Normally nothing fazed him. He was the boss—people came to him for guidance and advice. Yet right now he felt like raging at her. For sure he was losing it.

And she was the catalyst.

He pushed a hand through his hair. "Why did you have to come to the ball last night and cause trouble? Was it worth it? Was it worth telling Amy about your relationship with Roland?"

"I didn't tell Amy a thing."

Joshua relaxed slightly. So Amy didn't know that Roland and Alyssa were lovers. But surely Amy must have suspected Roland was embroiled in a heated affair with a woman because Joshua certainly had. All the signs had been there. The constant visits to Auckland, the cell calls that his brother took privately while talking in a low, intimate voice. By not denying her clandestine relationship with Roland, Alyssa had confirmed the suspicions he'd had about his brother for months.

"You must know that if Amy found out about you, it would devastate her. Not to say what it would do to my parents to discover that Roland had been two-timing Amy, their goddaughter. Right now they need to think about all the good things he's achieved."

Alyssa's eyes widened. "You think—" She broke off.

Joshua waited for her to refute that she'd been attempting to seduce Roland away from Amy. Deep down, he wanted that denial. Even though he knew it would be a lie. Instead she stood shifting from foot to foot, her eyes reflecting her inner turmoil.

Raking his hands through his already ruffled hair, he sighed. "It would be better if you left now and returned to Auckland."

"I haven't got your jacket here—it's back in my hotel room."

He shrugged. "I don't care about the jacket. I want you gone."

She said flatly, "I'm not going until—" her throat moved as she swallowed "—until it's all over. But Amy needn't worry,

I won't be staying a second more than I have to. I know when I'm not wanted."

Not wanted? Joshua suppressed the urge to groan. He *wanted* the woman standing in front of him more than he'd ever desired a woman in his life. But no good could come out of it. Not only had she assassinated his character in print, she'd been his brother's lover.

And he had no intention of following in Roland's well-worn footsteps.

Four

Alyssa felt terrible.

Joshua thought she and Roland had been lovers. Worse, he believed she'd come to Saxon's Folly to steal Roland away from his fiancée. She bit her lip to stop herself blurting out the truth. How could she refute what he believed without revealing the truth about her relationship to Roland?

Yesterday, just before midnight, his parents had demanded that she leave; now Joshua was ordering her to go, too. A sense of hurt settled around her. The sooner she got away from here, the sooner she could retreat to the solitary comfort of her Auckland apartment and lick her wounds in private.

But for now she had to shrug off the hurt. This morning she would hold vigil for as long as necessary. Because this wasn't about her. It was about her brother.

"Nothing to say?"

The words jerked her attention back to Joshua. He was watching her through dark, suspicious eyes.

"You should go upstairs," she said quietly. "You don't want

to miss what might be your only chance to say goodbye to Roland because you wasted time arguing with me." The thought of her brother lying there with little chance of regaining consciousness was unbearable…heartbreaking…and she sniffed back the fresh wave of tears.

"Do you love him very much?" Joshua's voice held a strange tone.

"Yes, I love him a great deal." Alyssa didn't look at him in case he read the depth of the loss and confusion in her eyes. Instead she stared at her feet and noticed that the laces of her left sneaker had come undone. What was a lace? So unimportant in the greater scheme of things.

"He never mentioned you."

She sighed. How tricky this had all become. Clearly Roland hadn't wanted his brothers to know that he wasn't a Saxon by birth. Now, because of her promise to Kay Saxon and out of her respect to her brother, she couldn't tell Joshua the truth—even though she desperately wanted to. They'd connected on some primal level, she and Joshua. She didn't like lying to him. Finally she settled for, "We hadn't known each other very long."

One brief meeting last night…she'd shaken Roland's hand. And this morning she'd touched his unconscious body.

From the old cuttings in the town's archives she knew he'd played rugby as a boy and captained his team to a regional win. She'd shuddered in fear as she'd watched television footage of Roland as a late teen riding his horse over solid fences with a determination that had won him numerous eventing titles. An article in a wine magazine had said Roland joked that he'd liked fast women and good wine. Alyssa had wondered what Amy had thought about that! A recent appearance on a lifestyle television programme hosted by a pretty blonde had revealed that he wore jeans with panache. Every last fact she could glean about him, she had uncovered.

Yet Roland didn't know her at all.

"Maybe he didn't say anything because he knew you wouldn't be pleased with his friendship with Alyssa Blake, despised journalist." Now, through desperation, she'd cornered herself into an outright lie. Before last night's meeting, Roland had only known her from the letters and e-mails…written in the name of Alice McKay.

"Friends?"

Joshua looked her up and down in a way that made her regret donning the ancient sweats. A disturbing prickle of awareness followed in the wake of his gaze. She shut it out ruthlessly. "Yes, friends. Why not?"

"I can accept that Roland didn't want us to know he was sleeping with you." Joshua's lip curled. "First, because he knows I think you're a hack writer and have no respect for you after that hatchet job you did. And sec—"

"Hack?" She glared at him in outrage. "I only did—"

He held up a hand. "Let me finish. Second, I'm sure Roland didn't mention you because you're of little importance— certainly not worth losing Amy over." Joshua gave her a long, hard stare. "Roland was always a bit of a ladies' man. But I'm not going to let Amy be hurt."

Alyssa drew a deep, steadying breath and counted silently to three before saying slowly and distinctly, "I have absolutely no intention of hurting Amy."

"Good. Then we understand each other." Joshua stabbed the button to summon the elevator. "You're trouble. As long as you keep far away from Saxon's Folly, my family—and Amy—everything will be fine!"

"You should go and see Roland," she said with urgency.

He gave her a snooty look. "My brother has the luck of the devil—he's a survivor."

Alyssa prayed to God that he was right. But his words caused a flare of hope. Joshua knew his brother. If he thought Roland might live…

"And when he's out of here, you stay far away from him."

No chance.

Joshua blamed her for the argument between Amy and Roland last night. She thought about the pretty TV-show hostess who'd interviewed Roland only a month ago. Alyssa had gone to see her. The woman had giggled that Roland was a great lover—and lamented the fact that he was already taken. Not that it had stopped him, she'd added, giving Alyssa a lascivious smile.

Maybe Amy had quarrelled with him over the hostess, but it wasn't up to Alyssa to reveal that scandal to Joshua. It might turn her stomach having Joshua accuse her of being Roland's lover…but no one except she and his parents knew how vile that accusation really was.

She wasn't the troublemaker Joshua had branded her.

Alyssa started as the elevator pinged beside her and the doors slid open. "Think what you want about me—I don't care," she said at last, suppressing the sting of his words.

Joshua strode into the waiting elevator. His gaze swept over her, cool and dismissive. "I'm sure you don't care about anything except yourself."

Alyssa decided that it was just as well she could seethe over Joshua's departing comments while she sat in the hospital café drinking stale coffee. But under her fuming she still fretted about how Roland was faring upstairs in that sterile ward.

Drained of all emotion, Joshua paused in the entrance of the coffee-cum-flower shop in the hospital lobby. His eyes burned. After almost twenty-four hours awake, he needed a shower, a change of clothing and sleep.

But right now there were other things—important things—to which he needed to attend.

His chest expanded as he hauled in a deep breath.

And the first that needed sorting was sitting at a table beside a rack of magazines, staring into a coffee cup, a napkin crumpled in her fist. Some sixth sense must have alerted

Alyssa to his presence because her hand tightened around the mangled, once-white napkin and she looked up.

The vulnerability in her eyes vanished the instant she spotted him, replaced by wariness. Okay, so this conversation wasn't going to be easy. But it couldn't be delayed. He started forward.

"Alice—" No, not Alice. "Alyssa," he corrected himself. He'd kissed Alice. He'd never willingly touch Alyssa. "My mother sent me to tell you…" He broke off and swallowed the burning bile at the back of his throat.

She was on her feet, her hand against her mouth. "Roland…is he conscious? Can I see him?"

He shook his head. An appalling sorrow splintered inside his chest. There was frustration and bewilderment, too.

"Why? Just for a few minutes? Please?"

Her eyes were wide, beseeching. As much as he disliked her, it was clear that she loved his brother, that she'd do anything, even beg, to be with him. Damnation! This was more difficult than he'd expected.

His legs carried him to her without his realising it. He cleared his throat awkwardly. "Alyssa—"

Her hand touched his sleeve. He flinched, and she jerked it away.

"I won't make waves. I won't do anything to cause Amy anxiety. I just want to see my—Roland." She was frantically shredding what was left of the paper towel.

He caught her flailing hands and tossed the napkin on the table, hating what he had to do. "Alyssa, you don't understand. Roland is dead."

"What?" She rocked on her feet, looking as if she was about to faint.

"Steady." He moved closer, shifting his hold to her shoulders, propping her up with his body.

Her eyes were wide, staring. Shocked. Little flecks of black floated in the unseeing smoky purple irises.

"Alyssa?"

"Is it true?" She pulled away from him, wrapping her arms around herself, looking shaken to the soul.

Joshua nodded, swept by a wave of terrible pity. She'd said she loved his brother. Had Roland known the depth of her love? Had he even appreciated it? Joshua doubted it. But he couldn't afford to relent. Family came first.

Alyssa Blake was more than capable of looking out for herself.

Besides, she was too much of a forbidden temptation. "So you'll be leaving in the morning?"

Her head came up. The magnificent eyes flashed. "I'll go after the funeral. Please, leave me alone until then."

And as he watched the tears pool, the foolish and chivalrous part of him wished he had the right to hold her, comfort her and wipe those tears of hopelessness from her eyes.

Alyssa crept in and stood in the back of the church, keeping her head bowed, and stared blankly at the order of service booklet that had been given to her by the usher at the door.

Yesterday she had called David Townsend, her editor at *Wine Watch* magazine, requesting a few days' leave, without giving him any explanations. If she mentioned the word *bereavement,* she suspected that the tears that dammed up the back of her throat might overflow. Once she started, she feared she might never stop.

David had given her two days.

Alyssa had told him she'd be back in the office on Wednesday. But standing here in the crowded church, work…and Auckland…seemed so far away. A numbing mist enveloped her. Beneath the booklet she held, her gray pin-striped pantsuit seemed woefully inadequate. She'd intended to wear the outfit to the one-on-one meet she'd coerced Roland into. A quick glance around revealed that the boutique businesswear was out of place among the designer black and sedate pearls.

She hadn't brought much with her—she'd only expected

to be in Hawkes Bay for the weekend. She didn't even have pins to put her hair up. The dark silky mass lay around her bowed face in a sleek wave. But shopping for mourning clothes and hairpins had been the last thing on her mind yesterday. Roland's death on Sunday had left her reeling.

She opened the order of service booklet and found herself staring at a photo of Roland…a piece about his achievements, a short eulogy where he was described as "the much loved son of Kay and Phillip, brother of Joshua, Heath and Megan."

Of course, there was no mention of his real parents, or the sibling who had been robbed of the chance to know and love him.

The hymns reverberated around Alyssa, moving her until her heart ached so much she thought it might burst. Then Joshua stood and started to talk about Roland, and her heart shattered.

By the time she arrived at the cemetery on the farm where Saxons had been buried for nearly a century, Alyssa was so wrung out by emotion that her legs felt a little shaky.

She'd debated about the wisdom of coming to the burial. She'd known it would be upsetting. The last funeral she'd attended had been her adoptive mother's—and that had been simply awful. But in the end, the need to see her brother—her flesh and blood—laid finally to rest had won out. Perhaps now she might get some peace, too.

The first person she recognised as she made her way through the white-painted picket gate was Joshua.

She hesitated. He hadn't seen her yet.

Alyssa halted a distance off from where the Saxons crowded around the grave and sneaked another look at Joshua.

His arm was around his white-faced mother and on his other side stood his sister, Megan, sobbing into a hanky. Behind them stood Heath and Phillip Saxon, looking solemn. Amy hovered dry-eyed at the edge of the raw grave, her expression bleak.

From her vantage point, Alyssa could see the rows upon rows of vines planted on the hills that lay below the cemetery.

They would only just be starting to bud for the coming summer. It struck her that, unlike the vines, Roland would never see another summer.

Blinking back a fresh prick of tears, she barely noticed the breeze that swept her hair off her face as she listened to the priest delivering the prayer.

"Amen," she murmured with the rest of the crowd as it ended.

"Don't plan on staying," Joshua said very softly from behind her.

She didn't turn her head to look at him. She hadn't heard him approach. But every hair on her nape stood up. "I won't."

"Good." He moved to stand beside her as the final hymn started. "I don't want Amy suffering any more than she already is."

Alyssa stared at the words on the sheet of paper in her hand and stifled an impatient sigh. Amy. His parents. That's all he could think about. What about *her?* "Please believe me, I'm not going to do anything to harm Amy."

He gave her a hard look. "I wouldn't let you." His eyes scanned her face. She could feel the intensity of his gaze, as he examined every inch of her face.

"Well?"

"You're beautiful." His tone was dispassionate. Unmoved. He might have been studying an inanimate block of marble.

"Thanks," she said tersely, her gaze dropping away from his. The knowledge that he considered her beautiful didn't bring satisfaction. Joshua didn't even like *her*—the real Alyssa Blake beneath the veneer—he'd made that clear enough.

A disturbing thought struck her. Perhaps he fancied Amy? And, now with Roland out of the way, did that mean Joshua expected a chance with his brother's grief-stricken fiancée?

She gave him a covert glance from behind her lashes. "Amy's beautiful, too."

He stilled, the skin over his slanted cheekbones suddenly taut. "What the hell is that supposed to mean?"

Her lashes swept up. Her eyes clashed with his frigid ones. "Just that you seem to admire her immensely."

"You think I have the hots for my brother's fiancée?" Darkness moved in his eyes.

"It would be understandable."

Amy would be the perfect wife for Joshua Saxon. She was even Kay's goddaughter. It was a no-brainer. "Amy is vulnerable right now. You'll need to take care that she doesn't view you as a rebound relationship."

"I don't need your pop-psychology advice. I don't poach my brothers' women." His gaze was bleak. "Or at least, I never did. Not until the night I met you."

What was that cryptic statement supposed to mean? A burst of adrenaline shot through Alyssa, quickly followed by a flare of desire.

What would happen if he learned Roland wasn't his real brother. And that she, Alyssa, was Roland's younger sister.

And what was the point of agonizing over it all. It was moot. Because Joshua would never learn the truth.

Despite the pale golden light of the sun, a cold shiver started at the base of her neck and inched down her spine, leaving Alyssa feeling like an emotional wasteland.

He moved away and Alyssa shut her eyes, and let the singing voices swirl around her. After what seemed an interminable time she heard car doors slam, the roar of engines starting.

Her shoulders sagged with relief. Conscious of the careless caress of the wind on her skin, of a tui whistling in a nearby phutukawa tree, Alyssa stood still as the cemetery rapidly emptied.

Finally, she opened her eyes. Only a few people remained. Joshua was gone. But the memory of his intensity as he'd told her that he didn't want Amy suffering any more than she already was, remained vivid. What would it be like to be the focus of all that masculine protection?

She wished....

What was the point of wishing? The connection she'd sensed

with Joshua had ended the minute he learned who she was. She was accustomed to being alone. As the indulged, only child of two older parents she'd grown up curiously isolated. She'd been thirteen when she'd discovered that she was adopted, that she'd been born Alice McKay—not Alyssa Blake.

She'd been so excited at the prospect of finding siblings… more family. But her mother had cried at the idea of Alyssa searching for her birth parents. For years Alyssa had put it off, fearful of upsetting Margaret. But finally she'd been compelled to make a start, secretly. Only after her mother's death three years ago had she been able to focus single-mindedly on her quest.

She'd never tracked down her birth father. But she'd found her vacant-eyed birth mother in an institute for stroke victims and she'd become a regular visitor. But from the moment Alyssa discovered that she had a brother, she hadn't rested.

She'd wanted to find him…Roland.

And now Roland was gone forever.

A cloud drifted across the sky and passed over the face of the sun, blocking out the sunlight and casting a shadow over the mound where Roland lay. Alyssa shivered.

Why? Why had she not forced the issue with Roland sooner, *made* him see her. They could've had a few weeks…months. She sighed. But would extra time have made any difference?

Alyssa supposed it wasn't a big deal to him. Roland hadn't needed a sister; he'd already had a sister—and two brothers. A whole proud, supportive family.

While, to her, finding her brother had become everything.

"Alice.…" Kay spoke hesitantly from beside her.

She gave a start of surprise. "Call me Alyssa." Alice was gone. Buried in the ground as surely as Roland was. Alice had existed only as evidence that she had once been someone else…someone with a brother.

Coming to a decision, Alyssa said flatly, "Joshua thinks that I'm Roland's lover." Alyssa still felt sullied by the accusation in his eyes. "I don't like it—especially not since Roland was already engaged. I'd like you tell Joshua the truth, please."

Kay shook her head, and gestured to the raw, new grave. "Roland is dead. Phillip and I don't want the trauma of explaining to the children that he was never their blood brother."

Children? Alyssa goggled at the older woman. Joshua Saxon was no child. "They're adults, not children anymore. Surely they'll understand?"

Kay looked uncomfortable. "It would mean their whole upbringing was based on a lie."

"They deserve the truth."

"It's too late for that." Kay shook her head and started to move away toward the white gate where Phillip stood, his back to them, talking with a group of mourners.

Frustration and despair pooled deep inside Alyssa's chest, setting a heavy lump.

"Why didn't you tell them sooner?" Then Roland might even have come looking for *her*. He'd have had time to come to terms with having a sister, of not being a Saxon by birth.

Kay stopped. "At first we intended to tell them, but the years passed, and then it was too late. Neither Phillip nor I want them to know now. It's not necessary." Kay faced Alyssa, her eyes a cool, implacable gray. "I'd like you to respect that."

Alyssa had known how Kay would react, but she'd hoped…

It wasn't to be. Roland was gone. Yet there was so much Kay could share about her brother. Maybe…

Alyssa's heart started to beat anxiously in her chest at the audacity of what she was contemplating. "Kay, I won't tell anyone. But only if you share your memories of Roland with me. Every day for a week. I want to see the photos of him, hear the stories of what he did, share the places he knew growing up."

"That's not poss—"

Alyssa read the other woman's refusal in her eyes. Thrusting her apprehension away, she firmed her lips into a determined line and stalked past the older woman. "Then I have no reason to give you my promise to keep my relationship with Roland a secret."

"Wait."

She turned her head.

"You can't do that." Kay looked horrified. "And if I do as you want? How can I trust you not to say anything later?"

"I'll give you my word." Alyssa sagged under the weight of the tension. "And I'll never break it, no matter what pressure I'm put under. This is important to me... It's all I'll ever have of the brother I've been searching for since I turned eighteen."

"Okay." Kay wore a peculiar expression. "Come to Saxon's Folly in the morning. You'd better bring your bags. You may as well stay for the week."

Alyssa felt a surge of victory...until she remembered Joshua's hard, judgmental gaze.

Five

Alyssa drove through the curving set of white gates of Saxon's Folly the following morning, nerves tying her stomach in knots. The beauty of the rows of vines stretching away on both sides of the long, oak-lined drive, still bare of the lush green growth of leaves that would come with summer, failed to calm her trepidation about encountering Joshua Saxon again.

At least she had her boss's blessing. She'd called her editor early this morning, telling him that she needed a few more days off. David's annoyance had evaporated when he'd found out she was in Hawkes Bay.

"Why didn't you tell me that last time you called? I heard that Roland Saxon was killed over the weekend. A terrible tragedy. You can do a story on the great loss that he'll be to the industry. Try get the scoop on who'll be replacing him as the marketing man of Saxon's Folly—and how that will impact on Saxon's Folly's place in the industry."

Her breath catching in her chest, she said, "David, I want to take time off."

"Are you ill? You sound strange."

To distract her canny editor, Alyssa announced in a rush, "I've been invited to stay at Saxon's Folly."

There was a short silence. Alyssa could almost hear the cogs turning in David's mind.

"Get a short obituary on Roland Saxon to me ASAP—if I have it by Friday, it can run in the next issue." There was a moment's silence. "You should've told me you were on visiting terms with the Saxons."

She had no intention of explaining about Roland. She'd promised Kay it would remain a secret…and it would.

Alyssa thought about the obituary she'd agreed to write while she walked through the town picking up some toiletries and clothing for her extended stay. She had a horrible suspicion that Joshua would not be pleased when he learned about it.

Typically, as she pulled up in front of the winery, the first person she saw was Joshua Saxon. When she got out of the car, his face hardened, radiating disapproval. Alyssa's gaze locked with his as he approached.

"The funeral is over." His obsidian gaze bored relentlessly into her. "I thought you'd be packed and gone by now."

Alyssa raised her chin. "I brought your jacket back."

"Oh, thanks." He had the grace to look slightly shamed as she got out of the car, popped open the trunk and drew out his jacket.

He took it from her and slung it over his shoulder. "Have a safe trip."

Staring at her overnight bag, Alyssa hesitated. To hell with it. He'd know sooner or later. "I'm not leaving yet. Your mother has invited me to stay for a week."

"You approached my mother?" He replied, openmouthed. "My mother is grieving the loss of her eldest son. She doesn't need an interloper barging in at the moment."

"I didn't 'barge in,' as you so delightfully put it. Your mother invited me." She drew a deep breath. "Inviting" was stretching the truth. She'd given Kay no choice. "Don't worry, Joshua, I'll be very sensitive of her feelings."

He bent forward and hoisted her overnight bag out, then cast her a disbelieving look. "Right."

Her heart started to race and apprehension shafted through her as his narrowed gaze raked her. He'd better never discover the truth of how she'd gotten her invitation. Quickly, she said, "Also, my editor has asked me to write a short tribute to Roland. I'll use this week to research that." No point hiding that.

"Oh, no, you won't! You're not poking around here for dirt on my brother."

She'd expected his reaction. She lifted out her handbag and slung it over her shoulder. "I'm not here to dig up dirt. I'm here at the invitation of your mother. But it's a good opportunity to talk to people about Roland, about what he meant to them, how he enriched their lives. Think about it, Joshua, there's nothing sinister about a tribute in *Wine Watch* to your brother. The wine community is going to miss him." And so would she.

Terribly.

He paused. She watched him weighing up her words, seeking the worst.

"I don't trust you," he said at last. "Don't forget I've been at the sharp end of your poisoned pen before. I want to keep an eye on you, hear the questions you're asking. You're coming with me each day."

Alyssa saw her dream of spending time with Kay, learning about Roland going up in smoke. "But—"

"That's screwed up whatever it is that you want." His eyes had narrowed to black slits. "So why did you gate-crash the ball? What is it that you really want, Alyssa? An exclusive interview?"

His derogatory tone caused her to say heatedly, "No, I came to—" Too late she remembered her promise to Kay.

"To what?" He pounced on her hesitation like a mountain cat.

She tempered her response. "I came to see Roland." Let him draw whatever damn conclusions he wanted from that.

"Why? You still haven't told me what you wanted with him."

"I thought you'd decided that." Alyssa couldn't stop the snippy retort as she slammed the trunk shut.

"To get him to break up with Amy?" He didn't take his eyes off her. "I'm still leaning that way, am I correct?"

"No!"

His eyes held cynical disbelief. "Then what? You had another agenda? Or do you still want me to believe that you and Roland were 'friends'?"

Joshua gave *friends* such a mocking intonation that she flinched. But she didn't give him the satisfaction of a response.

He tilted his head sideways, examining her. "You wanted something from him. Did you think Roland would feed you the story of a lifetime?"

"No, seeing Roland had nothing to do with any story."

"You're trying to tell me that hooking up with my brother meant more to you than the sniff of a story?"

She nodded. "That's exactly what I'm saying."

Joshua fell silent, a frown grooved between his guarded eyes. "You know, I'm starting to believe that Roland meant something to you. That you're grieving for him as much as we are."

Before Alyssa could respond to his unexpected concession, he'd set off with her bag in the direction of the main house.

They found Kay in the library, working at a big walnut desk overlooking the gardens that rolled down to where the vineyards started.

"Your houseguest."

"Joshua—"

"I'm sorry, Mother. I can't stay, I need to get back to the estate." Joshua set down her overnight bag and slung the dinner jacket onto a leather chair. "Don't forget that we arranged to go to see Amy tonight." He glanced pointedly at Alyssa. "It'll probably be better if you stay here."

"It would be rude to leave Alyssa. She can come, too."

"No, it will be too upsetting for Amy—if she ever discovers the truth about why Alyssa was so eager to attend the ball."

Kay blinked, the only sign that she'd remembered what Alyssa had told her in the cemetery about Joshua's belief that Alyssa was Roland's lover. For a moment Kay looked indecisive then she said, "If you think so, dear."

"I do." To Alyssa he said, "As soon as you've settled in, come find me. I'll be in the winery."

"Oh, but…I thought I would get to know Alyssa a little, especially if she and Roland were…" Kay's voice trailed away "…close." Her eyes darted everywhere—except Joshua's face.

But he didn't notice; he was too busy glaring at Alyssa.

"Behave yourself then," he growled.

Which she took to mean that she was not to ask Kay too many questions about Roland for the tribute she was writing.

After Joshua had gone, Alyssa turned to Kay. "I know this must be very hard for you. Rather than talk about Roland so soon maybe we can take a walk around the vineyard."

Kay sniffed but her eyes remained dry. "I want to talk about Roland. It happened so fast. Roland and Amy were due to get married in December. Phillip and I were looking forward to grandchildren—now he's dead."

"Children…I've never thought of children." Or a niece. Or a nephew. Or a sister-in-law like Amy. "I hadn't thought beyond finding Roland. He was the family I've been looking for since I learned I was adopted."

The stark statement hung in the air.

Kay's eyes darkened until the gray had turned almost black. "Oh, Alyssa…." She hesitated then she opened her arms.

Alyssa walked into them, conscious of the scent of lavender that clung to the older woman. At last she stepped away.

"I feel so…lost."

"What about your parents? Wouldn't it help to stay awhile with them right now?"

"My mother—adoptive mother—died of cancer three years ago. That was when I really stepped up my search for Roland. She'd never been keen on my finding my natural parents—or Roland when she learned I had a brother."

Kay gave her a peculiar look. "Maybe she feared she might lose you."

"How could she ever lose me? She was my mother, she'd raised me. I loved her."

"What about your adoptive father?"

"He remarried last year—his new wife wanted to live on Australia's Gold Coast with her daughter and two grand-daughters."

"So in a space of a few years you've lost your mother, your father has gone away…and now your birth brother is dead." Kay looked quite ill.

"Yes," Alyssa whispered, the pain of it all closing her throat. "But you're going to share a little of Roland with me…and that's so much more of him than I've had before."

Once the Saxons had driven off to visit Amy that night, Alyssa felt strangely deserted. Using the remote to switch off the television, she was plunged into silence and within seconds the vast quietness of the homestead enfolded her. Other than one solitary creak of the beams, the lack of sound was absolute. Picking up the photo album that Kay had shown her earlier, Alyssa started to browse through.

A sharp burst of nostalgia pierced her as she stared at the images. Roland as a baby with only a little ginger fluff on his head. As a toddler, holding a new-born Joshua. A photo of Roland on his first day of school, gap-toothed, his red hair slicked down, with Joshua and Heath in front of him, as different from them as fire from coal. Roland and Heath smiling like little devils while Joshua stared solemnly at the camera, his gaze already self-possessed and direct. No Megan yet. Just the three boys.

The next page showed Roland on a bay horse, grinning as he held a great, big silver trophy aloft while Megan and Joshua stood on either side of the horse's head, looking proud and pleased.

When she'd finished paging through the album, Alyssa set it aside and made her way to the kitchen, which Kay had asked Ivy, the friendly housekeeper, to show her around earlier. There was a tray set out for her. In the fridge was the slice of quiche and bowl of salad just as Kay had promised. But Alyssa didn't bother to nuke the quiche in the microwave. She set the empty wineglass to one side and made herself a cup of cocoa instead and, picking up the tray, made her way out.

At the foot of the stairs Alyssa paused. Her room lay upstairs, along with Megan's quarters, and Kay and Phillip's suite. Downstairs was the wing that housed Roland's rooms—and Joshua's. A wave of shame swept her at the memory of what had so nearly happened in Joshua's bedroom the night of the ball.

Curiosity propelled her down the stairs. At the base of the stairs the area opened up into an airy sitting room furnished with a large plasma-screen television, two brown leather sofas and a pair of armchairs. She'd caught only a glimpse of it on the night of the ball when Joshua had hauled her through.

An immense kauri bookshelf covered one wall that closer inspection revealed was filled with books on viticulture and a couple of rows of crime novels interspersed with classics. The opposite wall was filled by an abstract study of an incoming tide that looked like a John Walker. A narrow arch led to a sleek, streamlined galley kitchen gleaming with stainless steel appliances and beside it lay a cosy dining area.

Leaving the sitting room, Alyssa glanced both ways down the passage that led off the sitting room. At one end, a door stood ajar, at the other, the door was firmly closed. With soft footsteps she made her way to the closed door at the far end. The handle twisted under her touch. As she stepped through the doorway, her throat closed.

Without a doubt this was where her brother had slept.

It hurt too much to stand beside the double bed that he would never waken in again. Through an archway she glimpsed a desk. A few steps took her to what had clearly been his private domain. His trophy room. Two glass-fronted cabinets held an impressive array of silverware. A closer look revealed schoolboy medals for athletics, awards for rugby, while trophies for eventing were prominently displayed, holding pride of place.

She made her way back into Roland's bedroom, and stopped at the sight of a door leading off into a bathroom en suite. An electric razor lay on the marble slab, charging, awaiting its next use. Alyssa picked up the wooden-backed hairbrush. There were short strands of red hair in its bristles. She disentangled a hair, then pulled one from her own head. Laying them side by side, she compared the texture and colour. Hers was darker, his was coarser. She swallowed the lump in her throat and shook the two hairs free.

Closing the door behind her had a certain finality.

At the other end of the corridor the open door beckoned. She couldn't resist the call. Joshua's rooms. She stepped past a study, papers neatly stacked on a desk, past the walk-in dressing room with the bathroom that lay beyond. The instant she stepped into his bedroom, she smelled his scent. Familiar. Taunting. The dinner jacket she'd returned hung draped over a chair, and she lifted it to her face, inhaling the rich, living male scent that had surrounded her outside the chilly hospital. She dropped down onto the navy bedcover and fought back tears. She sat there for what seemed like an age. Finally she rose and returned the jacket to the chair. Collecting her tray, with the now-cold cocoa, from the landing, she made her way upstairs to her own room.

The silence of the empty house was suffocating.

A hollow emptiness pressed down on Alyssa. Here, in the heart of the Saxon family's home, she felt more alone than she'd ever felt in her life.

* * *

Joshua had swept Amy—along with his parents and Megan—off to dinner. It was good for Amy to get out. His eyes rested on his parents—and good for them, too. Yet as they sat at the window table of an upmarket-café overlooking Napier's Marine Parade, an unaccountable sense of guilt nagged at Joshua at the thought of Alyssa alone in the great house.

"Why so pensive?" He found Megan staring at him curiously as he set his knife and fork down.

"Just thinking."

She gave him a wicked grin. "About a woman?"

"No comment, wench."

She laughed. Then her cell phone pinged to announce a new message and she looked down at the screen with a secret smile.

"New admirer?"

A slight stain of uncharacteristic colour tinged his sister's cheeks. "Maybe."

"When do we get to meet him?" Kay leaned forward, looking interested, while beside her Phillip shook his head and laughed.

Megan rolled her eyes at Joshua. "See what you've started."

He grinned. "Serves you right for being so secretive." And she wasn't alone. Roland had been keeping secrets, too. A lover who no one knew about, for one. His gaze rested on Amy. She hadn't spoken much, but he thought she was looking happier since leaving her solitary cottage. Joshua had no intention of letting her find out about Alyssa's relationship to her fiancé.

Amy was the reason Alyssa wasn't here tonight. There was no need for him to feel guilty about not inviting her. But nor should Alyssa's presence at Saxon's Folly be kept secret. Amy worked as a PA at the winery. She'd find out soon enough.

"Did my mother tell you that Alyssa Blake, the wine writer, is staying with us?"

"Alyssa Blake?" Amy bristled in disbelief. "Really? After that article she wrote?"

"She wants to write a tribute to Roland for *Wine Watch* magazine." Joshua held his breath, waiting for Amy's—and his parents'—reaction.

To his surprise, Amy nodded. "It would be a nice way for Roland to be remembered."

His mother perked up. "I have some photos she can use… I'll have to find them."

Neither of them had fallen apart at the idea. Joshua started to feel as though he'd overreacted by telling Alyssa he'd be keeping her under his scrutiny…yet, from past experience, he felt he couldn't trust her.

What would she be doing right now? Eating in the salon, settled in front of the large picture windows that overlooked the garden? Or would she be in the bath, soaking out the stresses of the past days? He liked the idea of Alyssa naked in the bath, covered with frothing bath foam. He liked the idea far too damned much.

He shifted uncomfortably in his seat and censored the provocative images. How had this happened that thoughts of the woman could reduce him to a state of hot and bothered?

Restlessness drove him out of the café on the pretext that he had a call that he needed to make. Once outside, he stood on the pavement surrounded by smokers who had come out the restaurant for a quick smoke after their meal.

He fingered the keypad of his phone. He wanted to call home, speak to Alyssa and reassure himself that she was okay. His mother was right. It had been rude to take off and leave her alone. However much he disapproved of her relationship with his brother she, too, must be experiencing grief over his death—much like Amy was. And that disturbed him.

He stared at the phone. What reason would he give for calling her? It was unlikely that she'd even answer the homestead phone.

Finally he pocketed his phone. For the first time in his life he wished that he smoked. It might've helped to ease this unsettling tension inside him.

By the time he got back to the table, everyone was talking about one of the scandals in local politics. Joshua signalled for the bill. He wanted to leave. The feeling that he should not have left Alyssa alone on her first night at Saxon's Folly, with nothing but grief to keep her company, grew stronger.

As they drove up the long drive to the house, Joshua saw that the wing where Alyssa was staying was in darkness. He'd worried for nothing. She was already fast asleep.

It was the siren that woke Alyssa from a restless slumber and confused dreams full of disturbing, disjointed encounters with Roland and Kay and Joshua.

Disorientated by the shriek, uneasy from the aftermath of the nightmare, she swung her legs out of bed.

Men's voices filtered in through her window. Quickly Alyssa pulled on her robe, grabbed her bag and headed for the door. Kay had told her there had been a fire in the past, but the homestead had survived without great damage. Could it be happening again?

Downstairs the house was empty, the doors of the salon flung wide onto the verandah. No smell of smoke. No red haze to signal a fire. But Alyssa could hear the sound of motors. Fire engines? To the left she could see floodlights. Moving outside, she made her way down the stairs, toward the vineyards where she could hear the commotion.

It took the sound of the helicopter overhead to alert her.

Frost.

Of course. The siren had been a frost warning.

Alyssa glanced at her watch. Four o'clock in the morning. The roar of motors morphed into the drone of tractors. As she came closer she could see the giant fans hitched behind and whirring as the tractors drove up and down between the rows of vines. Overhead the rotors beat the warmer air down, desperate measures before the frost settled on the vines.

A figure materialised out of the murk.

Joshua.

"Did the siren wake you?"

Instantly she was aware of her hastily pulled on robe, which must look incongruous with her bare feet and the handbag slung over her shoulder. As he came closer she saw that his hair was mussed adding to the impression that he, too, had risen in a hurry.

"I thought it was a fire alarm."

"Not fire, only frost."

Only frost. There was little to be dismissive about frost. She knew the dangers of frost at the delicate budding stage. "Did you catch it in time?"

Joshua nodded. His eyes glinted in the light from the house behind her. "We've got good equipment. And all the local helicopter companies are on standby. Heath usually does a fly-over once he's finished his yards—he's a qualified pilot."

The air beat down on them, Alyssa's hair whipped across her face. She rocked on her feet and almost fell against Joshua.

His hands shot out. "Steady."

Pulling out of his grasp, she pushed her windswept hair off her face and gave a strangled laugh. "Sorry, it's the wind."

"You can go back to bed now, there's no emergency. You'll only get chilly standing out here."

She was conscious of his gaze taking in her dishevelled hair, her sleep-mussed face and the comfortable terry robe that was a world away from the glamorous, sophisticated image she preferred to present.

As the self-consciousness spread within her, she became aware of how isolated they were from the rest…how hidden and sheltered under the cover of night. Her pulse picked up, she breathed slowly, trying to hide her agitation. How could this man have such an effect on her?

"Okay, I'm going." Her voice was hoarse, a croak of sound in the night.

His gaze darted over her wind-ruffled hair, to where the

robe gaped in front. Alyssa yanked the sash tighter. He stilled. She sensed his tension, knew he'd picked up on what she was feeling. He cleared his throat. "I'm sorry you were woken."

"It's not a problem. I should catch another couple of hours sleep if I go back to bed now."

Immediately she wished she hadn't used the word *bed*. It brought an intimacy that she didn't want. And Joshua was aware of it, too. The utter stillness that surrounded him told her that. For one wild moment she felt herself swaying toward him, inching closer. Then she caught herself.

This was madness.

Joshua believed she'd been his brother's mistress.

Spinning away, she hurried back to the homestead, nerves of apprehension fluttering like drunken butterflies in her stomach when she heard his footsteps crunching on the gravel path behind her.

Alyssa set her bare foot on the first step and paused, not daring to look back. "See you at breakfast." She tried for a casual, throwaway tone, and knew she'd fluffed it up when he stepped closer.

"Not so fast."

She froze. Her chest rose and fell, and her toes curled into the cold stone stairs. She was eternally grateful for the fans, for the drone of the rotors. Hopefully Joshua wouldn't hear the thunder of her heart.

He stopped beside her. And touched her face. Gently. His fingertips cupped her cheek, turning her head toward him.

The thunder of rushing blood grew loud in her ears. She caught a whiff of his aftershave, the same scent that clung to his jacket. To her intense horror all the emotion she'd experienced in his bedroom welled up inside her. Joshua grew blurred. The tears she'd been suppressing since Roland died spilled over.

"Hey, don't cry."

"I'm not crying." She wiped frantically at her eyes. "I'm not." She faced him, blinking furiously.

His features softened in the light from the salon behind her. "Come here."

"I'll be okay," she choked out.

"Hush." He reached out and took her into his arms.

The storm of sobs caught her unawares and caused her shoulders to shake and her stomach to ache. His arms were strong and he cradled her against his chest, rocking her slightly. The merino lambswool sweater he wore was soft and warm under her cheek, and she could feel his heart beating steadily under her hand. It was comfortable and safe. Alyssa wished she could stay in his arms forever.

The tears fell faster.

Simply holding her, he let her cry, saying nothing.

The tempest subsided. Her sobs quietened.

And in the silence of the pre-dawn it all changed. Suddenly Joshua's hold wasn't only about comfort. There was something else, too. In slow degrees she became aware that the steady beat of his heart under her fingertips had picked up, that his breathing had become irregular. A sense of expectancy hung over them.

A moment of indecisiveness. To snuggle closer? Or push him away? She was desperately tempted to move closer.

Whatever she did now would change their relationship irrevocably.

But he made the decision for her, easing his grip. "My touch has never had that effect on a woman before. I've never made a woman cry before."

Alyssa knew he was trying to lighten the moment, trying to make her smile. But she couldn't.

She hiccupped. Mortification set in. How could she have dissolved into weak, womanly tears in his arms?

After a little silence, she said awkwardly, "I'm sorry, I'm crying like a baby."

"It's been a hell of a week." He pulled her closer again and rested his cheek against her hair. The unexpected contact was achingly tender. The pulsing sensuality had evaporated. "Cry all you want."

She regretted the loss of whatever it was that had stirred between them. She ached. But his tenderness made the tears flow afresh. Alyssa sniffed, furious with herself for appearing so vulnerable. "You must think I'm so dumb."

His arms tightened around her. "I don't think you're dumb at all." After a moment, he added huskily, "I miss him, too."

Six

A little awkwardness from her emotional meltdown still lingered when Alyssa entered the sunny glass-walled breakfast room later that morning. But she gradually relaxed once she realised the room was empty until Joshua strolled in from the kitchen.

"Oh, you startled me." Her heart started to race and not only from the shock of his sudden appearance. He looked utterly, heart-wrenchingly gorgeous. He'd changed. A black shirt and blue jeans replaced the sweats. The lambswool sweater that had been so soft against her skin earlier was gone.

"Where is everyone?" Her voice was annoyingly breathless as she fixed her attention on his face.

"Working. We rise early. No city hours at Saxon's Folly." His eyes scanned her, making her aware of how out of place her boutique-chic, pin-striped pantsuit and suede shoes must seem. At once she wished she'd worn the jeans she'd bought yesterday morning.

Today's early-morning encounter with Joshua had put her

on the defensive, forcing her to don corporate armour to withstand the devastating effect he had on her. Off balance, she said with a touch of acerbity, "Oh, then what are you still doing here?"

The beautiful bone structure tightened, and his mouth firmed into a sculpted line and all affability vanished.

"I've been waiting for you." There was not an ounce of gentleness in his narrow-eyed inspection.

"Why?" she asked baldly, tensing for a confrontation.

"Have you forgotten? You're accompanying me today. So eat up, I need to get moving."

She *had* forgotten all about it. Her brain had been short-circuited by the nightmare, then jolted by the siren. The crying jag and Joshua's show of sympathy had only deepened her turmoil. She met that granite gaze. "I don't need a guard dog."

"You don't have a choice."

His way or hit the highway. His flinty eyes and the rocklike set to his jaw warned her that there would be no point in arguing. Not if she wanted to stay at Saxon's Folly.

No hint of the gentle pre-dawn Joshua remained. She'd been duped into believing that he was empathetic. Nurturing. Safe.

Mistake.

This was the real Joshua Saxon. Too arrogant. Too sure of himself. Too darn *everything*.

But even knowing all that, she couldn't stop the sensual awareness that prickled under his penetrating regard. What a pity her body was so out of sync with her brain about the kind of man that was good for her.

Alyssa helped herself to toast, scooped on homemade marmalade, and let out the breath she'd unconsciously been holding, "So, what are you going to show me today?" She tilted her head to one side. With Joshua, attack was probably the best line of defence. "More etchings?"

"I'm a pretty straightforward kind of guy. I say what I

want. I don't need those kind of ploys—if I wanted you, I'd tell you." His grim smile held little humour.

So he didn't want her anymore. Alyssa withered a little inside and bit into her toast. Discovering her identity had killed his interest. After a few minutes of eating in silence, wishing she'd resisted the temptation to provoke him with the etchings dig, Alyssa followed him out to the Range Rover.

He took her to the vineyards first. "The vines are the heart of Saxon's Folly." Leaping down from the vehicle, he opened the passenger door for her to alight, then bent and picked up a handful of red soil and let it trickle through his fingers. "And this is the lifeblood."

Some hidden place deep within her responded to the passion in his voice. Standing a little distance from him, she fought it as she'd fought the hold he wielded over her senses. But she suspected this ability that Joshua Saxon possessed to get under her defences, deep into the heart of her, was more dangerous than the way her body responded so wantonly to his.

What was it about this man?

She examined him. Sure, he was tall, dark and dangerously gorgeous. But she'd never been one for looks alone. And, yes, the slanting morning sun struck his almost-perfect features giving his skin a rich, golden glow as he dusted his hands off. But it wasn't that alone that made her heart leap.

"This block was originally planted in 1916. Strange to think about it, isn't it?" He glanced at her. "Men from Napier, a few miles away were going off to fight in Europe during the Great War, and here, on this piece of land a world away from the war, a dozen Spanish monks planted vines. Even during times of death, life must go on."

And just like that he held her captive. Alyssa knew Joshua was talking about more than the vines that he touched with careful fingers. He was talking about Roland. About grief. About life continuing on the other side.

She resented him for it. Resented him bitterly for this uncanny ability to get through to her on the most elemental level, to hold her in his thrall.

In an attempt to break the sudden tension that snapped like a pulled string between them, she said, "What cultivar is that?"

"The monks thought they were planting Cabernet Sauvignon. Only years later when the grapes were ready to harvest did they discover their mistake. They're Cabernet Franc. Too late then to pull them out. They made their wine."

She assessed him. The way his Driza-Bone hat tipped over his forehead, the way he stood with his legs planted hip-width apart on the soil. Master of all he surveyed. "You love it out here, don't you?"

"Who wouldn't?" Pleasure lit up his eyes. A flash of white teeth transformed his face into breathtaking sexiness. Her stomach dropped as desire swept her. "Before Dad decided he wanted to step down as CEO of Saxon's Folly, I managed the vineyards. I never wanted to make the wine. I wanted to grow the fruit that winemakers like Heath and Caitlyn so magically transform into a nectar fit for the ancient gods."

The sheer beauty of the picture he painted touched Alyssa on a primal level. Here was a man with roots, who knew who he was. A man so solid, so confident in his own skin that she couldn't help but admire him...and want him.

Alyssa suppressed the yearning. She couldn't afford the distraction that Joshua presented. Drawing a shuddering breath, she said, "So you miss it?"

He nodded. "I still keep an eye on the vineyards. But I've appointed two vineyard managers. One here, and one for the blocks over at Gimblett's Gravels where most of the grapes for our reds are grown."

After an instant of hesitation, she asked daringly, "Do you miss having Heath to work with since he walked out?"

A frenetic buzz caused Alyssa to pull a vibrating cell phone out of her handbag. She glanced at the caller ID. David. She killed the call.

"Sorry." She smiled sunnily at Joshua. "You were about to say?"

His face expressionless, he said, "That last question sounded a little too much like an inquisition. Alyssa Blake in journalist mode. You should've taken your call."

Heavens, he was perceptive. Thank goodness he had no idea who had been calling. "I'll ring back later." Changing the subject, Alyssa gestured to the rolling vineyards around them. "And how did all this end up in your family's hands?"

"After the Great War the monks decided to move on. The land was sold. My Saxon forefather won it three years later in a poker game. The monks had planted vines for sacramental purposes—everyone laughed when Joseph Saxon said he was going to grow wine in commercial quantities. The land was barren, people told him. But he was determined to prove them wrong." Joshua's mouth slanted wryly. "Stubborn old bastard. The locals called it Saxon's Folly. The name stuck."

"So that's who you get it from."

He raised an eyebrow. "The name Saxon?"

She laughed appreciatively. "The stubbornness. The hard-nosed streak."

He touched his nose. "Soft as butter."

"Sure," she said, smiling up at him. And warmth rose within her as he smiled back at her.

But Alyssa was no longer smiling when, back in her bedroom, she managed to sneak a call back to her editor later that afternoon.

"I've been hearing things about Saxon's Folly…rumbles in the jungle," David said without preamble. "Let me see what more I can find out. I'll get back to you to see if there's enough for a story."

A story about Saxon's Folly?

Alyssa's heart sank. "I haven't heard anything…and I don't want to do a story now. Isn't there anyone else available?" She was no longer certain she could guarantee an impartial perspective. "I'm on leave, David."

"Maybe you won't need to use up your leave," he said cryptically. "I'll call you once I know more. And don't forget to send that obituary through by tomorrow."

Alyssa killed the phone. Oh, heavens, Joshua would have conniptions if he discovered David was considering assigning her a story about his precious vineyard and family. It would be best to say nothing. After all, David's rumbles might turn out to be nothing more than unsubstantiated rumours.

With that conclusion, Alyssa's step lightened. For now, she would put it out of her mind and concentrate on learning about her brother's life for her own satisfaction. Nothing more.

"Jump in," Joshua called to Alyssa late the following afternoon as he throttled back the engine of the Range Rover and drew up behind her.

A quick hello and she clambered into the cab, slinging her handbag at her feet. His rapid sideways glance showed long, feminine legs encased in dark blue denim and a purple T-shirt moulding curves that caused his chest to constrict and heat to shoot downward.

He forced his gaze away from her. "My meeting was unavoidable." His voice was suddenly husky. He cleared his throat. "What have you been doing?" Better, Joshua decided.

"Nothing much." Alyssa paused, pulling a notebook and pencil from her bag. "After you left I took a walk around the winery—Caitlyn kindly showed me around."

Joshua relaxed a fraction. He'd been uneasy about leaving Alyssa alone, uncertain what mischief she might wreak left untended. But he'd had no choice. Work came first. He risked another glance at her. Her hair was blowing around her face and her rosy lips tilted up.

Another surge of lust hit him. Shaken by the force of it, he tightened his fists around the steering wheel and focused on the track leading up the hill ahead.

"That's all?"

"And your mother showed me some family photo albums and told me about the stories behind Roland's trophies." The words sounded torn from her.

All feeling of relaxation vanished. He shot her a brooding look. "I don't want you upsetting my mother."

"I didn't. I promise. She wanted to do it. I think she found it therapeutic."

Was he overreacting? His innate distrust of the woman had him wanting to keep her in his view all the time. But his mother had invited Alyssa to stay at Saxon's Folly. He could hardly forbid his mother to talk to a houseguest. It might even be good for her to talk about Roland to a stranger. God knows he wasn't ready to talk about his brother yet. Certainly not to Alyssa.

They were climbing to the west, the sea behind them.

"Where are we going?" Alyssa broke the silence.

A sudden foreboding closed around Joshua. Perhaps this was not a good idea. "There's something I want to show you over on the other side of The Divide."

"The Divide?"

Joshua pointed through the windshield to where a winding pass cut into the hills ahead, which had they been higher might have earned the label of mountain range.

As they crested the summit of The Divide, he heard her breath catch. He flicked her a look and caught the entranced expression on her face.

Ahead of them lay a valley so beautiful it never failed to take his own breath away. But this time all his senses were focused on the woman seated beside him, a pencil gripped in her fist as she took in the vista of rolling hills, the wide plain, the river running through.

"So, what do you think?" Holding his breath, Joshua waited for her response.

"My God, it's beautiful," she said softly. "Too beautiful to describe in words." She tapped her pencil against her short-hand notebook.

Joshua started to smile inwardly. Satisfaction spread through him. Maybe it hadn't been a mistake to bring her here after all. "On a warm summer's day this is the best place in the world. See that river?"

Alyssa nodded.

"Chosen Valley Vineyard—Heath's home—lies on the other side. There are trout in the river. They lurk under the rocks. It takes time to coax them out."

"What a lovely picture. It's absolutely idyllic. Clearly you love it here and Heath must, too, otherwise he wouldn't live here." Alyssa fell silent for a moment. "What about Roland, did he love it, too?"

Joshua forced himself not to react to the way his brother's name fell so easily from her lips. Yet he couldn't stop the tension that settled between them, destroying the bond that had been forged in the last few minutes.

He gave a short laugh. "Roland didn't have the patience to land a trout. He was drawn to dangerous sports, fast cars…" he cast her a derisive glance "…and equally fast women."

She rose like one of the trout that lived in the stream to a particularly tempting lure. "You're saying that I'm fast?"

Joshua pulled the vehicle off the road and turned his head. "Fast lane? Fast tracked for success? Maybe. When last did you take time to reflect a little? To go hiking? To stand on the edge of a hill and wait for the sunset?"

Then he turned his back on her wide eyes and silky hair and the womanly fragrance that tangled him up in knots. Swinging out of the driver's seat, he slammed the door behind him, and walked to the road's edge, his back to her, his hands on his hips.

He heard a door slam, heard her footsteps crossing the hard ground. She stopped behind him.

His every muscle went rigid.

"You're right." She sighed, a soft, breathy sound that only served to ratchet up the tension inside him. "I've been working so damn hard."

"Why?" He stared blindly ahead, for once not seeing the beauty of the valley. "What drives you?"

"It's so hard to explain."

He swivelled to face her, his eyes searching her features. Her eyes were troubled, her mouth soft. "Try me."

For a moment he thought Alyssa might refuse. Then she said, "I was raised an only child…" Her voice trailed away.

Raised an only child? That was a peculiar way to phrase it. Joshua let it pass. She was clearly unhappy about the subject matter. And waited.

Eventually she spoke and the words were so soft that he had to strain his ears before the wind carried them away. "I was brought up to excel. Special tutoring. Piano. Drama. Art. Tennis lessons."

"Because you were an only child?" He eyed her profile. It would explain some of her hard edges, the ambition that drove her.

She didn't answer immediately. "My parents thought of me as their protégée…their chosen child. Eventually all their expectations became my own. I was expected to become someone. Don't think I was a cipher—I wanted that, too. For a long time I wanted success so much, even though my version was a little different from my parents'. My father was a judge and he wanted me to become a lawyer. It took a while for him to come to terms with my choice of career. I worked like a dog."

"But you got your success." Joshua couldn't help wondering if some of her father had rubbed off on her. "Maybe you're a chip off the old block after all."

Her lips curved into a sad smile. "I was always a bit of a

crusader. And my father made sure I had firm ideas about right and wrong from the time I was very young. Believe me, it's not easy being a judge's daughter. Especially when you're a teen. You can never win." Her eyes had regained a hint of sparkle. "But once I grew up, I realised he was right. The world needs people who stand up for what they believe in. For truth and honesty and all those old-fashioned values."

Joshua decided that this was not the best moment to remind her that trying to break up his brother's engagement was hardly honourable behaviour. But he didn't want to see the desolation return to her eyes.

"At least my mother lived long enough to see me become an award-winning wine journalist," Alyssa was saying. "A television personality instantly recognizable. But it cost me time I should have spent with her—though I never knew she was ill. Cancer," she added as she read the question he didn't ask.

"That would've been hard." There was compassion in his eyes. "She must have been proud of you."

"Oh, she was."

"I've never thought of what it might be like being an only child. About the pressures that go with it," Joshua mused, tilting his head to one side to study her. "We've shared all the responsibilities that go with Saxon's Folly. My life would have been empty without Roland and Heath to fight with, without Megan always wanting her own way."

"You're lucky." There was a wistful light in her eyes.

"Think so?" He gave a chuckle. "Sometimes I want to murder them. But I love them," he added hurriedly when he saw the horrified expression on her face.

"Maybe I was too driven," Alyssa conceded. "But that changed around three years ago."

"When your mother died?"

Alyssa's eyes were bleak. "I missed her." Her gaze focused on him. Direct. Disconcerting. "I wanted siblings…a brother. More than anything in the world, I wanted a family."

Maybe death did that to a person. He knew he would give anything to have Roland back. Pity for Alyssa stirred inside Joshua. Carefully he said, "I'm sorry that you lost your mother. Death is so final."

Emotion flared in her eyes. "I grieved for her."

"And your father?"

"He grieved, too. He remarried last year… He was lonely, I think."

She turned her head and gestured to where the sun had sunk a little more. "Somewhere along the line, I stopped looking for sunsets."

Joshua stood quietly beside her, staring out over the distant western hills at the orange-and-gold streaked sky as uneasiness filled him. He wished that her story had not moved him so much. He wished that the senseless attraction to her would cease.

He should have more sense than to want Alyssa Blake.

"You know, Joshua, I never thought that every splendid sunset means the death of another day—and that time is passing by at an alarming rate." She looked up at him, her eyes a haunting purple that would seduce him if he let them. "Maybe you're right. Maybe my life has become too fast."

A long-waited sense of satisfaction curled inside him. The impulsive words escaped him before he could curb them. "I didn't think I'd see the day that Alyssa Blake might admit that she was wrong."

Her eyes narrowed, the purple depths no longer soft as they shot sparks at him. "You're pretty fast, too. Vineyard manager of a sizeable estate. CEO of Saxon's Folly. Mentor to a full staff. Architect of employment practices that business schools studied," she reeled off his successes. "Are you any better? Saxon's Folly is a big business. You're the boss where the buck stops. Surely you're driven to achieve? Surely you set goals?"

He should've know she'd come back fighting. "Touché. Sure I do. But I'm not obsessed by goals."

"You're implying that I am?"

He shrugged. "You know my philosophy. Here at Saxon's Folly enjoyment is fundamental to the wines we make. How can people enjoy our wines, if the people who work with the wine don't have fun making it?"

She shook her head dismissively. "That's a pile of codswallop. I told you that back when you tried to sell me that line in the ten minutes you granted me for a *Wine Watch* interview."

"I was busy. You caught me in the midst of the harvest with a bad forecast on the way." He paused, not liking how defensive he sounded. "And I firmly believe that the happiness of the staff shows in the finished product."

He could see her fighting to hold her tongue. She wanted to tell him that his concern and benevolence was nothing more than an act. He could see it in her blazing eyes.

Finally she said, "You didn't strike me as the crusading type."

His own anger was rising. "No, you preferred to view me as the type who could dismiss someone arbitrarily."

Alyssa took up the challenge. "So why did you dismiss Tommy Smith? He maintained he was victimised, that you made his life a misery. That your 'happiness' philosophy was a sop."

"You know that's not true, you discovered he was dismissed from his next job only three months after I fired him. I know that the vineyard owner advised you." He'd asked Michael Worth to let her know. Her low opinion of him had rankled. It still rankled.

"That was long after the story was published," she protested. "And it was different. That time Tommy was dismissed for a sexual harassment of a fellow worker."

"And you don't think that I dismissed him for the same reason?"

Alyssa looked at him in horror. "That's why you dismissed him? Why didn't you *tell* me?"

"The last thing the victim needed was the story spilled over the papers."

"So who—"

But Joshua was shaking his head. "Sorry, I'm not at liberty to say. Even off the record."

Alyssa thought back to how dismissive she'd been of Joshua in the story she'd done, how she'd championed Tommy, the underdog. Her stomach rolled over. Had she misjudged Joshua…and Tommy…so badly?

Then her misgivings receded as he said with the arrogance that she'd come to associate with him, "Forget it. It's over and done with."

Any lingering liking for the man vanished.

A cool sea breeze swept over the hill they'd traversed. Alyssa shivered and rubbed her hands briskly up and down her arms, feeling her flesh prickling under the fingers of the wind.

"You're cold. We should go."

But Alyssa didn't move. "I didn't know that he'd harassed one of your staff. And by withholding that essential piece of information, how could I present your side of the story?"

His mouth curled. "I wasn't prepared to break my word to someone who trusted me simply to satisfy your curiosity."

Impasse. "But it cost you and Saxon's Folly."

He slanted her a cynical smile. "And lost *Wine Watch* any respect I'd previously held for the magazine."

"And any respect you might have had for me."

"Yes."

Annoyance—and disappointment—surged within her as he confirmed his poor opinion of her. What had she expected? A denial? Maybe. So when had his opinion become so important? She tried to brush the hurt away with a flippant comment, "So you didn't respect me the morning after the magazine hit the newsstands?"

The brightness of his eyes intensified. "That's what you want? My respect in the morning?" There was a sudden simmering heaviness in the air that hadn't been there a moment earlier.

"Joke," she said hastily, "that was a joke." And, as much as she craved his respect, the crack had not been appropriate.

Alyssa could've bitten her tongue out. "My mouth runs away from me sometimes."

His gaze dropped to her mouth. "Funny, I had you pegged as calculating rather than impulsive. I have the impression that you think rather carefully about every word that comes out of that delectable mouth."

And suddenly he was much too close. Blood rushed to her head, she could feel herself flushing. Alyssa tensed. Yet even as she pressed the lips he'd mockingly referred to as *delectable* tightly closed in annoyance, she experienced another betraying flare of heat.

Joshua's expression didn't change. But a muscle in his jaw tightened, the only warning she had. Alyssa didn't move. His head lowered, slowly, his lips parting. She felt his breath against her mouth and a wave of desire ripped through her. His mouth claimed hers. For a moment he stilled and then his tongue entered her mouth, and Alyssa melted against him.

His body was big and warm and she no longer felt chilled. His arms came around her, pulling her against him. She was fervently conscious of the hardness of his chest beneath his shirt, of the flimsy cotton of her own shirt and her nipples tightening with excitement. So when his fingers slid into her hair, cradling her head, holding her exactly where it was comfortable, all her senses responded and he kissed her with deep intensity.

The tingle started under the touch of his fingers against her scalp and spread down her spine, along nerve pathways she hadn't known existed, until Alyssa felt like every inch of her flesh was electrified.

He lifted his head. "You taste of peaches."

Alyssa opened her eyes, stunned by the emotion that had exploded within her, and stared at him blankly. *"Peaches?"*

"Luscious and sweet like a fine Prosecco." His mouth came down again before she could retort. She couldn't help noticing he tasted of the wind, cool and wild with a hint of mint.

The kiss was thorough, his tongue exploring her mouth, the soft inner skin, the sleekness of her tongue until Alyssa felt that he'd overpowered her senses. She clung to his shoulders, not wanting it to end, not sure whether her legs would support her if he let her go.

When he finally raised his head, her breathing was ragged. He slid his hands down behind her back, linking them, supporting her, their lower limbs touching. Denim brushed against denim. Intimate. A whisper of sound that carried in the velvet silence of the evening.

Alyssa glanced up and found Joshua watching her.

"So, can you respect a woman who responds with such abandon to your kiss?" She tried to sound casual...dismissive... sophisticated. Instead her voice came out thin and thready.

"I respect the honest emotion I discovered," he said throatily.

And her heart flipped over in her chest. Maybe he did want her. Maybe discovering her identity had not staunched the desire.

Even though he fought against it.

Right then Alyssa realised that Joshua was far more complex, far more dangerous to the yearning woman deep inside her, than she'd ever suspected.

That evening Alyssa was the last to arrive at the dinner table in the smaller dining room used for cosier family meals. Her first dinner with the family—last night she'd eaten on a tray in her room. Everyone had already settled in their seats, leaving only one chair empty. Roland's. The place her brother had occupied for years.

Her chest tight, she sank down on the chair where her brother had eaten countless meals. Opposite her sat Joshua with his mother on his right side, and his sister, Megan, on his left. Phillip and Caitlyn Ross, the Saxon's Folly winemaker, sat on either side of Alyssa.

"How was your day?" Caitlyn asked with a polite smile.

"It was fabulous," she replied mechanically, and Joshua shot her a quizzical glance, his eyebrow raised.

Oh, heavens! He was thinking about their kiss. That had been more than fabulous. Earthmoving. Mind shattering. Nothing as mundane as fabulous. Not that she intended him to know any of that.

"I learned a lot," she said lamely, then started to flush as his expression turned incredulous. So she quickly added, "Well, it's so beautiful here."

"Heaven on earth," said Caitlyn.

Alyssa stilled.

Not heaven. Not with Roland gone.

But for the first time she managed to think of her brother without the wild grief and searing regret that had so shaken her. There was still sadness, but the anger and resentment at missing the opportunity to know him was receding and acceptance of his death was starting to settle in. In some peculiar way talking about her mother's death to Joshua had helped.

"If you want to see something special, you need to get the boss to take you to the waterfall," Caitlyn said, with a glance at Joshua. "The best way to get there is by horseback, to hike there takes forever. It's a fantastic ride."

"I haven't ridden much." Alyssa thought back to her childhood, when her adoptive mother had signed her up for two terms at pony club, but with all the other scheduled tuition, she'd never had the time to learn to ride well.

"You can ride Breeze, she's very gentle," said Megan.

"I don't know…" Alyssa hesitated.

"Roland always loved it at the falls." Kay entered the conversation. "He used to beg to go on picnics there as a child. As a teenager he loved to hang out there with friends."

Alyssa started to pay attention. A place that Roland had loved? "Maybe I'll consider it." Perhaps there she would capture that spiritual closeness that she was seeking. Perhaps she'd finally lose the loneliness that lurked inside her.

"Did you know Roland?" Megan was staring at her with a puzzled frown.

Damn. Had she given away too much? Apprehension filled Alyssa. Her gaze shot to Kay, who had stilled at her daughter's question. Then moved on to Joshua. His mouth was set in a hard line.

"Uh…no."

The stuttered denial didn't sound convincing to her own ears. And the force of Joshua's glare told her that he was convinced she was lying.

But thankfully she appeared to have deflected Megan's interest. Alyssa let out a silent sigh of relief. That had been far too close.

Kay turned hurriedly to Joshua. "Do you remember one night you terrified me by arriving back covered in blood? You and Roland had some sort of competition that I never quite got to the bottom of."

Megan glanced from Joshua to her mother. Joshua's mouth tightened. "Teen garbage," he said dismissively.

"For a few years you all thought you were bulletproof." Phillip spoke for the first time.

"We grew up," Megan said quickly.

"Think carefully. You'll be sore if you're not used to riding—it's a fair distance," Joshua murmured as Ivy arrived to collect the dishes.

Looking at him, Alyssa realised that he didn't look wild about the idea. "If you're too busy, we don't need to go."

"I can probably find time to take you on Monday, the winery is closed to the public after the weekend, so it will be quieter."

Had he offered Monday because he knew she was supposed to be back at work then? But if she stayed, that would give her an extra day at Saxon's Folly. Despite his grumbling, David wouldn't mind, she never took leave. And seeing a place that had been special to her brother would be worth a bit of extra stiffness.

"I'd probably survive." She threw Joshua a quick smile, saw his double take and stopped smiling. "As long as I'm back in Auckland by evening. I'd like to do it—if you don't mind taking me."

There was a gap in the conversation. Then Caitlyn said, "I heard that you've decided against attending that European wine show, Megan."

Megan glanced tellingly in her mother's direction. "The timing was all wrong. I wanted to be here, with the family. There'll be more shows next month, starting with the show in Paris."

She'd stayed because of Roland's death. Megan didn't need to say it out loud. But her meaning was clear.

After a short pause, Caitlyn said with forced humour, "That should be fun. Those French vintners can be very charming."

Megan's lashes fell, hiding her eyes, but a small, secret smile curved her mouth revealing a dimple in her cheek. "Oh, I intend to have a lot of fun. I want to taste some of those deliciously sexy wines."

"Frenchmen are supposed to be legendarily sexy, too," Caitlyn responded.

"It's the language," Alyssa said. "Even though I don't speak it, everything sounds so sexy in French."

"Passez-moi votre verre de vin, s'il vous plaît."

Everyone started to laugh as Alyssa stared at Joshua in bewilderment, until Megan took pity on her and said, "He asked for your wineglass."

"No more for me, thanks," Alyssa said, feeling warm and fuzzy inside at the good-humoured amusement on Joshua's face, coupled with an intensity that made her heart melt.

At last he glanced away and the discussion moved onto Chardonnay, becoming increasingly technical—temperature and malolactic fermentation. Alyssa couldn't help noticing how easy the relationship between Caitlyn and Joshua was. Had he ever dated the winemaker? It would be such a sensible relationship, the winery boss and the stellar winemaker, a marriage would truly cement the relationship. She couldn't help wondering whether Joshua had ever considered keeping his winemaker happy forever.

The notion caused her a stab of something like discomfort... she didn't want to label it anything as significant as envy. Or, even worse, jealousy.

On Saturday, David called Alyssa to tell her that the rumours were definitely buzzing and that Saxon's Folly was in the thick of it all.

"It's all about a Chardonnay that was entered in the Golden Harvest Wine Awards. One judge is muttering that what's available in the shops, isn't the same as the wine he tasted in the competition."

"So what happens next?" Alyssa asked.

"They'll give Joshua Saxon the option of withdrawing the wine before the scandal becomes public, I suspect. Although there is a rumour that an investigator has been appointed. But it's all under wraps right now." David was speaking quickly now. "See what you can find out, Alyssa."

"Hey, I'm back in the office next week. Tuesday probably."

"That gives you three days." David didn't say a word about the extra day she'd added on.

"I'm not doing this story, David. I'm on leave." He was still trying to convince her when she ended the call. And the rest of the day passed in a lazy fashion.

The next morning when Kay broke the news that two of the casual workers—students who regularly helped on the weekend with the tastings and cellar door sales—hadn't turned up on Sunday, Alyssa leapt into the fray.

Kay looked relieved. "Thank you, Alyssa. Joshua is there now, he's pitching in, too. He'll tell you what to do and give you price lists."

The car park beside the winery was packed with vehicles glittering in the morning sun. Alyssa couldn't believe the amount of visitors who came for the weekend tastings and tours.

Joshua looked harried. "At least with working for *Wine Watch* you'll know how tasting works."

"Don't be so sure." She gave him a teasing grin. Within minutes she'd settled next to him behind the counter, bottles of wine uncorked beside her, a list of wines with prices. Alyssa scanned the labels of the bottles in front of her out of interest. A Sauvignon Blanc, a Cabernet Merlot and a Semillon. And even a Chardonnay. Could this be the controversial vintage David wanted her to find out more about?

A brief lull followed.

"It's been so busy," said Joshua in disbelief, "now it's gone all quiet."

"Maybe I killed off all the customers," Alyssa joked.

He shot her a dark look. "Maybe."

"Hey, that was a joke."

"It wasn't funny." But his lips curled into a smile inviting her to smile back.

"Why aren't you married, Joshua?" That sounded so blunt. But it had been on her mind since Friday night when she'd seen how at ease he and Caitlyn were in each other's company. "Or at least attached. You're an attractive man—"

"Thank you." He gave her a slow smile.

She felt herself flush. "Don't get me wrong, this isn't a proposition. I'm—"

"In journalist mode?" This time the smile held an edge. "Don't worry, I never did consider it a come-on."

"What a relief," she said, a little barb to keep him from realising how interested she, Alyssa the woman, not Alyssa the journalist, really was. "So are you going to answer?"

"Always the journalist," he said, and the irony was not lost on her.

She didn't respond.

Finally he sighed. "I've never found anyone that I want to

spend my life with." He gave her a crooked smile. "My parents set a tough example to follow. They met each other at a dance and knew from the first moment."

"You expect the same?"

He gave her a strange look. "Perhaps."

"Perhaps their romance has grown in the telling."

"They love each other. They always have. There's never been anyone else for either of them—ever."

Alyssa felt a moment of envy at his certainty. "I hope you find it—the once-in-a-lifetime love that you're looking for."

He shrugged. "I'm not looking for it. But if I find it, I'll recognise it and embrace it. And in the meantime I'm not settling for second best."

"Don't you get lonely?"

He shrugged again. "Not really. I date. I've got friends—"

"And family." Joshua had friends, he was highly respected, he ran a successful winery. Yet more than anything Alyssa coveted his family.

"Yes, my family is important to me."

"And your staff…" She waved a hand around the tasting shed.

He nodded, his eyes softening. "Saxon's Folly is more than a workplace, more than a winery. It's home."

"If you ever marry, your wife is going to have to love this place."

"It's in my blood," he said with a simple acceptance that she envied.

"What about Caitlyn?"

He blinked at the sudden question. "What about her?"

"Have you ever dated her?"

"Caitlyn?" He gave a surprised laugh. "What makes you think that?"

"It seemed like such an obvious partnership. The wine-maker and the winery boss."

"I like Caitlyn. She's smart—a great winemaker. But she's always been one of the boys. There's no chemistry."

"One of the boys?" Caitlyn? Alyssa stared at him in astonishment. Was he blind to the other woman's tall, slim strength? Granted, she wore jeans and boots and men's shirts that gave her a tomboy look. But her light blue eyes, dusting of Celtic freckles and strawberry-blond hair had an undoubted charm even if her hair was always pulled back in a no-fuss ponytail and she wore no make up, but she hardly resembled a boy.

Men! Alyssa shook her head in disbelief, but she couldn't prevent the relief that flowed through her that he'd never been attracted to the other woman.

Joshua leaned toward her. "Here come your first customers. Are you ready?"

She looked up to see three women and two men in their late twenties approaching. Alyssa gave them what she hoped was a welcoming smile and waved them onto the barstools in front of the counter.

"What would you like to taste?" She lined up five tasting glasses. One of the women and the two men chose the Cabernet Merlot, the other two women pondered indecisively. Alyssa poured the red wine into the three tasting glasses and watched as they picked up and swirled it around.

"I'll try the Semillon," said one of the two who had been undecided.

"Sav Blanc for me, please," said the other.

"Black currants," said one of the men, sniffing at the dregs of the red in his glass. "It smells of black currants."

The others laughed. "I tasted red grapes," said the blonde who had tasted the red.

"You wouldn't be wrong to say black currants," Joshua's voice was low and serious.

"And I suppose the Sav tastes of grapefruit?" The woman with the Sauvignon Blanc gave him a flirtatious look from under her lashes.

Unaccountable annoyance rose within Alyssa. "The Saxon's Folly Sauvignon Blancs are known for their stone fruit flavours." She forced herself to smile blithely at the flirt.

"Stone fruit?" The woman gave her a blank look.

"Yes, peaches and nectarines." Alyssa poured a little more wine in her glass.

"Can you tell the difference between a Sauvignon Blanc and a Chardonnay," asked one of the men, giving her an interested look.

"Yes." Alyssa took out two clean glasses and placed them before him. She poured a little Chardonnay in the one and a sample of Sauvignon Blanc in the other. "You're looking for taste on the palate. The Chardonnay will have hints of oak—it's been barrel fermented—not in the bottle. It's also a little buttery, whereas the Sauvignon Blanc is fruitier. Have a taste of each."

"Ooh, can I try, too?" one of the women asked.

"Sure." Alyssa repeated the ritual for her.

"I taste a hint of peaches," said the woman.

Joshua had said she tasted of peaches when he'd kissed her up on the hill. A tremor ran through Alyssa. She flashed him a sideways look from under her lashes—and found him gazing at her, his gaze hot, his eyelids heavy.

A flare of excitement ignited deep in her belly.

"The stone fruit flavours are very specific to this region, if you travel down to Marlborough, you'll discover that the flavour's grassy, reminiscent of gooseberries." Joshua's voice washed over her talking about fruit and flavours and she listened to the mesmerising cadence of his voice, words like *peach* and *smooth* and *creamy* creating a sensuous flow that surrounded her.

"Can you taste the differences between the same wines?"

"You mean, from different producers?"

The tall man nodded.

"That's called horizontal tasting. So Saxon's Folly makes Sauvignon Blanc, and over the hill at his winery my brother makes Sauvignon Blanc, too. They're different. He's a fine winemaker…but so is Caitlyn Ross our winemaker—"

"A woman makes wine here?" One of the men sounded shocked.

"Good wines, too." Alyssa found herself bristling a little.

"Of course you'd say that, you work here."

"Actually I'm a journalist—"

"Ooh, you're doing a story? How exciting. Which newspaper?"

Alyssa told her the name of the magazine.

"I know you," said the tall man. "You're Alyssa Blake— you have a column in the Sunday papers, too. And I've seen you on television. So what do you think of the wines here?"

Alyssa gave him a smile, aware that Joshua was growing tense beside her, his hand tightening around the bottom of the wine bottle. Did he really believe that she would say something that might be detrimental to Saxon's Folly?

"You taste and tell me what you think," she responded, passing a glass to the man who had spoken. Out of the corner of her eye she noticed that Joshua's grip had relaxed a little, his knuckles were no longer white.

"Make sure you get some photos of him—" the flirt pointed at Joshua "—I might even buy a copy of the magazine." The woman batted her eyelashes in that way that Alyssa found intensely irritating. But she swallowed her annoyance and said nothing.

In the end the group walked away with a purchase of three cases of wine and Alyssa let out the breath she'd been holding.

"Hard work?" Joshua asked, a glimmer of laughter in his eyes.

"Let's just say it's not quite the easy sell I thought it would be." She looked up at him. "So you can tell the difference between the wines you brew and those that Heath makes, hmm?"

He nodded.

"And I suppose you can tell the difference between different Saxon's Folly vintages?"

"Piece of cake."

"And then you try and tell me that the samples you supplied for judging in the Golden Harvest Wine Awards taste the same as the same label available for sale in the supermarkets?"

Joshua froze. "Trying to ambush me?" he asked very softly.

Alyssa refused to be intimidated. Joshua made a big deal about his reputation, about how honourable he was. She was entitled to know if that was the truth. What she wasn't sure about yet was what she would do if she discovered it was all lies. She didn't want to hurt Kay and Phillip Saxon—or their children. Not now. Not while they were grieving. And she couldn't bear to find out that Joshua was dishonest.

It surprised her how much she needed to believe that he was as solid and real as the hills surrounding the vineyards he loved. She badly wanted to accept his word.

But she owed a duty to the public. The consumers who were possibly being scammed. She couldn't rely on her feelings, her desire to find the best in Joshua. Growing up, her father had drummed into her that people lied. All the time. Facts counted. She needed proof. Hard evidence.

It tore her apart to think of what she might discover....

"No," she said finally. "Just trying to get to the bottom of a disturbing rumour that the Chardonnay Saxon's Folly supplied for tasting in the recent competition is far superior to what's available at the retail outlets."

Seven

"So that's why you gate-crashed the ball."

Joshua had known all along Alyssa had an agenda. Bitter disappointment corroded the fondness and respect that had been developing against his will. He'd been right not to trust her.

He propped one elbow on the tasting counter and swivelled his body to face her. "And that's why you inveigled an invitation to stay at Saxon's Folly."

Her eyes flickered. "I told you before, your mother invited me."

"Right." Disbelief and sarcasm loaded his voice.

"Honestly, I didn't know about this until recently. I haven't agreed to do the story."

He should've known *Wine Watch* would be on to the story. "I'm supposed to believe that?"

"Yes."

Her amazing eyes widened ingenuously. But he wasn't about to be taken in by a pair of purple pansy eyes and an act of injured innocence. She'd known, all right. And he'd *almost* been suckered. And Alyssa Blake would not turn down the opportunity to do such a story.

Then the thought crossed his mind that Roland might have let something slip to her. Pillow talk after a hot session between the sheets.

Anger twisted his stomach into knots.

Pushing away from the tasting counter, he straightened to his intimidating height of six foot two inches.

Alyssa didn't flinch.

Roland had known about the dark cloud hanging over one of the premier Saxon's Folly wines. As soon as Joshua had learned there was a potential problem with the wine judging, he'd told Roland. He cast his mind back. The conversation had taken place a few days before the ball. He'd wanted to pull the wine from the competition. Roland had assured him there was nothing to worry about, that the sample provided for tasting was uniform and no danger of adverse publicity existed.

Would he have told his lover about the debacle? Joshua didn't want to believe that Roland had let something so confidential slip to a wine writer who'd already slated Saxon's Folly in the past. Joshua assessed her. But the wide eyes and patient smile revealed little.

Was it possible that Alyssa had found out from another source? The competition organisers? Highly unlikely. Wine-tasting competitions were run with rigorous secrecy.

Roland *must* have told her. He must have been taken in by Alyssa's inviting eyes and confiding manner. Damn! Annoyance at his brother's gullibility shook him. Being led around by the libido was the oldest trick in the book. Joshua could hardly believe Roland had fallen for it. But Roland had never been able to resist a pretty face.

Joshua scrutinised her. Shiny, dark red hair framed her face in a smooth sheet, the wide-spaced pansy eyes promised untold sensual delights. Yup, definitely a very pretty face. His gaze moved lower. Long legs went on forever in the new denims and the stretchy top, the colour of the lavender that grew outside the homestead, moulded the generous curve of her breasts.

No doubt about it. Roland would've have been utterly infatuated. Okay, so maybe he could understand why Roland had blabbed. Alyssa Blake was certainly the sexiest thing he'd seen for a long time. In Mata Hari mode she would be lethal.

He ignored the whisper in his head that suggested he might be every bit as susceptible as his brother had been; that Alyssa Blake had him tied up in knots. He narrowed his eyes. This crazy wanting had never happened before. Why now? Why *her?*

How was he supposed to deal with the fallout when she reduced him to this damn idiotic state of constant arousal? He fought to get his thoughts in order.

While she knew there was a problem with the judging, it didn't appear that she knew much more, otherwise she wouldn't be here, digging for a story.

The story she insisted she wasn't doing.

Maybe there was still time for damage control. He gave her a grim smile. "There will always be some variations between batches—it's only the small vineyards with small outputs that can almost guarantee that every bottle will taste the same. We bottle thousands of cases of Chardonnay. There's going to be a little variation—"

She gave a snort of disgust. "I'm not talking about a small amount. I'm talking about a huge difference—enough to make it taste like two completely different wines. Please don't take me for a total idiot."

Joshua held on to his temper with difficulty. "What you're suggesting is not possible. When we have a batch that comes out so much better, we bottle it as a reserve selection. Why would we pretend it's the same? Especially when we can command a higher price?"

"To garner awards? To deliberately entice the public to come out in droves and buy an award-winning wine when the one they get is vastly inferior to what they're expecting? Not that they'd ever find that out."

His brows drew together at the accusation. "We would *never* do that."

"Maybe I should ask Caitlyn that question, since she makes the wines." Alyssa started to turn away.

She was going to confront Caitlyn? After he'd told her not to question his staff? She was challenging him, walking away from him, after all but calling him a liar. He glared at her shapely back, irate that he noticed how her hips flared in the snug jeans. "It's not necessary. I am the boss. I speak for Saxon's Folly. We don't indulge in questionable practices designed to mislead the consumer. You can quote me on that in your damned article."

Looking past her he saw that a new group of tasters were heading in their direction. "We've got company. Better behave yourself," he said softly, and he knew by the sudden tension between her shoulder blades that she'd heard.

Arranging his features in a pleasant, welcoming smile, he added, "You leave tomorrow. My final word is that you're not to go to the winery…or try to interview my staff without me present."

She threw him a searing look over her shoulder. "I've no reason not to behave. I'm telling you the truth, Joshua. I've no intention of writing this story. I'm too close to…everything."

But instead of feeling relief at her revelation, Joshua felt annoyance because it underlined how much his brother had meant to her. *Too close to…everything.* His irritation was exacerbated as Alyssa flashed the wide smile that caused his body to snap to attention. Even more irritating was the fact that it wasn't directed at him, but at the approaching enthusiasts.

He couldn't trust her for a moment. She would do exactly what was best for Alyssa Blake, as always. He started to seethe.

Mata Hari indeed.

* * *

When Alyssa stirred on Monday morning, an appalling sense of dislocation rocked her at the thought of leaving Saxon's Folly later today.

The end had come before the beginning had started. She still had so much to learn about Roland. Grief eroded to a raw ache as she walked down to the stables for the last time with an unusually silent Joshua beside her.

Earlier, she'd considered calling off the ride, given Joshua's annoyance with her yesterday. But now as Alyssa watched Joshua saddle the two horses, she found she was looking forward to visiting a place that Roland had loved.

It would give her a chance to say goodbye. Closure. That's what she was looking for.

Then she could put Roland finally to rest. She wished that she could tell the Saxon siblings the truth. She'd come to like them all very much. She watched Joshua tighten the girth. With him the connection went deeper than fondness. The last thing she wanted was to leave him with the wrong impression of her relationship with Roland.

But she'd promised Kay....

In return for her silence she'd gotten a week to trace Roland's footsteps, learn about his life. And that week of time had a high price: her secrecy. She'd given her word and she could not go back on that. End of story.

Joshua led Breeze toward her, his expression unreadable. "Come, I'll give you a leg up."

She approached a little nervously. Breeze turned her head, pricked her ears and gave Alyssa an enquiring look.

"Bend your leg."

Alyssa obliged. The next moment Joshua hoisted her through the air. She landed in the English saddle and picked up the reins, while he adjusted the stirrups.

She stared down at his dark head. His hand brushed the inside of her jean-clad thigh, causing a frisson of heat. Her breath caught. She hated this tense awkwardness that yawned between them like a chasm and craved a return of the Joshua who had shown her around the vineyards. The Joshua with love for the land and passion in his eyes.

Even though she'd told David she couldn't do the article, Alyssa couldn't help wishing that Joshua would cooperate on the story. That way he'd have a chance to air his side of the situation to the public and she'd be able to do the article that David wanted so badly—and even clear up the damage she'd done to Joshua's reputation last time.

The end result would be win-win all round. Then she and Joshua might be able to resolve this friction between them. Become colleagues or even—

"How does that feel?"

At the question she abandoned her wishful thinking and stood up in the stirrups. Both legs felt even. She pulled a face. "Wobbly. Like I haven't been on a horse in a very long time."

Joshua's head tilted back and his black-as-midnight eyes clashed with hers. Her heart flopped over.

"Your stirrup leathers…are they even?"

"They'll do." Alyssa made a pretence of fiddling with the reins—anything to avoid looking at Joshua, not to feel that shameless heart-stopping surge of want that simply glancing at him aroused.

"Okay." With economy of movement, Joshua swung himself easily up onto the bay's back. Alyssa watched furtively through lowered lashes as he settled himself. He sat straight, totally at one with the horse beneath him; the broad shoulders tapering down beneath his blue-and-cream-striped shirt to where his faded jeans rode low on his hips. She didn't even see the command he gave to make the bay move. No doubt he'd been riding all his life.

As they rode out of the stable block, a black horse trotted poker-legged along the length of the fence, neck arched, his head held high. Beautiful but defiant.

"I'm glad you're not riding him." Alyssa tipped her head in the stallion's direction.

"I want to enjoy the ride." Joshua turned his head to look at the horse. "And I won't if I ride that animal. It takes hours to catch Ladykiller."

Alyssa gave the stallion a look of sympathy. But the horse belonged here. She didn't—and never would.

Joshua had made that very clear.

An hour later the rolling grasslands ended. The trail entered dense, overgrown bush and narrowed dramatically. They rode in single file with Joshua ahead.

Alyssa looked around with interest. Roland would've taken the same path and passed beneath the same trees. She called out, "So how much farther to go?"

Joshua turned in the saddle. "Not long now. We're nearly there."

Birds chirruped in the canopy overhead and bits of sunlight dappled the lush green ferns under the trees. Alyssa's heart lifted. She banked the scents and sounds to remember later, when she was back in the rat race of Auckland amidst the hurly-burly of deadlines and rush-hour traffic.

"Hold tight," Joshua said a few minutes later.

Alyssa's breath caught in her throat as she saw the incline that he planned to ride down.

She tugged on the reins to slow Breeze down. "I can't go down there!"

"Yes, you can. Believe in yourself. Lean back a little, hold the pommel of the saddle and try to relax. Come, follow me. You can do it."

Already he was descending. Alyssa could hear the scrabble of loose stones under his mount's hooves, could see his back swaying in time to the horse's stride. Rigid with apprehension, she let the reins slide through her fingers as Breeze extended her neck, lowered her head and pricked her ears forward. Alyssa grabbed at the pommel, and stared through the space between the mare's ears and hoped frantically for the best.

At the bottom of the incline she let out a whoop of triumph that caused Breeze's ears to flicker back. "I did it!"

She couldn't believe the sense of achievement she felt.

Joshua was waiting. He shot her the first grin he'd given her for what felt like a century. "Of course you did. Did you think I would've let you get hurt while you were in my care?"

As she heard the words, a penny dropped. Joshua was the boss. The final responsibility always stopped with him. Shielding a female worker from ugly gossip after she'd been harassed, making sure his mother wasn't upset while she mourned her dead son, protecting Amy from any sexual indiscretion that Roland might have committed. How many more burdens did he assume?

The boss. The guy who carried all the weight. Didn't he ever tire of it?

"Don't you ever want to share the load a little?"

"What load?" The grin disappeared and he stared at her blankly.

Alyssa wanted the grin back, wanted to see the flash of white teeth and the way his eyes lit up and crinkled at the corners. "The load of taking care of everyone around you. It must grow exhausting."

"Not really. I like to see people grow and achieve things that they doubted they could." He nodded at the incline. "Like you did there." He wheeled the big bay around and moved forward.

And that was the quality that made him such a great boss. She'd watched him at work in the winery. He had the ability to encourage people to try new things, to strive to do their best. Alyssa was thinking so hard about Joshua, she almost missed the first view of the waterfall as they rode into a sunlit clearing, and Joshua reined in ahead of her.

Her breath caught at the sight of the water tumbling down the sheer rock face, frothing into a lazy pool at the bottom.

Roland must have spent hours here. A perfect swimming hole for a hot summer's day.

Breeze stopped alongside Joshua's bay.

"I didn't bring togs to swim in," Alyssa said.

"The water is icy this time of the year. In a month or so it will be warmer. We can eat instead."

Hunger rumbled in her stomach. "I didn't even think of food."

"I brought some lunch," Joshua revealed, dismounting. "We can eat that beside the waterfall."

"You made food?"

"Not me, Ivy made it."

But he'd remembered to organise it. Alyssa had always considered herself organised, but Joshua's attention to detail was overwhelming.

He helped her off the horse, his hands firm at her waist. Alyssa suppressed the flare of awareness. Relief overtook her when Joshua moved away to tether the horses. She sat down on a soft mound of grass above the water's edge. From here the view of the waterfall was spectacular. It bubbled over a ledge of rock and plummeted over the drop into the dark green pool below, the sound oddly soothing. A sense of peace stole over her.

"It's beautiful. I can see why Roland loved it here."

Joshua flung himself down beside her and started to unzip the saddle pack he held. "It wasn't the beauty that Roland loved. It was the danger the place represented."

"Danger?" Alyssa stared at him. "Where?"

"See those rocks?" He pointed to boulders at the side of the ledge over which the waterfall flowed. "Roland liked nothing more than challenging a friend to dive from there."

Alyssa's heart sank like a stone as she took in the sheer height of the drop. "Was he insane?" The words burst from her.

"He loved the adrenaline rush. Roland never felt fear."

She had to ask. "Didn't anyone get hurt?"

Joshua nodded. "Roland had a friend who slipped and

broke a leg climbing up there—of course, the parents never knew the full story. Once, I cut my head on a rock in the pool when I hit the water headfirst."

Alyssa swallowed at the thought. He could've drowned! "You were equally reckless."

"I did it to stop Heath. Roland bet him that he couldn't, that he was too chicken to dive in. I took Heath's place. Although if I hadn't been hurt, Heath would probably still have dived in. He was as mad as a snake that I'd taken his turn. So my big gesture was probably for nothing," Joshua said wryly. "The joys of being sixteen—and impatient to be a man."

And the man had become every bit as responsible as the boy had striven to be. She eyed him furtively. Gorgeous, too. And loyal to the point of fault.

Alyssa remembered his mother saying she hadn't known how he'd been hurt. So he'd never dobbed his brother in. She didn't know if the loyalty was stupid or admirable.

"Here, have a bagel." He held out a paper bag.

"Thank you." It was perfect. Fresh and slightly chewy, filled with smoked salmon, avocado and cream cheese. Eating distracted Alyssa from what she'd been going to say next. But at least Joshua was talking to her again. She'd had enough of the silent treatment to last her a lifetime.

Next he produced a bottle of Pinot Gris and two glasses out of the pack. Once he'd filled the glasses, Alyssa took a sip. The slightly sweet, well-rounded sturdiness of the wine took her by surprise.

"Very nice," she said appreciatively, squinting at the label. "I didn't realise Saxon's Folly produced Pinot Gris."

"Not in large amounts," Joshua said. "You need to be on our loyal client mailing list to even get a chance of snapping it up. We hold the grapes on the vine until early May, so it's essentially a late-harvest wine." He swallowed a mouthful. "Mmm, the really special thing about this wine is that we sourced the vines from an ancient Alsace clone."

Alyssa dusted her fingers of the last of the crumbs from her bagel. "Alsace? In France?"

"Yes, imported into New Zealand in 1886."

"That *is* ancient."

Joshua topped up her glass. "And to complement fine wine…" His voice trailed away and he dug into the pack again. With a flourish he drew a punnet of strawberries and a container of chocolate dipping sauce.

"Oh my, this is decadent." There was something incredibly sexy about a man who provided food. A primitive leftover from ages past when the male had been the hunter. It was disgusting to be so impressed. There should be no need to feel so nurtured. She was a modern woman, totally able to take care of herself. Self-sufficient and sensible enough to be able to forage for herself.

Alyssa glanced around the clearing but couldn't see anything in the surrounding bush that would've appeased the appetite that the fresh air and ride had whetted. Not even the birds that called from the treetops.

Then there would be the little problem of catching them, cooking them. She slid a glance at the man beside her, his fingers long and tanned against the bright red berries. Okay, so he'd probably make a plan to find food in the bush. While she'd only poison them both.

City girl.

Fast lane….

Joshua's words came back to haunt her. So what if she was out of her comfort zone? This was Joshua's world. He'd been born and raised here.

"Try this." He held out a strawberry that had been lightly dipped in the chocolate.

She took it and bit into the ripe red fruit. Juice leaked over her fingers, her lips. She gave a little self-conscious laugh as she licked them. "Juicy, aren't they?"

He didn't reply.

She looked up into blazing black eyes.

"Joshua?" she whispered, her nipples hardening under the pink cotton T-shirt she wore, warmth flowing through her body to pool between her legs. The heat and desire and that other emotion…something terribly primal…in his eyes set her instantly alight.

"God, but you are the most provocative woman I have ever met."

She stretched her eyes wide. "What did I do?" But she already knew. The fire in his eyes was unmistakeable.

She'd turned him on.

"You bit into the berry," he said, his voice cracking.

The hoarse sound caused shivers to spread across her skin. Alyssa didn't know how this had happened. Didn't want to think too much about it. She only knew that she wanted more of the heat, the exquisite arousal that softened her body, the excitement that churned in her stomach.

She picked up a strawberry, swirled it through the chocolate sauce and offered it to him, her pulse racing. "Your turn to bite."

"Oh, yes," he drawled, his eyes dark and slumberous. "My turn."

Eight

The heat that scorched through him at Alyssa's offer turned Joshua's lower body to fire. Bending his head, he took a bite of the strawberry she held. His teeth sank into the soft flesh of the fruit and instantly his mouth was filled with an assortment of flavours.

The succulence of the strawberry.

The sweetness of the chocolate.

The complexity of the Pinot Gris.

There was another flavour, too. The unmistakable spice of desire. Slowly he chewed, swallowed, then raised his head.

A hectic flush staining her cheeks, Alyssa quickly popped the remaining half of the berry into her mouth. Their eyes held. She swallowed. Joshua groaned and leaned forward.

His mouth closed over hers. She tasted sweet. Of fruit and juice and wine. He moaned, licking the soft inner skin of her cheeks, sealing her lips tightly with his lest any sweetness escape.

His head spinning, he finally lifted his head. He cradled her chin between his cupped hands and stared into her glowing eyes. "Was that good?"

She nodded.

"Tell me you want more."

She hesitated. An unfamiliar emotion flickered in her eyes. "I want more."

Satisfaction settled in him. She'd come with him for this. And he wasn't objecting. Instantly Joshua wanted to take her mouth, slake his hunger for her. What was it about this woman? With one searing look, a couple of words and she made him throw all his customary caution to the wind. He'd had girlfriends...lovers...women that he'd easily kept at a distance while he waited for the right one. But no one like Alyssa. Never this hunger.

Why her? This woman could never be right for him.

His brother's lover....

Alyssa Blake, the woman who had once before humiliated him in print. Compromised his reputation and Saxon's Folly's profits. And would do so again in a flash. A woman who took what she wanted, to get what she wanted. To desire such a woman was *his* folly.

He forced himself to slow down, told himself he was in control of his senses, his tight-wound body. Sure, he was. He told himself he could control this reckless desire as easily as he controlled a busy and successful vineyard, told himself that he could take his pleasure and watch her walk away later today with no regrets.

He almost believed it.

"So you want more." He coupled the gentle taunt with a deliberate, measured smile and watched her breasts rise and fall as her breathing quickened. He picked up another strawberry. The strange colour of her eyes deepened. Clearly she'd expected him to kiss her, not feed her.

"Oh, no, my beauty," he whispered softly. "We're going to take this slowly."

A trace of fear flitted over her face. If he hadn't been watching her so closely, he wouldn't even have seen it. And that was what concerned him most about Alyssa Blake. She wasn't easy to read. He never knew what this woman was thinking. Hell, he still didn't even know what had been behind her gate-crashing of the masked ball.

Why had she come to Saxon's Folly?

To patch up a relationship gone wrong with Roland? And if so, then why the hell had she let *him* kiss her that night? If Heath hadn't interrupted them…she would have made love with him. In his bed.

For revenge? Because Roland hadn't done what she wanted? Except Joshua couldn't forget how those kisses had sizzled. How could she have wanted Roland back…yet have kissed *him* with such abandon?

Was it possible that she had come to the ball intending to seduce *him,* the CEO of Saxon's Folly Estate & Wines, hoping to get a scoop on the story she was after? The story that she now denied chasing….

Was that why she'd leapt at riding out here with him alone today? Had this been her intention all along? His head felt as if it was about to explode. His body, too, as her lips parted and he glimpsed the tip of a pink tongue. Without planning, his hand moved closer, the juice of the berry staining his fingertips. Joshua felt himself hardening as her lips closed over the fruit he held.

And why the hell was he hesitating? She was less than an arm's-length away. Her pink tongue a hair's breadth away from his fingers. If she wanted to seduce him…well, hell, he was more than willing. He craved her. Right now he didn't care if he would regret it later…after she was gone.

He wanted her…would have her.

Every sexy inch.

"Taste good?"

Even to his own ears his voice sounded hoarse.

She nodded and her tongue ran over his fingers, licking off the sticky strawberry juice.

It was enough.

Joshua took that as consent. He placed his hands on her waist, and hauled her toward him. She landed in his lap with a gasp of surprise. She filled his arms with soft, womanly warmth, her curves fitting against the hard angles of his body. Exotic perfume clung to her skin, her hair. He inhaled sharply. She smelled of sweet strawberries, jasmine…and desire.

This time his kiss was careful. Joshua was conscious of stepping into the unknown as his tongue probed her mouth, tasting the sweetness within. Of the shifting boundaries between them. Their relationship wouldn't—couldn't—be the same again.

The want that swirled in his lower abdomen was strong and hungry. Astonishingly so. Joshua suspected that he was going to be thinking about Alyssa Blake long after she'd returned to Auckland…that this interlude would change him, even if he never saw her again.

He told himself that her leaving was for the best.

But his body didn't agree.

She wriggled in his arms. Under his fingers, her top rode up. The smooth skin of her bare stomach was silken to his touch. The feminine feel of it tipped him over the edge. He pulled her closer, filling her mouth with the ferocious hunger that was building within him, threatening to explode, threatening to destroy everything he'd ever believed about women…about sex and desire…and love.

She didn't hesitate. She kissed him back with everything he desired, her purpose clearly the same as his. To make love…and the hell with tomorrow. Her tongue moved under his…giving as much as he took…as much as he wanted. With a hoarse groan, Joshua rolled, taking her with him, mouths locked, landing on his back in the cushioning grass. Pulling her above him, he shoved his hands under her top and his fingers ran riot over her back. Around them the air was redolent with the pungent scent of sweet, crushed grass. And Joshua felt his tightly leashed control start to slip.

In a staggering moment he realised that the forbidden attraction he'd been fighting had taken over. It was stronger, more powerful than anything he'd experienced. He surrendered to its force.

Even as the relentless hunger took him, he knew he had to have her. Just once. Before he let her leave Saxon's Folly.

Joshua's torso was solid beneath her. She felt safe…not exactly loved…but certainly cherished. It felt like coming home.

"This is in the way," Joshua murmured.

"This" turned out to be her T-shirt. Alyssa shifted, lifting herself so that he could push it up, then her breath caught as his hand slipped forward…further up…under her bra and touched her breast.

"Ah." She sighed and her head fell forward against his shoulder.

His other hand fiddled with her bra clasp. It gave. Then his hands were cupping her, shaping her, holding her apart from him. Eager to help, to prolong her pleasure, she braced herself on hands planted on the grass beside his shoulders.

Another gasp—sharper this time—escaped her as his head lifted and his mouth closed on one nipple then the other. Then his fingertips took over from his mouth…massaging…until an achy sweet sensation pierced her.

A hand moved between their bodies in restless little circles over her stomach. Down. Under the waistband of her jeans.

She was panting now. The sound loud in her ears. Alyssa shut her eyes. Patterns danced across her eyelids. He touched her where she was already wet with wanting. Blood rushed through her ears. She felt as if she might pass out.

Then he was rolling again, and she lay flat on her back,

while Joshua rose above her. Alyssa kept her eyes closed, focusing on the stroke of his hands as he ran them over the skin that his caresses had laid bare.

"You're hot and soft."

The throaty drawl was uttered against the bare skin of her belly.

His hand moved again. She heard the rasp of a zipper.

Alyssa's eyes shot open. Ohmigod. "What are we doing?"

His lips curved, sensual, satisfied. "Isn't this what you wanted?"

His words shocked her. *"What?"*

Maybe it was what she wanted. But she hadn't even admitted that to herself. How on earth did he know?

"That's why you came here with me...to be alone."

"You—" Words failed her. She pulled away from him, disappointment piercing her heart, and tugged her T-shirt down, uncaring that her bra was ruched up. Right now she wanted her breasts...her belly...covered.

"No need to be shy about it. We're consenting adults." The dark eyes simmered. "I have to admit it's a huge turn on to be seduced by a woman who knows what she wants."

"Knows what she wants...?" Alyssa stared at him. The smoked salmon...the strawberries...the Pinot Gris. He thought she wanted...this. He'd planned it down to the last detail.

Damn, but she'd been dumb.

She covered her face. How could he have misunderstood so badly? "I wanted to come here because Megan said that Roland had loved it here...that it had been one of his favourite places."

"Roland." His tone was peculiar, flat, dead.

After a long moment she pushed her hair back and looked up at him. "Yes, because of Roland."

He gave a laugh, but it held no amusement. "I thought you wanted something from me."

She blinked. "Why would wanting something from you involve coming here alone and—" not making love "—having sex?" What kind of woman did he think she was, for heaven's sake?

"Something you wanted enough to allow yourself to eat strawberries from my hand while your eyes promised me untold delights."

Alyssa felt the flush start on her chest, spread up her face. But she forced herself to hold his gaze.

"Something you wanted enough to forget your lover."

Her lover? Oh, yes, Roland.

She bit her lip at that. "And what was I supposed to want so much?"

"The big-break story. The insider's report on whether we lie to our consumers."

"Oh, for heaven's sake. I told you I'm not doing that story."

His intense, disquieting eyes stayed locked with hers. "So if you came on this ride today only because of Roland, why did you kiss me…respond to me…so convincingly?"

Alyssa gulped. How was she supposed to answer that? Tell him that he confused her? Bewildered her? Tied her up in knots? Made her feel emotions she'd never known?

No way was she handing him that much ammunition! He'd never believe her anyway. He'd think it was another seduction attempt. How utterly humiliating….

But his question hung in the air. Why had she kissed him…responded to him so wildly? Alyssa groped mentally for an acceptable explanation.

"Grief?" she offered at last.

"Grief?" He looked poleaxed.

Sorry, Roland. "Yes. Grief does strange things to people." She was babbling now. She wanted to run away. Hide. "Everyone reacts differently. Being here—" she waved a hand at the waterfall "—thinking and talking about Roland set me off. I'm leaving today. I'll never see you again. I didn't think you'd mind. I mean, guys don't take sex as seriously as women…" She stopped talking as anger ignited in his eyes.

"Didn't think I'd mind? I suppose I shouldn't care that it's just my bloody bad luck to be the butt of my brother's clandestine girlfriend's lustful grief attack."

Alyssa couldn't think of any suitable response to that.

It was just as well that she was leaving.

Thank goodness she hadn't agreed to do the story David had wanted her to do. If she stayed any longer, there was a very real danger that she was going to do something incredibly stupid…like fall in love with Joshua Saxon.

They headed home in silence. As the bush gave way to grassy fields, Alyssa scanned the surrounding countryside with nostalgic eyes. Even though she'd come with the express purpose of being closer to Roland, Alyssa knew she would never think of dense green bush and cascading water without remembering the tall, commanding man who rode beside her.

She cast him a sideways glance. A frown carved a deep furrow between his brows. She glanced quickly away before he could catch her looking at him, her silly heart in her eyes.

As they drew closer to the stable yard they heard a commotion.

"What the—" Joshua broke off as they were met by the sight of the black stallion racing up and down along his paddock fence, his tail held high like a banner and his nostrils flared so wide that the inner red tissue showed. In the adjacent paddock horses whinnied frantically, milling around in a tight bunch.

"What's upset them?" Joshua nudged his horse into a trot.

Alyssa followed more slowly.

The black horse, still galloping along the length of the fence, slammed to a halt at the gate and trumpeted with rage. It was then Alyssa saw the two youths in the paddock, half concealed behind the trunk of a gigantic oak.

"Hey," Joshua yelled.

The pair took one look at Joshua and ran across the field,

vanishing round the back of the stables. A moment later an engine roared and a motorbike came racing out from nowhere.

"Look out!"

But Joshua's warning came too late. The stallion came catapulting over the paddock fence, rushing headlong toward them. Breeze had gone rigid between her legs. Alyssa snatched at the mare's mane. At the last moment the black horse swerved around Breeze, so close that Alyssa could smell his sweat, and galloped past, his iron-clad hooves ringing on the ground.

Unsettled by the motorbike, the enraged and screaming stallion, the mare shied violently to the side.

Alyssa lurched in the saddle. For a moment she thought she might stay on, but then she felt herself tossed skyward. She hung suspended in the air for a moment, conscious of the plunging distressed horse below her. Then she was spinning toward the ground, sound and colour rushing past.

"Let go of the reins." It was a frantic yell.

Alyssa opened her hands. Breeze bolted free. The impact of the cobbles was bone-numbing. Alyssa sobbed with pain, which turned to fear as she discovered that she couldn't breath.

"Lie still."

Joshua's voice boomed above her. His black boots came into her line of vision and then he crouched down beside her. She caught a glimpse of dark, worried eyes.

She gasped, trying to speak.

"Hush, you're winded. Don't talk."

A moment later a sound escaped her throat. Agony.

"Does your head hurt?" His voice was urgent.

She shook her head again. "My back," she sobbed.

He went white, his lips pale. "Don't move. I'm going to call an ambulance."

There was the sound of light feet running on the cobbles. Caitlyn? Joshua turned his head and barked out a terse order.

Then a fresh stab of excruciating pain stopped her thinking. "My hand!"

"Breeze must have stepped on you." Joshua touched her fingers.

"Ouch!" She nearly blacked out.

He pulled his hand away. "The ambulance won't be long."

Alyssa was barely aware of the ride to the hospital as she shifted in and out of consciousness. But even as everything closed in and went dark, Alyssa knew that Joshua sat beside her, his eyes full of concern, never leaving her face.

After her examination in the emergency room had been completed, Joshua entered the curtained-off area where Alyssa lay.

"How are you feeling?" he asked.

Terrible. She hated the hospital. The sterile smell, the hushed sounds all brought back the nightmare of Roland's accident—of Joshua breaking the devastating news that her brother had died.

"Sore," she said finally, coming back from the hellhole to find his gaze fixed on her face.

"They'll operate on your hand soon. Is there anyone you want me to call?" Concern etched deep lines into his face. And there was something more. Something that made her heart tremble.

"To call?" she said stupidly, closing her eyes so that the gorgeous features with the misleading concern would go away. Joshua didn't give a damn for her. He thought she was the kind of woman who seduced men for career gain. Allowing herself to build hopes on his concern for her would bring nothing but heartache.

"Your family. Your friends. To let them know what has happened."

Her editor.

It reflected the barren state of her life that the only person who came to mind related to her work. Her boss…not family…not a friend. But David could wait until after the operation.

Thankfully the emergency-room doctor had confirmed that

there was no damage to her spine—only some bruising on her back, and damage to her fingers where the reins had wrenched the ligaments and the fracture of her thumb where Breeze must have trodden on her. It would need setting. And perhaps a pin, the doctor had said. Nothing life threatening.

No, there was no one who desperately needed to know. No one who would drop everything and rush to hold her mangled hand. A tear slid out the side of her closed eye.

Alyssa turned her head away, reluctant to let Joshua witness her bout of self-pity. The silence lengthened. He—her nemesis who was being so unexpectedly kind—was waiting for her reply. She moved her head from side to side against the regulation hospital pillow.

"No one?"

Was that disbelief she heard? Swallowing the lump in her throat, she opened her eyes. "My father lives in Australia with his new wife and her children," she murmured huskily, her throat raw from suppressed tears. She gave him a tremulous smile. "He's taking his retirement from the bench seriously."

"I'm sorry you're alone." Joshua sounded more subdued than she'd ever heard him, no sign of his usual take-charge arrogance remained.

Clearly he'd remembered that her mother was dead, that she was an only child.

"What about friends?" he asked. "Can I call anyone?"

"They have their own lives...families, children."

"They're all married?"

"Yes. All except Lanie, my best friend, but she recently moved to Christchurch."

Emotion flashed in Alyssa's eyes. An emotion that caused Joshua to blink. Pain? Vulnerability? Loneliness? He looked again. But her eyes were already closing.

"I'm tired," she whispered.

And Joshua wanted to kick himself for interrogating her when she least needed it.

"Rest," he said feeling utterly powerless to do anything about her misery. "It shouldn't be long until they operate."

In the end, Joshua waited until the operation was over and had been declared a success by the surgeon he'd arranged—the best in the region. Once Alyssa had been moved to the private ward he'd booked, Joshua sat beside her while she blinked sleepily after a hefty dose of painkillers.

The surgeon would be doing rounds before he went home, and Joshua had every intention of cornering him to discuss Alyssa's prognosis.

He looked down at her. She'd been a real trouper. Uncomplaining. Pleasant to the nurses. A dream patient.

On cue, almost as though she'd heard his thoughts, her eyelids fluttered.

"My boss is going to be mad. I'm going to need even more time off work." She gave him a sleepy look from under heavy eyelids and pushed the covers back with her uninjured hand, revealing a white hospital-issue flannel gown.

Instantly his body stirred. God, the woman was hurt... drugged...and one sleepy glance was all it took to electrify him. To bring back the memory of strawberries and soft skin and—

He pressed his mouth into a hard line.

"Have no fear, I won't be staying at Saxon's Folly," she muttered, misinterpreting his frustration.

"Yes, you will." It had been bothering him ever since the doctor had asked who would be looking after her. "You're staying. I'm the boss, remember? What I say goes."

"I thought you couldn't wait to be rid of me?"

"So did I," he growled.

But she didn't laugh as he'd half-intended. Instead her irises darkened her eyes to an unfathomable shade. "What of your concerns that I might stir up trouble with your mother... and Amy?"

"I'll confine you to your room—so seeing Amy won't be

a problem." Joshua smiled to make sure she knew he had no real intention of locking her away. "And for some strange reason your presence seems to be doing my mother good." He hadn't expected that. "Everything she says is prefaced by 'Alyssa thinks…' It's her latest craze."

Her expression softened. "I like your mother very much, too. I couldn't impose on her. She has enough on her plate emotionally without an invalid in the house."

"You don't have a choice." Joshua stood and stretched, his back aching from the hard hospital chair that he'd occupied for the past hour. "You're staying at Saxon's Folly."

"Because you feel that what happened was your fault?"

Trust Alyssa to see through his offer to the self-blame that lay beneath. "Yes." He raised an eyebrow and added with barbed humour, "And because I don't trust you not to rush away and get legal advice so that you can sue Saxon's Folly. Consider my invitation an attempt to save on legal costs."

That managed to raise a smile. "Okay, then I definitely have no choice. But don't accuse me of trying to seduce you."

"I wouldn't dream of it." He couldn't blame her for her reluctance to stay. He'd done all he could to drive her away, scared that she might hurt his family. And then there was his other unspoken fear.

The fear that stirred whenever she came too close.

The deep-seated fear that she could seduce him anytime she chose seemed unreasonably absurd when, eyelids drooping, she said softly, "Thanks, Joshua."

The fear melted away beneath her gratitude.

"My pleasure."

The hands of the clock on the wall moved forward, and Joshua sat quietly by Alyssa's side as her eyes remained firmly shut. Not even the bustle of activity when the night staff came on duty caused her to stir.

He stared into her pale face. She was beautiful in sleep, her features perfect. The straight nose, the curved lips, the ivory skin and dark auburn hair that spilled against her fine-grained skin. How could he have missed her perfection?

Awake, Alyssa was so animated—so opinionated—that all consideration of her beauty was driven from his mind. He was always aware of *her*…the spirit of her…the very essence that was Alyssa. She annoyed him. She frustrated the hell out of him. And, yes, he'd admit she intrigued him more than any woman in a long, long time.

The night of the masked ball his attention had been captured by her figure, her poise, her assurance…and the in-your-face challenge that she radiated. Once he'd held her in his arms…well, hell, his hormones had taken over.

And then at the hospital, when his only concern should've been for his brother, he'd discovered he'd been turned on by Alyssa Blake, his dead brother's forbidden lover.

The discovery had shaken him to the core.

Now he stared at her, remembered the flash of vulnerability when she'd spoke of her married friends with their families.

The loneliness in her eyes had called out to him.

Did she yearn for a family…children? Had she expected to find them with Roland? Or had his sometimes obtuse older brother caused the emptiness he'd glimpsed hidden inside her?

Then there was Amy, the woman who Roland had been supposed to marry before Christmas. Joshua had been eager for Alyssa to leave—before Amy found out Roland had been screwing around with another woman.

He felt torn between looking out for Amy, his mother's goddaughter who he'd looked out for all his life, and the responsibility he'd acquired to Alyssa. She was hurt, in hospital, with no one to call on to tell about her operation.

Tough, opinionated Alyssa Blake needed *him*.

Watching her, something heavy shifted deep inside his chest. Alyssa wouldn't be able to leave tomorrow. And even when she'd recovered enough to drive, how could he let her go back to Auckland, where clearly there was no one to take care of her?

Suddenly Joshua wished Roland had lived so that he could throttle his brother. How dare Roland have been so irresponsible? He'd always been a bit of a playboy…but to mess around with two women simultaneously was stupid. Hadn't he expected them to find out about each other? And now Joshua was stuck with the mess.

Joshua stared at Alyssa. The worst of the whole mess was that he was starting to suspect that if she crooked her little finger at him, he'd come running.

He wanted her for himself.

A memory from earlier in the day flashed into his mind. Of her head tilted back, her eyes shut and her glorious hair spilled over the grass beside the woodland pool. God. He'd nearly damn well had her. He'd touched her pale skin, kissed her soft, sensitive breasts. He'd taunted Alyssa, asking if she wanted more. The raw truth was he'd craved more. Much more.

If the knowledge that she'd gone with him only because she'd wanted to see Roland's favourite spot hadn't been flung over him like a bucket of icy water, he would've taken her.

He almost wished he had.

A soft groan of shock escaped him.

What kind of man lusted after his brother's lover…a brother who hadn't even been buried for a month?

Nine

Alyssa woke to find pale gray, early-morning light filtering in through the half-closed blinds. Outside the ward she could hear the clank of heavy trolleys, hear the attendants offering patients tea down the corridor.

She started to sit up. A movement in the corner of the still-dim room startled her.

Joshua unfolded himself from an armchair. "Let me help you."

"Thanks." She leant forward. He bent over her and immediately his masculine scent embraced her. Sun and earth and a hint of lemon and something a little spicy. He propped a pillow in behind her back.

She couldn't help thinking how unfair it was. She must look a mess, her hair rumpled, her eyes sleepy. Whereas the hollows beneath Joshua's eyes gave him a jaded appeal that simply made him more attractive. The events of the past week had added edges and angles to his handsome features. Shadows darkened his eyes to black pits and in the depths she could discern his turbulence.

"Don't tell me you stayed up all night?" she asked.

He nodded.

She clicked. "You should've gone home. That chair must've been terribly uncomfortable. Did you get any sleep?"

He came closer, till he stood beside the hospital bed. "Not much. There's a lot on my mind."

She could imagine. Joshua took his responsibilities seriously. And right now they must be piling up almost out of control. Saxon's Folly took up a huge chunk of his time. He had his parents' emotional well-being to look after…and Kay had told her that he was the executor of Roland's estate. And beyond that lurked the threat of scandal about the tastings in the wine competition. No wonder he looked drained. All those matters must weigh heavily on his mind.

His eyes scanned her face, inspecting every feature, until Alyssa started to feel self-conscious. "What is it? What are you thinking about?"

The dark eyes met hers squarely. "You told me once that you loved my brother a great deal."

He seemed to expect a reply. Alyssa swallowed hard, not knowing what to say. At last, she simply nodded.

"But you let me kiss you." He brushed her lips with his fingertips. "Here. And here." His fingers skimmed her neck, touching the base of her throat.

"Joshua!" Eyes stretched wide, she objected to his touch.

His hand moved to rest on the covers beside her. "I'd like to think that you would not have responded to me like that if you loved Roland."

"I loved him." It was a squeak of sound. Alyssa found that she couldn't hold his gaze. She glanced down. His hand lay on the crisp white bedcovers. She jumped as he lifted it and placed a finger under her chin.

Tilting her head, he looked down into her eyes and asked, "Did you ever sleep with Roland?"

Her pulse started to hammer. She swallowed nervously. "What kind of a question is that?"

"Answer me."

She shook her head.

Something gave in the bleak, black gaze. "Now we're making progress. I don't believe that you'd sleep with one man, and then respond to me like you did down at the waterfall so soon after his death. Not if you really loved him—not with your black-and-white views of the world. Not even because of grief."

Trapped, she stared back at him. Better she remain silent.

Five seconds dragged past. "What do you say about that?"

Alyssa thought of her promise to Kay. Not to tell. Ever.

This time when she shook her head, his mouth tightened. "You know what I think? I don't even think you wanted him to break off his engagement to Amy. I don't think you were waiting for him to come to you. Because after yesterday, I no longer believe that you loved him."

"I did love him." This time the silence stretched until Alyssa's nerves started to fray.

Joshua finally broke it. "I'll get to the bottom of this."

She believed him. His jaw was set. She had no doubt he was going to do his best. But she had no intention of breaking her word. "The answer is staring you in the face."

"What do you mean?"

She'd said too much. "I can't tell you!"

"Why not?"

Because she'd promised. And she never broke her promises. She shuddered and covered her face with her hands. "I just can't."

"Staring me in the face." He narrowed his gaze. "It's something to do with you."

She lay unmoving, refusing to look at him.

Taking great care not to hurt her hand, Joshua lifted her hands away from her face and gently set them down. "Help me here." His eyes held hers. Intent. Demanding answers she could never give.

"This isn't some game of charades, Joshua." She sighed. "I can't help you. I shouldn't even have said as much as I did."

"What are you so worried about?"

Again she shook her head. "No more. Don't ask me." She closed her eyes, refusing to answer. But when his hands landed on her stomach they shot open. "What are you doing?"

Joshua didn't respond. Instead he examined his hands moulding her belly. He couldn't bear thinking of her carrying Roland's child. After a pause, he said, "You can't be pregnant with Roland's child. Not if you never made love. So it's not that. But it must be physical."

He studied her, searching for something that was staring him in the face. Her colour was good. Her eyes didn't look dull and lifeless. "You're not suffering from any dread disease, are you? I helped complete your admission and surgery forms—there was nothing you felt a compelling need to share. So it can't be that. It's not linked to any medical condition you have that Roland might have been a match for…blood, bone marrow, kidneys."

He was fishing now. Alyssa pursed her lips in a straight line. She'd seen through his ploy. Joshua could see that she wasn't going to tell him a thing.

He stared at her, feature by feature. From this close, he could see the fiery lights in the dark red hair. The pansy eyes were more navy than purple right now. And even lying in a hospital bed the scent of jasmine and some spice—cinnamon perhaps?—clung to her. Joshua noticed something he'd never picked up on before. A feeling of disbelief swept him. "You know something…you share the same colouring as Roland. I never saw it before, because I wasn't looking for it."

She tried to laugh. "That's ridiculous."

"Good, you're talking." He was on the right track. He knew it. He frowned as the implications hit him. He touched her hair. It was soft, silky. "Your hair is red, not the bright shade of Roland's, but darker. Your eyes are such a dark blue that they appear purple in some lights. Roland's eyes weren't black—they were navy blue." He touched her cheek, the skin was smooth under his fingers. He heard her breath catch. Instantly his blood surged, and heat shot to his head. He fought to stay calm. He needed to. "Your skin isn't pale, nor does it bear freckles. Nor did Roland's, despite his red hair. Surprised?" He cocked a brow at her.

At that moment the tea trolley arrived. Relief swept Alyssa's face, and she accepted a cup of tea with a warm smile to the attendant.

Fingers drumming against the overbed table, Joshua waited impatiently for the attendant and the tea trolley to depart. Why had none of them noticed Alyssa's resemblance to Roland before? It explained her misery when he died…her insistence on staying for the funeral…and her endless questions about every aspect of Roland's life—even to the point that she wanted to visit the waterfall he'd enjoyed swimming at.

Once the attendant had left, a simmering silence remained. Joshua broke it. "I'm interested in why you feel you can't you tell me the truth, Alyssa."

She gave him a hesitant look from under her lashes. "I made a promise."

He pounced. "To whom?"

"It doesn't matter!"

"I think it does." His tipped his head to one side. "Cousins?" he mused. "Am I on the right track?"

"I'm not discussing this." She turned over in the bed and presented her back to him.

A startling thought struck Joshua. His heart started to pound. It couldn't be…or could it? Slowly he said, "When we were kids, Roland used to be teased that he was a foundling—the parents didn't know about it. The teasing stopped because we were three tough boys. Only fools took us on. I haven't thought about it for years. But now I'm starting to wonder—"

"Don't." She rolled back and gazed at him with a horrified expression. "Don't wonder. He was your brother."

Triumph surged through him. "But what was your relationship to him, Alyssa?"

"I can't tell you!"

"So there was a blood relationship."

She stared at him stonily. "God, you're sneaky."

"Brother and sister?"

It had to be that...there was nothing else it could be.

She shut her eyes. "Please go," she whispered.

"That would mean Roland was adopted." He paused, weighing it up. It was possible. He considered how he would feel if it were true. Nothing changed. Roland was still—would always be—his brother. But why had they never been told? "Not something that my mother and father were likely to miss. Did you promise my parents you wouldn't tell?"

The pansy eyes were full of guilt. "They didn't want you to know."

"I worked it out. I should have realised something was amiss about Roland. You were so desperate—"

The smile she gave him was twisted. "That's why you decided that I had to be Roland's mistress."

"You loved him."

"Never in that way."

"But it was the only explanation that made sense. The truth was too far out of left field for me to even suspect—until I took a damn hard look at you." He gave her a small smile. "You didn't break your promise, you never told me anything. But there are questions I need to ask my parents. I want to know if he's my half-brother—"

"He's not." She put her hands over her mouth. "Damn, I

shouldn't have said that. You must ask your parents. But please wait till after I'm gone."

He nodded. He would ask. Later. He wasn't allowing Alyssa to leave. Not yet. "I won't say a word. First you need to recover."

David Townsend, *Wine Watch*'s editor, took the news of Alyssa's continued absence from the office far better than she'd expected. But there was a price, David warned her. He'd be expecting a terrific exposé about the Golden Harvest Wine Award tastings to show for her absence from the office.

A hollow weight settled in the pit of Alyssa's stomach as she found herself telling David that she would do her best. She couldn't refuse him anymore. He'd let her extend her leave, now he hadn't complained about her accident leave. She had to pay the price—and he would expect her to pull out all the stops.

It was enough to make her feel queasy.

On Wednesday morning, packed, her head still ringing with the doctor's discharge instructions to start physical-therapy sessions as soon as possible, Alyssa glanced up as footsteps slowed outside the door of the private ward.

Joshua stood in the doorway. He wore a pair of chinos and a white button-down shirt. He appeared tall, dark and totally overwhelming.

"I've come to take you home," he said. With the truth about her relationship to Roland out in the open, the tenderness that shone from his eyes jerked at her heartstrings.

Home to Saxon's Folly.

A complex mix of emotions raged through her. Relief…guilt that she'd had no choice about the story…and beneath it all shimmered the confusing hot need that Joshua's proximity evoked. Alyssa knew she should flee back to Auckland at super-sonic speed. Before she reached the point of no return. Instead, she let him take the bag of toiletries and feminine fripperies she'd accumulated and followed him out to the Range Rover.

Back at Saxon's Folly a welcoming committee awaited her on the stone stairs in front of the homestead. Kay. Phillip. Megan. Caitlyn. And even Heath Saxon.

"Really, I'm fine," Alyssa protested as they ushered her into the living room where Ivy waited with a tea tray. "Oh, a cup of tea will be lovely."

"Shouldn't you go to bed?" Kay asked.

"After two nights in hospital, I'm tired of being in bed," Alyssa said with brutal honesty.

"You can rest here." Joshua patted the chaise lounge beside the window.

"I'll feel like a Victorian invalid," Alyssa objected.

Kay and Caitlyn started to laugh. Then Caitlyn said, "The Saxon's are determined to cosset you, I suggest you give in gracefully."

Alyssa shot the winemaker a sparkling look. "You're saying I should surrender?"

Caitlyn nodded emphatically. "Enjoy it while you can."

Alyssa settled onto the chaise lounge, then Joshua claimed the armchair beside her. Again the wariness resurfaced. She had to take care. It would be all too easy to be seduced by this softer Joshua...particularly when he was being thoughtful and caring. And there was the seductive charm of his wonderful family.

It was vital to remember that Joshua would never fall in love with her. His view of her as an ambitious hack writer, out to get a story at any cost, hadn't changed. He still blamed her for blackening his—and Saxon's Folly's—name.

It lay between them like an unscalable abyss. Not even the new tenderness he showed to her, or the knowledge that she wasn't Roland's lover would change that. No doubt about it, falling for Joshua would be crazy. A sure road to heartbreak.

Hurriedly, to get her mind off him, she said to the room at large, "I can't wait until all these dressings come off." She held up her left hand. "I'm supposed to start physical therapy in a day or so."

"Let me know when your appointments are, I'll take you," Joshua said, his eyes smiling down at her.

Alyssa couldn't look away. "No need for that."

Joshua glanced pointedly at her bandaged hand. "Your hatchback has a gear shift. How do you propose to drive?"

He had a point. "I'll call a cab."

"I could drive you, too," Megan volunteered.

"Thanks." Alyssa smiled at her in gratitude.

The warmth faded from his eyes. Alyssa felt the absence. "I don't want to be a burden," she said lamely.

"You're not a burden," said Joshua firmly. "The accident should never have happened."

His eyes held hers. Alyssa's breathing quickened and happiness rushed through her at his caring expression. The knowledge that she was playing with fire, risking the danger of being painfully burned sank in.

If she had any sense, she'd keep herself busy. The story for *Wine Watch* would be a start. But Joshua didn't know that she'd agreed to do it.

Her contentment faded a little. He would not be pleased when he discovered that. Better to let him think she was otherwise occupied. "Is there anything I can do? I'm bored out of my skull."

"You could help with some press releases I need written," Megan said.

Joshua shook his head. "Alyssa needs rest."

His refusal stung. Did it stem from concern for her? Or distrust? What did he believe she could do to harm Saxon's Folly? The reality sunk in. He was justified in distrusting her. She'd agreed to write the article David wanted.

By morning Alyssa was back on her feet, dressed and ready to accompany Joshua to work. Spending the day in the winery and driving around the vineyards would be far easier than being cooped up in the intimacy of the homestead with Joshua.

But Joshua had other ideas.

"You're staying home. You're hand needs to heal...and the bruises on your back, too."

"The pain is much better," Alyssa said. "If I spend another day lying on the chaise lounge, I'll go stir-crazy."

"Rest," he barked out.

She rolled her eyes to the ceiling. They were still arguing when Joshua's cell phone rang. After a few moments, he pocketed the phone. "That was Caitlyn. There's a problem with one of the stainless steel vats. I'll see you later."

Alyssa sank onto the chaise lounge, relieved at her unexpected reprieve. Joshua popped in intermittently through the day to make sure that she had everything she needed. Over the next week Alyssa felt like a total fraud as everyone took turns to sit with her and keep her amused.

Megan drove her into town for a check up, and took her to two physical-therapy sessions. While Kay had decided to create a Roland scrapbook out of photos and mementos and had asked for Alyssa's help. Although Alyssa suspected it was a ploy to keep her occupied, she was thrilled to when she saw how much joy the project gave Kay. It brought her even closer to Roland's mother.

But Alyssa found that she couldn't relax. She was worried about Joshua's reaction to the story she was already working on.

Since he'd discovered that Roland was her brother, the barriers between them had been collapsing. She didn't want to deceive him. She couldn't go on like this, she decided, as she put away the notes that she'd compiled. When he came home that night, she cornered him in the lobby and said abruptly, "I need to talk to you. Alone."

Joshua slung an arm around her shoulders and guided her through the French doors of the salon. Outside, in the rosy light of the evening sun, she trembled beneath his touch.

He released her and leaned against the railing, radiating a relaxation he didn't feel. "Okay, what's on your mind." Whatever it was, was clearly worrying her.

"I've told *Wine Watch* that I'll do an investigative piece on the tastings." Her face was tense as she waited for his response.

Joshua nodded slowly. So much for her claim that she had no intentions of doing the story. Disappointment edged through him, chilly and sharp. Alyssa would never change—the story would always come first.

"I tell you what, I'll cooperate and answer any questions you choose to pose about the competition tasting."

Alyssa pinned him with a sharp glance. "You'll answer all my questions? No holding back?"

He nodded. "But there's one condition: all your questions must be directed at me. No one else at Saxon's Folly is to be badgered."

"I have your word? You won't back out?"

He nodded again. "Why should I back out?"

"You might not like the angle I take."

"I doubt you'd write anything to sully Roland's memory."

She looked at him. The slanting light turned his handsome features into a mask of gold. Then she looked past him to where the Nikau palms whispered in the breeze. Her fears about Joshua's reaction when he found out she'd agreed to take the story, dissolved. He was going to cooperate. She let out a shaky breath and brought her attention back to him. "I've already sent in the tribute I wrote for Roland. This is an investigative piece. About the rumours that the samples provided for tasting in the Golden Harvest Wine Awards differ from what's available in the stores. My editor won't go for a romantic, rose-tinted article," she said warningly.

"You can't do that without compromising your brother, too." His jaw was thrust forward. "Isn't that a conflict of interest?"

Alyssa considered that. Anything negative she wrote about Joshua or Saxon's Folly, would rub off on Roland, her brother, too. Which was exactly why she'd felt her objectivity for this story was compromised from the outset. It was a pity that her promise to Kay hadn't allowed her to share that insight with

David. "I have no choice but to take that risk. I'm not known for being soft," she warned again. But despite her tough words, the delight was spreading. She could hardly believe that Joshua had conceded, that the solution had come so easily.

He narrowed his eyes. "If I didn't know better, I'd think you were trying to scare me off."

She threw him a smile that revealed some of her pleasure. "If there's one word I'd never use to describe you, Joshua, it would be *cowardly*."

"Thanks." His jaw relaxed slightly. "I think. Do I want to know what words you will use to describe me?"

Gorgeous. Sexy. Endearingly protective.

But those gave away too much.

"Hmm, let me think." She tilted her head to one side, and assessed him. Finally she said, *"Suspicious…"*

His eyes sparked. "You bet! And I'm not going to let you out of my sight while you pursue that story. I intend to watch every move you make."

"Distrustful…"

"Hey, I'm letting you do the story…I'm even cooperating," he protested.

It didn't take Alyssa long to discover that Joshua meant what he'd said. He watched her like a hawk and clearly had no intention of letting her talk to anyone other than him on the estate.

She'd barely taken out her pocket Dictaphone in the vicinity of Caitlyn, when Joshua came bearing down on her, a frown blackening his expression, making him look like a gorgeous—but fearful—fallen angel.

"This is not what we agreed, Alyssa." His anger was molten.

Caitlyn gave her an apologetic smile and disappeared with a mutter about getting to work before the boss fired her.

Joshua didn't even grin.

And once Alyssa met his fulminating glare, trepidation filled her. "Hey, Caitlyn didn't refuse."

"She likes you. You took advantage of her good nature."

"She's a grown woman."

"But she's not nearly as wary of you as she should be. She thinks you're her friend. She sees the whiteness of your smile, but misses your hunger for a story."

Ouch. Alyssa's shoulders started to sag. Then she squared them, refusing to let him get to her. "I only want to find out the truth. Caitlyn has become a friend. I wouldn't take advantage of her by asking her questions that would be a problem."

"Ask me. That was our deal. I'm available now."

She gave him a speculative look. He'd calmed down a little. Alyssa let him lead her to the rough-hewn, heavy wooden table and benches that sat under a trio of silver birch trees on the southern side of the winery. Her Dictaphone hit the wooden tabletop with a thud.

A challenge, Joshua decided.

The impression was reinforced when Alyssa said, "You don't mind if I record, do you?" And her pansy eyes dared him to object.

"I don't mind."

"That way you can't accuse me of putting words in your mouth." Her grin was edged.

Joshua suppressed his retort and contented himself with raising an eyebrow. "Feel better?"

"My hand is not as sore as yesterday." She looked mollified.

Joshua didn't have the heart to point out that he'd been referring to her barbed comment—and whether that had made her feel better. He let her take his comment at face value.

"I'm glad to hear that." Joshua was relieved that she seemed to have bounced back to her confident self. He watched her fumble one-handed with the Dictaphone and switch it on.

"So Saxon's Folly would never deceive the public?"

Joshua picked his words carefully. "When you're producing the volume of wine that we do, it's virtually impossible to guarantee that each batch will be identical. This is wine we're talking about, not manufactured widgets. There isn't a mould to make it from. It's science mingled with art. A fluid process. The winemaker will strive to bring out the best in the harvest, to make it consistent with the character that the winery is renowned for."

Alyssa paused the recorder. "I need to talk to Caitlyn—otherwise I'm not going to get a full picture."

"No!"

His face was tight. His jaw hard. Alyssa could see she wasn't going to move him. This was the Joshua Saxon who'd gotten under her skin. Arrogant. Opinionated. Certain that he was right.

Always.

"How can it hurt?" she wheedled.

"Plenty." He laughed. It held no amusement.

Alyssa gave up with a sigh and asked a string of questions. The answers he gave were insightful. It was going to be a great article. Finally, the sun prickling on her back, she brought the interview back to the point that was central to her story. "I'm aware that there might be certain subtle differences between vintages…but that's not what we're talking about. Here the issue is deliberately misleading the public. What do you say about that?"

"Saxon's Folly would never do that."

Looking at Joshua, Alyssa felt her conviction waver. "So you would never try to win awards with a superior batch of wine and flood the stores with an inferior version?"

He shook his head. "Not deliberately. As I said before there might be variations between batches, but only a very experienced taster would be able to detect the minuscule differences."

"I'm not talking about subtle differences."

"I've tasted them—I assure you they're substantially the same. But I'm certain you won't accept my word." A muscle flexed in his jaw. "I bet you wouldn't be able to taste the difference." He warmed to his topic. "I challenge you to a blind tasting, so that you can taste for yourself what the judges get and what the public buys. Let's see if your palate can detect the difference you believe exists."

Alyssa didn't hesitate. "Fine! I'll take you up on that—as long as I get the same samples you sent the judges."

"Of course." He inclined his head. "You'll be eating your words. In print. For all the world to see."

The look on his face was implacable. For the first time, apprehension shuddered through Alyssa. What if there was no difference? David would be expecting a story with substance. Then she straightened her backbone. Whatever happened, she would tell the truth.

That night Alyssa came downstairs to find the grand salon full of people. She paused at the high double doors, instantly aware of Joshua standing by the large sash window talking earnestly to his father.

Then the crowd dissolved into familiar faces. Megan sitting with Kay, and a quiet Amy. Caitlyn and Heath were chatting to the only man in the room who Alyssa didn't recognise, while Ivy bustled around setting down platters with hors d'oeuvres on the side tables.

Alyssa noticed that the discussion between Joshua and Phillip had come to an abrupt end with her arrival. Her journalist instincts went on full alert.

"What can I get you to drink?" Joshua came toward her.

She gave him a careless smile, determined not to show her curiosity. "I'll have a tall glass of lime and soda please." And glided across to stand beside Caitlyn.

Heath gave her a welcoming smile. And Caitlyn said, "Alyssa, did you meet Barry Johnson at the winery this afternoon?"

The stranger grinned at her and answered for them both. "We didn't have that pleasure."

Quickly Alyssa said, "I had a rest this afternoon." And held up her bandaged hand.

"Barry's here to investigate some ludicrous claims that Saxon's Folly entered fraudulent samples in a wine-tasting competition," Megan said, joining them. "I've no doubt that you'll tell the organisers what a bunch of rubbish that is, Barry."

Barry's smile was noncommittal before he requested a re-count of Alyssa's accident. The next few minutes were spent talking about the dangers of horse riding—with Megan laughingly labelling Barry's more outrageous recounts of his own youthful experiences as urban legends.

"Alyssa's fall was certainly not funny while it was happening," Joshua broke in from behind Alyssa. "I blame that stallion. He caused Breeze to bolt. He's been an accident waiting to happen for a long time. I don't know how many times I told Roland to get rid of him."

"What happened to me wasn't the horse's fault," Alyssa objected as she took the drink he held out. "The two guys upset him."

"Yes. And I'll deal with them as soon as they're caught."

Alyssa shivered at the slashing tightness of Joshua's mouth. She had no doubt he would. She almost found a little pity for them—despite the lingering ache in her hand.

"Is there a possibility that they came to taste the wines?" Alyssa asked, taking a sip before setting the drink down on a nearby table.

"No. There's closed-circuit surveillance in the tasting shed and we didn't catch any footage of them. The investigating officer suspects that they're young hoods, part of a gang that has been causing some problems recently. They're determined to apprehend them."

"Good," Megan sounded fierce. "As long as they don't take too long about it."

Alyssa caught Joshua's eye and both of them started to grin.

"What are you two laughing at?" Megan eyed them suspiciously.

"You sound so bloodthirsty."

Megan snorted. "They could've hurt Breeze...or that black devil horse."

"That black devil can look after himself. It's Alyssa who could've died." Joshua gave her a brooding look. "She didn't escape unscathed."

A surge of warmth swept through Alyssa. For a moment the outlandish thought crossed her mind that Joshua really cared.

"I'm feeling a lot better," she said softly.

"I'm glad." His voice was smooth and deep.

Out of the corner of her eye Alyssa caught Megan's start of surprise. She felt herself flush a little with embarrassment. She didn't need another witness to this insanity she felt about Joshua Saxon. It was an infantile infatuation. All about sex. About being too long without a man. It was totally crazy. And it had no hope of surviving. Heavens, he didn't even trust her to do a story.

Joshua lifted his Baccarat wineglass and took a sip of Saxon's Folly's Pinot Gris. His meal finished, he watched Alyssa flick back the fall of spectacular hair that glowed in the dim lighting. Instantly his senses were assaulted by the memory of the last time he'd tasted the full-bodied wine.

On Alyssa's lush lips, mingled with strawberries.

Damn!

"Joshua?" He jumped as a hand touched his shoulder. "Sorry, I startled you."

He moved his high-backed chair a little as Caitlyn slid into the unoccupied seat beside him.

"Barry was asking me questions earlier."

"About what?" Disquiet rocked Joshua. The hairs on the back of his neck started to rise.

"That this isn't the first time that Saxon's Folly has been

suspected of misrepresenting samples," Caitlyn murmured, keeping her voice low.

"That's bull."

"Is it?" Caitlyn's eyes were wide and worried. "What if Roland did submit a better batch?"

"He didn't." Joshua refused to believe that of his brother. In life, Roland might have been reckless…fiercely competitive. But he'd never been stupid.

And intentionally substituting better samples would've been stupid.

"It's not illegal to use a better batch of the same wine," Caitlyn said falteringly, as if already trying to create spin.

"But it's misleading. While we all know there may be some variation, it shouldn't be so great that the wine the public buy off the shelves is vastly inferior. That's tantamount to a breach of trust." Or fraud. Now he was starting to sound like Alyssa. But it was what he'd always believed.

"Roland did like to win." Caitlyn sounded subdued. "He got a kick out of collecting the gold medals for our wines. He loved admiring the display case in the tasting shed. He used to say, 'The end always justifies the means.'"

Joshua finished the Pinot Gris and set down the glass on the damask tablecloth. "That was a joke."

"You think so?"

Joshua didn't like the doubt on Caitlyn's face. "You think he did it."

She drew a deep breath. "I don't want to leap to incorrect conclusions, but I think it's possible. There were better batches."

"But we used those for the Special Reserve."

Caitlyn's eyes didn't meet his. "What if…" Her voice trailed away.

What if Roland had used those batches as samples? That's what she didn't want to say. Joshua hesitated. Caitlyn was an experienced winemaker. She knew the quality of every batch they produced. Then he conceded, "The reserve batches would've been substantially different. Substantially better."

This time she met his gaze, and he read the worry. "Exactly."

Double damn.

"I don't want to—"

"Think about it?" Her eyes were apologetic. "I think you have to."

"I was going to say, I don't want to believe it. He was my brother."

"You're too loyal, too protective." She paused. "You and Roland were fundamentally different. You didn't always react in the same way." There was sadness in her eyes. "You're a born defender. But you can't defend the indefensible."

"I know. But I want more proof. Roland is dead. I can't allow his memory to be muddied." He glanced over the subdued glitter of antique silverware to where his parents sat at the head of the table. "I can't let that happen to them."

"Well, you can't bear the blame yourself, so you may have no choice."

So that would mean that Alyssa had been right all along. Her cynicism about Saxon's Folly had not been displaced. She'd simply misidentified the culprit.

How would Alyssa feel when she found out the wrongdoer wasn't the Saxon she detested? That it was Roland, her brother? It would place her in the intolerable position of blowing the whistle on her own brother. Joshua knew he would do whatever it took to soften Alyssa's pain—even stop her from writing the article she so badly wanted to do.

Not for the first time, he wished that he'd never agreed to cooperate on this damned story.

On Sunday Joshua found Alyssa in the tasting shed. He stopped behind her as the group she'd been tending made their way to the cash register and he frowned as she unconsciously shielded her injured hand.

"What are you doing here?"

"Helping out. It's busy today."

"If your hand hurts, take a break."

She turned her head, her eyes startled. For an instant he caught a glimpse of emotion in her eyes that caused his chest to tighten and his blood to pound. Then it vanished and her eyes became shadowed.

Joshua opened his mouth to reveal there was a good chance that she'd been right all along, that the Saxon's Folly entries in the competition tasting had been compromised.

"It's been busy. I might take that break." She stood and flexed her hand.

As she turned away, a stream of tourists from one of the buses that stopped regularly at the estate entered the shed. The next few minutes were hectic, and Joshua stayed to help Kay and the two students who worked in the tasting shed on the weekends.

But it was a struggle to concentrate. He found his thoughts wandering to Alyssa. Finally he abandoned the tourists to his mother's care and stalked outside.

To the southern side of the winery, Alyssa was talking to Barry in a courtyard planted with olive trees. Joshua felt himself bristle with annoyance.

What was she after? And what had Barry told her? Tension coiled tight in his chest.

Alyssa was a journalist. Nothing would be off the record. The last thing he needed was a huge scandal that dropped the share price and lost the public's confidence in Saxon's Folly wines.

And then there was Roland's memory.

He didn't want any hint of scandal attached to that. He walked forward with a stiff gait.

"What are you two discussing so intently?"

Barry frowned. "We were talking about food if you must know. Mediterranean cuisine. The olives prompted it." He gestured to the trees. "Have no fear, I'm not discussing the progress of the investigation with a member of the press." He glanced at his watch. "Which reminds me, I wanted to talk with Caitlyn about something."

"Perhaps I can hel—"

"No, stay here in the sunshine with this lovely woman," Barry said with heavy gallantry. "Caitlyn has the records I want to see."

Joshua smiled at the older man, hoping that none of his apprehension showed…but knowing that Caitlyn would never reveal her reservations.

After Barry had left, the tension between him and Alyssa grew worse as the seconds stretched past. Finally Joshua flung himself down onto a stone bench and patted the seat beside him. "Sit. If you have any further questions, you can ask me now."

Alyssa continued to lean against the low white wall that bordered the courtyard, the sun striking her hair and turning her eyes to an impossible shade of violet. Again he felt the relentless twist of desire.

Then she said, "I've already asked everything I need to know from you."

"You have everything you want from me?" His stomach dropped as the colour of her eyes deepened. The desire was sharp now. Urgent. He rose to his feet and advanced on her. The wind lifted her hair, swirling it around her face. Almost against his will, he raised his hand, sliding his fingers under her windblown hair, cupping the smooth, warm skin of her nape. He moved his fingers, rubbing gently, caressing, and he heard her gasp, "I don't think so. I think there's more."

Their eyes tangled.

Several emotions flashed in the depths of hers. Hunger. Apprehension and something more.

Refusal, perhaps?

But she didn't voice the hesitation he glimpsed. So he stopped analysing, pulled her toward him and simply kissed her.

His lips moved gently against hers, parting them, tasting her sweetness, and he tangled his hands in her hair and held her where he could taste her best.

It was a kiss full of fire, brimming with all his frustration and desire. Her hands came up and pushed at his chest. Hard. Josh staggered back. They were both breathing heavily.

"No, Joshua."

Disbelief surged through him. What little air remained in his lungs rushed out. "You responded. Right now you want me."

Colour rose in her cheeks. "Do I?"

Annoyance flashed through him at her prevarication. "You want *this*. Your lips are so soft. You're as hungry as I am."

Her lashes fluttered down. "Maybe I am. But not now. Everything's too…" Alyssa's voice trailed away "…too much. I need to keep some distance—from you."

"With all that lies unfinished between us?" Joshua bit the curses that threatened back.

She met his eyes. "Let me finish this story. Help me with that."

The imploring look in her eyes told him this was important to her. How the hell was he supposed to battle that? Short answer was, he couldn't. He sighed inwardly. "I've already agreed to cooperate. So what comes next?" he asked flatly.

"You promised I could taste the wines." She slanted him a sideways look. "To see if I can taste the difference."

He wanted to taste her…not wines. But her mind was on the damned article. Her work came first. He had to respect that. It was part of the woman she was. And he'd already committed to cooperating. Joshua gathered his wits together.

As he held her unblinking gaze, he thought about Caitlyn's concerns that Roland might have entered fraudulent samples in the Golden Harvest Wine Awards, about Barry's task here at Saxon's Folly to get to the bottom of it all. He thought of his parents' frail state of mind. He thought of the raw grief he'd felt when his brother died. And, of course, he thought about Alyssa, the tumbling want that had consumed him since the night he'd met her.

Unstoppable.

Relentless.

Consuming.

Alyssa, who was the fuse to the devastating powder keg of desire that hovered between them. He narrowed his eyes, thinking furiously. The sooner her story was done, the sooner he could get back to the unfinished business between them. This time he wouldn't let her push him away, wouldn't allow her to use her job to put a distance between them—even if he had to use this formidable sizzle to seduce her. Alyssa would own up to the attraction that burned between them. He'd make sure of that.

"What are you thinking?" she asked, the first flare of alarm brightening her eyes.

He smiled slowly, deliberately. "You'll have your tasting. This evening."

Ten

Alyssa hadn't expected Joshua to arrange the tasting so fast. Nor had she expected him to set it up in the underground cellar beneath the main winery building. If she'd thought about it at all, she'd have imagined an informal meal at the homestead and a few samples afterward.

But here in the cellar they were alone, with no one to witness her findings. Was that deliberate?

She scanned her surroundings, taking in the ancient oak barrels that marched along one wall and the refractory table covered with a white cloth in the centre of the room. A row of glasses topped the table. At the far end, a leather chesterfield was grouped with two leather wing chairs. It all felt very masculine.

"The cellar was originally cast out of concrete and used as immense vats where the wine was made." Joshua moved to stand beside her. "It was hard work in those days. Before I was born my father had this fitted out as a place where he could retreat and taste the wines he'd created."

"Very masculine." Alyssa examined the rough concrete

roof and the racks filled with wines that lined the sides of the cellar. She was conscious of his size, the warmth radiating from him. She fought her response, fought to keep this about business…about the story, about tying up the loose ends that had to be tied.

"Why did your father need a refuge from your mother?"

Joshua started to frown. "Don't misunderstand me. My parents' marriage has always been very happy. I don't want you printing any rumours to the contrary."

Alyssa raised her brows. Then why had Phillip Saxon needed a place to which he could retreat? Why not retreat to the homestead and the comfort of his wife? But seeing the annoyance in Joshua's eyes, she let the subject drop.

"Sit down," he said, pulling out one of the bentwood chairs for her.

"Aren't you going to join me?" she asked, gazing up at him through half-lowered lashes as she lowered herself.

He leaned forward. "In a moment."

He was too close. Too overwhelming.

"Where do I start?" Hurriedly Alyssa turned her attention to the tulip-shaped tasting glasses on the table. "I don't see the wine."

"I'm not risking having you read the labels." Joshua flashed her a heart-stopping grin as he produced three bottles from a slender box.

"I wouldn't cheat."

"I want you to rely on taste and smell. Nothing else." Joshua picked something up. A white silky length of fabric. "I'm going to blindfold you."

A thrill of dark emotion assailed Alyssa. She fought not to let the illicit excitement show on her face.

"But I want to see the wine, the colour, the way the light moves within the liquid," she objected as her heartbeat drummed wildly in her chest. She braced her hands on the table in front of her, and was amazed to see that there was no tremor.

Joshua stood behind her. His body blocked out the light from the lamp. She sensed him coming closer. But still she started as she caught a glimpse of the white strip of silk that passed before her eyes. Then the world went blank.

The pressure of the blindfold against her eyes, the touch of his fingers against her nape, caused her breath to shorten to shallow gasps. White-hot heat rushed through her veins, setting her senses ablaze. She resisted the urge to clench her fingers around the edge of the table and fought to keep her breathing steady.

She was damned if she was going to give him any clue about what he was doing to her.

"Here…" He slid a glass into her right hand, his fingers brushing hers. "Taste this."

Alyssa swirled it around awkwardly with her right hand, raised the glass and inhaled. Then she took a sip. The wine filled her mouth. She swished it around experimentally.

Blindfolded it was impossible to spit it into the spittoon she'd seen. She swallowed and it slid down her throat like velvet.

"What's the verdict?"

"Nice," she croaked as his hands rested on her shoulders.

"Nice? That's all you can come up with? And you wield words for a living?"

Words. Work…keep it about work.

"It's definitely a Chardonnay. Richly fragrant, with toasty oak aromas. It has a ripeness." She struggled to find the words to describe the elusive flavour. She tried again. "Hints of butterscotch and honey."

There was a sharp silence.

Joshua didn't move. No rustle of his clothes. No clink of glass against the table.

"Let me try the next one," Alyssa said hurriedly, eager to shatter the unnerving, ringing silence.

"First you need to cleanse your palate."

He was very close now. She could sense him beside her, the power of his body, the subtle tang of expensive aftershave.

"I'm going to give you some mineral water."

A glass rested against her bottom lip. She took a quick sip, swirled the water around and gulped it down.

"Open your mouth, Alyssa."

Heat swarmed over her skin at his command. It sounded unbearably erotic and she could feel the colour rising over her throat, over her cheeks. How in heaven could this be work?

Slowly, hesitantly, she opened her mouth. He placed a piece of biscuit on her tongue, crumbly and savoury. She closed her mouth and chewed.

"Ready?"

Ready? For…?

Images assaulted her. Dancing with Joshua in the moonlight. The touch of his hands on her bare back. Joshua bending his head, his full sensuous lips against hers.

Then she came back to earth. She reminded herself she'd wanted distance between them. Joshua wasn't doing this deliberately. He was simply talking about the next tasting. Nothing more.

"I'm ready." Could he hear the huskiness in her voice? God, she hoped not.

This time his fingers closed around hers as she took the glass. She lifted it, the glass cool and smooth under her fingertips and his hands cupped hers.

"Relax, I'll make sure you don't spill wine over yourself."

Alyssa sipped blindly, all too aware of his fingers wrapped over hers, the warmth of his breath against the side of her face. The disorientating darkness of the blindfold confined her to a highly charged, supersensitive world she'd never entered before. A world where every sense was magnified and every sound amplified.

She swallowed too quickly, overwhelmed by sensation.

"What do you think of that sample?"

"I didn't taste it properly…I need another sip." Her voice was husky. Barely recognisable. She coughed to cover up the real cause. "It's a little dusty down here."

"Can't say that I've noticed." He released her hand. His jean-clad leg brushed against the back of her chair, and the fabric rustled. "I'll close the door, perhaps there's a draft."

The tension within her ratcheted up another notch. Great. Now the intimacy was even more enforced. Her pulse was slow and heavy, each beat measured. Her body had picked up on her thoughts and taken it to the next level.

As long as Joshua didn't notice.

She raised the glass and concentrated on the wine. It smelt rich, ripe with the fullness of oak. Next she tasted. This time she held the liquid in her mouth. It was smooth and mellow, showing all the best characteristics of a Chardonnay.

"So, what do you think?" Joshua's voice sounded loud from beside her. Alyssa started and swallowed. Too quickly. The wine went down the wrong way. She started to sputter.

Joshua thumped her on the back. "Are you all right?" His fingers went to the blindfold, pushing it back.

Through streaming eyes, she caught sight of his face, directly above hers. His eyes were velvety with the now-familiar concern.

"I'm fine," she murmured hoarsely.

The concern changed to something else…something darker. Intense and a little dangerous. Her heart plummeted then started to pound with unmistakable purpose.

Picking up a cracker off the plate, Alyssa tugged the blindfold back into place. She popped the biscuit into her mouth, doing her best to get her body's responses under control. "Give me the next glass."

There was a moment's silence. Then, he said, "You haven't told me what you thought of that wine."

"It's a Chardonnay."

"Same vintage or different?"

She hesitated. "It's definitely familiar. But the same as the first sample? I don't think so." She held her breath, but he didn't respond. "I'd guess it's an earlier vintage. It's even better than the last sample, I assume the time in the bottle might've added to it."

He remained silent.

"Am I right?"

"I'm not answering any questions until afterward."

"I'm sure I'm right." Alyssa started to relax. "Even though I'm not a trained judge."

"But sometimes the obvious is not the truth."

Was he talking about wine? Or the story she'd done a long time ago? Or was he talking about Roland being her brother, not her lover.

"Are you saying that I'm wrong?"

She could hear him moving glasses, the sound of wine splashing into a glass, then the thud as the bottle landed on the table.

"No, I'm not saying you're wrong."

He was talking about wine. Alyssa relaxed a little. "Unfair," she countered. "You're trying to confuse me."

The glass touched her hand. This time she made sure their fingers did not connect. "It's okay, I've got it. You can let go."

"Always so independent."

"Yes." But she thought about his pointed observation. When her mother had died and her father had remarried and left for another country, her response had been to cling to her independence. She only had herself to rely on.

For a while she'd hoped for an emotional connection with Roland. But even that tenuous bond had been ripped from her.

"At least I can look after myself." She lifted the wine and took a small sip and forced herself to concentrate. Lovely rich, ripe flavours. Cream and butterscotch. "This is wonderful. You should taste some."

"I will." His voice held an odd note.

She heard liquid swirling into a glass. Lifting the tulip-shaped tasting glass, she took a tiny mouthful.

"I'll taste it now, I think."

She felt an instant of heart-leaping shock as his mouth closed over hers.

And then she yielded.

His tongue sank in, searching out the flavours of the wine she'd consumed. It tasted. It explored. It devoured. Desire exploded within her. Alyssa met his hunger with her own.

When he finally lifted his head, she could barely think, much less talk.

"Velvet smooth and darker than midnight."

It took her a moment to realise that he must be talking about the essence of the wine that lingered on her tongue.

"Open your mouth."

She hesitated, then realised he intended to feed her another sliver of biscuit. Too late now to baulk. That would be too revealing. Her lips parted, her tongue slipped out and ran along her bottom lip.

She heard his breath catch, giving her an instant of warning. When his mouth claimed hers again, she was ready for him.

From behind the blindfold it was easy to pretend that these desires didn't belong to her—Alyssa Blake—that they belonged to the mindless, sightless tasting cipher he had created.

But she hardly cared. All she cared about was the feel of him. He lifted her, she grabbed for the table, and a moment later she landed across his lap as he slid beneath her.

His arm circled behind her back, pulling her close.

"What about the tasting?" she murmured, one last, desperate attempt at levity.

He moved. Then she felt smooth, cool glass against her kiss-swollen lips. "Taste then."

She sipped. Immediately his tongue swept her lips, parting them, plundering her mouth, stealing the wine.

God.

She wasn't sure whose prayer it was. All she knew was when his head lifted, she gasped for air…and fought for composure. No easy task half sitting, half lying in his lap, while he supported her.

"I think that's the same wine as the first you gave me. You must've mixed up the bottles."

He growled, a low, deep sound in the back of his throat. "I didn't. But I don't really care."

This time the kiss went deeper still. His hand cupped her breast and all thoughts of keeping a distance between them fled. Alyssa arched upward, every inch of her responsive to his touch.

Why him?

Why this out-of-control attraction to Joshua Saxon, of all people? Why couldn't it have happened with someone safe? Someone who respected and admired her?

His fingers fumbled with her blouse. The edges parted. Cool air blew across her skin. Alyssa bit her lip…waiting.

He didn't disappoint her. His hand closed over her breast, and sharp slivers of desire stabbed her, cutting deep.

She arched again, moaning. There was a moment of waiting. His fingers loosed the ties behind her head and the silk fell from her eyes. Alyssa blinked against the sudden light.

Then Joshua's head bent, and her heart twisted over.

It seemed like forever before his lips left her breast and his shoulders bunched under the cotton shirt he wore. Alyssa squeaked as he lifted her. The hardness of the table was a shock after the comfort of his lap. She felt stretched out, more exposed than when she'd been cradled in his arms.

Apprehension feathered down her spine. She tried for humour. "You never did tell me what you thought of the wine."

"I've forgotten the taste. I'll have to refresh my memory."

As his head came down toward her, she gave a little laugh and murmured, "I no longer taste of wine."

"No, you wouldn't," he agreed.

He picked up the nearly empty tasting glass, his eyes heavy with intent.

A thrill of desire ran through her. But instead of tossing the wine back, he leaned over her. The glass tipped, and her breath caught as the liquid spilled onto her skin where the blouse lay open. His head swooped, and she watched as he licked the liquid from the valley between her breasts. Her nipples stiffened into tight peaks, almost as dark as the rich wine. She shut her eyes with a groan.

A second later his mouth closed on the peak closest to him and her world rocked as a bolt of lust, unlike any she'd ever experienced blasted through her. Her eyes shot open. She watched wide-eyed as his mouth worked her flesh, sending wave after wave of pleasure through her.

What was he doing to her? She didn't recognise herself. She'd been kissed—loved—before. But no man had unleashed the raw, primal response he ripped from deep inside her.

Who the hell had she become?

Even now he was advancing further, expertly unfastening the last buttons of her blouse. His fingers were frantic now and his shirt was off, too. She stared at his naked torso gleaming under the electric lights, the muscles bunched, ready for action.

He couldn't possibly know how new this wild wanting was to her. Could he? She shuddered, uncomfortable with the idea that he might know exactly how far he'd trashed her boundaries.

He stripped his jeans off, revealing long muscled legs. Then he was leaning over her, and sliding the denim down her legs. Her panties followed.

Bare legs, brushed against bare legs. His body was heavy and warm against hers. Joshua's hand brushed her hair off her face, he looked down into her eyes and then his hips drove forward.

Alyssa closed her eyes as he filled her, stretching her, pleasuring her with slow, deliberate strokes. She bit her lips as the tension tightened within her, pulling tighter and tighter. Lights danced against her eyelids as the instant of ecstasy took her by surprise. Shivers streaked through her bloodstream, hot then cold, and Joshua made a wild, keening noise.

There was a moment of utter bliss, then the shudders came. Alyssa let them embrace her, and finally she dared to breathe. Opening her eyes, she looked into Joshua's hot, molten gaze. Incredibly, she knew he'd experienced the same wonder as she had.

Afterward, still dazed, Alyssa sat on the edge of the table and pulled her jeans on, then slid her arms into the sleeves of the blouse.

"Wait." Joshua held a white linen cloth in his hands. "There might be some residue from the wine." He licked the corner of the cloth and gently wiped the damp edge over the soft skin between her breasts. But when the cloth moved over her breasts she said, "I can do it."

He looked at her then. And he gave her a soft, sweet smile. "I know. But I wanted to do it for you."

And a sensation of falling into a deep void, of entering the wide unknown overwhelmed her.

Alyssa gulped, and didn't say another word as he fastened her bra and buttoned her blouse with fingers that were a lot steadier than hers.

It was only when he opened the heavy cellar door that she realised that anyone could have walked in on them. She shuddered again. The stunned sense of shock at the passion that Joshua had unleashed in her was starting to sink in. How could she have allowed that to happen? She wanted Joshua to take her seriously, respect her professionalism.

Stupid!

Alyssa slipped off the table and hurried past him.

"Thank you," he said from behind her. "You blew me away."

She turned her head, took in the slight flush high on his cheekbones. He wasn't unaffected by what had passed between them. In fact, he seemed to share her mood…shaken, uncertain.

"The final tasting I did was contaminated. I was distracted…" She flushed and he started toward her, stopping when she said, "You don't mind that I wasted your time?"

"Wasted my time?" His unaccustomed uncertainty fell away, his high colour had subsided, but his black eyes still smouldered. "What happened back there was no waste of time."

She halted at the bottom of the stone stairs as his words struck her. The sense of wonder that had encased her after their intimacy, the fragile joy, shattered.

What happened back there was no waste of time. His lovemaking had been no spur-of-the-moment impulse. She swung around. "Did you plan what just happened?" The urgent words escaped before she could temper them. For a brief moment he looked discomfited, then he smiled, and the confident Joshua Saxon was back.

"You did plan it!" It was there in the dark edge of guilt in his eyes. "You planned to seduce me," she accused. Joshua had used the relentless attraction that simmered between them for his own ends, to distract her from pursuing the story, to stop her getting to the bottom of the imminent wine-tasting scandal.

The smile that curved his lips held irresistible wickedness. "So what if I did? You responded. Hell, you enjoyed it."

She hadn't been able to help herself. But no way was she ever admitting that. Annoyed that she'd been so easy, so gullible, that she'd fallen into his arms so readily, she said, "You deliberately derailed the tasting."

All humour vanished from his face. Without a word he brushed past her.

"Joshua," she called. "Wait…"

But the only answer was the sound of his footsteps against the stone floor. Right now she felt dazed, so disoriented she could barely find her way back to the house, much less around the labyrinth of half-truths surrounding the scandal that threatened Saxon's Folly.

Alyssa pressed trembling hands against her mouth. Had Joshua been distracted, too? Could he be as confused as she was? Was he every bit as ruthless and calculating as she'd ever thought?

Or had she made a terrible mistake? Was he simply the sexiest man alive—the man her hormones recognised as different from anyone she'd ever met? The man who could be incredibly empathetic and caring and make her feel like the most special woman on earth. Had his lovemaking been intended to make her recognise the force of the power that lay between them?

Oh, God…please not that.

She wanted to bury her face in her hands as the revelation came to her.

The truth that she'd fallen hopelessly in love with Joshua Saxon.

Eleven

There was an unmistakable air of tension at dinner that evening. Kay had invited Heath over and by the time Alyssa came down, Heath and Phillip had already argued and a sense of gloom hung over the family.

Kay and Joshua sat at either side of Phillip with Megan opposite her father, flanked by Alyssa and Heath. Caitlyn had excused herself from dinner to show Barry around the nearby art-deco town of Napier.

But none of the family's frictions touched Alyssa. The devastating discovery she'd made earlier cocooned her from everything. *She loved Joshua Saxon.* And she'd probably mucked up any chance of telling him…horribly.

Alyssa sneaked Joshua a quick look. His face was set, until their gazes clashed. Sparks flew, and his eyes glowed like burning coals. He'd been right. They had unfinished business.

How was she ever going to resolve their differences? The distance that she'd begged for lay like a chasm between them now. Too far to bridge.

But it had always been too late for them. The secret of Roland's birth would always divide them... It was a truth Joshua could never acknowledge. For his parents' sake. Any relationship between her and Joshua had never stood a chance.

What was love without trust? She didn't trust his motives for making love to her—seducing her—during the tasting. So how could she ever tell him she loved him?

During the meal Heath kept her wineglass filled. By the time the main course of roast chicken was served, Alyssa felt more relaxed, and the warmth from the wine and food had spread through her body, although nothing could fill the hollowness inside her.

After Ivy had cleared the dishes away, Kay rose to her feet. "Phillip and I have something to tell you." Her voice faltered.

A grave-looking Phillip pushed back his chair and placed an arm around his wife's shoulders. "These last weeks have been incredibly draining for all of us. Kay and I have had the terrible task of burying a son...something no parent should ever have to do, while Megan, Heath and Joshua lost a brother."

Phillip's gaze caught Alyssa's for a moment and then slid away. The bubble that she'd been existing in for the last few hours burst. Alyssa clenched her fists against the edge of the table.

After a minute she glanced up. For a moment her eyes tangled with Joshua's. His gaze softened. He made an involuntary gesture of comfort toward her, then stopped. But she knew he'd glimpsed the emptiness...the hopelessness...in her eyes.

Before she could react, Phillip was speaking again.

"With Roland's death came a very tough time for Kay and I—" He broke off and glanced at his wife.

Kay put her hand on his arm. "What Phillip is trying to say is that we were faced by some decisions to make. And I fear that we made the wrong ones."

"What do you mean?" Heath was the first to speak, his earlier annoyance with his father gone. "What decisions?"

"Many years ago, I struggled to get pregnant—"

"I never knew that," Megan said.

"It was a painful time, a time I try not to dwell on," Kay murmured. "I became quite depressed—"

"After a lot of thought we decided to adopt a baby boy," Phillip finished gruffly.

"Roland," said Kay softly.

Alyssa's heart started to thunder. She couldn't believe what she was hearing. She glanced around the dinner table. Heath sat openmouthed with astonishment, even Megan had nothing to say. As for Joshua…he was staring at his parents…tension in every line of his body.

"But—" Heath was the first to rouse himself. "I'm not adopted am I? Hell, I look just like Dad, like Joshua…even Megan."

"Thanks," said Megan. "But I'm prettier."

"No, you're not adopted. None of you are." Kay's smile was tremulous. "It was a miracle. After adopting Roland I fell pregnant. It was as though those barren years had never been."

Finally, Joshua spoke. "But why did you never tell us?"

Phillip shrugged, looking trapped. "We intended to. But as the years passed, it became increasingly difficult. In the end, we never told Roland he was adopted."

"We were concerned that Roland might feel like an outsider." Kay's hand tightened on Phillip's arm until her knuckles turned white.

"So why tell us now?" This time it was Heath.

"Because—" Phillip stopped. "Your mother and I haven't handled this as well as we should have."

Kay's gaze flickered to Alyssa. Joshua's eyes followed. His gaze caressed her, she could feel the tenderness, the support.

"For a few months a young woman has been trying to contact Roland. At first she sent letters…and later…e-mails." Now Kay didn't look in Alyssa's direction.

"What did she want?" Megan asked apprehensively.

"Was she pregnant?" Heath interrupted. "Did she want money? Was she blackmailing Roland?"

"It's obvious what she wanted." Joshua's voice was loud in the sudden silence.

Kay made a sound that was halfway between a groan and a laugh. "She wasn't Roland's lover. She was his sister. His younger sister."

Pandemonium ensued. Everyone was talking at once. But Alyssa only had eyes for Joshua. Unsmiling, he was watching his mother. Alyssa couldn't see his face, had no idea what he was thinking. Had he set this up? Had he asked his parents to confess the truth?

Then he turned is head as if he'd felt her gaze on him, and mouthed, "Okay?"

She nodded, feeling comforted.

Kay sighed. "The only blackmailing she did was to tell me that if I didn't tell her all about the brother she'd been seeking for years...then she would tell you all that Roland was adopted."

"So you agreed to her blackmail," Heath said.

"Oh, poor girl. We want to meet her." That was Megan.

"You already have." Joshua's voice resounded around the room.

"What?" Megan turned to him.

"She's sitting right here."

The family grew utterly silent. All eyes fell on Alyssa.

Megan was the first to move. She pushed her chair back and came around to hug Alyssa. "Why didn't you tell us you were Roland's sister?"

"I couldn't." She looked over Megan's shoulder at Joshua. "None of you knew that Roland was adopted. I promised your parents I would never reveal that. I kept that promise." Joshua had guessed, she reassured herself, she hadn't told him.

At last Joshua said, "What I can't understand is why Roland never told us that he was adopted."

"He never knew, either," Phillip answered.

"But what about the e-mails and letters from Alyssa? Surely he confronted you and Mother with them?" Joshua's frown cut deep into his forehead.

"He did," Kay said very softly, lines of worry creasing her face. "We told him that Alice McKay must be crazy or a fraud. That of course he was our son. We convinced him not to respond, that it was an extortion ploy. He wanted to go to the police—we had to talk him out of that." Kay's shoulders rose and fell as a deathly silence fell over the room.

A sense of horror rocked Alyssa. Roland had thought she was a crazy, a stalker? Then reality settled back. But that meant that Roland had not rejected her....

She shook her head, trying to clear the confusion. "But you told me that he wanted nothing to do with me. That he chose his Saxon heritage over the opportunity to be reunited with me, his birth sister."

Kay's eyes met Alyssa's. "I'm very ashamed of what we did. Alyssa, I wish we could turn the clock back."

Alyssa bit her lip to stop herself from saying the bitter words that wanted to spill out. She found it impossible to hold Kay's gaze without letting her condemnation show. She'd liked Kay…laughed with her. Yet Kay and Phillip had betrayed her, lied to her brother and killed any chance of their fragmented little family ever finding each other.

"Mother!" Megan had let Alyssa go. "How could you and Father have done such a thing?"

"I thought if he found out he was adopted, he'd reject us." Kay's shoulders sagged. "You have to believe, if I'd known that Roland would die…that Alyssa would never get a chance to know her brother… That's why I called her when Roland was dying…to give her a chance to say goodbye. I couldn't keep Alyssa from him any longer."

Kay dropped her face against Phillip's chest.

Her husband's arms closed around her. "Kay has gotten to know Alyssa very well. She couldn't carry on the deception."

So Joshua hadn't spoken to his parents....

Alyssa didn't feel the relief she'd expected. Instead she felt more shattered than the three Saxon siblings looked. Megan was clearly more excited than upset, Heath stared at her with interest...and as for Joshua, well, he was impossible to read. All Alyssa could think about was that there was no longer any reason to stay at Saxon's Folly. As Kay left Phillip's side and went to hug each of her three children, Alyssa sneaked out of the dining room, seeking the solace of her bedroom to come to terms with what she had learned.

Joshua entered her bedroom while Alyssa stood staring out the window into the darkened night. She'd changed into her sweats and a T-shirt and was trying to summon up the energy needed to finish packing the bag that gaped open on her bed.

He didn't knock. But she heard the door squeak open, heard the soft fall of his footsteps as he came up behind her.

"Why are you leaving?"

She swung around at the sound of his deep voice. He looked unbearably dear and familiar. But his face was etched with lines that had not been there on the night they'd met. The night of the masked ball. The night they'd first kissed. The night Roland had crashed.

How could he ask that? Did he not know how that scene downstairs had devastated her? "I think we all need some time. I'll leave in the morning."

At some level she wanted...needed...him to persuade her to stay. Alyssa searched his eyes. There was concern. Even a little anger. But she couldn't find the emotion she was searching for. The emotion she wanted above all else. Right now she couldn't even spot desire.

Too much had happened.

She'd been insane to think that she and Joshua stood a chance together.

He nodded slowly. "Perhaps you're right. Come have a nightcap with me."

She paused. Was it possible to reach a truce? "A cup of tea would be nice."

But he didn't take her to the main kitchen, instead they made their way down the old servant's staircase to his suite. He settled her on the overstuffed sofa in the living room he'd shared with Roland and slipped into the state-of-the-art kitchen next door. He was back before she'd even had time to gather her thoughts, with a mug of coffee for himself and a cup of tea for her.

"My parents should never have lied to Roland. It was wrong of them."

Alyssa picked up the teacup. "I know. There were times I wished I'd never promised your mother that I'd keep it a secret."

He was angry. She could see it in his eyes. But it wasn't directed at her. "Of course you couldn't break your word. Your integrity and crusade for truth is part of what makes you special. Hell, you even felt the need to defend Tommy Smith because you believed he'd been unfairly dismissed."

"His version checked out." Alyssa said, as he settled beside her. "I even called you for a comment on it."

"And I never called you back. But I was critically busy. First with the harvest, then with a fire in the winery." He stroked her hair and drew a deep breath. "I'm so sorry that you were robbed of time with Roland. He would've loved you…your grit…your sharp tongue…your fierce loyalty."

The prick of tears caught her by surprise. "Thank you. You're a very kind man."

"Nothing kind about me." But he reached for her and took her in his arms. There was nothing sexual about the embrace. There was only comfort and understanding. How had she misjudged him so badly? A curious sense of belonging in the safety of his arms swept Alyssa.

Alyssa finished her tea and set the cup down. They sat in a companionable silence, his heartbeat slow and steady against her ear. She dozed a little, until she felt herself being hoisted up.

"Sleep," he murmured as she stirred and uttered a protest.

Seconds later a mattress gave beneath her. Then Joshua's arms surrounded her again. Alyssa let herself float into a dreamless sleep.

In the bright morning sunlight that slanted through his bedroom window Joshua looked down at the sleeping face of the woman in his arms. A surge of tenderness overwhelmed him. Her eyelids fluttered up and she blinked as the light registered. Then she turned her head and snuggled into his chest.

Heat flooded Joshua.

She'd lain in his arms, her bottom pressed up against his stomach all night. He'd barely slept. By the time dawn had broken, he'd been ready to quietly come apart.

But things were different. The basis of their relationship had shifted. Publicly. Irrevocably. Alyssa was almost family.

Everyone knew she was Roland's sister.

He couldn't have a reckless, no-strings-attached affair with her. He could never do casual with this woman. She might look tough and uncompromising...but he'd seen the vulnerability beneath. He owed her more protection—even from himself. With a sigh, he started to move away.

"Where are you going?" her voice was husky with sleep, sexy as sin to Joshua in his aroused state.

He asked the question he knew he shouldn't. "Do you want me to stay?"

"Please." She stretched a little, like a supple, slender cat.

His blood started to pound.

He pulled her toward him and she came without resistance, her eyes sleepy. She was beautiful to him with her clear skin and tangled hair, her body warm from a night under the covers beside him. And the bittersweet emotion that blossomed in his chest was wholly unfamiliar.

Her hip brushed his belly. He heard her breath catch as she felt his hardness. Her eyes met his, wide and startled, suddenly very much awake.

"*Joshua?* Now? Here?"

"Whatever you want."

She came to him, slipping off the T-shirt she'd slept in. He'd already removed the sweats the night before so she wouldn't cook in the night. Her breasts were full and beautiful. Then her panties were off. She lay back against the plump pillows and curved her lips in the most provocative smile he'd ever seen. And waited.

Joshua growled.

His hand smoothed over her belly, down between her legs. She was already moist.

"Open for me, babe."

She obeyed. He slipped one finger into the secret heat, then another. She groaned. "Joshua, you only touch me and I go up in flames."

Her words were enough to tip him over the edge. Pulling her over him, her breasts against his chest, he nuzzled his lips against her neck. Little kisses against soft skin. Then by some magic, he was inside her.

They moved slowly, in concert, until the pleasure that had started in his groin spread through to every part of his body. As the intensity grew, his thrusts sped up. He felt her internal muscles tightening…contracting around him. And then he was falling through space, Alyssa's heart thundering against his.

When they surfaced, a sense of power overwhelmed Joshua. He felt invincible. He gave her a brilliant smile.

"Wow."

She wrinkled her nose at him. "Just wow?"

"Just wow," he agreed. "Anything more could kill me."

Then her face grew serious, and he wasn't sure that he would like what was coming.

"Where do we go from here?"

He relaxed a little. He'd thought she might talk about leaving—and never coming back. He couldn't let her go. Even if she was Roland's sister.

"You said you wanted time to come to terms with last night. There must be a part of you that's furious."

She brushed her hair off her face. "No, I meant what happens to us?"

She wanted to know what his intentions were. Joshua drew a deep breath and felt he'd stepped off into uncharted territory. "A little later we'll tell my family that we have a relationship." He didn't think it would come as a surprise.

"But you live in Hawkes Bay and I work in Auckland. That's a little problematic."

That brought his mind back to the real problem: the damned story that she was doing. Sooner or later she would discover that it was highly likely that Roland had intentionally submitted samples from a superior batch of wine for the competition. It would kill her to have to do that story. Of course, there was a good possibility that she might decide that she had a conflict of interest and have her editor assign the story to another writer. But Joshua suspected once she knew the truth, she'd view it as a failure of her duty to the public not to report it.

Last night she'd looked shaken. It had hurt him to see her in that state. If she did the story, her pain would only increase. "Alyssa, drop the story."

She pulled away and sat up. *"What?"*

"Give it up. There'll be other stories."

"You can't ask that of me. Not when you say it's my defence of truth that you admire. I can't believe you're saying this." She scanned his eyes. "Or do you know? You know who submitted the samples. You know who committed the fraud. Was it Caitlyn?"

He shook his head. "This has nothing to do with Caitlyn."

"Who are you protecting this time? Was it Phillip? Your

mother? Last night proved they will do whatever they think necessary."

"They thought they were protecting Roland." Joshua felt compelled to defend his parents' inexcusable actions.

"They were mistaken. He should have been allowed to make up his own mind. He's an adult, not a child."

"I agree with you. But this story will hurt them, too. Surely you can see that?"

"Who are you protecting? Megan?" She paused, looking poleaxed. "Or was it you, after all?"

Her distrust tore him apart. He reminded himself that he was doing this for her. "I'm not answering, Alyssa." He paused. "Pursuing this story is going to hurt you."

"You're asking me to drop it, because of you?"

Joshua stiffened at her tone. Clearly she believed him involved. He wasn't prepared to muddy her vision of Roland. To let her suffer more hurt. But was he prepared to risk losing her over it? Finally, he said, "Yes, drop it for me."

She'd never looked more gallant…or more upset…as she said, "I don't think I can do that. Not even for you. It's my career—what I do. And I do it well. But it's more than that. You're asking me to turn my back on everything I believe in, all the values I was raised to fight for. Truth. Justice. What I do is about keeping the industry clean and the players ethical. It's about doing the right thing."

And the betrayed expression in her eyes told him that she thought he was motivated by ruthless self-interest to protect himself and his family at all costs. Joshua knew he wouldn't be telling his family that he was romantically involved with Alyssa. His demand had killed any chance of that. And he was damned if he'd tell her the truth to save a relationship built on such shaky ground.

Twelve

An unwelcome suspicion crossed Alyssa's mind as she made her way to the winery an hour later to say her final farewells to the Saxons. If Joshua had made love to her in the winery cellar to stop her tasting and identifying the wines, was it also possible that he'd made love to her this morning with the sole purpose of getting her to drop the story?

She didn't like the idea one little bit. But she couldn't help remembering that after she'd spoken to Barry outside the winery, Joshua had asked if she had any questions, then kissed her. Had even that kiss that had seemed so sweet and tender been given to distract her?

Then she shook her head. No. It couldn't be true. She remembered his sensitivity...his vulnerability. She would never fall in love with a man who was so devious and manipulative.

But still the suspicion festered.

She needed time, she told herself. Time to put everything into perspective.

The first person she saw as she walked into the winery with

its immense stainless steel vats was Barry Johnson. She forced herself to smile in greeting.

"Well, I might was well give you a break," he said. "But you're not to run it in the next twenty-four hours. I know *Wine Watch* has a longer lead time, but you're not to run this in your newspaper column until I tell the competition organisers."

"You've come to a finding?" A tingle of fear vibrated down her spine. She couldn't help feeling a wave of pity for Joshua…the Saxons…at the thought of the coming bad PR. This would mean share-price drops all over again.

He nodded. "I've satisfied myself that there was no irregularity."

Alyssa gaped at him in surprise. Because of Joshua's behaviour, she'd been so sure Saxon's Folly had entered trumped-up samples. And if they hadn't, then why hadn't Joshua denied it when she'd demanded to know who he was protecting?

Joshua…

She groaned silently. How he must despise her. She'd all but accused him of being the culprit. She said goodbye to Barry and walked blindly on.

"Alyssa."

She swung around as Caitlyn appeared from behind the nearest vat, her faded jeans splattered with the residue of grape pulp. "I heard the news."

For a moment Alyssa didn't know what Caitlyn was talking about. So much had happened. Then she realised that Caitlyn meant about Roland being adopted and the news that she was his sister.

Caitlyn hugged her. "No wonder you seemed familiar. It's the red hair and your features at certain angles."

"I'm going back to Auckland," Alyssa told her.

"Today?"

Alyssa nodded.

"Oh, no. I suppose you need to get back to work?"

It seemed easiest to let Caitlyn believe that. Then Alyssa said, "I also heard the good news about the investigator's findings—you must be thrilled."

"I'll tell you, I had some worrying moments when Barry told me that it wasn't the first time that Saxon's Folly had been suspected of entering samples of better batches. So I searched through all my records of the batches and cross-checked which bottles had come from which barrels—everything is numbered and electronically tracked, you know." Caitlyn paused to draw a breath. "Then I triple-checked Roland's paperwork, to make sure he hadn't entered any of the batches that we'd earmarked for Special Reserve. Fortunately it was all clear."

But Alyssa was riveted on one fact. "Roland did the entries?"

"Well, yes, he was the marketing manager. He always did the competition entries and decided which contests to enter and which wines would do best. Didn't you know?"

Slowly Alyssa shook her head. "Did Joshua know all this?"

Caitlyn gave her a strange look. "Of course. I told him the other night at supper that I was very afraid of what Roland might have done. Roland liked to win. And he could be reckless." Then she put her hand over her mouth. "I'm sorry, I shouldn't have said that."

Alyssa's heart sank. "No, you should always tell it as it is."

That made Caitlyn look even more worried. "You won't write about that? It's speculative, off the record. We don't even know for sure if Roland did it in the past. Joshua drew bottles from the same batches that I was looking at, to taste himself. He didn't want mud to be slung at Roland. He's determined to protect his brother's good name."

"No, I won't use it in my story." She didn't tell Caitlyn that Joshua had demanded that she drop the story, that she'd refused. Then someone called Caitlyn from the other side of the winery. She gave Alyssa a final hug, told her to visit again soon and hurried off.

Alyssa stared blindly at the floor. All the time, she'd suspected Joshua was protecting someone.

It had been Roland.

Alyssa was touched by Joshua's loyalty to his brother, his determination to let Roland retain dignity in death. Had he been protecting his parents against more hurt, too?

Another possibility struck her. Was it possible that Joshua had been protecting her? What had he said? *Pursuing this story is going to hurt you.* She'd taken that as a challenge... even a threat...he'd said it out of concern. For her.

Then she remembered something. Caitlyn had said that Joshua had drawn bottles out of the same batches she'd cross-checked to taste. She started to run.

In the cellar under the winery the bottles still stood on the table, beside the empty glasses and the discarded blindfold.

Alyssa thought back, trying to remember. She'd been so distracted by what Joshua had been doing, his touch, his kisses that she could barely remember.

Concentrate. Two wines had tasted identical—or at least to her palate they had. She read the labels on the bottles. Two were recent vintages, one of which had been bought from a local outlet and still had the price on. The third was a vintage from three years ago and also bore a price sticker. She poured a little of each wine into three different glasses. Then she raised them and sniffed each one carefully. The one she'd thought was an older vintage was fuller, fruitier...it was a Chardonnay Special Reserve. But according to the markings on the bottle this was not what had been sent to the competition. It still had a price sticker from the store where it had been bought on it. The other two were identical to her fairly well-developed sense of smell. Of course, Barry would be an expert.

Joshua had not been trying to distract her.

He'd given her a sample from a bottle available from the shops, and a taste from a bottle that came from the same batch of wine that the competition sample had been sourced.

If she took the bottles to Caitlyn, she was certain it would all check out.

Joshua hadn't attempted to mislead her. Nor had he crowed when she'd announced that they were the same, vindicating Saxon's Folly.

He'd been too caught up in their lovemaking. She'd been at the forefront of his focus during the wine-tasting, he'd put her ahead of Saxon's Folly.

Alyssa knew that she owed Joshua a massive apology. But she was done with talking, this time she'd do it in print. A public apology. She owed him that. It was the only way she could begin to make up for her lack of trust.

Thirty minutes later Alyssa found Joshua in the vineyards behind the homestead. The leaves on the vines had started to unfurl in the warmth of the summer sunlight.

"I've come to say goodbye." She stopped in front of him, noticing how tall he was, how utterly gorgeous.

The sun gave his features a golden cast as he looked down at her, the expression on his face unreadable. "You've decided to leave then."

"Yes, I need to write my story. And I need time to come to terms with—" she fumbled for words, not wanting to accuse his parents of anything that she would later regret "—what happened."

He only nodded. Alyssa hoped he would understand, prayed she hadn't already lost him. There was so much she wanted to say, but she couldn't. She'd said hurtful, distrusting things and she needed to set that right. When she sent him the article, he would recognise that she was humbling herself with a public apology.

"I'll walk you to your car."

"Joshua, I probably should've trusted you—"

Hot emotion flared in his eyes. "Yes, you should've." He turned away.

So this was it. It was over. Her heart contracted in her chest, a sharp, painful sensation. Then she followed him. Her luggage was already in the trunk. Beside her car, they paused, and there was a moment's awkward silence.

Finally Alyssa plucked up enough courage to lean forward and kiss him on the cheek. "Goodbye, Joshua."

His eyes darkened but he didn't reach for her, didn't kiss her in the way that he had early that morning. Instead he opened the car door for her. Alyssa turned the key and the engine took the first time. She unwound her window.

As the car started to roll forward, she stuck her head through the window. "I'll send you the story as soon as it is done."

His mouth slanted and he shook his head. "That's not necessary. I'm sure I'll find out what you've written as soon as the magazine hits the newsstands."

"You need to trust me, too—trust cuts two ways." Then more softly, she said, "You also need to know that I love you."

Her last view of Joshua in her rearview mirror was of his shocked, incredulous expression.

The story was done.

Alyssa had sent it in to David two days ago. And she'd posted a copy to Joshua, telling him that she'd never before shown her copy to anyone prior to publication, but she was happy to do it with him. She trusted he was satisfied.

She hadn't heard anything from him. But then, she hadn't expected to.

What she and Joshua had briefly shared had been over before it had even really started. Alyssa knew that it would take her a long time to get over Joshua. She'd gone to Saxon's Folly to find her brother. She'd found so much more—a family of strangers who had become so important to her. But more important than anything was the love that she'd discovered there. The love for Joshua.

But she was proud of the article. It had been the most difficult piece she'd ever written. The story was fair. She celebrated Roland's life, the successes of Saxon's Folly...and underpinning it had been the pain of her hopeless love for Joshua.

It was done. She'd vindicated Saxon's Folly publically, quoting Barry liberally. In a couple of weeks *Wine Watch* would be out there on the newsstands—her apology to Joshua.

The doorbell rang.

With a puzzled frown Alyssa made her way to the door. Who could be calling on a Friday morning?

Joshua stood on the doorstep, his beloved features wearing an expression that made her heart leap. "Can I come in?"

"Of course." She scanned him hungrily. There were still shadows under his eyes, and the hint of sensuousness in the bottom lip still made her insides turn to liquid. He was dressed more formally than usual—a dark suit, with a pin-striped white shirt...but no tie. As always, he looked gorgeous. The attraction that he held for her remained unchanged. It always would. And so would her love for him.

He must've received the article.

Why hadn't he called first? What did he want from her? She stood aside to let him in, hoping, hardly daring to breathe.

Inside he looked around at the mix of creams and grays with splashes of lilac and blue, and the windows positioned to take advantage of the light. "This is nice."

"Yes, it's a lovely bright sun trap."

He sucked in a deep breath. "I came to give you this." He held out an envelope. Alyssa took it from him. The paper was heavy. One corner bore the crest of Saxon's Folly. Her gaze met his. "What is it?"

His mouth slanted. "An invitation."

Oh, how she'd missed the quirk of his mouth, his wry humour. "It's not dark blue, embossed with silver, so it can't be to the ball." She sought refuge in humour.

He started to smile. It crept up until his dark eyes gleamed with laughter. "No, it's not an invitation to the ball. That's past.

I'm afraid you remain a gate-crasher. But you're welcome to attend next year. If you choose."

Her heart sank a little. She'd had such high hopes when she'd first seen him on her doorstep. That he'd come to tell her he loved the story…that he'd recognised and accepted her apology…that he wanted her back.

Ridiculous.

She didn't deserve it.

She slit the envelope open with her finger to find the invitation he'd deemed important enough to deliver himself and drew out the card inside. On the outside was an image of the gracious homestead surrounded by the rolling green vineyards that she'd grown to love. She flipped the invitation open. The Saxon family welcomed her to attend a planting of a new cultivar in honour of Roland Saxon.

It was to take place the coming Monday.

"It's very short notice, I know," Joshua said quickly. "But we wanted to do it four weeks after his death. It's been a mad rush these past few days to get it all organised."

"I understand." She swallowed her disappointment and looked up. "I'll be there."

It would be painful to return to Saxon's Folly. It would be even harder to leave afterward. Leaving Joshua once had been a wrench, this time it would break her heart. But by her distrust she'd forfeited any chance with him. All her life she'd placed so much stock in values like truth and justice. She'd thought that they needed to be underpinned by hard evidence. But that hadn't allowed for emotion. And she hadn't known how to deal with the feelings he'd roused in her. She'd doubted him. Despite the signs that he was the most caring, responsible person she'd ever met. She'd failed to trust him. It would haunt her forever. Slowly she placed the card carefully back in the embossed envelope.

She gestured to the love seat under the window. "Would you like to sit down?"

"I can stay awhile." He moved to the sofa, shrugged off his jacket and dropped it over the back of the love seat.

Alyssa hovered uncertainly. "Can I get you something to drink?"

"No, come sit." He patted the empty space next to him.

Heart pounding, Alyssa made her way across the room and dropped onto the plump cushion beside him. Instantly his warm male scent surrounded her. She inhaled deeply. She'd missed that, too.

"Alyssa…" He paused. "I know now how badly you wanted to meet Roland…to get to know him. I'm sorry it never happened." He shook his head. "And I'm sorry for mistakenly believing he was your lover."

She turned to face him, propping her back against the padded arm of the loveseat. "I couldn't tell you in the beginning. I'd promised your mother—I always keep my promises."

"I know." His eyes met hers, their dark depths soft and tender. "It must've been very difficult for you."

Alyssa thought back to the confusion she'd experienced, the sense of being torn. "It was."

"My mother—and father—hope you'll forgive them. When you come next week, you'll find them very contrite."

"Of course I will." But Alyssa knew that it would take her some time to come to terms with what Kay and Phillip had done. But they'd tried to make amends. She had more than she might've had. "I will forever thank your mother for at least giving me the opportunity to say farewell to him."

Joshua was talking again, his black gaze intent. "I can never give your brother back. But I can share my family with you. If you want that. Anytime you want, my family would be proud to welcome you to Saxon's Folly."

His words were incredibly moving. Her throat tightened. How could she ever communicate how much his offer meant to her? She knew that she would take him up on it. Even though it meant that every time she visited her heart would be torn out by seeing him…being close to him…and then leaving again. "Thank you," she said huskily. "I'd like to share your family."

"But, I'm warning you, if you want a brother, you're going to have to make do with Heath."

Alyssa stared at him. Then her heartbeat rolled into a drumming that resounded in her ears.

"Because I want a wife. A lover."

"What are you saying?"

"That I love you, that I'm asking you to be my wife." His dark eyes were intent. "We can start a family of our own. Will you be part of my dream?"

Joy rushed through her. Tears of happiness blurred her vision. "Oh, Joshua, I'd *love* that."

He closed the space between them, scooping her up in his arms. "I hoped you'd say that."

It was warm in his arms. Like being cocooned in sunshine. A safe, familiar place that Alyssa knew would always be home. "I can't believe you want me…after I trusted you so little."

Joshua bent his head. "I don't only want you. I love you. More than you can ever know."

He brushed his lips across hers and instantly excitement tightened in her stomach. She sneaked her arms around the back of his neck, holding him tight, as though she would never let him go. His mouth was soft and tender on hers, telling her so much more than words about his feelings for her…about his relief at her reaction.

Alyssa wanted to save this magical moment in her memory forever.

When he finally lifted his head, it was to say, "But to be fair, the mistrust wasn't all on your side. I didn't trust you, either—I jumped to the wrong conclusion about your relationship with Roland. I'm sorry. It was only once I got to know you, once I knew what was developing between us, that I realised that my mistake couldn't be right."

She brushed a finger over his full bottom lip. "Thank you

for granting me that, for giving me credit. Because I would never have been able to tell you the truth."

"It was hard," he admitted. "Especially because I kept defaulting back to my dislike of Alyssa Blake, wine writer."

"I wish I'd never done that story in the past," she said, bitter regret filling her. "But at the time I believed I was doing the right thing, my research backed it up."

"I know. And my attitude at the time didn't help." His arms tightened around her. "But I couldn't tell you what Tommy had really done, it wasn't my story to tell. But I'll have the person tell you herself, then you'll understand. And how could I expect you to accept that? You had a job to do."

And by the sincerity in his eyes, Alyssa knew that he loved her…trusted her.

Alyssa smiled up at him. "You were so arrogant, but you had the sexiest voice I'd ever heard."

He looked discomforted. Then he growled, "It was dumb of me. You were part of the media. But I was—"

"Busy with the harvest."

He nodded. "And that takes precedence over everything else."

Once he mentioned the past story she'd done, Alyssa couldn't help herself. "So what did you think of my article?"

A blank look settled over the features she'd come to love. "What article?"

She pulled back in his arms. "You didn't receive it?"

He shook his head. "Not yet."

"Rural mail." She rolled her eyes. "I thought that's why you were here."

"Nope." He tilted her chin up. "I came because you told me you loved me. I would've been here sooner, but you wanted time."

"I needed to finish that story. I sent you a copy. Do you know what a concession that is?" She gave him a smile that held all her love. "I've never let anyone see an article before it was run. But this was different, I owed you an apology." But he hadn't waited to see the article, he hadn't needed her apology, he'd come anyway. He'd trusted her not to hurt him…or Saxon's Folly…in print. The last bit of restraint inside her melted away. "I love you, do you know that?"

Then without giving him time to answer, she wriggled out of his arms and returned with a sheaf of papers a minute later. "This is for you."

Joshua pulled her back onto his lap. Resting his chin on her shoulder, he scanned the pages swiftly. Then he planted a kiss on her cheek. "Apology accepted. Thank you, Alyssa. It captures the heart of Saxon's Folly. The sense of family we have, and how we try to put that joy into every bottle of wine we make."

Warmth filled her. The happiness spilled out of her and she couldn't seem to stop smiling. "I'm glad you like it. That means a lot to me. I only wrote about what I found at Saxon's Folly."

Josh met her eyes squarely, the glow subsided a little and her smile faded. A wave of apprehension swept her at what was coming. Then he said, "You're a city girl. Will you be happy living at Saxon's Folly?"

Was that what he was worried about? Relief shook her. "Joshua, I'd be happy living anywhere you are." She gave him a look filled with all the love she felt. "I love you. Where you are, my home is."

He gave an audible exhalation of relief and tightened his arms around her. "You are my heart, do you know that?"

She couldn't imagine Joshua being happy living anywhere else. She gave a laugh. "Were you really worried that I wouldn't want to live at Saxon's Folly?"

"Very much." The big body relaxed against hers. "We'll remodel the suite downstairs. Or, if you want, we can build a new home on the estate."

Alyssa inched up the sofa, snuggling closer to him. "You know I love your family but when we start that family of our own we may need a new house." Right now she didn't even want to think about a family. All she wanted to concentrate on was Joshua.

Starting now.

She stretched up and kissed him. The top button of his shirt was already undone, she searched for the second button and undid it. "Do you have anything planned for the rest of the day?" she asked throatily, pressing a kiss against the skin she'd just revealed.

"Right now I can think of nothing more important than staying here," he said.

"Good."

"Alyssa?"

She glanced away from the third button that she'd been loosening with single-minded determination and looked up at him. "Yes?"

"You haven't said you'll marry me." Joshua gave her a grin filled with teasing and love. "Promise you'll marry me? Make an honest man of me?"

"I promise." And Alyssa knew it was a promise she would never break, that their marriage vows would be a promise she would keep her whole life.

* * * * *

Don't miss the next book in Tessa Radley's
THE SAXON BRIDES *trilogy.*
Spaniard's Seduction *is on sale in October 2009
from Mills & Boon® Desire™.*

Turn the page for a sneak preview of
High-Society Secret Pregnancy
by
Maureen Child

This glamorous first story in the
PARK AVENUE SCANDALS *mini-series*
is available from
Mills & Boon® Desire™ in October 2009.

High-Society Secret Pregnancy
by
Maureen Child

"**D**amn it, Julia, answer the phone," the deep voice growled into the answering machine, and Julia Prentice winced when the caller hung up a moment later.

She'd been dodging Max Rolland's phone calls for two months now, and he still hadn't given up and gone away. Not that he was stalker material or anything, Julia reassured herself. No, he was just an angry male looking for an explanation of why she'd been refusing his calls since their one amazingly sexy night together.

The reason was simple, of course. She hadn't been able to think of a way to tell him she was pregnant.

"Whoa." Julia's roommate and best friend, Amanda Crawford, event planner extraordinaire, walked out of her bedroom. "He sounds royally pissed off."

"I know." Julia sighed. And she could even admit that Max had a right to be angry. She would have been, too, if she'd been in his shoes.

Amanda crossed to her, gave her a brief hug, then said, "You've got to tell him about the baby."

Sounded good in theory, Julia thought as she dropped into the closest chair. She looked up at her friend and saw the gleam of sympathy in Amanda's gray eyes. "How'm I supposed to do that?"

"Just say the words." Amanda sat down, making their gazes level, which she pretty much had to do all the time. Julia was short, at five feet two inches, and Amanda was eight inches taller. Built like a model, Amanda had short, choppy blond hair, beautiful gray eyes and a loyal heart.

"Easier said than done," Julia said, smoothing one hand over the sharp crease in her pale green linen slacks.

"You can't wait forever, honey," Amanda told her. "Sooner or later, you're going to show."

"Believe me," Julia said, "I know. But that night I spent with him was an aberration. I mean, things got all hot and heavy so quickly I didn't have time to think and then the deed was done and Max was telling me he wasn't interested in anything more than a mutually satisfying sexual relationship."

"Idiot," Amanda offered.

"Thanks for that." Julia smiled. "Anyway it seemed that that was the end of it, you know? Max wanted uncomplicated sex and I wanted more."

"Of course you did."

She dropped her head against the chair back and stared up at the ceiling. "Now everything's different and I don't know what to do."

"Yeah, you do. You just don't want to do it."

"I suppose." Blowing out a breath, Julia said, "He deserves to know about the baby."

"Yep."

"Fine. I'll tell him tomorrow." Decision made, Julia actually felt a little better about things. After all, it wasn't as if she was going to ask Max to be involved in his child's life or even to pay child support. She could afford to raise her baby on her own. So, all she had to do was break the news of impending fatherhood, then let him off the proverbial hook.

"Why have I been obsessing about this?"

"Because you're you," Amanda said, smiling. She gave her friend's knee a pat. "You overthink everything, honey. You always have."

"Well," Julia said wryly, "don't I sound exciting?"

Amanda laughed. "Hey, don't knock it. You overthink and I act on impulse too often. We've all got our crosses to bear."

"True. And it's time to pick up yet another cross." Julia pushed herself out of the chair, then tugged at the hem of her white linen blouse. "I've got to go to that residents' meeting."

"Lucky you."

"I really wish you could come with me," she said.

"Not me, thanks," Amanda countered. "I'm meeting

a friend for dinner, where I will have a lot more fun than you will tonight. Personally, I'm glad to be only a roommate, with no place at those meetings. I'd be bored to tears in ten minutes."

Sighing, Julia said, "Five."

* * * *

Don't forget High-Society Secret Pregnancy
is available in October 2009.

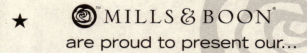

are proud to present our...

Book of the Month

Expecting Miracle Twins
by Barbara Hannay

Mattie Carey has put her dreams of finding
Mr. Right aside to be her best friend's surrogate.
Then the gorgeous Jake Devlin steps into her life…

Enjoy double the Mills & Boon® Romance
in this great value 2-in-1!

Expecting Miracle Twins by Barbara Hannay and
Claimed: Secret Son by Marion Lennox

Available 4th September 2009

*Tell us what you think about
Expecting Miracle Twins
at millsandboon.co.uk/community*

millsandboon.co.uk Community

Join Us!

The Community is the perfect place to meet and chat to kindred spirits who love books and reading as much as you do, but it's also the place to:

- **Get the inside scoop from authors about their latest books**
- **Learn how to write a romance book with advice from our editors**
- **Help us to continue publishing the best in women's fiction**
- **Share your thoughts on the books we publish**
- **Befriend other users**

Forums: Interact with each other as well as authors, editors and a whole host of other users worldwide.

Blogs: Every registered community member has their own blog to tell the world what they're up to and what's on their mind.

Book Challenge: We're aiming to read 5,000 books and have joined forces with The Reading Agency in our inaugural Book Challenge.

Profile Page: Showcase yourself and keep a record of your recent community activity.

Social Networking: We've added buttons at the end of every post to share via digg, Facebook, Google, Yahoo, technorati and de.licio.us.

www.millsandboon.co.uk

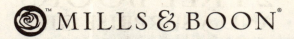

2 FREE BOOKS
AND A SURPRISE GIFT

We would like to take this opportunity to thank you for reading this Mills & Boon® book by offering you the chance to take TWO more specially selected books from the Desire™ 2-in-1 series absolutely FREE! We're also making this offer to introduce you to the benefits of the Mills & Boon® Book Club™—

- **FREE home delivery**
- **FREE gifts and competitions**
- **FREE monthly Newsletter**
- **Exclusive Mills & Boon Book Club offers**
- **Books available before they're in the shops**

Accepting these FREE books and gift places you under no obligation to buy, you may cancel at any time, even after receiving your free books. Simply complete your details below and return the entire page to the address below. You don't even need a stamp!

YES Please send me 2 free Desire stories in a 2-in-1 volume and a surprise gift. I understand that unless you hear from me, I will receive 2 superb new 2-in-1 books every month for just £5.25 each, postage and packing free. I am under no obligation to purchase any books and may cancel my subscription at any time. The free books and gift will be mine to keep in any case.

Ms/Mrs/Miss/Mr_____ Initials _____

_____

Surname _____

Address _____

_____

_____ Postcode _____

Send this whole page to: Mills & Boon Book Club, Free Book Offer, FREEPOST NAT 10298, Richmond, TW9 1BR